In Praise of *Chasing a Blond Moon* (2003, The Lyons Press)

"Top-notch action scenes, engaging characters both major and minor, master-ful dialogue, and a passionate sense of place make this a fine series."
— *Publishers Weekly*

"An absorbing narrative twists and turns in a setting ripe for the corruption that inevitably occurs when obscene profits encounter a simpler way of life."
— *Dallas Morning News*

In Praise of *Blue Wolf in Green Fire* (2002, The Lyons Press)

"A gripping plot, replete with memorable surrounds and spiky characters, makes this second in the series (after *Ice Hunter*) an excellent choice for most collections. A good pick also for readers who enjoy outdoor mysteries by such authors as Nevada Barr or Dana Stabenow."
— *Library Journal*

"This second Woods Cop procedural is well written, suspenseful, and bleakly humorous while moving as quickly as a wolf cutting through winter woods. In addition to strong characters and a compelling romance, Heywood provides vivid, detailed descriptions of the wilderness and the various procedures and techniques of conservation officers and poachers. The tricky, evasive behavior of federal officials recalls the atmosphere of *The X-Files*, while the police procedure and banter evoke K. C. Constantine's Mario Balzic series. Highly recommended."
— *Booklist*

In Praise of *Ice Hunter* (2001, The Lyons Press)

"Crisp writing, great scenery, quirky characters, and an absorbing plot add to the appeal of the memorable first entry in a promised series of Woods Cop mysteries."
— *Wall Street Journal*

"Heywood builds his surrounds slowly . . . peopling his novels with memo-rably idiosyncratic characters and conveying an overall sense of reverence for nature. An engaging read and a promising series debut."
— *Library Journal*

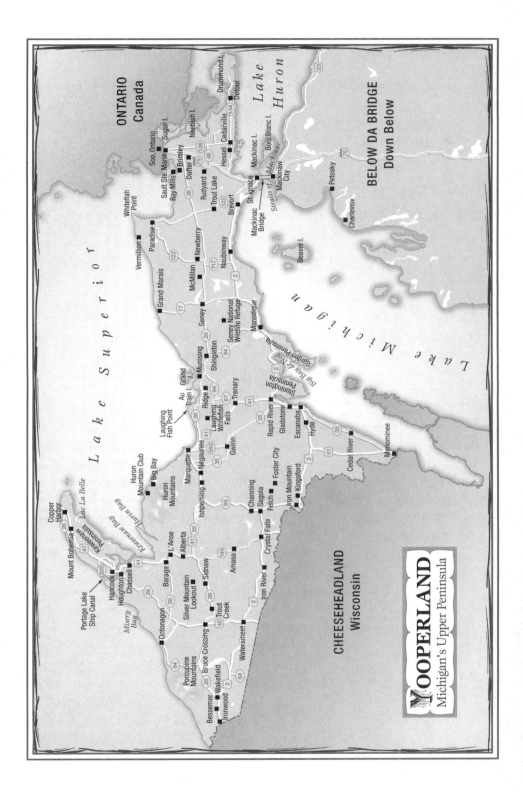

JOSEPH HEYWOOD

BLUE WOLF
IN GREEN FIRE

A WOODS COP MYSTERY

THE LYONS PRESS

GUILFORD, CONNECTICUT

AN IMPRINT OF THE GLOBE PEQUOT PRESS

This novel is dedicated to Michigan's conservation officers, who learn to see what we can't and do the things we won't while exercising courage, intelligence, empathy, common sense, and tenacity.
And to their families, who sacrifice so much.

· 1 ·

G rady Service got out of bed, tugged on his ratty gray sweatpants, and went down to the kitchen where he made coffee, set the table for one, poured orange juice, boiled water for instant oatmeal, and heated a cinnamon roll in the microwave.

Maridly Nantz padded to the table with hair wet from her shower and warily eyed the breakfast he had laid out for her. Newf came down behind Nantz and sat beside her chair. The dog was a female Canary Island mastiff, a breed developed in Spain to protect cattle and known there as *Presa Canario.* Newf was 130 pounds and all muscle. Her color was brindle, an ugly mix of brown, gray, and ochre all slopped together like cake mix in a bowl. She had alert light brown eyes and a wide black snout.

Nantz nodded at his empty chair. "You're not eating?"

"Breakfast with the captain," he said, placing her vitamins by her juice, and went back to the counter to pour boiling water in the instant oatmeal. He brought the hot cereal and cinnamon roll back to the table.

She nodded. "It slipped my mind."

"You okay?" he asked. Nothing ever slipped her mind.

"Sure," she said without conviction.

"Anything I can do?"

She stared across the room and shook her head. "Go see your captain."

Newf sat beside Nantz, watching her closely. Outside the house, Newf stuck to Service; inside the house, Nantz got most of her attention.

After showering and dressing, Service came downstairs and kissed Nantz on the top of her head as he passed through the kitchen. She didn't bother to look up at him. This was not at all like Maridly Nantz, the ultimate morning person and eternal optimist. Whatever it was, he reassured himself, she'd tell him when she was ready

Newf followed him to the door. Cat was already there, waiting to be let out. Until Newf came into his life, courtesy of his former girlfriend Kira Lehto, he had been afraid of dogs—all sizes, all breeds, all temperaments. Newf had begun to change this but he still respected and admired Cat's independent and ferocious ways. He had found the animal in a cloth bag of eight kittens that somebody had drowned in Slippery Creek. Why this one survived was beyond him, but she had lived and turned into a feline misanthrope that he had never gotten around to naming, which made her an animal he could relate to.

For most of his time in the Department of Natural Resources, Grady Service had lived in a 1953 Airstream trailer that he moved from campground to campground. Fifteen years into his career he had finally bought twenty acres on Slippery Creek, not far from the Mosquito Wilderness Tract. Others called his place a shack and worse, but the opinions of others rarely concerned him. It was two stories with one large, open space on each level. The upper level was for expansion and remained empty, a place where Cat dismembered lesser creatures and held sway in nature's violent chain. On the ground floor he had a kitchen area, a bathroom behind unpainted doors he had propped up to provide privacy, his communications equipment, and a dozen O.D.-green military-surplus footlockers. He slept on a thin mattress on three of the footlockers stretched end to end to accommodate his six-foot-four height.

Kira Lehto, a woman he had dated for a couple of years, had begun to change his lifestyle, and for a time he had actually slept in a real bed with her. But Lehto, like all the women in his life before Nantz, couldn't deal with the risk and demands of his work. The fact was that he'd never had a relationship with a woman that endured, much less felt right, including his ex-wife — until Nantz. Since last summer it had been a new world for him. He still had his place at Slippery Creek, but most of the time he lived with Nantz in her sprawling house on the Bluff in Gladstone. The screened porch of the house overlooked Little Bay de Noc, and at night they often sat on the porch sipping martinis and watching the sun sink in the west toward Green Bay.

He cracked the door and Cat shot outside with an acknowledging whirp while he rubbed Newf's chin. "If you learn anything, call me." The huge dog wagged her tail. He watched Cat sprint across the yard, either happy to be outside or intent on killing something. With Cat you never knew.

It had been quite a summer, he thought as he slid into his truck and radioed the district office and county dispatcher to report that he was on duty. Actually, he'd only just returned to duty the week earlier after a sixty-day suspension. He and Nantz had spent countless hours over the summer wandering the Mosquito, harvesting wild strawberries and blueberries. Come spring there would be morel mushrooms, and he couldn't wait to show Nantz his secret spots, some that his father had revealed to him, more that he had discovered on his own and never shared with anyone. This fall chinook salmon would come up the Mosquito River to spawn and die, and he would show Nantz a gathering of eagles and bears she could not imagine. His wilderness had, to his way of thinking, only one deficiency. Wolves, which had started coming back into the state in 1989, had yet to move into the tract, and he wondered why. He had been with his friends Gus Turnage and Shark Wetelainen last summer and seen wolves in the Misery Bay area and had been moved to tears by the sight. Someday they would come to the Mosquito, he told himself. Someday.

His suspension had turned out better than he expected. Last summer he had arrested a man who had murdered two people and in doing so spoiled a scam among diamond explorers that threatened the Mosquito. His actions had pissed off the ardently pro-development Governor Samuel Adams Bozian, who had retaliated by ordering the suspension. The Michigan Conservation Officers Association and state employees union had wanted to fight it, but he had accepted it, and when he came back to duty on Labor Day he had been promoted to detective, the DNR's way of telling the governor that while he had the clout to order the suspension, the department had its own ways of countering. His position was new, an extension of a concept already established in the Lower Peninsula. He was the first detective in the newly created Wildlife Resource Protection Unit for the Upper Peninsula. He wasn't sure he was cut out to be a detective, but he had few regrets about how it had all turned out. Most of all, he was pleased that he had been able to keep the Mosquito from being ravaged by diamond miners.

This had been his second scrape with the governor, whose critics called him "Clearcut." Bozian was not a man who liked to be opposed. Service knew the next time might be his third strike, though with Michigan's term-limits law, Bozian was in his final term. Whoever got the job next could hardly be worse than Bozian when it came to caring about, much less protecting the state's natural resources.

Michigan was a huge state comprised of two peninsulas. The lower half of the state held most of the population. The Upper Peninsula was the size of Vermont and New Hampshire combined, with less of a population than greater Grand Rapids. But the U.P. contained most of the state's remaining wild places. Some of the areas were well known and popular with tourists, but others, like the Mosquito, were virtually unknown and little used, which was exactly as Service thought it should be. In his more than twenty years as a conservation officer he had done all in his power to protect the tract. Poachers and violators were not treated gently and he pressed every charge he could, making sure the word went out loud and clear to violators: Screw with the Mosquito Wilderness and you are fucked.

Grady Service constantly reminded himself that if he had loved the women in his life with half the ardor he had lavished on his wilderness, his life might have turned out differently. He had never had a great deal of luck in relationships with women, but he was certain that this reflected his deficiencies, not theirs.

The Mosquito had a river cutting more or less through its center and a population of native brook trout with a beauty that often left him speechless. Most of the tract had never been logged and was filled with old-growth white pines and cedars hundreds of years old, bears and coyotes, deer and moose, bobcats, martens, fishers, skunks, coons, and uncountable varieties of birds.

Failures of his love life aside, he knew with certainty that he loved the Mosquito Wilderness. His father had guarded it before him, and it had fallen to him to be its steward for future generations. Like most conservation officers, Grady Service took his responsibilities seriously and passionately. It was not so much about doing a good job as it was upholding a sacred trust.

Nantz's mood had gotten his day off to a shaky start, and breakfast with Captain Ware Grant had only added to his uneasiness. Grant was the DNR law boss of the Upper Peninsula, an often unruly region filled with individualists and fringe livers. A taciturn man with white hair and a carefully groomed beard, always polite and proper, the captain had grilled him about progress on his first case as a detective in the DNR's Wildlife Resources Protection Unit.

Service still couldn't believe he was a detective. What bothered him most about the promotion was that after more than twenty years of playing doting mother to the Mosquito, it was no longer his responsibility. Because of his unexpected promotion, defense of the Mosquito had passed to Candace McCants, his fellow CO and friend. Relinquishing the Mosquito to someone he respected didn't make the change any easier to stomach. If there was a downside to what had happened over the summer it was that he felt less connected to the area he loved so deeply, a place whose moods and currents he felt as keenly as his own.

Sixty days without pay was unprecedented, and had it not been for Nantz he would have resented the punishment more. In fact it had turned out to be a badly needed break, which Nantz referred to as his sabbatical. He could not recall ever having taken a legitimate vacation. After graduation from Northern Michigan University he had enlisted in the marines, and after serving in Vietnam and satisfying his military obligations he had attended the Michigan State Police Academy in Lansing. Then there was a two-year stint as a road cop. He had hated patrolling the interstates. When openings developed for conservation officers in the Department of Natural Resources he had applied for a transfer and been quickly accepted. After a year on probationary status when he worked all around the state, he had been assigned to the same territory that his father had covered and he was so intent on doing his job that he rarely thought about vacations. If anything, he resented rules that prevented officers from working seven days a week. Poachers and violators didn't watch clocks; why should woods cops?

He had expected to find himself unhinged by the lack of work, but with Nantz's gentle urging he had taken advantage of his newfound freedom to get to know her and help her with her duties as a fire officer.

It had been a wet and rainy summer with the fire threat remaining low, and he and Nantz had spent a great deal of time fly fishing in the Mosquito and Slippery Creek. But summer was behind them now, his enforced break over, and he was back at work.

Captain Grant had been raised in south Louisiana; though most of his accent had faded, a hint of it persisted. "Where are we in the investigation?" he asked when they were seated in the rear of Elliott's Lake Trout Café in Marquette, where the captain, a widower, ate breakfast every morning at the same table.

"I'm still getting organized," Service said. He'd been at his new job only nine days. There was no investigation yet in the case, which had been transferred to him from the Wildlife Resource Protection Unit in downstate Mio. They had heard rumors and gossip about a gang of poachers killing trophy bucks for big dollars, but had no substantial evidence. There was a potential source in the Kent County Jail, but he wasn't talking. The man had been arrested last fall near Grand Rapids with three trophy buck heads in his vehicle. The man, Kaylin Joquist, refused to answer questions, a sure indicator that he had had previous encounters with law enforcement. But Joquist's past had nothing to do with fish and game violations. His lawyer had gotten the trial delayed several times over the year, and the client had shown no great interest in getting back on the street, which suggested he had reasons for wanting to stay inside.

Sometime soon Service planned to drive down to Grand Rapids, talk to Joquist, and see what he could nudge loose. In all probability the man had nothing to do with his case, but Service's gut told him it was possible. There was no doubt about a commercial poaching operation; rumors and gossip in the Upper Peninsula were invariably based on shreds of truth.

"What's your plan?" the captain asked.

Service started to roll out the usual evasive bullshit COs reserved for their superiors, but stopped himself. "Captain, we don't have diddlysquat. We need something concrete. I'm talking to informants and trying to work them. Eventually I'll get something and then we'll see where it points."

The captain nodded. "Thank you for being straight with me."

"I've got a meeting this morning with a fella named Griff Stinson."

"The bear guide in McMillan," Grant said.

In the short time he had worked with the captain, Service was continually amazed by his superior's memory for names and details. "Yessir, Griff's a bait-and-wait man, no dogs." And every year Griff's clients took a couple of five-hundred-pounders because he was a consummate woodsman, knew the animals' behaviors, habits, and their likely locations. "Griff hates cheaters," Service added. "He says he's found a dead bear he wants me to see. He found it last night and he's camped on it to preserve the site."

"What about the animal?" Grant asked.

"He wouldn't say. I'm meeting him at noon north of McMillan."

"A bear isn't a deer," the captain reminded him.

"Things can link together in peculiar ways," Service said. "I like to keep all options open."

"Keep me informed," Grant said with a forceful nod. "A major poaching ring sends out ripples and upsets the balance. It's one thing for one person to poach to feed his family or because he can't resist temptation, but it is another thing entirely for someone to organize the endeavor for profit."

In the world of fish and game law, most sins were relative.

Service promised to keep his superior in the loop and headed for McMillan with plenty of time to get there. At 9:20 A.M. he was just east of Munising when his cell phone squawked.

It was Nantz, her voice tight and cracking like thin ice. "Have you heard?!"

"Heard what? Are you okay?"

"I felt it this morning," she said. "In my bones." He heard her sob, catch herself, trying hard to check her emotions.

"Felt what?"

"Grady, about fifteen minutes ago an airliner struck the north tower of the World Trade Center in New York City and a couple of minutes ago another airliner hit the south tower. I *saw* the second plane hit on the TV, Grady! It was horrible, honey. Terrible, like some sort of movie special effect, only this was *real*. The talking heads on TV are calling it a possible terrorist attack."

He tried to get his mind around her words. Terrorist attack, New York City? "Are you all right?"

"No," Nantz said. "I'm sick. I *felt* something coming, honey. I *felt* it. I had the heebie-jeebies all night."

Service let her talk. He understood the power of instinct and intuition. It had taken all of his nearly fifty years to learn to trust his own gut.

"If terrorists did this . . ." she said, not finishing her thought. "I'm going to keep watching," she said. "I love you."

When she was off the line he tried to call the captain, but got a busy signal. Instead he checked his voice mail and found a message from Lorne O'Driscoll, the DNR's law enforcement chief in Lansing. The chief's message informed all law enforcement personnel that in the wake of the morning's tragic events, they should go about their business; if they were needed for special duty they would be contacted directly by the Michigan State Police Emergency Management Division.

Terrorist attacks on the United States. How did you go about your business in the wake of that?

The phone rang again. It was Nantz, sobbing. "There are going to be thousands of dead, Grady, thousands! Another plane has crashed into the Pentagon, Grady. *My God!*"

She hung up before he could speak.

· 2 ·

Commercial radio stations had abandoned their computer-fed formats for call-in chaos. Jocks were yapping about Pearl Harbor, pounding the war drums and talking to anyone who would add a shrill voice to the hype and hysteria, all without a single shred of evidence of a crime, much less a suspect.

Service fiddled with his tuner and switched to the National Public Radio station out of Marquette, and listened carefully to a retired defense intelligence analyst, now a professor at the University of Michigan, discuss the possible involvement of Muslim extremists. The professor ended his report by warning listeners not to jump to conclusions, reminding them that the Oklahoma City bombing was reason enough for such prudence. That disaster had been spawned by homegrown terrorists, whom he described as fundamentalists in their own right, there being zealots and extremists in all cultures and religious faiths.

Then NPR had opened its phone banks and even the station's liberal callers were expressing a desire for justice and payback for the perfidy in New York, though only if the government could clearly identify the perpetrators.

Service heard shock in callers' voices. He could feel it himself and in Nantz's calls. Surely something being seen as Pearl Harbor would demand national political action, and he had no doubt that given what George Bush Senior's administration had done to mobilize public opinion in favor of liberating Kuwait, President Bush Junior's crowd would do no less in pulling public opinion into their corner, for whatever lay ahead. You couldn't use military options without public support.

There had been no such mobilization of public opinion by Washington during Vietnam, and by the time politicians understood the need, it had been too late. But this was different from Vietnam. If this truly was terrorism, America had been attacked and citizens would demand both justice and revenge. Without a draft, war now would fall only on the shoulders of a few, all of them volunteers.

In McMillan, at the intersection where he intended to turn north, he saw a silver Lexus SUV nosed against a telephone pole, which looked ready to topple. A battered gray Ford pickup was jammed into the trunk of the Lexus, and a white Luce County sheriff's cruiser was hanging over the curb of the parking lot of the Shanty Bar. The bar's sign was in bright red letters several feet tall. Underneath there was a motto: WHERE GOOD TIMES AND OLD FRIENDS MEET. A crowd of people milled around, looking agitated, not exactly the atmosphere advertised on the sign over their heads. Service thought about driving past to get to his meeting, but instinct and a sense of duty to a fellow officer told him otherwise. He pulled over and got out of his truck.

A deputy stood with three men in suits. Another man hung back from the fringe of the four. One of them had a sleeve ripped off and was holding a handkerchief to a bloody nose. The other two looked equally disheveled.

Service looked at the deputy and nodded. "Got a problem here?"

The deputy was unfamiliar, a short emaciated man with thinning hair. His black baseball cap was on the ground, his bony face flushed.

"Idiots," the deputy said. His metal nameplate read TELEMANSKY.

"This is patently unfair," the man with the bloody nose grumbled in pain. He was of average height, with a dark complexion, silvering black hair, and scraggly beard. "We were passing through and trying to stop to get coffee when that *animal* rammed my vehicle and drove us into the pole." He pointed to a man in a faded and threadbare green plaid wool jacket.

"Fucking terrorists!" Green Jacket shouted, surging forward, but Deputy Telemansky blocked his way and pushed him back. "*You're* the animals, towel head!" Green Jacket screamed in rage.

"I am *American*," Bloody Nose said forcefully.

Service saw more vehicles arriving, people drifting into the parking lot, a gawking crowd growing restless.

"Camel-fucker!" Green Jacket shouted, shaking his fists. "We liberated fucking Kuwait and this is the shit we get in return? How many Americans did you murder this morning?"

Bloody Nose turned to Service and fumbled, trying to reach into his suit coat, and Deputy Telemansky tried to stop him, but Service blocked the deputy's hand. The man brought out a crumpled business card and handed it to Service. It read JUDGE SAMIR BAAZ. The address was Dearborn, a suburb of Detroit. "My friends and I are going to Marquette for a meeting. That *man*," he continued, pointing at Green Jacket, "rammed us."

Service passed the card to Telemansky, who looked at it and raised an eyebrow.

"Are you all right, Your Honor?" Service asked.

"My nose isn't broken."

"Did that happen in the vehicle?"

"No," the judge said. "After the collision I got out to see what this fool was doing and he attacked me.'

"I'll do worse, you don't get the fuck out of America," Green Jacket said with a snarl.

Service stared down the loudmouth. "Did you ram this man?"

"Fucking eh," Green Jacket said proudly. "Pieces of shit like this don't belong in our country."

"I was born in *Marquette*," Baaz said, his voice breaking. The judge's companions remained quiet and looked frightened.

"Your blood ain't ours," Green Jacket snapped back.

"Telemansky?" Service said.

"Yah, I got 'er." He turned to Green Jacket. "Verlin, you asshole, you can't be trying to kill people."

"I didn't want to kill him, just run his sorry Arab ass out of town."

Telemansky took out his handcuffs. "You're under arrest, Verlin."

"Fuck off, Deputy Dawg," Green Jacket said, earning a laugh from a few of the onlookers.

Service reached over to the man called Verlin and pinched a nerve in his neck. The man's knees buckled. "Stick out your hands, Verlin." The man tried to resist, but Service tightened the hold until the man relented and stuck out his hands so that Telemansky could cuff him.

"This ain't over," Green Jacket said.

"It is for you, Verlin," Telemansky said.

"Break it up," Service said to the onlookers. "This show's over."

The crowd began to disperse, and several people came forward and put blankets over the shoulders of the judge's companions. "Don't judge our country by the actions of a few," an elderly woman said.

"I am *American*," the judge growled in exasperation.

Service stayed until Verlin was in the back of Telemansky's county cruiser and a tow truck summoned from Newberry to haul the damaged SUV there for repairs.

The judge's nose had stopped bleeding by the time arrangements were made. The owner of the bakery across the street from the bar escorted the men inside and gave them coffee and cinnamon rolls, the Yooper equivalent of chicken soup.

Service told the judge and his companions that their vehicle would be towed, another Luce County deputy would drive them to Newberry, and a room would be arranged until their vehicle was repaired.

"Or," he continued, "we can get someone to take you on to Marquette so you can make your meeting."

Judge Baaz looked at Service. "The meeting can be rescheduled to tomorrow," he said, adding, "I never expected to be rescued by a game warden. Thank you."

"You were in good hands with Telemansky," Service said. The deputy had been bewildered by Verlin's attack, and though Service didn't know the man, he wasn't certain he would have reacted any better or faster than Telemansky in quelling the situation.

"All I know is that the situation was not getting resolved until you arrived," the judge said. "This tragedy in New York . . ." He didn't finish the thought. "Thank you."

Service nodded.

"This is the start of a terrible chain reaction," the judge said.

Service nodded again, and thought the judge was right.

"I never felt like a foreigner until today," Baaz said with sadness in his voice. "Never."

Service patted the judge's arm. When their escort arrived he made his good-byes and headed for his meeting with Griff Stinson.

The old hunting guide was sitting in his truck at the end of a two-track, listening to the radio when Service pulled up behind him.

"Have you heard?" Stinson asked with a nod at the radio.

"Yah."

"Sometimes it seems like this bloody world wants to pull itself apart," Stinson said.

He took Service to a green tarp. When he lifted it, Service saw a large black bear with coarse, matted fur. Griff got down on one knee and lifted the animal's front left leg to show its chest cavity. "One round put her down. All they took was the gallbladder," he said.

They both knew what it meant. There were several cases a year of the same thing. The gallbladders were shipped to agents on the West Coast for sale to Asian customers who believed that powders from the organs had aphrodisiac powers.

Griff poked at the entry wound and rolled the bear over. The bullet had torn a massive exit hole. Stinson had fought in Korea and been decorated. "I'd say a fifty-caliber. Not your usual poaching weapon."

Not just unusual, Service thought, but unprecedented. Still, he reminded himself, people up here loved their guns, so no doubt there were some strange and illegal weapons floating around, or somebody had bought himself a single-shot fifty-caliber from one of the many specialty manufacturers who played to male fantasies about being mercenaries or soldiers of fortune. One kill didn't amount to anything, but it was something to file in his memory. Something related might pop up down the road. First thing tomorrow he'd put the word out to U P. COs and tell them to keep a watch for a fifty-caliber weapon.

"Thanks, Griff."

The old guide touched the bill of his faded Red Wings hat and took out his pipe. "You think this world will ever get to the point where there are no more wars?"

Service didn't answer.

"I guess a cop has to think that way," Stinson said. "Thanks for coming over."

When Service called Nantz, she was sobbing. "Come home, honey," she said. "*Please.*" It was a one-word order disguised as a plea.

Just east of Seney there was a portable marquee propped on a flatbed trailer in front of a church. The sign said PRAY: GOD ANSWERS KNEE-MAIL.

Grady Service doubted God answered anything. He probably sat in heaven shaking his head at the shit he saw back on earth. All the way home he noticed that American flags were sprouting in front of homes. They hadn't been there on the way to McMillan. If the intent of the people who'd attacked New York City and Washington D.C., had been to arouse American emotions, they had succeeded. Maybe this *was* another Pearl Harbor, he thought, shuddering at the implications

· 3 ·

Nantz had awakened him before daylight, her soft lips trailing butterfly kisses across his chest. After a long embrace, flesh against flesh, Maridly had straddled him the way she liked, holding her hands gently against the sides of his head, making love to him slowly, relishing the sensations and the buildup, lingering with each movement, sliding downward almost lazily, and when they came together she lay her head next to his ear and whispered, "I love you Grady. Just you, in all ways, always."

Later they had gotten into the shower together and she was as relaxed as he had seen her in the almost three weeks since September 11.

In the shower she held him tight as water cascaded over them. "You are a great fuck, Service. For an old guy." She punctuated the punch line by tickling him. He retaliated until she squealed for mercy, and they ended up outside the shower with Nantz sitting on the counter, her legs wrapped around him, raptly watching them in the mirror

"I thought it was men who're visually stimulated," he said as they moved together.

"I'm New Woman," she said, her breath coming in bursts. "And I am *close.* You there?" she asked, her words clipped. "Grady, *there?*"

"When you are," he said, keeping cadence with her hips.

"Yep," she said. "Yes, there she is, there she is . . . God!'

All the while Newf was scratching on the bathroom door trying to tell them to hurry up, that she had her own needs to tend to.

After they had finished Nantz began to run water in the tub. "I'm gonna take a long soak, hon. I hear they don't give you time for real baths at the academy."

They both laughed.

Tomorrow Nantz would depart for downstate to attend the nine-month DNR Law Enforcement Academy in Tustin, a town south of Cadillac. By next spring she would be in her probationary year as a new CO. They had been living together since July, and Service had enjoyed their routine and closeness. Now they would be apart for much of the coming twenty-one months.

16 · JOSEPH HEYWOOD

Maridly had a good idea of what lay ahead. She had talked at length with Kate Nordquist, who had graduated from the academy the previous spring and was now field-training with Eddie Moody, the CO in Manistique. Moody had a nose for finding illegally killed animals and was known in the force as Gutpile. He was an immense officer who could charm people one moment and petrify them with fear an instant later. Nearing forty, Gutpile still attacked his job like a new officer. Kate Nordquist, twenty-three, told Nantz that he was "way cool."

Nordquist had been to the house in Gladstone several times, and she and Nantz had become friends. The new CO was tall and lean, an attractive woman with a good mind and a model's face, an attribute that could work for or against her, depending on circumstances. Gutpile told Service that Nordquist was "solid," high praise coming from him.

"Kate says the school's tough," Nantz said as she tested the water with her toe and slid into the tub. "They make you stand at attention and spray Mace in your face."

Service had heard. The DNR Law Enforcement Academy had been created three years before under their state training officer Captain Chamberlin, who looked faintly like a sleeping owl but was a raptor in his work; he was called Blood Hawk behind his back. Chamberlin was a longtimer who had made it clear to all who would listen that he intended to make the academy far more demanding than Troop School—the vaunted Michigan State Police Academy. The DNR academy would be longer and tougher.

In Service's day new recruits could graduate from any police academy program where they learned basic law enforcement, then join the DNR for specialized fish and game training. Blood Hawk had put together a program that combined basic police work with fish and game law enforcement, and so far it seemed as tough as advertised. The idea was to put new officers into the field with a much stronger preparation for the job and to test them early and often in order to weed out those who didn't belong. Service and Gus Turnage had been asked to serve as instructors for the tracking module. And Service would also teach the search and rescue section—if his new job would allow it, and if his suspension had not turned Chamberlin off to him. Chamberlin was fanatical about appearances.

He had heard about the Mace-in-the-face drill and wasn't happy that Maridly would have no choice in undergoing this. In his Troop School class it had been strictly voluntary; not undergoing it had not been held against trainees.

But he felt like he knew Nantz well, and he knew she could handle it. He had seen her in action as a fire officer. Despite all the wealth inherited from her late father, she had shown an incredible devotion to the resource and her work.

But Blood Hawk had a different notion of how the world was, and Nantz would have to endure it.

"Did you get Maced at Troop School?"

He nodded.

"Was it awful?"

"Yah."

"If you can do it, I can do it," she said.

While Maridly lolled in the tub he took Newf downstairs and let her out, made Nantz's favorite almond-flavored coffee, and started the batter for lemon-raspberry muffins.

There would be no work today. He had one mission and that was to heap his attention on Maridly and help her to pack. She would depart tomorrow after lunch and drive to Cadillac where she and several other recruits would spend the night at Jerry Openlander's Cast-and-Blast Inn. Jerry was a longtime officer who had retired with a medical disability after a nasty snowmobile crash near Mesick. He had moved smoothly from law enforcement officer to hotelier and his business seemed to be working out. Monday morning all recruits were to report to Tustin to begin their ordeal.

This would be their last full day and night together, perhaps for months, and Service planned to shower Nantz with affection, good food, and good wine. Only sex took priority over food in Maridly's scheme of life. She would say, "Great sex, great food, and humor make for great love, and a couple with great love and challenging work make for a great life." She never talked about children or motherhood, which he found curious, but he didn't press her on it. They had not discussed marriage, and if this was how she wanted it, then he did too. She was thirty-two and he was nearly fifty, an eighteen-year difference. He wondered if there would soon come a time when she began to feel her biological clock running out.

He set the oven to 425 degrees, took frozen raspberries out of the freezer, dumped them in a bowl, and strained away the syrup. After dolloping the muffin mixture into a pan, he slid it into the oven, set the timer for nineteen minutes, poured a cup of coffee, and started preparing the crabmeat egg casserole. When the buzzer sounded, he took the muffins out, reset the oven temperature, and put the casserole in.

By the time Nantz came into the kitchen wearing only underpants, Newf was back in the house and Cat was bumping against his legs to irritate him. Nantz nuzzled his shoulder and sat down.

Nantz seldom wore clothes around the house. "You're almost fully clothed," he said teasingly.

"Practicing for the academy," she said with a smirk.

It still wasn't clear to him why she wanted to be a CO, only that she seemed determined, and in their three months as a couple he had learned that when she set her mind on something, she would not be swayed. Earlier in the week he had asked her how she wanted to spend her last day of freedom and she had said, "Eating like a pig and fucking like a nympho."

"Nymphomaniacs can't get off," he said.

"Okay, so I'll be a pseudonympho," she shot back.

She sat in the chair nursing her coffee and sniffing the air like an animal.

"It smells so *good* in here!" He had never met a woman so attuned to scents and aromas.

When the two-quart casserole was ready, he removed it from the oven and let it stand five minutes before scooping out wedges.

"Oh God," she said with her mouth full. "You think they'll have food like this at the academy?"

He laughed. "Overcooked meat, soupy taters, frozen veggies, and semifresh fruit."

"Savages," she said. "I guess I can lower my standards."

They ate in silence for a while. "You and Gus will be teaching, right?"

"I hope," he said. She eyed him curiously. "The suspension sort of tarnishes me. Cap'n Chamberlin may decide he doesn't want all you academy virgins soiled by my presence."

"Well, the captain better not mess up my plans," she said. "I'm going to be first in my class to fuck an instructor," she added with a leer.

"I don't know if that will be possible."

She rolled her eyes. "Don't you worry, Detective. *I'll* handle the logistics."

He opened a bottle of 1971 Cuvée Dom Perignon and filled two flutes. He put small shot glasses of orange juice beside them.

"Bubbly for breakie. My favorite." She held the bottle in front of her and studied the label. "You must've dipped deep into your piggy bank," she said approvingly.

He grinned.

Her tone turned serious. "You know champers makes me horny."

Now he rolled his eyes and grinned. "You are terminally horny."

Lifting her glass for a toast, she said, "To us."

"To you," he said, their glasses clinking a delicate musical note. "You'll do great downstate, Mar."

She closed her eyes when she sipped the champagne. "Definitely the *good* stuff."

Nantz ate like she was starved.

At one point she suddenly put her fork on her plate and looked at him. "Grady, I have something very important to ask you."

He put down his fork and looked at her. He had no idea what was coming. With Maridly, it could be anything.

"When I'm on my deathbed, will you pull the plug for me?"

"You'll outlive me," he said, grimacing.

"I'm serious, Grady. Will you pull the plug or won't you?"

"If that's what you want."

"Right answer. Next question, will you fuck me in the hospital bed before you pull the plug?"

He started laughing and couldn't stop.

They skipped lunch and loaded her truck with her gear and clothes. As always, she was organized in every way; his only job was to mule her gear down to the truck and store it under the cap.

It was a warm afternoon for fall, in the upper fifties, and they took his truck to the Mosquito Wilderness, parked, and walked down to the Mosquito River. Brook trout were wearing their spawning orange and were gathered on the gravel runs, the females in front of several males that jockeyed and pushed each other around, trying to be first to spew milt on the eggs.

"Gawd," she whispered. "There's sex everywhere we turn!"

He spread his jacket on the grassy bank and they sat together to drink in the sounds and smells of the forest. "I'll miss this place," she said.

On their way back out of the tract three hours later, they found Candace McCants parked behind his truck, sitting in her state vehicle.

McCants was in her fifth year as a CO. She was Korean-born, a muscular five-six, afraid of nothing, and had inordinate common sense. Unlike other young officers she wasn't a health freak. They found her puffing on a cigarette.

"Hi Candi," Nantz greeted her.

"Hey," McCants said with a sly grin and a stare at Service. "Afraid I'm not taking care of the Mosquito?"

Nantz intervened. "I leave for the academy tomorrow," she said. "Not that it's the state's business, but if you insist on being nosy, we were fornicating like animals beside the river. He does it really good," she added.

McCants coughed, grinned, and shook her head. "You two are made for each other."

Service turned red.

Nantz laughed. "Philosophically and physiologically, I can assure you that everything fits."

Service felt his blush deepen. Both of the women saw his embarrassment and began to laugh together at his discomfort, the sisterhood at work.

"Why'd you tell her that?" he said when they were in the truck.

"We did it in my mind," she said. "Doesn't that count?"

Nantz pottered outside the house while Service made dinner. He had put a lot of thought into the meal and began preparations while Newf followed Nantz around outside. Through the kitchen window he watched Maridly throwing sticks, which Newf retrieved, barking for more. Cat sat on the porch looking disgusted at the dog's suck-up behaviors. Things seemed so perfect at the moment that Service began to wonder if it would last. It never had for him. Maybe life was not meant to be perfect. He certainly didn't deserve Maridly Nantz, but now that they'd found each other, he wasn't going to let her go.

The challenge of a big meal was similar to an investigation. You had to bring several things along on parallel tracks so that they all finished at the same time. He baked a mushroom and Stilton galette, which he would reheat before serving, then made a harvest fruit salad, and started on an oven-braised venison ragout. Once the prelims were done, it would be in the stewpot in the oven for ninety minutes.

Dessert would be baked apples with Calvados custard sauce, which he would make later in the evening before they went to bed.

When things were coming together he decanted two bottles of the Armagh, Jim Barry 1998 Shiraz, to breathe and set the table, using Nantz's china. He mused over the fact that only a few months earlier he'd been using a G.I. mess kit to eat from. When he had moved in with Nantz he had brought virtually nothing but Cat and Newf and some of his gear. He was nearly half a century old and a man without possessions because he had liked it that way. But he also had to admit to himself that he was enjoying Maridly's things, her comfortable bed, dishes that matched, furniture that fit the contours of their bodies, a lawn, and hot water that never ran out. It occurred to him that he was getting soft and losing his edge, which at the moment seemed irrelevant. Nantz and Newf came in while he was checking the venison, which fell apart under his fork.

"Mmm, it smells good in here!" she said, grabbing him and kissing him hard. "Will you always be my chef?"

He put on a disk, *The Best of Miss Peggy Lee*, and turned up the sound.

"Is that woman's voice pure sex or what?" Nantz said. Peggy Lee was one of her favorites.

When she tasted the wine, her eyes rolled back. "Oh, man," was all she said. She picked up one of the bottles. "The Armagh. Honey, your piggy bank's gotta be getting empty. How much?"

"It's not important."

"Grady."

"One-oh-one."

She thought for a minute, then circled the table and threw her arms around him. "Ten-one, the date I start the academy. God, you are *such* a romantic, baby. Don't ever change and don't let the rest of the world know who you really are."

They began with the galette, had small portions of acorn squash soup with toasted walnut butter, small harvest fruit salads, and the braised venison. Not much wine remained when they were done.

After dinner they sat on the couch while Nantz went through her paperwork for the academy for the umpteenth time. "I can't believe I'm really going," she said.

"You're ready." He had tried to give her an edge by starting her training as soon as she announced that she had been accepted for the academy. She'd been running and lifting free weights every day. She was a short woman, five-three on her tiptoes, but with large hands, well-developed upper arms and back, and she was powerful. She had the thighs of an athlete and endurance that was remarkable. More important, she was quick.

He had used a game his father had used with him to develop his hand–eye coordination, tossing colored BBs into the air and yelling a color when he released them. It was her job to grab all of that color that she could, an exercise that most people could never come close to mastering, but she had. In basic defensive tactics, her speed and quick response time served her well.

Only in her firearms training had he found potential weakness. She handled a shotgun all right, but the forty-caliber SIG Sauer handgun seemed to freeze her. She stuck with it, though, and now she could shoot respectable scores and would be able to avoid rubber gun school, the remedial firearms training that seemed to be the destination of a proportion of female officers. She would face challenges and surprises, but she was ready.

"I'm going to do my best," she said. "For us. It would be awful for Grady Service's woman to disgrace him."

"It's *your* program, honey. You couldn't disgrace me if you tried. I seem to do that just fine on my own."

She kissed him gently on the cheek. "Are we going to have dessert?"

He went to prepare the apples and rejoined her while the dessert baked.

"I've got a buzz on," she said as she started to undress with a gleam in her eye. They finished making love just as the timer buzzed.

Nantz tasted her apple and sighed. "Almost as good as sex. *Almost.*"

In the shower in the morning she said seductively, "Wanna go again?"

He put both hands up in surrender. "I can't," he said, shaking his head.

"Thank God!" she said, laughing. "If I have to have a pelvic as part of my medical tomorrow I don't know what the doctors will think! What's for breakie?"

"Fried eggs and asparagus, orange juice, and Trenary toast."

"No champers?"

"You have to drive today."

"Ever the cop," she said.

For lunch he made shrimp and feta cheese pasta and filled a thermos with coffee for her five-hour drive to Tustin. She had been pensive all morning and when he walked her to her truck, she clung to him for a long time. When he looked down he saw tears in her eyes.

"You can do this," he said. "You're ready."

She blotted at her tears with the back of her hand and laughed. "Not the academy, you dolt. Us. I can't stand being apart, I really can't, Grady. I feel like we're halves of one person now, joined at the hip."

"Wrong location," he said.

She punched him lovingly in the arm "You."

"Us," he said, turning serious. "Us." No other words would come out.

She said, "I adore you, Service." They kissed and hugged tenderly for a long time while Newf sat watching them.

He stood beside her truck as she started the engine.

She rolled down the window.

He said, "I'm proud of you."

She looked at him, tears cascading from her eyes, rocked and pulled away, but stopped after a few feet, jumped out and ran back to him, hugging him with such power he almost fell.

When she got back into the truck again, she stared at him with her focused look and said, "I'm going to drive down to that academy and knock their dicks off."

I t was his fiftieth birthday and Grady Service was alone, missing Nantz and feeling down. She had been gone nineteen days and it seemed like forever.

It had been a typical morning in his new job. An e-mail from the director of the Ralph MacMillan Center at Higgins Lake reminded DNR personnel of the meeting facility. Service didn't blame the guy for trying to keep the center full. Under Bozian, budgets were always at risk. At one time the RAM had been earmarked almost exclusively for DNR use, but DNR budgets had been chopped and the RAM had been forced to look elsewhere for users. Now on rare occasions when DNR personnel needed to use the place, there wasn't space.

A half dozen e-mails came in from headquarters in Lansing pointing out deadlines for various reports.

He had another e-mail from Glen Sheppard, editor of *The North Woods Call*, asking for the name of a man at Wakely Lake who was developing a new form of bluegill popper.

An e-mail from Parks and Recreation provided a preliminary report on summer state campground use and explained that the new advance reservation system for camping permits was a success in its first season.

There had been eight phone calls. He passed a question about deer hunting in the Mosquito to McCants after fighting the temptation to take care of it himself. A woman from Gwinn called to complain about illegal trash dumping on state property. A magistrate from Escanaba called for clarification of a ticket Service had written last spring. Lansing called to say they were forwarding a pile of computer reports of non-residents who had used false ID to buy resident hunting and fishing licenses.

Pure scut work, the whole lot.

Too damn much time talking on telephones, he told himself. Twenty years on the job and he had been reduced to this. A recent talk with Hoagy Chalk still lingered in his mind. Chalk, the commercial fish specialist assigned to Naubinway on Lake Michigan, had stopped by for a beer a few days after Nantz left for Tustin.

Having spent many years in open boats on the Great Lakes, Hoagy was always tan. He was a short man, built like a miniature sumo wrestler. He had been in Vietnam as a Navy river rat, been wounded twice, and came home with a Silver Star.

"You hear about Laurie Aho?" Chalk asked.

Aho was a retired CO who had covered the Keweenaw for years, a dour Finn who did his job and never had much to say. Aho's wife claimed they would sometimes go months without passing a word.

"The cancer got him," Chalk said. "Another horseblanket into the ground."

The little fish specialist didn't wait for a response. "Guess we're both getting to that age," Chalk continued. "I see these old horseblankets going and I think I've gotta get out of this shit so I can live a little before I become worm chow." He took a slug of beer and burped. "I've put in my papers, Grady. When I go, you'll be about the last of the Vietnam guys left," he announced. "When are you going to hang it up and get a life?"

Service grinned. "They'll have to carry me out in a box," he said.

Chalk didn't laugh. "It's getting tougher out there, Grady. It's a game for the young officers, not old dinosaurs like us. Hell, those kids look at us like we're horseblankets."

Service had never thought of himself as a dinosaur or a horseblanket. Horseblankets, what the real old-timers were called, worked 24/7 and never stopped chasing a poacher until they had him in court. In those days juries often decided the outcomes and more often than not they let the worst poachers off, fearing retribution if they brought in guilty verdicts, but that didn't stop the horseblankets from hauling the same perps in over and over. Some of these contests raged on for years and took on legendary status. The real dinosaurs were his father's contemporaries, the generation of COs who had been through the Second World War and did their jobs without complaint or expectation of better pay, much less promotions.

"You learn to work smarter," Service countered.

"Maybe," Chalk said. "Right now hanging it up seems the smart thing to do."

It had been an unsettling conversation. He had called Maridly that night and talked to her about it.

"You should hear the way they talk about you down here," she'd said.

"I can imagine." He'd been in and out of hot water throughout his career.

"The instructors believe in you, Grady. They tell trainees about you, how Grady Service does things."

"How will I know when it's time to retire?" he asked her. He couldn't imagine it being an arbitrary date on a calendar.

"You'll know, honey."

He wondered if he would. Was he really the last of the Vietnam guys? It was a disconcerting thought.

Captain Grant had called Service at the house while he was lifting weights at 6 A.M. and told him he wanted him to move his office to Marquette to be nearer to him. Rationally the decision made sense. His office was a cubicle in the District 4 office in Newberry and he was seldom there. Another change, he thought. Everything was changing around him, people retiring, retirees dying.

Later Lieutenant Lisette McKower called to wish him happy birthday, saying nothing about his office move, which left him wondering if she knew. McKower was the senior officer in Newberry. Then Candace McCants dropped by unexpectedly with fresh cinnamon rolls from Gerties in Kipling and they drank a pot of coffee.

"Missing Nantz, eh?"

He nodded.

"Ain't love grand," she said.

"Why don't you get your ass out in the dirt where working wardens are supposed to be," Service said with a playful growl.

She laughed and gave him an upside-down left-handed salute. "On my way, Your Surly Detectiveness."

Moving his office would be a pain in the ass. He would have to drive two and a half hours to Newberry, load his truck with his files, and backtrack to Marquette to new digs. He didn't want to move, but the captain's tone was serious and there was no point in delaying things, he told himself. Some birthday this was turning out to be.

When he got into his truck, the cell phone sounded. He picked it up, flipping open the lid to activate it.

"Goddamn *motherfuckers!*" Nantz screamed. He held the phone away from his ear.

"Maridly?"

"Cocksuckers!" she said with a hiss, barely containing her temper.

He had never heard her so angry. "Calm down, honey. What is it?"

"I'm out," she said.

"Out?"

"Like out of the fucking academy!"

He wasn't sure what to say or even what question to ask next. What could she have done? "Out of the academy?"

"Yes," she said. "Blood Hawk pulled me aside this morning after our run and told me that I am being transferred to Lansing."

This made no sense at all. "They don't transfer trainees."

"They're transferring me to something called Task Force 2001. It's part of the state Emergency Management Division."

"What exactly did Chamberlin say?"

"He said that upon reevaluation of the state's emergency preparedness in the wake of September eleventh, a determination has been made that EMD needs to be beefed up. Because I am a state employee and because of my past experience I've been tapped for the duty. I'm supposed to report there this afternoon."

Reevaluation of emergency preparedness? Service's gut began to rumble. "Reporting to whom?"

"No name, just a fucking address. I am pissed, Grady, really, really pissed."

And hurt, too.

"I do not understand this, honey," she said. "I do *not* understand this. Somebody is fucking with my life and I am pissed."

"Calm down, baby. We'll get it figured out."

"I'm ready to march over to the captain's office and tell him to shove EMD up his tight ass."

"Don't do that," he said.

"Why not?"

"Because I'm asking you not to."

She sputtered momentarily. "I would do this only for you, Grady."

"I know."

"So I just pack up and go to Lansing?"

"No choice if you're under orders."

"Fucking assholes," she said.

"Do you want me to drive down?"

"No, I'm a big girl and if I'm going to be a CO I need to deal with this shit. I'll call you after I get to Lansing. Now I'd better get moving. You seen Kate yet?"

"Kate Nordquist?"

"Yeah, Kate. She's got your birthday present. I love you, Grady, and I'm sorry to be such a bitch."

"You're not."

"I'll call you tonight, honey. I love you, Service."

He didn't tell her about his office move because it suddenly seemed irrelevant. His move was no more than an irritating detail. Hers was serious. What the hell was happening to her?

Service telephoned Captain Grant.

"I just talked to Nantz. She's been yanked out of the academy and is being transferred to something called Task Force 2001 in Lansing. What's going on, Cap'n?"

"Are you moving today?"

"I was just about to leave for Newberry. I'll be back this afternoon."

"See me when you get to Marquette."

Did the captain know? There was no way to read his boss. He usually knew everything that went on in the DNR throughout the state.

He was in a dark mood when he got to Newberry.

His office was a tiny cubicle filled with boxes and stained paper cups. The walls were gray, there was no nameplate, and there were no mementos or decorations. He loathed offices, hated every minute he had to sit in a chair.

Lieutenant Lisette McKower came in as he angrily threw the last of his files into a cardboard box.

"Hey birthday boy, you planning to do some homework?"

"No, I've been ordered to move my office to Marquette."

Her mouth hung open, but she recovered quickly. "Well, it will give you faster access to the west side and you won't have to drive so far."

Service glared at her. "I don't like being jerked around," he said, picking up the boxes and storming out to his truck.

McKower followed him outside.

"What's wrong, Grady?"

"I'm following orders!" he said, snapping at her. "We're *all* following orders. Nantz has been yanked out of the academy. She's been reassigned to some task force in Lansing."

McKower said, "That can't be done."

He glared at her. "It *is* being done."

The DNR office in Marquette was not far from the ancient state prison that housed the "worst of the worst" of the state's burgeoning population of felons. He left the boxes in the truck and went directly to the captain's office. Captain Grant was talking to his secretary, Fern LeBlanc, and when he saw Service in the doorway, he motioned for him to come in. Fern slid out quietly and closed the door.

"I talked to Chief O'Driscoll. The transfer order originated in the executive branch," his captain said apologetically. "Until the EMD releases her, Trainee Nantz is stuck there. I talked to the chief and we're keeping her position open. If she misses too much time and can't get back into this class, she will have a slot in the next academy class."

"Thanks, Captain, but this sucks."

"It's not for you, Detective. It's for the department. Nantz is standing at the top of her class right now, and we do not want to lose an individual of her quality."

"She's angry, Captain."

"Talk to her," Grant said.

Executive branch? Service suddenly understood the game—the governor's office. It was Clearcut again. Nantz's transfer was intended as a message to him; the coward was using her to get at him.

He told himself that somehow, some way, he would get even with Sam Bozian.

Nantz called at 10 P.M. She had reported into the office on the south side of Lansing. The office was empty; she was the only person there. A woman from EMD's human resource unit had dropped by, helped her set up her computer and e-mail, and gone through a quick orientation to the building and its facilities. When Nantz asked to whom she would report, the woman said vaguely that the task force was in the process of being formed and at some point others would begin to arrive. Until then, Nantz was to keep regular state office hours and check e-mail for instructions.

"I feel like a prisoner," she said.

"Do you want the CO job?" he asked her.

"Goddammit, you know I do."

"Then you have to hang in there and stick it out."

"When did you become an organization man?"

"This is Bozian's work," Service told her.

"Sam?"

"It's aimed at me, not you."

"Sam. Jesus," she said. Her voice said she couldn't believe it.

Nantz had known Bozian for much of her life. The governor had been a friend of her father.

"Where will you live?" he asked.

"I'm at a Motel Seven for now. The HR broad said something about housing at the Troop School, but I don't want that."

Another little shot at him through her. Pull her out of the DNR academy and let her live so she could watch Troop recruits experience what she was being denied.

"Captain Grant talked to Chief O'Driscoll. Your slot is being held for you in Tustin."

"Yeah, but when will I get back to it? I don't want to fall behind, Grady. You can't believe the load there."

"The captain said you are at the head of your class Maridly."

"I am?"

"Number one."

"How the hell can I stay number one if I'm down there and my class is racing along ahead of me? I hate this, Grady!"

He did too. The whole thing had one goal: to drive her to resign, and to get back at him.

"You want to be a CO, baby?"

"Yes."

"Then let's just ride this thing out. The captain and the chief are in your corner." He didn't tell her she'd have a slot in the next class if she were away from the academy too long to finish with this one. She had suffered enough blows for one day. "Bozian will get his," he said, as much for him as for her.

"Maybe I should just call him up and talk to him."

"Don't do that."

She waited to answer and said gently, "You're right I'd blast out his eardrums. But he wasn't *always* an asshole, Grady."

Service had a different view of the governor. "What's the hotel and your room number?" He wrote them down as she spoke and added, "I moved my office to Marquette today."

"Why?"

"The captain's idea. So he and I could be closer—or so he can keep an eye on me."

"Our whole world is turning upside down," she said.

"We'll get it righted," he said, hoping he wasn't whistling in the dark.

"I miss you, Grady."

"Hang in there, honey."

"I'll try," she said skeptically. She sounded really down and trying to be brave.

"Seen Kate yet?" she asked, her tone lightening.

"No."

"You will."

At 11 P.M. Gutpile Moody and Kate Nordquist pulled up the driveway and came to the door.

"What're you two doing here?" Service asked.

Nordquist handed him two boxes and said, "Happy birthday." Then she kissed him firmly on the mouth, prying it open with her tongue. "*That's* from Maridly. But it was pretty good for me too," she added with a giggle.

The larger box felt like a cake. "Are you two working tonight?"

"We had to interview a loser in Kipling," Gutpile said. "We're on our way back to Manistique now."

"Have some cake with me."

"We can't," Nordquist said.

"I can," Gutpile said.

Nordquist took Moody by the arm and started leading him back to the truck. "We're going now." She glanced over her shoulder and winked at Service. "Enjoy your cake, birthday boy."

He sat down at the kitchen table and opened the box. The cake was covered with purple frosting, and in the middle was a photograph of Nantz totally nude, posing suggestively. In the second box was a Marble knife with a carved curly maple handle. The Marble Arms Company in Gladstone made some of the finest edged weapons in the world.

He laughed until he cried and then slid the cake into the freezer. He would save it until they could enjoy it together. He called the hotel and asked for her room.

"I can't believe you had Kate deliver *that!*" he said.

"I wish we were together tonight, Grady, so I could give you a *real* birthday present."

· 5 ·

The day was off to a fast and rocky start. E-mails were pouring in from COs and Lansing, and Grady Service's telephone wouldn't stop ringing.

Fern LeBlanc, the captain's secretary, stepped into his cubicle with a couple of call-back slips and put them on his desk. "It used to be quiet around here," she said.

The necropsy results of Griff Stinson's bear had come back from the state wildlife laboratory at Rose Lake, the bullet fragments recovered from the dead animal confirming it probably had been killed by a fifty-caliber weapon.

The state's Report All Poaching (RAP) Line in Lansing had gotten a tip from a man in Menominee who claimed knowledge of an illegal commercial minnow operation. The RAP people had passed the tip to him, expecting him to investigate.

CO Vilnus Balcers called from Carlshend. A farmer had found a black bear sow and two yearling cubs dead in one of his pastures. The animals had four arrows in them. The arrows were marked and belonged to a retired air force master sergeant who lived at Little Lake. The sergeant had been arrested for illegal bears twice in the past three years. He was claiming the arrows had been stolen, but he had not reported the theft to the local police. Did Service want to take a look?

Virgil Haluska, a forester in the Baraga office, called about the suspected theft of timber from state land near Channing and thought maybe it was a crew who had been working the area for nearly two years. He could use some help in developing a case.

CO Bob Putnam called from Stephenson. He had busted an unlicensed taxidermist in Wallace and found ten boxes of live massasaugas. The Michigan rattlesnakes were endangered and protected by the state's Endangered Species Law. Did Service want in on the case? The taxidermist told Putnam he was selling them to collectors and was willing to deal.

Minnows, dead bears, stolen trees, illegal snakes? Grady Service had his mind on the commercial poaching case. He was thinking it might make sense to drive down to Grand Rapids to interview Kaylin Joquist, and—being so close to Lansing—maybe he could pop over to see Nantz. He definitely wasn't going to chase after other shit right now. He didn't need new cases to work. He was worried about Nantz, who called him every night and sometimes during the day, her own mood growing fouler.

Simon del Olmo called while Service studied the necropsy report.

"When did you transfer? I called Newberry and McKower said you'd moved to Marquette," del Olmo said. Simon had been an officer going on five years. He had been born near Traverse City to migrant workers who worked Michigan in summer and spent their winters in Texas. Despite a peripatetic life Simon had gotten all the way through the University of Michigan and had served as an officer in the Air Cav during the Gulf War, where he had been involved in a fight with the Republican Guard inside Iraq.

"Not long. The dust is still settling," Service said.

"Cool. I got a call from a woman who claims her ex-boyfriend is poaching."

"And?"

"You called me back in September and asked me to be on the lookout for big-buck specialists."

Service had called several COs as he took over the case, hoping one of them would kick loose something useful. To get leads you sometimes had to put out a wide net.

"She claims he's looking for trophy racks. I thought you might want to come on over and we'll take a look," del Olmo said. "The woman told me where this guy hunts. She said he's staked out a couple of animals and is doing his work in broad daylight."

"You believe her?"

The young officer chuckled. "Well, there's a jealousy factor. She says he dumped her for another woman, so she wants to get even. It wouldn't be the first time we got righteous info from an outraged woman."

"When?"

"She says he'll be out there this afternoon. He's working the hardwoods near Lower Hemlock Rapids on the Paint River."

"Okay. Two hours?" Anything to get out of the office.

"*Si, jeffe.*" The aggressive young officer gave Service the coordinates of their rendezvous and added, "Wear your mouthguard. The roads out there will rattle your choppers. I'll bring lunch. Sommers subs. Got a favorite?" Sommers was a sausage shop in Crystal Falls, its meats and sub sandwiches renowned across the western Upper Peninsula.

"Italian meatball on a rye bun, lots of onions and jalapeños. See you in two hours," Service said.

Downstate cops liked their doughnuts, but Yoop COs preferred cinnamon rolls and sub sandwiches, when they remembered to eat, which some days took on a low priority. Service wondered why a retired CO had never opened a sub shop.

"The area's on the west side of the river," del Olmo said. "Take US Forty-One to CR Six Forty-Three, then south. As soon as you cross the bridge over the Paint by the gravel pits, take the first dirt back to the north. Keep working your way north until you get up into the hardwood country. We'll meet about five miles north of the gravel pits."

"In two hours?"

"Think throttle, *jeffe*," del Olmo said with a laugh as he hung up.

Service told Fern LeBlanc he was heading toward Crystal Falls. She seemed relieved. He radioed the office in Newberry from the truck to let them know he was in his vehicle and moving. They could look at the Automatic Vehicle Locator computer to see where he would end up.

It was only 9 A.M., but the temperature was aleady in the high forties, at least twenty degrees higher than normal. The sun felt good coming through the windshield as he headed west on US 41 past Negaunee and Ishpeming.

He was glad Simon called, but he didn't like relying on others to send him work. He'd spent his career taking care of his own business, and he reminded himself with some bitterness that it was not as if he had chosen this job. He had been placed into the position more a bureaucratic thumb at the governor than an earned promotion. Ironically, if he hated the job or flubbed it, the governor would get the last laugh. At heart he was a field officer, happiest when he was in the bush. Despite his misgivings, he had to admit that so far the captain had proven to be a boss he could work with, but Fern LeBlanc was a potential problem. She was used to quiet and having the captain to herself.

In two weeks the firearm deer season would kick off. If there was a commercial poaching operation, it would be in full-blood mode from now through early December. He reminded himself that if you kept your focus on a case sooner or later something came your way, either because of the path you followed or through serendipity, which to his way of thinking amounted to the same thing.

Simon's warning about the roads turned out to be not so much a joke as an understatement.

Several days of steady rain had left the logging roads deep in mud and ruts. Grady could imagine four-G loads as his truck lurched and banged slowly along, scraping bottom, first pressing him upward against his seat belt, then dropping him down into the seat heavily, a compressed roller coaster that threatened to rip the steering wheel out of his hands. At least the sun was shining today, which helped his mood. In the old days officers could choose a vehicle that suited their individual needs, but now department policy offered no choice. All officers drove new Dodge Laramies with double cabs and loose transmissions. The old single-cab trucks had been better in the dirt; the Dodges were better on the highway, which was not where working wardens did their real business. The rough road turned the Dodge transmission into a kangaroo, making it pop out of gear into neutral and forcing him to drive with one hand on the steering wheel and the other hand on the gear shift. Focusing on the driving helped keep his mind off Maridly's emotional state, and his own. The metal pedestal that sat between the front seats to hold his laptop computer rattled and clattered like the wagon of a Gypsy tinker. He had stuffed a heavy winter glove in the handle of the computer's carrying case to mute some of the cacophony. It helped, but not much.

Service reached the rendezvous in Section 14 before del Olmo and parked on a spot of dry ground. He buzzed down the electric windows and sat listening to the chucking and chattering of the dry autumn leaves and felt the breeze. This was more like early summer than late fall. Any day now they would get an infusion of arctic air and the snow would come and remain in the swamps into May. There had been four or five inches of snow on the ground before Halloween, but it was gone now, the ground still too warm to hold it. Nature did things in its own time and its own way. When you lived in the Upper Peninsula, you accepted this or found somewhere else to live.

The report of a rifle broke his reverie. Not the big bark of a high-caliber weapon, but the sharp, toylike crack of a .22 mag or .223, a poacher's tool. He grinned at the thought. It was possible that a squirrel hunter was in the hardwoods, but squirrel hunters nowadays tended to be kids or old men, and neither was likely to be out in an area like this. Instinct and experience suggested a violet—his own term for a violator.

Service got out of the truck, carefully leaving the door slightly ajar, took his binoculars, and walked slowly through an area of blowdown toward the sound. He was in a relatively open stand of oak and beech, with a cedar swamp at his back. Deer were still in the hardwoods, pigging out on the mast crops, but soon they would head for heavy cover and stay there until overcome by the rut and the need to copulate, which put animals and humans on an even footing. Where sex was involved, dumb decisions could get made with disastrous results for either species. When you had your mind on sex, you didn't have it on other things, a factor that led to human miscalculations and a lot of dead bucks. He made a mental note to remind Nantz of this, but she was so pissed off these days he doubted her libido was engaged.

After a cautious ten-minute stalk through still-green ferns, Service spotted a figure at the base of some beech trees about a hundred yards ahead. He guessed by the way the figure was hunched over that he probably had a deer down.

He circled the kneeling figure and got into a position that would put the sun in the man's face.

The man was gutting a gray-black buck with a handsome set of antlers, as thick as fists at their base.

There had been a single rifle shot, but the orange-and-green fletching of an arrow protruded from the animal's neck. Coincidence maybe, but Service doubted it. They were in an extremely isolated area, and it wasn't likely that two hunters would be out here at the same time. Hunting deer with a firearm before November 15 was against the law. Killing a deer with an arrow was still legal. Poachers seeking heads liked neck shots. Bowhunters preferred lung shots.

Service approached the man cautiously and silently. He looked to be midtwenties, with long scraggly hair, decked out in full camo.

"Nice buck," Service said.

The hunter lurched at the sound of the voice and squinted to find the source of the voice.

"DNR," Service said. "Good shot."

"Yah, I been watchin' dis galoot coupla weeks, eh. Seen him a half dozen times." The hunter was nervous, his face twitching.

"Get him from a tree stand?" Service asked.

"Nah, brush blind." The man's eyes betrayed panic.

"Where's the blind?"

"Back over dere." The man nodded in a direction that could take in half the compass.

"You hear a rifle shot?"

"Shot?" The man said, shaking his head.

"Could've been the wind," Service said, knowing full well what he had heard. When you dealt with violets, it helped to put them at ease before you pounced. The best approach was to get them talking, then trap them with their own words, a contest he enjoyed. "The wind plays tricks on old ears. Can I see your license?"

"See my license?"

"Yah, your license." When somebody started repeating your questions you could be reasonably sure they were trying to buy time to think.

"She's back in da blind, eh."

"Ought to have it on you so you can tag the buck."

"Dude, I was gonna to tag 'er."

Dude? "Let's walk back to your blind and get that license. Your bow there?"

"Yah." The man got up and Service fell in a step or two behind him, letting him lead the way.

"Where's your vehicle?"

"You mean da truck?"

"Right, da truck," Service said.

"She'd be oot to da road. I walked in. Figured if I got lucky I could drive 'er in, pick 'er up."

It was not at all likely that a hunter who was after a specific buck, especially one with a handsome ten-point rack, would risk leaving it in the woods to be stolen by somebody else. Service had seen no trucks on the way in. The area had been logged over and was crisscrossed with a varicosity of tote roads. It would be easy enough to stash a truck somewhere close by.

"How far did he come after he was hit?" Service asked.

"A ways." Service would check for a blood trail later.

The hunter led him into an area of slash, and as Service looked for footing in a pile of fallen logs, the man bolted, running full out. Service scrambled through the tangle, barking both shins, and began to pursue, but stopped. The man had a good lead and was moving at a fast clip, his skinny ridge-running arms windmilling. Service knew he had no chance of catching him unless he fell.

Service hustled back to his truck and got on the radio to Simon. "Three One Twenty-Two, where are you?"

"Half mile southwest of your position if you aren't lost."

"I've got a runner heading your way. He's in his cammie-jammies. He ought to cross your path soon. You want to put the hook on him? He won't be expecting two of us."

"You're not in hot foot pursuit?"

"Experience makes an officer smarter."

Del Olmo laughed. "Experience or age? Don't worry, *jeffe*, I'll nail his sorry behind. You want me to bring him to you?"

"That would be peachy. Wait for me by my truck."

"Stopping now. I think I see your man All camo?"

"Yah, with hair like Samson."

"And the build of Barney Fife?"

"That would be him."

"See you."

Service returned to the buck and knelt down. The arrow was not lodged in the way modern arrows tended to penetrate. He put on a latex glove and wiggled the arrow gently, suspecting that beneath it he would find a small slug or pieces of one, but to be safe they would take the animal into Crystal Falls and ask a biologist at the district office to do the extraction.

It was forty minutes before del Olmo appeared, his prisoner cuffed and sitting in the suicide seat beside him, the man's head slumped, hair glistening, nose bloodied. Simon didn't look much better off, his gray shirt torn, his green trousers stained with mud.

Service helped the prisoner out of the truck. "Where's your rifle?"

The young poacher chewed his bottom lip and refused eye contact.

Service studied the man's jawline and guessed he was going to clam up.

"Taking a deer with a rifle in bow season," Service said. "Fleeing and eluding."

"Resisting arrest," del Olmo added. "He wanted to wrestle. Add assault."

"Sounds like jail to me," Service said. " 'Course there're easier paths, eh."

The hunter would not look at him.

"Any ID?" Service asked his colleague.

"Empty pockets."

"No hunting license? Not even a small-game ticket? You need that just to carry a rifle in the field now."

"*Nada*," del Olmo said, running a hand through his hair. "Like Mama Hubbard's cupboard."

"Let's call Iron County, let the deputies transport our sport," Service said, turning to the man. "Be a lot easier on you if you talk to us. Silence doesn't take you anywhere but deeper into the cannibal's pot."

The man said nothing.

Service shrugged and looked at del Olmo. "Call the county."

His friend radioed the Iron County dispatcher and arranged to meet a deputy on the hardtop county road. There was no way someone could negotiate this terrain in a patrol car.

Simon read the man his Miranda rights and had him sign a card. He signed with an X. The younger officer showed it to Service and raised an eyebrow.

"Don't be a jerk," Service told the man. "We're gonna find out who you are. That's a given."

"Name's Jason Nurmanski. I can't write, dude."

The two officers looked at each other. This didn't happen often, but neither was it a rare occurrence. "Makes things sort of tough, doesn't it?" Service asked.

Nurmanski shrugged and stared at the ground.

Service said, "Okay Jason, we're gonna take you out to the hardtop and a deputy will take you into Crystal. The deputies will get you cleaned up and get you something to eat. I'm leveling with you, Jason. You really screwed up, but your cooperation will go a long way toward making things easier. Where's your rifle?"

The hunter remained silent.

"What about your bow? You leave that stuff out here and somebody will come along and that'll be the last you'll see of them. You got enough money to lose your gear?"

The man shook his head and Service knew he wasn't going to talk.

"You can call a lawyer from the jail."

Again, there was no response.

"I'll be back after I drop him," del Olmo said.

Even with two of them searching it took most of the remainder of the afternoon to locate the rifle. It was a twenty-two magnum made by Remington, a new bolt-action single-shot model with a four-power Weaver scope mounted on it. There was no ground blind and no bow or arrows. It looked like the man had shot the buck with the rifle and carried in one arrow to try to disguise what he had done. No license either. Service found where the man had stood and one spent cartridge on some dead oak leaves. The serial number on the weapon had been filed off, an indicator that it was stolen, which suggested another reason for the man's reluctance to talk.

They took the weapon back to the truck. Service got out a thermos of coffee and lit a cigarette. "This kid is having himself a most shitty day," del Olmo said. "Sandwich?" The two men unwrapped their subs and ate in silence, drinking coffee.

"Pretty fast, wasn't he?" Service said.

"Had his adrenaline rockets lit full burner."

"He put up a pretty good scrap?"

"Desperation—a flailer. Must be a nightmare to not be able to write or read," del Olmo said.

"He the one you got the tip on?"

"Yep, but I didn't want to let on we were tipped. Some of these young palookas got some strange values. A woman turns her old man in to a cop, she's gonna be toast."

"New rifle," Service said. "Somebody will have reported it stolen."

"Let's hope," del Olmo said. "It's a big state."

"It'll be local. Our boy doesn't look like a traveling man."

"You want this?" del Olmo asked, holding out a dill pickle.

"You dropped it on the ground, right?"

"Five-second rule," del Olmo said, grinning. "I love it when these yahoos want to wrestle," he added. No matter how violent a scrap with a violator, conservation officers always called it wrestling, their typical understatement.

"I like it when they don't run so damn fast," Service said, as much to himself as to del Olmo.

The other officer grinned and nodded "He was fast."

"Not fast enough today," Service said. 'It sucks to be him."

"You wanna go with me to talk to his lady?"

They drove to the district office and put the deer in the truck bed of one of the district biologists. Service left his vehicle in the parking lot and rode in del Olmo's truck.

The woman lived in a trailer not far from the old Mansfield Mine, which had been the scene of the state's worst mining tragedies back in the late 1800s. A tunnel had collapsed, and dozens of men had drowned. Many of the bodies were still entombed. The woman's trailer was close to the road. There was a dilapidated Datsun parked in front.

Simon knocked, and when the woman finally eased open the door, she said, "Go away! Geez, what's wrong with youse guys, comin' oot here in da daylight?"

"There aren't any neighbors," Simon said.

"Da woods got eyes," the woman said.

She stepped out onto the small wooden platform that served as a stoop and shielded her eyes from the sun. She wore a soiled white cardigan over a T-shirt. The sweater was buttoned once—up high—and a swollen belly protruded beneath. Her hair was disheveled, her skin broken out in some sort of rash.

Service thought she looked to be seventeen, maybe younger.

"We arrested Jason this afternoon," Simon told her. "You can bail him out."

"Hell wid 'im," she said. "Been porkin' some chick over to Gogebic. You guys got 'im, you can keep 'im."

Service got the rifle out of Simon's truck. "You recognize this?"

"Da chick, she give it to him. She was gonna pay him."

"For a buck?" Simon said.

"Only a big guy," she said.

"He told you this?"

"Yah, get Jason in bed and he blabs, eh?"

"Did he tell you the woman's name?"

She leered. "He'd a done that, I'd a cut off her tits. Bastard said wun't be right to tell her name, so I called youse." She quickly added, "You see 'im, don't be telling 'im who called youse, eh?"

They met Jason Nurmanski in a small room in the jail, which was attached to the Iron County courthouse on top of the hill in Crystal Falls.

"So, Jason," del Olmo said. "We're looking at fifteen hundred dollars for a fine here, some jail time, and your rifle's gonna be condemned."

"I got no rifle."

"We found a Remington twenty-two Mag out where you popped the buck."

"I used da bow, dude."

"There wasn't any bow, Jason."

Nurmanski scowled. "Some fucker musta tooken it. The woods're filled with gankers these days."

"Who's the woman who gave you the rifle, Jason? What was she going to pay?"

Nurmanski locked angry. "You talked to that bitch Marcie!"

"Who's Marcie?" Simon said. "We've got a report from Gogebic. The Remington was stolen."

The young poacher glared and stared at the far wall. "I don't know shit."

The officers got up to leave. Nurmanski said, "Tell that bitch Marcie I'm gonna superglue her mouth shut."

Out in the dark hall, Service said, "You played that nicely."

"Ironic," Simon said. "It can be a crime to tell a lie, but it's not a crime to tell a lie to catch a criminal. Some system, eh? You want to let him make bail?"

"Can you talk to the judge, tell him we have a rifle without a serial number, get him to jack up the bail?"

"No problem. By the looks of Jason, fifty bucks would be too high."

On the way home to Gladstone, Service got a call from del Olmo on the cell phone.

"He'll be arraigned tomorrow. We're adding possession of stolen goods to the charges. The judge will boost bail, but I don't think Nurmanski wants out."

"Did he call a lawyer?"

"Says he doesn't want one and I get the feeling he's happy right where he is," his young colleague said.

Kaylin Joquist had been caught downstate with trophy heads and still sat in jail in Grand Rapids. Now this kid in Crystal Falls was acting the same way. Could the two men be linked? Grady Service wondered as he drove east.

As he pulled into the driveway at the house his cell phone rang.

"Service, Lars Hjalmquist in Ironwood. You know that fifty cal you asked us to keep an eye out for?"

"You found one?"

"I busted a guy named Cacmaki today. He took a shot at my grouse decoy from his truck. He's one of my regulars, and this is the second time this fall he's pulled this stunt. He told me he saw a fifty being used."

"This was unsolicited?"

"Not exactly. Last time I bagged him I told him to watch for a fifty and if he located one, I might owe him a favor." This was the sort of thing most officers did, using what they had to get more, banking and trading favors. Hjalmquist had fifteen years of experience and knew what he was doing.

"Where'd he see this?"

"Up in that rolling country southwest of the Porkies."

"You buy what he says?"

"He's an old-timer who doesn't want his knuckles rapped again. His old lady will stick it to him."

"You make the trade?"

"It's not like I won't get him again. He can't help himself. I gave him a warning. He was one very happy old coot. He says there's a woman named Wealthy Johns. She's the one he saw using the weapon. She works for Skelton Gitter at Horns. She's also his housemate, if you get my drift."

"Do you know her?"

"Seen her around and heard about her. Good-looking barfly with bittuva rep with the boys. She shoots over to South Superior Gun Club all the time. Supposed to be a helluva shot."

"Was she alone?"

"Just her, and old man Cacmaki said it sounded like a howitzer. What do you want me to do?"

"Gitter's supposed to be legit." The man was a well-known taxidermist with a big shop in Ironwood. He sold guns and fishing gear and won awards for his mounts. "How about you go over to the store when she's working, inquire about the fifty, see what she says."

"It's not illegal to have one."

"Unless its been modified to automatic. Just tell her you're interested and let her take it from there. I want to know how she reacts."

"I've got a pass-day tomorrow and Joan and I have to do something over in Hurley, but I'll get over to Gitter's the next day and give you a buzz afterward. That work for you?"

"Thanks, Lars. Way to keep your ear to the ground."

"Sometimes I think my ear's glued to the ground."

"Think of it as an occupational advantage."

"That's a good one," Hjalmquist said with a chuckle.

Service felt good when he got out of the truck. If there was a fifty in the U.P. it had to turn up sooner or later. Maybe this was the break they needed.

6

L ars Hjalmquist called back the same afternoon that Jason Nurmanski was arraigned in Crystal Falls.

"I talked to Wealthy Johns," Hjalmquist said. 'But I wasn't
alone. Brakelight Bois stopped by for coffee and I took him along. I didn't
figure he'd be too threatening."

Service laughed. CO Jamie Bois of Bessemer had twenty-three years
in the field and long ago had lost whatever fire he'd started with, which
had not been much. When younger officers got a call, they tended to ac-
celerate toward the action. By contrast, Bois tended to step on the brake
and debate the pros and cons, earning him his nickname. His reluctance
to engage meant he wrote few tickets, preferring to spend time in coffee
shops and talking to school groups. Alone, information developed by
Bois tended to be suspect, but Bois had only tagged along with
Hjalmquist and Lars was the kind of professional you could depend on
in any circumstance.

Hjalmquist continued. "I told her I'd heard she had a fifty and I was
curious about it, said I'd never seen one. She said Gitter owned one but
sold it to a guy from Indiana. She said it was a bolt-action made by Harris
Gunworks in Phoenix."

"Not her weapon?"

"She said Gitter owned it until he sold it."

"Did you ask for paperwork?"

"No, she seems pretty sharp and she'd know that we don't look at
records unless there's a crime under investigation and rarely without a
subpoena. I didn't want to stir her up. I just made a polite inquiry and
she answered politely."

"No concern on her part?"

"None. She was calm, friendly, businesslike, like a visit from a couple
of woods cops was ho-hum."

"What does she look like?"

"Nice, I guess." Lars was married to Joan and she was the only
woman he seemed to see.

"Describe her."

"Okay, let's see . . . five-two to five-four, severely short black hair, blue eyes, well built, good figure. Do you want me to go back and push her?"

"No, let's just keep our eyes and ears open and see if the weapon turns up again. If it's gone to Indiana we may have to take a look at that angle later."

"Why the interest?"

"A fifty was used to pop a bear over near McMillan in September. The shooter took the gallbladder and left the rest to rot."

"I never heard of a woman poacher," Hjalmquist said thoughtfully, "especially not one shooting a fifty-caliber cannon, but I guess there's always a first time, eh? If any woman could shoot a fifty, Johns could. The newer commercial models have a kick no worse than a twelve-gauge. Give a shout if you want anything else."

Service was pleased and quickly informed the captain, who agreed they should not press the woman unless there was evidence of her doing something illegal with a fifty. If the weapon was sold and gone, there was no point in stirring the pot.

Late that day he learned of a new wrinkle in the Nurmanski case.

The young poacher had been arraigned as planned, but contrary to his claim of not wanting a lawyer, he had somehow gotten connected to Severino "Sandy" Tavolacci, who pled him not guilty. Service hadn't been there, but Simon sat in and called afterward to fill him in. Nurmanski had refused to post bail and seemed to prefer to sit in jail. What the hell was Sandy doing with Jason? Tavolacci was the mouthpiece-of-choice for major poachers across the western Upper Peninsula, but he made a point of keeping on good terms with DNR law enforcement personnel. Service made a note to call Tavolacci at some point and talk to him. Jason Nurmanski wasn't the sort of client Sandy handled: too small in scope, too young, not enough money. Tavolacci's involvement didn't make sense.

It was just after 7 A.M. and Service was sitting at the table in the kitchen, waiting for the coffee to be done. Nantz had called him just after 3 A.M. saying she was having "those feelings" again. She had awakened him from a sound sleep, and her voice immediately turned his thoughts to sex. He had said something dumb and she had snapped at him.

"Not *those* feelings, Service! It's what I felt before September eleventh."

She had rambled on about how she hated having premonitions. He had tried to reassure her that most of them didn't materialize, and she had growled at him, "*Mine* do."

He had tossed and turned the rest of the night. She was alone and unhappy and there was nothing he could do to help her. He definitely needed to take that trip to Grand Rapids, talk to Kaylin Joquist, and get over to Lansing.

Despite a lousy night's sleep, he was out of bed. his morning weight-work done, and determined to get enough caffeine and nicotine into his bloodstream to help get him moving.

The telephone rang just as he reached for the coffeepot.

"Service, Joey Pallaviano." Pallaviano was the sheriff of Iron County. "I just left your buck-whacker Jason Nurmanski. He's in the mood to talk. You'd better get over here."

"Is his lawyer going to be there?" Service had dealt with Tavolacci several times and didn't like the man. In his mind the lawyer was worse than the criminals he represented.

"No, the kid dismissed Sandy this morning and the little shit's been on the phone to me and the prosecutor trying to argue his way back in, but Nurmanski's adamant. He said he doesn't want a lawyer, *especially* Sandy. He's jacked up pretty good."

"Be there in two hours," Service said. "Thanks, Joey. Can you call del Olmo?"

"I called him first," the sheriff said. "He asked the same questions you asked. Do they make you guys with a cookie cutter?"

Service was filling a thermos and smoking his second cigarette of the day when the phone rang again.

It was Captain Grant. "Joquist, that fellow sitting tight in the Kent County Jail, committed suicide late yesterday afternoon under circumstances being described as suspicious. The Kent County people are investigating. I meant to call earlier, but I heard that Fish and Wildlife have been visiting Joquist."

"Working on a deal?"

"I heard they were talking and that's all I can verify."

Service tried to get the new information in perspective. Kaylin Joquist had been a possible link to the poaching operation, and he and his lawyer had done everything in their power to keep him inside. Now he was dead, and suddenly another poacher who seemed equally content inside wanted to talk.

"I just got off the phone with Joey Pallaviano," Service told his superior. "Jason Nurmanski wants to talk."

There was no need to remind the captain who Nurmanski was.

"Interesting coincidence," the captain said.

"My thought too," Service said. "I'm headed over there and I've asked del Olmo to join me." Were the two events related? And if Joquist's death wasn't a suicide, had his conversations with Fish and Wildlife been a causative factor?

"Let me know how it goes," Grant said.

Service closed his eyes. He should have gotten his ass down to see Joquist and Nantz. He cursed himself for not moving more quickly. It wasn't speed that killed investigations. It was procrastination.

Two hours later he pulled into the parking lot behind the Iron County Jail, and Sandy Tavolacci hurried toward him with mincing steps. The lawyer was short and wide, dressed in his usual black trench coat with a turned-up collar.

"Hey Service."

"Sandy."

"I got a client here."

"Me too," Service said.

"I heard my client wants to talk to you fellas. He oughta have the advantage of my expertise, am I right?"

"Who're you talking about, Sandy?"

The lawyer looked befuddled. "Da fuck ya tink? Jason Nurmanski."

"You're the attorney of record?"

"Yah, on paper. Dis kid, up dere he ain't got it wired so good, eh?" Tavolacci put his forefinger at his temple, made a swirling motion and shrugged.

"What's that supposed to tell me?" Service asked.

"Just dat he don't seem ta be tinkin' too good. He coulda walked on bail. I told 'im if he didn't have money, no problem-o. I got a cousin who can post bond, eh? But dis kid says he likes it where he is. Who woulda thunk it?" Tavolacci shrugged again. "It's a pain workin' wit amateurs, eh?"

"Where did your client get the money to afford you?"

"It's pro bono, I gotta heart. Da law ain't all money, eh."

Service let him talk.

"I get a pro, we come in, I plead 'im, we post bail, powdee-pow, we're outta dere and I bill maybe an hour, two tops. A good lawyer don't gotta cost you both your nuts. I just wanna help this kid, maybe get him going straight."

That would be a first, Service thought. Tavolacci was as peculiar as the clients he represented, but despite his dunce act, he had a sharp mind and he had put a lot of people back in the woods who didn't belong there. But he also had to interact with a lot of woods cops and when he thought something wasn't quite right, he usually found a way to signal his concern. In this case Service had a pretty good idea what Sandy's concern was, if not why. Tavolacci handled pros, not amateurs, so how had he gotten hold of Nurmanski, and why?

Sheriff Pallaviano suddenly appeared in the parking lot and walked directly to them. "He's waiting," he told Service. "Simon's already in there."

Tavolacci started to walk with Service but the sheriff grabbed the lawyer's sleeve. "Not you, Sandy."

"Da kid's mixed up, Joey. I'm 'is fuckin' lawyer."

"You'll have to take that up with your former client, but you'll have to do it later. You're not on the A-list today."

"Hey Service," the lawyer yelled out. "Yer an asshole, just like yer old man."

"Who tipped Sandy?" Service asked when the sheriff joined him inside the building.

"Loose lips," Pallaviano said. "The little fuck makes it a point to know county employees. You know how things work up here."

Jason Nurmanski looked even more spooked than he had the afternoon Service and del Olmo arrested him. He was dressed in an orange jumpsuit, his hair still oily and matted. They met in a tiny interrogation room in the jail. Simon stood by the door, while Service sat at the table with the prisoner.

"You want to talk, we're here to listen," Service said. "What's on your mind, Jason?"

Nurmanski opened his hands in a gesture Service took as a plea. "Dude, I done wrong. I fucked up and I know I gotta pay, but not here, eh."

"Iron County's accommodations not to your liking?" Service asked.

The prisoner's eyes hardened. "I got information. You get me moved, different name when I get out, da whole thing. You dudes can do dat."

"Michigan doesn't have a witness protection program, Jason," Service said. "That's federal."

"I don't give no fuck who you gotta talk to," Nurmanski said. "This ain't no fuckin' joke." The panic in his voice was rising.

"Why the sudden change of heart?"

"I got my reasons," the young poacher said.

"Anything to do with Kent County?"

The prisoner's eyes flashed with fear. "Why don't matter. What I got is what matters."

"Well, let's hear what you have. We don't buy until we see the merchandise. Where'd you get the Remington?"

"It was give to me."

"It's stolen."

"If you say so, dude."

"Receiving stolen goods is a felony."

"Do you want to hear what I got or not?"

Service nodded.

Nurmanski reached out a hand. "Gotta smoke?"

Service set a pack and his lighter on the table.

The prisoner lit up and inhaled deeply. "Couple weeks before I seen you dudes I was up to Wakefield, place called da Copperhead Inn. I met dis chick inna bar. A little older den me, but pretty good, ya know? A player, major babe. We threw down a few and pretty soon she's yankin' my snake under the table and I tell her we ought to get outta dere. She drove me to da Mer-can over to Iron River."

"The American Inn?"

"Right, the Mer-can, right, on da left as you go down the hill into town."

"We know where it is. What room number?" Simon del Olmo asked.

Nurmanski shrugged. "How do I know, dude? You don't pay attention to dat shit when you got a hard-on, know what I'm sayin'?"

"Right," Service said. "Iron River's a good hour from Wakefield. Why so far?"

"She said she's married, dude, din't want her old man findin' out."

"Did she already have a room there?"

"No, I went in an' got it."

"Did you pay?"

Nurmanski looked embarrassed. "No, dude, she said it was her treat."

"So you signed in. Single or double?"

"Single, no sense wastin' money, dude."

"Did you register in your own name?"

"Yah."

"Whose license plate number did you use, hers?"

"No man, I made one up. Dey never check dat shit."

"Okay, so you checked in. Where was she?"

"Out in da truck. She come in tru da back door"

"She never went through the lobby?"

"No, dude. I went out and tolt her da room number and I go in first and open da door and den she slips in."

Simon interrupted. "I thought you didn't remember a room number."

"I forgot. It was one forty-three. So, we like scromped all night, dudes—"

"Scromped?" Service said.

"Did it, got it on, like that," Simon said acting as interpreter.

"Right on, dude," Nurmanski said. "Next mornin' she asks me I wanna earn some cash. How? I ask. She says, 'Bring me a big buck, ten-point at least, and you get five hundred cash, which is worth twice that if you had to report it to da IRS.' I told her I don't pay no taxes and she said, 'You want da goodies or not?'"

The poacher took a puff on the cigarette and continued. "I tolt her sure. We go out to her truck and she brings Remington outta case. Says it's new but clean, it's da best for poppin' deer. Shoots straight, not much sound. I thought what da hell, and she said when I got back we'd get it on again. She was so hot, eh? I said yes and right dere in da parkin lot in broad daylight she goes down on me. Dudes, it wasn't da money as much as I'd like ta get down wid dat again."

"You got the buck, but you didn't keep your date."

"Right. But she showed up here yesterday morning. She had ID saying she was my sister, only I ain't got no sister. She told me she heard I'd gotten busted an' dat when I got out I better keep my mout shut. She said another guy down in da Kent County lockup was about to learn da hard way to keep quiet." Nurmanski fumbled to light another cigarette. "When I seen her walk in, I was like that." The poacher held up his fore-arm and fist. "After she talks to me, I'm like Jell-O. She scared da shit outta me. Dis mornin' I hear coupla guards talking about a suicide in the Kent County lockup yesterday and I decide I'm not made for dis shit. I called da sheriff."

"Who is she?" Service asked.

"All I know is Kate from Wakefield."

"You're putting me on," Service said.

Jason Nurmanski made the sign of the cross. "*Honest*, dude. Says she lives Wakefield. She's got my snake in her hand under da table. I'm gonna ask for ID, dude? I never met a woman who give it up da way she did."

Service looked back at del Olmo, who shrugged.

"What's she look like?" Service asked.

"Long red hair, dude. Straight like a hippie. Big tits, bush-hair same color as da hair on her head. *Bright* red, man. You oughta see dat!"

"So this woman hired you, but you don't have a contract or the money, right?"

"No, dude. Tings don't get done like dat. C'mon, you know dat, right? I bring back da goods and she pops da cash."

"You think this is enough to get you into federal witness protection?"

Nurmanski leaned forward. "Dude, she told me she works da whole Midwest, see? Dat's like federal shit, over state borders an' such? Dudes pay big cash for racks an' she gets 'em. She gets da guys like me to do da work. Buck horns, bear paws and gallbladders, all sortsa shit. Do I get da deal or what?" Service thought about it. Antlers and bear gallbladders. Could this finally be a link to Griff Stinson's bear in McMillan? Not likely. McMillan was nearly 150 miles east. In twenty years he had known only one poacher who ranged across the entire U.P. and that was Limpy Allerdyce.

Service pushed a cassette recorder in front of the prisoner, took out the old tape, put in a new one, and pressed the ON button. "Tell the whole story, Jason, from the time you met the lady and she offered you the money through her visit yesterday. When the tape is done we'll have a court recorder type it up. Your lawyer will read it to you and you can sign your X to verify it's the statement you made."

"No lawyer, dude. Specially not dat wop Tavolacci. She sent dat little prick to me. I don't want *nobody*. Just read it ta me and I'll sign."

"No promises, Jason. You give us everything you've got and we'll see what we can do. That's the best we can do for now."

"I *gotta* get outta here," the man said. "If she can reach a dude down below, she can get ta me."

"The Kent County death was a suicide."

"Right," the prisoner said. "And Santy Claus don't scromp wid 'is missus all summer."

If this mystery woman had the reach to get somebody inside, her operation had to be large, powerful, and well protected. Sending Sandy Tavolacci was an indicator of clout and provided an explanation of how and why the lawyer had hooked up with Nurmanski. And she had identification that depicted her as Nurmanski's sister, which suggested some sophistication, if there had actually been ID. "We'll see what we can do to move you," Service said.

"Cool, dude." Nurmanski began talking into the recorder.

Service and del Olmo stepped outside.

"Paranoid," the younger CO said.

"Maybe, but check yesterday's visitor roster and see if you can get a description."

"I doubt the person who admitted her saw her pubic hair," del Olmo said with a grin.

Service winced. "I'm gonna call Barry Davey in Grand Rapids." Davey was the U.S. Fish and Wildlife Service agent responsible for the U.P. Unlike the FBI, the BATF and USF&WS had their agents live elsewhere and travel into the area. "Sit on our boy and make sure he doesn't fuck up the tape."

"On it now."

Service went to his truck, got his cell phone, and called Barry Davey.

"Grady Service, I'm in Crystal Falls."

"Howyadoin Service?" Davey had a thick New York City accent.

"Good. Listen, we have a prisoner up here who claims he was hired by a commercial poaching operation. He claims that someone from the organization told him yesterday morning that someone was going to be taken out in the Kent County Jail yesterday afernoon. This morning he heard there'd been a suicide."

"Kaylin Joquist," Davey said. "It was a suicide."

"Our guy thinks otherwise. He's under the impression that Joquist was trying to cut a deal and somebody decided to shut him up. Have you or your people been talking to him?" Davey's office was in Grand Rapids, and there were federal aspects to Joquist's crimes.

"He's jerking your chain for a deal."

Davey hadn't answered his question, which was an answer in itself. "This guy has a room-temp IQ, Barry. His dipstick barely reaches oil. His mind doesn't work deep or fast. He believes what he's saying."

"Most nuts and cons do."

"He wants out of the Michigan system and I'm inclined to go with it. Can you work something out?"

"What do we get?"

"Look, I'll need undercover help. If this op is as big as this kid makes it out to be, they'll have resources. Maybe you can send one of your people to give us a hand." Sending in a fed as an undercover in this case didn't sit well with Service because he had never had full confidence in federal agencies. He knew his own people and what they could do and couldn't do, but his gut told him this was the way to go this time.

"You got a target?"

"Yes." Wealthy Johns and Skelton Gitter were not part of the Nurmanski deal, but what the hell, he could use undercover help. Nothing else had developed from afar. It was time to try to put somebody in close. Davey wouldn't admit to dealing with Joquist either. Maybe Wealthy Johns was Kate from Wakefield. He smiled at the irony, then dismissed it and told himself to keep his mind on the puck.

Davey asked, "What's the scope of this alleged operation?"

"Midwest at least."

"That's not peanuts," Davey said. "Here's what I'll do. We've got an arrangement with South Dakota, and we can put your boy out there until we dope this thing out and see if it's worth more trouble. I've got an agent named Pidge Carmody. I can send him up to scope out the situation. He's the best I've got, and I was just about to give him a break after he finishes something he's doing for me, but he likes to work."

"How quick can you get him up here?"

"Let me get back to you tonight."

"Fair enough." Service gave him Nantz's home phone number and rejoined del Olmo and Nurmanski, who was slugging from a bottle of Classic Coke and smoking another cigarette.

Simon handed him a Xerox copy of the guest log. A name was highlighted in yellow. Name: Kate Cunny, Wakefield, Michigan. Relation to prisoner: sister. Service wrote a note to del Olmo on the back of the paper: "Find who checked her in, get a description, and see if there was ID." He doubted there would be. Security in county jails was notoriously lax.

While del Olmo took the tape out to get it transcribed and to find the person who had checked in the visitor, Service sat with Nurmanski. "We've got the start of a deal, but still no promises. We're looking at moving you to another state. Nobody will know you're there. You won't even know where until you get there."

"She knew da guy was in Kent County."

"This is federal, Jason. When they bury you, you'll stay buried."

"I don't like dat word, dude," Nurmanski said.

"Keep telling your story and we'll see what we can co for you, Jason."

"I appreciate it, man. I can't believe a little pussy got me into dis mess."

"Shit happens," Service said. "Sometimes the fucking you get isn't worth the fucking you get."

"I hear ya, dude," Nurmanski said disconsolately.

Simon returned after Nurmanski was returned to his cell. "She never showed an ID. Visitors are supposed to, but it didn't happen this time. The description matches. Straight, long red hair. The guy I talked to said she's a knockout."

That night Barry Davey called back. A copy of Nurmanski's statement had been faxed to him. "Okay, Service. Carmody will come up across the bridge. You got a meeting site in mind?" Service did. "Carmody's the best," Davey said, but his tone told Service he was trying to sell him something.

"What about Nurmanski?"

"A federal marshal from Minneapolis will drive over and pick him up. They'll fly from St. Paul to Rapid City. He can sit out there until we see how this is going to go down."

"Thanks," Service said. "When can I meet Carmody?"

"November ninth is the earliest. He's got something to finish for me first. He'll call you, and you two can set the time and place for a meet."

Service gave Davey his cellular number. Service had just slid under the covers when Nantz called. "Guess what?"

"What?"

"I think I can get away from Lansing for a couple of days."

"When?"

"Friday through Sunday before deer season opens," she said.

"Really? What're the dates?"

"November ninth through the eleventh," she said.

"You're sure about those dates?"

"What is it with dates, Service? Aren't you more interested in the fact that our drought is going to end?"

"Of course. Are you sure you can get away?"

"Right now it looks that way. I hope so, don't you? I love you, Grady."

"Good night, babe." Why couldn't he tell her how he felt about her?

What a fall this was turning out to be. Still, November 9 was beginning to look like a day to look forward to.

The next morning he was at his office in Marquette and stepped into the break room to get coffee. The radio was on. "Bombs," a voice on the radio said and Service immediately reached over and turned up the volume.

"A Michigan Tech public safety officer discovered two explosive devices at three thirty-five this morning before they could be detonated on the campus of the university in Houghton," the announcer said. "One device was outside the school's forestry school and the other outside the adjacent U.S. Forest Service Laboratory. A Michigan State Police bomb squad is on the scene now."

Service returned to his desk and immediately called his friend Gus Turnage, the CO in Houghton. They had joined the DNR the same year and worked together ever since.

"Turnage, DNR," Gus answered.

"Hey Gus. Are you involved in that bomb thing at Tech?"

"Not yet. Wink Rector called me a couple of hours ago and asked if I could be available for tracking if the need arises. I told him sure." Rector was the FBI's resident agent for the Upper Peninsula, a one-man office in Marquette. "The FBI and BATF are here. Wink is going to lead the investigating team: FBI, BATF, Houghton city police, Troops, Tech public safety, Houghton County sheriff, what a bloody monkey-fuck that will be, eh? Glad I'm not part of it."

"*Real* bombs?"

"Damn straight. Five-gallon pails filled with flammable liquid and wired to igniters. Wink says it looks like work typical of some environmental loonies, the Earth Liberation and Animal Liberation Fronts."

"The ones who burned the federal forestry lab in Wisconsin last year?"

"Yah, and they claimed responsibility for putting the torch to an ag biotech program at Michigan State the year before that. Wink says both groups like incendiaries. They like fire. They say it purifies."

"Good thing the university cop was paying attention."

"No kiddin'. A professor up to the college told Rector one of the buildings had enough chemicals stored inside to leave a six-story hole in the ground."

"This has been one fucked-up fall," Service said

"You betcha," Turnage said, "and BOB will soon be upon us." Blaze-Orange Brigade was the term some conservation officers used to refer to hunters who were required by law to wear hunter orange during the firearm deer season. "Guess we'd all better have eyes in the backs of our heads from here on."

"Nah," Service retorted. "We'll just let technology take care of it."

Gus Turnage laughed. "Yah, technology, that's a good one."

It was an inside joke. Under the previous state DNR law enforcement chief there had been a move to make up for the shortage of law enforcement people with increased technology, but so far not a lot of it worked as advertised and budget constraints were such that there weren't enough maintenance personnel to keep the equipment working. When equipment malfunctioned or failed, it could be a long wait to get it back.

Every CO in the state knew that technology could never replace officers. The same thing was in evidence in Afghanistan, Service reminded himself. The United States had satellite pictures out the wazoo but few assets on the ground to tell them what terrorists were thinking. Current state law enforcement chief Lorne O'Driscoll was not as enamored of technology as his predecessor, but his hands were tied by Bozian's budget cuts, and even replacements for retiring officers were slow.

"Be careful," Service told his friend.

A minute later the phone rang again. It was Nantz. "Well?" she said in her confrontational I-told-you-so tone.

"You were right."

"I wish I wasn't," she said, softening her voice. "Have you heard anything?"

"I talked to Gus. They found two devices, now disarmed. No casualties. Wink Rector is handling it. They're thinking ecoterrorists."

"Ecoidiots," Maridly Nantz said. "They'd burn the whole world to save it."

Echoes of Vietnam, Service thought. "People with passions don't necessarily have their brains fully engaged."

"You mean like when we're rattling the bedsprings — not that I can remember what that's like."

"Hang in there, honey," he said. "November ninth, right?" He didn't want to think about their situation now. It was too depressing and he missed her more than he was able to adequately express.

"It's been more than a month, Service. When I was at the academy I didn't have time to think about sex and now all I have is time and that's *all* I think about. What's on your agenda today?"

"I've got choices: illegal minnows, stolen timber, and rattlesnake trafficking. Or I can rattle a lawyer's cage."

"I miss you, honey."

"November ninth," he said.

"Yah, yah, don't you go trying to disarm any bombs, you hear me?"

"No problem."

"I mean it, Grady. My wants have merged with my needs and we are talking burgeoning, do you hear me?"

"I hear you." Did she think their separation wasn't affecting him?

"Okay, you may now go chase your little fishies and snakes."

He laughed out loud, hung up, and filled his coffee mug. *Weird fall* was an understatement. September 11 had been followed by the yet-unexplained anthrax contamination and now there were bombs at Michigan Tech. How much weirder could it get?

He decided to call Sandy Tavolacci.

It took ten minutes for the lawyer's receptionist to put him through.

"This is the son of the asshole," Service said when Tavolacci finally picked up.

The lawyer laughed. "Okay, okay, I was out of line on dat one. I apologize."

"Who's Kate from Wakefield?" Service asked.

"Da fuck should I know?"

"She hired you to take Nurmanski's case."

"Prove it," Tavolacci said defiantly, hanging up.

Captain Grant walked into his office. "Bad day, Detective?"

"Lawyers," Service said.

"Look at the bright side," his boss said. "You won't have to deal with them in heaven."

7

November 9 had arrived, Nurmanksi was gone to South Dakota, Grady Service had reluctantly arranged for his former girl-friend Kira Lehto to take care of Cat and Newf at her veterinary clinic until he got back on Sunday, and the days had dragged as he tried numerous avenues to develop information on Wealthy Johns, getting nowhere. Today he would meet the federal undercover agent, stop to see a troublesome old friend near Brevort, and finally see Mandly Nantz at a B&B in Mackinaw City. He could hardly contain his anticipation.

Pidge Carmody had called two days ago and Service picked a place for their meeting, a nameless roadside rest area two miles east of Naubin-way, which in Ojibwa means "place of echoes."

The meeting site was only an hour from St. Ignace and the bridge. Twenty-five years ago the shoreline south of US 2 and west from Rapid River to Naubinway had reverberated with the sounds of clashes between white and Native American commercial fishermen. The DNR had been caught in the middle of what was now known as the Garden Wars, and had absorbed the anger and frustration of both sides as judicial rulings earmarked large areas of the Great Lakes exclusively for Indian fishermen, thus sealing the fate of the white operations, which were marginal under the best of conditions. Yooper distrust of government was never far from the surface, but the court rulings had caused an explosion of pent-up violence. With a lot of luck and professionalism, law enforcement had gotten through the mess without a fatality.

Service remembered a night in the late 1970s in Big Bay de Noc off Garden Bluff when he and Sergeant Blake Garwood had boarded an illegal fishing tug in total darkness. They had drifted in with their lights out and gone over the gunwales. The captain immediately cranked his engines and tried to run while his crew turned on the two COs. Blake had been thrown over the side during the melee, managing to yell before he splashed. Service screamed for the captain to come about, and when he kept the tug racing away from Garwood, Service fired two shots through the cabin roof. There was a heavy fog on the water and Garwood, a veteran of the Garden conflict, always carried a maritime flare gun attached to his life vest by a lanyard. He used his flares to help them find him and get him aboard. The captain and his crew had gone to jail, but Service still shuddered when he remembered how close he had come to losing his sergeant. Garwood had since retired to the mountains of Tennessee with no desire to be near, much less in a boat on the water. A sign of age, he told himself, when you start remembering the old days.

This time of year, most state-owned rest areas and pull-overs in the U.P. were closed until spring, but this was one of the few left open to service travelers. Before the reign of Sam Bozian, rest areas on both peninsulas had been open year-round. Never mind that snowmobiles had led to a greater influx of tourists to northern Michigan and the Upper Peninsula in winter than in summer. Clearcut had slashed everything he could, and services to winter travelers had been among the first to go. Here a small cedar log building housed rest rooms and vending machines. The facility was only a couple of years old, which made Service suspicious. It wouldn't surprise him if one of Bozian's relatives owned the company that sold the prefab structures to the state. Service left his truck a hundred yards from the building and walked the rest of the way. It was just after sunrise.

There was one man in the small lobby and he was bumping the pop machine with a Frisbee-sized hand. He was tall with massive shoulders and long auburn hair showing hints of gray and tied back in a bobtail. A red goatee made it look like he had chugged a mug of blood. He had a gourd-shaped head and a thick neck bulging with muscular cords. His nose trended toward bulbous, and his cheeks showed webs of blue veins just under his ruddy skin. He wore an electric-green T-shirt proclaiming IRISHMEN LAST LONGER.

DNR Detective Grady Service paused to scrutinize what he was seeing. If this was Pidge Carmody, he was not at all what he had expected. Carmody looked nothing like a cop and even less like a top undercover man. Most successful UCs were nondescript people who could blend anywhere. Carmody would stand out in a circus. But Barry Davey of the USF&WS had given Carmody his highest recommendation, and Davey wasn't one to bestow compliments or respect unless it was hard earned over a long period of time.

"Anything good in the machine?" Service asked.

The man in the green shirt turned and squinted with the eyes of the nearsighted. It was a strange first impression to be sure.

"Just disgustin' nonalcoholic shite," the man said in an Irish brogue. "You'd be Service?"

"That's me."

"Carmody," the big man said, not extending his hand. "Let's be done with da fookin' gettin'-to-know-you games and have us a ramble."

Service wasn't sure what to do. He knew how to develop and run snitches, but working a federal undercover agent was uncharted water. It was difficult to tell Carmody's age. Fifty, maybe fifty-five, he guessed.

The man led the way down a groomed path from the rest area onto a rocky beach of Lake Michigan. Service automatically noted that the water level continued to be way down despite a wetter-than-normal summer and autumn. The water had been falling in the Great Lakes for years, but Bozian had announced a plan to pipe water to other states. Leave it to Clearcut to turn a pimple into a boil, Service thought.

"Davey did a fine job describin' you. What's this job you've got?"

"You in a hurry?"

"Let's not be fookin' with each other, Service. We've both jobs to do, so let's get on with it."

Service was not prepared for such directness. "How much did Davey tell you?"

"Shite-all, the usual. There's a job needin' doin'. You'd be fillin' in the blanks."

"He didn't have all the details to share."

Carmody's shaggy left eyebrow arched almost imperceptibly, and Service knew the man was wondering what he had on Davey to get a top federal agent assigned undercover to a state operation. He'd let Carmody stew on that for a while.

Ordinarily the DNR took undercover personnel from their own ranks, pulling officers from other parts of the state, but this poaching operation at least circumstantially seemed well organized and virtually invisible, which suggested a greater degree of sophistication than normal, and he'd decided he wanted an agent who was unlikely to be inadvertently exposed and compromised. He'd not been entirely candid with Davey in their negotiation around Jason Nurmanski, but now that he had Carmody, he intended to use him to the fullest. Maybe Nurmanski would be relevant to the bigger case, maybe not. Davey had agreed because he'd seen the possibilities of a major bust.

Service explained the situation. "At the end of last year's firearm deer season, an Indiana man named Kaylin Joquist was stopped for speeding by Michigan State Police between Grand Rapids and Kalamazoo. He blew point-two on the Breathalyzer. They had him cold on DUI, but he was not too happy about being stopped and got abrasive. They found ten pounds of wacky weed and three trophy buck heads in his truck. The Troops called us, and one of our District Twelve people responded. The guy refused to talk about anything and got a Chicago lawyer. Every time the case came up, the lawyer got a delay."

"Where was his client in the meanwhile?"

"Cooling it inside the Kent County lockup. Ten pounds of dope and two priors took him out of the bail picture. It turned out that he had two previous felonies, both for distribution, one in Indiana and one in Illinois. He did a year in an Illinois facility."

"Did the lad have a go at bail?"

"Technically, yes, but what his lawyer did was pretty much pro forma. He didn't even begin to push all the buttons."

Carmody nodded solemnly. "Suggesting a symbolic gesture intended to appease outside eyes, and Joquist's happy enough plopped on his arse amongst the brotherhood of perverts and fudge-packers."

"That's how we read it."

Carmody's bushy eyebrow wiggled again.

"Joquist was found dead in his cell about a week ago. He'd hanged himself."

"And you'd be thinkin' it's not a suicide."

"Possibly. There's an investigation, but you know these things don't break unless somebody spills."

"If your boy is in the ground, he can't be affectin' a seasonal business above it."

Carmody was sharp.

Service nodded. "We've gotten information about a poaching operation specializing in trophy deer heads and bear parts. Our info says they operate throughout the Midwest. You want a trophy, you make a bid, and high bid wins. Earlier this month I busted a young guy with a ten-point out of season. His name's Jason Nurmanski. He'd stuck an arrow in the bullet hole hoping to pass it off. Like Joquist, he seemed content to stay inside and wasn't interested in cooperating initially, but last week he changed his tune, dismissed his lawyer and said he wanted to deal. His lawyer was a guy named Tavolacci. He specializes in big-league poachers. We couldn't figure out why Tavolacci would be interested in Nurmanski, but he was and he didn't like being fired."

"Jailhouse percussionists put a beat on the wire," Carmody said with a nod. "Nurmanski learned about the suicide."

"Not a suicide, he claims. He says the person who hired him to take the deer showed up at the Iron County Jail the day of the suicide and told him that a man in the Kent County facility was going to be taught a lesson that same day. The next morning he heard about the suicide. He hoisted the white flag and asked for a deal."

"By his reckoning, it was a hit."

"Right, and he was very hinky. We interviewed him and took his statement. He claims he did his shooting for a woman from Wakefield named Kate. He didn't know her last name and we haven't been able to identify her, but his story seems to check out. He registered at a hotel with her. We thought it interesting that she drove him an hour south to Ironwood from Wakefield and paid for the room. The next morning she offered the cash-for-horns deal."

"And the lad agreed?" Carmody asked.

"She threw in some enticements," Service said. "Kate from Wakefield has bright red hair upstairs and down. She's five-two or five-three and she wants to hire poachers for cash. A woman doing this is unusual."

"Tiz a fact," Carmody said with a grin.

"Nurmanski didn't want a lawyer, but then Tavolacci showed up. We see him a lot. He works for big-time poachers in the west end."

"And Nurmanski isn't of that caliber."

"Exactly. He says that Kate of Wakefield hired him to take his case. Here it starts to get complicated. In September a bear guide found a bear near McMillan. The animal had been shot once with a fifty-caliber rifle and only its gallbladder removed. I put out an alert for other COs to be on the lookout for a fifty, and about a week ago I got a call from one of our people in Ironwood. He stopped a man for shooting at a grouse decoy and the old man told him he'd seen a woman shooting a fifty-caliber rifle near the Porcupine Mountains. He identified her as Wealthy Johns."

Service stopped for a breath. "Johns works for Skelton Gitter, a taxidermist who owns a gun shop called Horns in Ironwood. She also lives with him. I sent our people to see her, express an interest in the fifty-cal, and see what flopped out. She said it had been owned by Gitter, but he'd sold it to a man in Indiana. Wealthy Johns is five-two or five-three, with short black hair, and she's a gun expert who hangs out at a bar called the Copperhead Inn in Wakefield."

"The place where the lad met the mysterious Kate," Carmody said.

"Right, and Johns is a regular at the South Superior Gun Club and said to be an accomplished shooter. Gitter's been in business nearly thirty years. He's always been clean when we've inspected his taxidermy operation, and BATF has never had a violation on him. In fact, he's usually first to blow the whistle on competitors who step over the line."

"The paragon of the public-spirited citizen. God save us from righteous bastards."

"Gitter has a reputation and he *is* good at his craft. He's done mounts for all sorts of species and has clients all over the world. He's won international awards for his work."

Carmody made a face. "Cosmetics. An undertaker can't bring the dead back to life."

"The woman Nurmanski described closely resembles Johns except for hair color, so we've been quietly taking a closer look at Johns, but there's nothing there. It's like she landed in Ironwood fully grown with no history. What we know is that she's a gun expert and spends a lot of time at the gun club."

"Johns is to be the object of my attention then?" Carmody asked.

"Yes, but if this operation is real and as big as it seems, we need to assume Gitter and Johns are in it together until we determine otherwise. Gitter is one of those types who are always in full control and well connected."

"I know the type," Carmody said.

"I want you to set up in the Ironwood area and hang out at the Copperhead Inn. Nurmanski met Kate there. They threw back a few drinks and nature took its course. He insists she offered serious cash for big racks and he claims she bragged her clients are not just in Michigan."

"You agreed to a deal with Nurmanski?"

"Your people have moved him to another state. When his time is done, he's on his own. When you get to Ironwood, buy yourself a new rifle at Horns and ask about a gun club you can join where you can practice. Gitter will probably vouch for you to join South Superior. He does this routinely for customers. If you can buy from Johns, even better, but if you don't meet her there, you'll see her at the club."

Carmody grinned.

Service added, "I expect to hear from you at least once a week, and you're to keep me in the loop every step of the way. We want the whole operation top-down, not just another Nurmanski or Joquist. Davey is covering the cost of the investigation, but you take your directions from me, understood?"

"Aye," Carmody said. "Now for my rules, boyo. We meet only when I call for it and never closer than thirty miles from the operational area. I'll be pickin' the places and the times and your arse will be there. *Capisce?*"

"Works for me," Service said.

"There can't be too many women in those parts like the two you're talking about, boyo," Carmody said with a grunt.

"If Kate doesn't show at the Copperhead, you'll find Johns at the South Superior Gun Club. Anything else?"

"More here than I usually have to start a case," Carmody said. "If there's something of substance, I'll find it" he added, rubbing his nose and winking.

As Carmody got into a dented, rusty Black Land Rover, Service felt edgy. There was something about the undercover man that didn't quite sit right, but Barry Davey had backed him and Service needed him. There was no way he could take the risk of slipping an undercover state CO into the case. It was Carmody or back to the drawing board. Time would tell. It was a lot easier to work alone, he reminded himself as he got into his truck and headed toward Brevort.

In six days Michigan's Department of Natural Resources law enforcement forces would find their resources stretched beyond limits as they patrolled the forests and farmlands of the state, citing trespassers and violators, nabbing night shooters, finding the lost, rendering aid to heart attack victims, calling ambulances for those who shot themselves or each other, breaking up fights over wounded deer and wily women, nabbing drunk drivers, and tending to vehicular accidents. Close to a million well-armed and often overly lubricated hunters would be afoot and afield for some or all of the two-week season, primed to shoot at just about anything that moved. Sometimes their bullets would even hit what they were aiming for.

More women hunted now than in past years, but throughout the state, deer season tended to still be largely a male enterprise—if you ignored the fact that while the men went out to their camps to play Dan'l Boone, hunters' red-suit widows banded together and, looking to even the score, still-hunted hometown bars for out-of-town nimrods while their hubbies and their buds bonded in their deer camps. Women and men on the tavern trail caused a lot of trouble for cops and COs. It was the time of year all conservation officers both looked forward to and dreaded, a time when the North Country plunged into chaos, a time when anything could happen, and often did.

This year promised to be worse than normal as the pall of September 11 hung over the country. The day before the terrorists attacked, survivalists were seen as right-wing-fringe loonies; now even liberals were trying to buy gas masks and antibiotics to fend off bioterrorism.

Of potentially more immediate effect, the Michigan courts had the previous summer let stand a new law that required the state to prove why people should not have concealed weapons permits. Under the old system residents had to prove their need and fitness to carry a handgun. The effect of the ruling was to provide a concealed weapon to just about anybody who wanted one. Despite the fact that the governor backed the law, dozens of Republican prosecutors and their deputies had resigned from county gun boards in protest. Because of the change, there would be more handguns in the woods this year. Just what woods cops needed, Service told himself.

It was Friday and the firearm season for deer would not open until the following Thursday morning, but the highways were already jammed by an armada of vehicles: mini vans, Mercedes and Beamers, rusted-out pickups with dangerously tilting campers, cars and SUVs of every description, all of them streaming north to cross the Straits of Mackinac. The hopeful nimrods would be slugging down tepid coffee, lousy doughnuts, road beers from longneckers, root beer schnapps from pocket flasks, and puffing on homegrown dope and store-bought cheap cigars. They would be of all ages and all occupations and this year, with all the problems and layoffs among Detroit's auto companies, a lot of them would be headed into the Upper Peninsula for the full two weeks, rather than a few days. Every deer-hunting season took on its own personality and no two were the same. This one would be no different in asserting itself, but Service's gut told him this one would be memorable for him if for no other reason than he would not be covering the Mosquito.

He couldn't wait to see Nantz. Since her posting to Task Force 2001 she had been assigned every weekend to immediate-call status, meaning she couldn't leave Lansing.

Until she telephoned yesterday to confirm that they could meet, he had feared that she would be trapped in Lansing again. He had already decided to drive there if he needed to.

"Tomorrow at noon, Banger," she'd said. This had been his nickname during his college hockey days. "At the Brigadoon in Mack City," she added. "The room's my treat and you won't need a change of clothes."

"Has this been cleared?"

"All the boys down here must be thinking only about bagging their bucks. I think they forgot to assign me to my weekend cage."

"I'll be there," he said quickly.

"Damn right you will," she said, laughing with a lightness he had not heard in her voice for a long time.

They would have this afternoon and the next two days to themselves. It promised to be a sleepless time.

But before that he had one more item of business to tend to.

A couple of miles east of Brevort he pulled north onto a long gravel driveway, stopped at a closed gate, got out of his truck, and stared up at a small video camera several feet above him.

"You in there, SuRo?"

"No meat eaters may violate these hallowed grounds," a raspy voice replied. "Got any extra smokes?"

Service laughed and countered, "Tobacco is grown in fields fertilized with animal offal and harvested by pork-eating rednecks."

The voice chuckled. "C'mon in, rockhead."

A buzzer sounded and the gate swung open.

Summer Rose Genova was founder and operator of the Vegan Animal Rescue & Reclamation Sanctuary. Service had known SuRo for nearly eight years. He had happened upon her during an altercation with two hunters who had gut-shot a handsome buck. When they followed the injured animal out of the cedar swamp they found her squatting beside the dead animal, smoking a cigarette. She had shot the animal once through the head to put it out of its misery. The men demanded she surrender their trophy and she refused. One of them leveled a Remington 30.06 at her and she responded by pointing a nickel-plated .380 Walther PPK at him. Service was passing by, saw the pointed weapons, read the situation in an instant, and stopped.

He ordered the men to put down their rifles. SuRo put her automatic back in its holster and, before Service could react, charged the men, knocking one aside and punching the other in the nose, splattering it. When the second man recovered, he tried to intervene, but SuRo dispatched him with a crisp elbow to the jaw that sent him sprawling into a deep ditch. Fight over. After a long and heated discussion he sent the men back to their camp, and ordered the woman into his truck. He drove her into the town of Rock to buy her coffee.

"You can't take an animal from hunters," he said as they drove. "And you can't beat the shit out of people."

"Fucking idiots couldn't piss on a barn if they were resting their pencil-dicks against it."

"That's not your business."

"Fucking eh! It's yours, rockhead. You goddamn grayshirts let people run around who are dangerous to themselves and the animals."

"The law doesn't require hunters to be marksmen."

"It ought to."

She had a point. "I enforce the laws as written, not as I might want them to be. What were you going to do with the deer?"

"Bury it. What the hell else would I do with it?"

He had stopped the truck and stared at her.

She said, "I save animals that can be saved. If they can't be salvaged, I put them out of their misery."

"You'd waste the meat?"

"I don't eat meat."

"Who the hell are you?"

"Summer Rose Genova, DVM. I just moved up here. I've got property near Brevort. I'm going to establish an animal recovery and rehab sanctuary."

"There are laws regulating that."

"I know the laws, rockhead. I do everything by the book."

"Like carrying a sidearm?"

"I have a CCW permit," she said, taking it out of her purse.

There was something about the woman he liked. "I'm Grady Service."

"People call me SuRo and you can help me by telling your fascist colleagues about the sanctuary. They find an injured animal, they can call me."

"Even if they're meat eaters?"

She grinned. "Hell, I can overlook depravity if it serves the animals."

"You could have . . ."

She interrupted with a sarcastic laugh. "Gotten shot by those morons? More likely I'd have had them both on the ground before their fingers got to the triggers."

"That would be murder."

"Murder is what the state licenses them to do."

They spent nearly an hour sharing coffee and cinnamon rolls. Genova was over six feet tall, built like a linebacker and as opinionated as a revolutionary. But Service sensed a gentle heart and a genuine interest in providing a service that was badly needed in the eastern Upper Peninsula. He told her he would talk to the hunters she had tangled with and smooth it out and he had, though it had not been easy. At first the two men were adamant about filing charges for assault against the woman. He had to explain to them that it was their word against hers and that he had found them all pointing weapons at each other. If they didn't let it go, he'd arrest all three of them, confiscate all their weapons, and put it before a judge, which would not happen until long after deer season, in which case the two hunters would be done hunting for the year. The men reluctantly agreed that a complaint would not solve anything.

Since then SuRo had established herself and, in the process, become well known and respected throughout the U.P. Approaching her sixties, she seemed more stooped now, but as vigorous as when he had first met her.

The sanctuary consisted of 400 acres closed in by twelve-foot-high cyclone fencing. She lived in a one-room cabin attached to a larger building where she tended her animals. In recent years she had become a major proponent of the state's wolf recovery program, which was a misnomer because the wolf packs had developed from a few animals that had drifted in on their own from Wisconsin and Minnesota, or across the winter ice of the St. Mary's River from Ontario.

Genova was standing outside her cabin holding a wriggling buff-colored bobcat when he pulled up. He grabbed a couple of extra packs of cigarettes and held them out to her. The cat's fur bristled as it pressed against her chest for protection.

"You ought to smoke a better brand," she groused.

"I only smoke these because you hate them."

"That's my rockhead," she said, turning her head to the side for a kiss on the cheek. "What the hell have I done this time?"

"Hunting season starts Thursday."

She grimaced. "Don't remind me. The bridge packed?"

"Probably like sardines."

"Always with the meat metaphors. Breakfast and coffee?"

"I thought you'd never ask."

He followed her into the cabin. The young bobcat launched itself onto a bed and circled to paw a nest in the covers while Service sat down at the table in her kitchen area. He watched as she whisked pancake mix and brewed a new pot of coffee.

"Where'd the cat come from?"

"Her mama was hit by a pickup over by Pickford. Some kids found the kitten and now she's trying to take over the sanctuary. Rumor has it that Grady Service and Kira Lehto are toast and the rockhead has a new squeeze. Word is she's hot."

Genova and his former girlfriend were both veterinarians and good friends.

"Is she better in bed than Kira?"

"None of your business."

"*Everything* is my business, rockhead! What's your hotty's name?"

"Nantz."

When the coffee was brewed, SuRo lit another of his cigarettes and filled his coffee cup.

"You hearing anything out of Vermillion?" she asked.

Vermillion was the federal wolf laboratory north of Paradise on the south shore of Lake Superior. "Should I?"

"Just wondering."

SuRo wasn't big on small talk. When she asked about something she usually had a good reason.

"It's said they have a blue wolf up there," she said.

Service laughed. "Do they keep it next to a white buffalo?"

SuRo didn't smile. "Why do the ignoramati always dismiss what they don't understand?"

He had to search his memory and the best he could come up with was, "A blue wolf, like the one the Ojibwa believe brings bad luck?"

"Only to those who harass it—or cage it," she said, scooping dollops of viscous pancake batter into a huge black skillet. "And it's not just bad luck, but massive disruption."

"There's no law against people believing what they want. A cult over by Helps believes God is coming back to earth in a UFO."

Genova turned around and arched her eyebrows. "You mean *she's* not?"

Service went to the refrigerator and poured two glasses of orange juice for them.

"You look good," Service said, setting the glasses on the table.

"Knock on wood," she said. "Nothing wrong a sweaty romp in the kip wouldn't cure."

"How's Howard?" Howard Genova, M.D., was her estranged husband, estranged in the sense that she lived in the U P. while he practiced thoracic surgery in Ann Arbor. He couldn't tolerate the people or weather of the north and she couldn't abide flatlanders and their ways. They tended to meet when their moods coincided, which apparently wasn't all that frequently. SuRo did not talk much about her marriage.

"All surgeons are board-certified assholes," she said. "You may quote me liberally."

"What about the blue wolf?" Service asked, his curiosity piqued.

"You *don't* know, do you?"

He shrugged. "First I've heard of it."

"I guess feds are feds," she said, "always playing the secrecy game."

She placed a plate with a half dozen small pancakes in front of him and sat down across from him. "Is this Nantz thing serious?"

"You never can tell," he said.

"I can," she said, grinning. "I hear she's at the academy. How are you two gonna mix work and noogies?"

"We'll manage," he said.

"I imagine you will, rockhead."

· 8 ·

It was an easy fifteen-mile drive from SuRo's to St. Ignace. Traffic south across the Mackinac Bridge went smoothly while the northbound lanes inched along only feet away. As Service reached the highest point of the bridge he glanced back at the northwestern sky and thought it looked like a storm in the offing. The color was right, but the winds were calm, the temperatures unseasonably warm. Rain maybe, sleet if the temperature dropped. There were better odds in playing the state lottery than guessing the weather at the Straits of Mackinac.

The Brigadoon was a sprawling pale yellow building with green-tile gables, Victorian or Queen Anne; he couldn't remember which. There was no sign of Maridly's truck in the bed-and-breakfast's small parking lot, or along the curb of the facing street.

When he walked in and identified himself, the reception clerk grinned crookedly and jerked her head toward the stairs to her right. "Room Fourteen, the Forget-Me-Not. You're already registered and I expect you'd better get yourself down to business PDQ. That woman up there is antsier than a deserted cat on a rock in a rising river."

He wondered where her truck was as he made his way upstairs and down the brightly wallpapered hallway. When he pushed open the door he saw a naked Nantz sitting on the edge of a king-sized bed. Her clothes were in a heap on the floor, her shoes flung against the baseboard of the wall.

She looked coyly over her shoulder at him.

"You're late," she said.

"It's not noon yet."

"If you're not here before me, you're late." She turned around and pointed her finger at him, forming a pistol. "Drop 'em, Banger."

When he reached for his belt buckle, she jumped up and flung herself on him, her arms holding so tight around his neck that she pulled him down onto the bed.

"Forty-three damn days," she said. "That's biblical, a damn lifetime. I love your ass, Service."

"Just my ass?"

Three hours later they walked down to the tourist district near the Shepler Line docks that were home to jet boats that carted summer Fudgies back and forth to Mackinac Island. They settled themselves into a booth on the ground floor of the Oz Marsh Club. They sat beside each other and found themselves surrounded by men decked out in faded red plaid wools and new blaze-orange camo coveralls, most of their faces bristling with whiskers that might reach some semblance of beard status over the next two weeks. The hunters were boisterous, brimming with optimism for the coming hunt.

"Two more weeks," he lamented as they ordered a pitcher of draft beer. "How'd you get here?"

"I flew," she said.

"Into Pelston?" It was the closest commercial airport.

"To here. I flew myself."

"What do you mean you flew yourself?"

She rolled her eyes. "I . . . fly," she said. "I'm a pilot. My own plane? A Cessna One Eighty. You still don't get it, Service. I told you I was *loaded.* I got a lift over from the airfield. I've been hangaring my bird in Lansing for a year or so. Just haven't gotten around to moving it up to Escanaba, and I figured it was time to get the wings out of the hangar. If this 2001 shit drags on, it'll save us time. Smart thinking, huh?" She playfully nudged him with an elbow. "You got a problem with girl pilots?"

He shook his head dumbly and grinned, unable to think of a thing to say. She was so nonchalant about her wealth that he rarely thought about it. She was a *pilot?* What other surprises would Maridly Nantz have for him?

After drinking half a glass of beer, she leaned her head on his shoulder and rubbed his inner thigh. "I'm not hungry. For food."

On the quick walk back to the B&B, Service noted that the temperature was falling fast as they made plans for their belated Thanksgiving. Because the holiday this year fell during the middle of the firearm season, they would have to celebrate in early December. If she could get loose from Lansing, they would meet at her house in Gladstone and cook a turkey and all the trimmings. If the damn task force didn't interfere. If it did, he'd go to her.

"How's Newf?" Nantz asked.

"She and Cat are bunking with Kira."

Nantz poked him in the ribs. "When you pick up our dog and cat that's *all* you'd better be picking up. I don't *share* my man."

Just after midnight, Service's cell phone awakened them. As usual Nantz was instantly alert and got to it first.

He heard her say, "He's right here, Captain."

Service took the phone. It was Captain Grant. "Yessir?"

Service grunted as he listened. "When?"

Another grunt. "Injuries?"

"Yessir, right away." He hung up and felt his shoulders slump.

"What?" Nantz asked.

"The federal wolf lab at Vermillion. They've had an explosion."

"When will this shit end, Grady?"

"Two fatalities. It looks like somebody touched off a bomb to release some wolves. That wrinkle makes it my business. I've got to go."

"This instant?" she asked.

"I suppose we can take ten minutes for us."

"Make it twenty," she said, pulling him down beside her and rolling on top of him. "This has to last us a *looong* time, baby."

· 9 ·

Their allotted twenty minutes turned to thirty. When Service finally negotiated the severe curve that merged with the bridge approach, he was shrouded in heavy fog and it was just before 1 A.M. At this hour he expected the traffic to be lighter than what he had seen earlier, but it was even worse than before; he was hemmed in by the crush. By the time he left, Nantz had decided to go back to Lansing the next day, knowing he was going to be tied up. She was clearly disappointed but didn't say a thing about it, knowing this was the job.

Captain Grant had made it clear that he should expedite getting to Vermillion, which with luck, sparse traffic, and a heavy foot lay about an hour north of the bridge. He turned on his blue lights to goose the traffic along, and most vehicles squeezed right so he could pass. As he carefully crawled past cars and trucks, he remembered the chaos that had prevailed before there was a bridge. Before 1957 five state-run ferries carted vehicles across at a rate of about four hundred an hour, each crossing taking just short of an hour under ideal conditions. Some years, on the night before hunting season, cars had been backed up fifty miles below the straits with waits as long as twenty-four hours. Now, under ideal conditions, you could be across in ten minutes. This morning's conditions were the antithesis of ideal.

There were seagulls hanging suspended in the air at the apex of the bridge, illuminated by lights strung on the three-foot-thick cable housings. The temperature seemed to be rising. The weather at the straits and above could change with breathtaking speed, from good to awful in a near blink. There had been no more snow since Halloween. But it would come, as it always came. Without snow, hunters would be complaining, and with this warm spell continuing, the deer would not move around and hunting would be tougher. In a warm spell deer wouldn't move much during the day, and hunters would quickly start complaining that the lack of sightings meant there were fewer deer—and that this was the fault of wolves.

It didn't matter that there were fewer than three hundred gray wolves roaming the U.P., and that they each ate nine or ten whitetails a year for a total kill of fewer than three thousand deer. Vehicles killed close to twenty thousand deer in the U.P. every year, and the hunters wouldn't be blaming them. A difficult winter would claim another hundred thousand or more, and a severe winter twice that. If hunters weren't finding deer, it wasn't the fault of wolves, but facts seldom mattered when hunters began shooting off their yaps. The reality was that the last winter had been tough, and the deer herd was down in numbers.

A year ago he'd run into a hunter who said he'd stopped hunting near his home in the southern part of the state because the DNR had planted coyotes that were decimating the deer population there. Service had to explain that the DNR had never planted coyotes in the state, but the man refused to believe him, preferring to have an excuse for his inability to bag a deer, an event that many Michiganders took as an entitlement.

On the St. Ignace side he cut through a lane reserved for official vehicles and noticed an unusual amount of activity at the state police post west of the row of tollbooths. There were several National Guard vehicles and soldiers in camo fatigues, more spillover from September 11. Two weeks before, California's governor had gotten tips from the intelligence community and warned his citizens of possible terrorist attacks against the Golden Gate and other California landmarks. Sam Bozian had quickly and publicly beefed up security by sending the National Guard to the Mackinac Bridge and Soo Locks. Service wasn't aware of any specific warnings about Michigan targets, and didn't bother to examine the governor's motives. If Bozian could get in front of a camera, he'd do it—no matter how stupid or petty he looked. In the political world there was no such thing as bad publicity. Regardless of the governor's motivation, increased security in these times was probably smart.

Before racing north, he checked his fuel gauge and cut west onto US 2. He had enough to get to Vermillion, but knew from experience that keeping a full tank was the safest and most practical course—especially on the cusp of seasonal changes. It was warm enough now, but this could change any moment. He pulled into a Jet gas station and saw emergency vehicles converged in the parking lot of the McDonald's next door. Squad car light-bars flashed blue and red under the garish yellow arches. Two town cops and two Mackinac County deputies milled around the restaurant's parking lot.

He watched the activity next door while gas ran into his tank. There were faster pumps at other stations, but Jet had the cheapest gas in Iggy and even with his state credit card he tried to find bargains. After all, the money behind the credit card came out of his taxes too.

A blue state police Yukon joined the other vehicles and Service recognized the trooper who got out; Sergeant Lungo Ocha was known as Bilko by other Troops because of his office gambling pools and various schemes to make money for his retirement

Bilko saw Service, puffed up his chest in an effort to hide his beer belly, and strutted over.

"What brings you this way?" Bilko asked with his customary cockiness.

"Stuff to take care of before the grind begins. What's up over there?" Service asked with a nod toward McDonald's.

Bilko grimaced. "Some assholes busted the front window to get inside. They spray-painted all over the place."

"It begins early," Service said.

"There it is," Bilko said, shaking his head.

"What was spray-painted?"

Bilko pursed his lips and said with a sigh, "Meat is Murder. Mickey D is McPorkers."

"Did they sign their work?"

"AFL."

"I thought they merged with the NFL."

Bilko grinned. "Animal Freedom League or some such shit. Buncha middle-age pinkos and college kids. I guess we should be happy it's not that bin Laden fuckstick."

Service wished the trooper luck, headed north on I-75, and sped up until he got to the M-123 cutoff. He cursed when he found the two-lane M-123 jammed with campers and trucks all wending their way north into the bush; six days until deer season began and the BOB was already out in force. He used his blue lights to surge past clots of vehicles, through Moran, Greene, Kenneth, past Ozark into Trout Lake, and from there north to Eckerman Corners. At the M-28 he saw that east–west traffic was as congested as the north–south 123. He couldn't remember traffic this heavy in previous hunting seasons. Most people might be hunkering down in fear because of terrorist threats, but not hunters. He didn't welcome the influx, but there was some comfort in knowing that some Americans were still out and doing. Maybe carrying guns boosted their confidence. Guns had never done much for him. In fact, in twenty years he had tried never to draw his weapon. Once a weapon was unholstered you were deep in shit-happens-land where all outcomes were seriously in doubt. He'd been forced to pull his weapon on a few occasions, but he had never shot anyone, a distinct change from his tour in Vietnam.

The traffic thinned north of Eckerman, allowing him to settle into a steady eighty miles per hour through the fog, trying to keep an eye out for deer and other animals along the roads. He slowed to a moderate speed only when he reached Paradise.

It was twenty miles to Vermillion, but the road was a washboard from all the rain this fall; he drove cautiously to keep from bouncing into a ditch. He eventually crossed a half-mile-wide marsh where the road had been built on a steep berm and came to the main gate of the federal wolf lab, more commonly called Vermillion.

The lab was two miles east of where the old Vermillion Point Life-Saving Station had once been located, chosen because it was one of the most isolated places in the Upper Peninsula and adjacent to major shipping lanes from the iron fields of Minnesota and the U.P. to Cleveland, Detroit, and Chicago. The lifesavers had been called storm warriors, and six of them and their families had lived at the station until the 1930s. Winter supplies and mail were brought in back then from Whitefish Point, ten miles to the east, winter trips taking eight hours by dogsled. As much as he loved the bush, Service couldn't imagine living near the southern shore of Lake Superior, taking her nasty winter blasts for as much as seven months a year. His old man had always called the taiga-like area Michigan's Siberia, an especially apt description in winter. A group called Piping Plover Pals had recently acquired the old lifesaving station and turned it into a conservancy.

The gate to the federal wolf lab normally was attended by a security guard, but this morning it was standing wide open and two Chippewa County patrol cars were blocking the road. He had been to the Vermillion facility twice before, once two winters ago with other COs for a group snowmobile patrol and once just a month ago as part of Captain Grant's directive that he introduce himself around in his new capacity as a detective in the Wildlife Resource Protection Unit. That time he'd met Dr. Barton Brule, the lab's director. Brule had been gruff, not particularly friendly, and obviously irritated to have a visitor interrupt his routine. Brule was a lumbering man with long gray hair and sagging jowls.

He wondered if Brule was one of the victims.

A deputy sheriff waved him past the roadblock where he parked his truck off the side of the road. He headed east on foot along the road, which passed through tamaracks and cedars in the lee of the sand barriers that lay between him and the largest and deepest of the five Great Lakes.

Through the fog he saw the blinking of emergency lights — two fire trucks, two more Chippewa County sheriff's cars, and two ambulances, all of them pulled up near the lab. There were also two state police cruisers and a lot of people milling around with flashlights. He saw no hoses from the fire equipment, but firefighters were plodding around in their dark, bulky gear.

Service walked toward the knot of people and saw that one side of the building was gone, as were several sections of twelve-foot-high steel fencing that surrounded the compound behind the building. He could smell smoke, see plumes rising from the debris, hear steam hissing. He could also smell the residue of an explosive, but couldn't identify it.

It was difficult to tell now, but the building had been new, less than three years old. Now half of it was in a pile. Service recognized only one of the Chippewa County deputies, a thin woman named Altna Lodner. She was a lethargic, even-tempered professional who took her work seriously, seemed a little stiff around strangers, and didn't leave much of an impression on most people she met.

Lodner nodded when she saw him. "Service. They call you out too?"

"My captain," he said.

"Bad news travels fast."

"What have we got?"

"Two bodies, one male, one female. Prelim says Dr. Larola Brule and Dr. Lanceford Singleton, staff biologists. We're leaving everything alone until the Troop crime scene team gets here."

"Brule, related to the director?"

"His wife," Lodner said.

Service hadn't known Brule's wife worked at the lab. The director had not been chatty the day he'd met him.

"Crime scene team coming from Negaunee?"

The deputy sheriff nodded, and he walked on. Negaunee was a long 160 miles west of Vermillion. The Troops had put their lab there to create a central location to serve the entire U.P., but it was more in the west than the east.

Service pulled his six-cell Mag-Lite from its holster, snapped down the red lens cover, pulled up the collar of his green Thinsulate coat, and walked over to the fence, which was made of ten-by-ten gray steel panels with golf-ball-sized perforations. The fence was connected to the building that housed the wolf lab by a narrow tunnel of steel panels. He had no idea what the tunnel was for. His previous tour had been cursory; Brule had made him uncomfortable and he hadn't asked many questions, figuring it wasn't likely he'd have much contact with Brule or his facility in the future. At least four panels of the larger enclosure had been blown away where the wall was attached to the building. Shreds, strips, and scraps of metal gleamed in the beam of his flashlight.

Service walked around the exterior of the lab building and saw mounts for security cameras. Were there cameras on the gates, elsewhere along the fence? He'd have to check.

He cupped his hands to light a cigarette and continued walking. The wolf compound was oval in shape. He found nothing of interest near the destroyed sections and decided to make the full circuit of the perimeter fence, not sure how far it was. He flicked on his light periodically to study the ground or scan part of the fence.

The morning dew would preserve tracks like disappearing ink, the rising sun quickly melting them away. Dew in November? More strangeness. Usually there was frost—or snow, and up here a lot of snow. Thirty minutes into his tour he saw a small light flicker along the fence ahead of him and stepped under some overhanging cedar branches. When the light got to within ten feet, he said, "Looking for something?"

The light tumbled, sending its beam flashing around, like a drunk with a laser pointer.

Service illuminated the small figure and saw wild, long gray hair and a prune face that reminded him of Yoda.

"DaWayne Kota?"

The man bent over to retrieve his light and flashed it at Service. "Twinkie Man," Kota said with a smirk.

Service had earned the name in a highly publicized case in which a poacher claimed to be intoxicated by Twinkies, a defense that had failed miserably.

"Little off your beat, DaWayne." Kota was the recently appointed tribal game warden for the Bay Mills Indian Community near Brimley. The reservation was at least thirty miles southeast of Vermillion.

"You heard about the blue wolf?" Kota asked.

"Just yesterday."

"I heard on my police band tonight there was goin's-on out this way. Thought I'd better have a look."

Why? Service wondered. He decided to see what Kota volunteered.

"I think it got loose," the Indian said.

"How many wolves were here?" Four, he thought he remembered, but he wasn't sure. No wolves had been visible on his last visit, and there had been no mention of a blue wolf. Had it arrived after he'd been here?

"Don't know for sure how many," Kota said.

"You find tracks?" Service asked.

"Not yet." Kota was reputed to be a fine tracker, but Service had his own expertise and preferred to look for himself.

"Nothing back the way I came," Service said.

Kota hunkered close to the ground, dug out a tin of Wintergreen, and held it up to Service.

"No thanks," he said, taking out his cigarettes.

They squatted in silence, listening to more sirens from the direction of the lab building.

"The blue wolf supposed to be bad luck or something?" Service asked.

"Shit," Kota said, spitting on the snow. "Some of the old ones believe that, but it's just an animal." Kota had been a cop in Saginaw before taking the Bay Mills job.

"Bad luck if it's caged, right?"

"Some say," Kota said.

"And if it's running free?"

"Some dumb fuck will probably shoot it."

"Killing a blue wolf isn't bad luck?"

"For the wolf," the tribal game warden said.

Kota was a difficult man to read. Just an animal, yet here he was looking around. Why? Did he suspect people from Bay Mills were involved? The Indians looked out for each other and, given their history and experience with white justice, Service couldn't blame them.

Service flicked his cigarette away and stood up. "Guess I'll move on," he announced.

Kota remained where he was, chewing his tobacco.

The detective said, "Why don't we join the others and get some coffee."

"Gives me the shits," Kota said, not moving.

Service went back to walking the fence line, doubting there was any-thing to find, but he had decided to make the circuit and he would, just as Kota would go in the other direction. They were a lot alike, he de-cided. Loners, set in their ways, overly suspicious, detail-oriented.

It took another thirty minutes to complete the perimeter tour and when he got back to the wolf lab he saw Wink Rector with two men in dark parkas that said FBI in large yellow block letters on the backs. An-other jacket proclaimed BATF. Rector was the resident agent for the Upper Peninsula and rarely had visits from his colleagues. The nearest major Feeb office was in Detroit. Gus Turnage said Rector was heading up the bomb investigation at Tech.

Spotlights by the forensics truck illuminated personnel who were busily erecting a tentlike shelter and setting up folding tables. Service saw Barry Davey of the USF&WS near the truck. It was very strange to find Rector *and* Davey at the same crime scene. Service's antennae began to vibrate.

Wink Rector nudged Service's arm and handed him coffee in a Styro-foam cup. "The shit's hitting the fan tonight," the Feeb said.

"Anybody got a read on this?" Service asked.

"Animal rights freaks," Rector said. "They hit a McDonald's in St. Ignace, another in Marquette, released animals from a mink farm near Curtis, cut nets from fishing tugs in Naubinway, and painted a veal operation near Rudyard."

"All of that was tonight?"

"I suspect we'll hear more," Rector said with a nod.

"Where'd your compadres come from?"

"They flew into the Soo about an hour after the Iggy deal."

"Who are they?"

"Peterson, the guy with the beard, is CT—counterterrorism—out of the Bureau. Phillips is the Detroit ASAC—assistant special agent in charge."

"Peterson was in Detroit when this went down?"

"He's touring field offices with the monthly dog-and-pony CT brief-ing. It used to be quarterly. What're you doing here?"

"Checking for wolves."

Rector grunted.

"You see Barry Davey?" Service asked.

"Yep, looks like the whole crowd is descending on this one."

"Barry's usually in Grand Rapids."

"Deer season and September eleventh. Talk about a shitty combo," Rector said.

Maybe, Service thought. But so many agencies in one place so quickly was a curious coincidence.

"I talked to Gus Turnage. Any progress on the Tech investigation?"

"You mean, a bomb here and bombs there and are they related?"

"Something like that," Service said.

"No progress yet and thank God, no bodies in Houghton."

"Everybody behaving?" Service asked.

Wink Rector snorted with a little laugh. "Like trying to herd cats, eh? And all of 'em in feisty moods."

Service left Rector and walked over to Barry Davey. The USF&WS man did not look happy.

"Howyadoin, you see Carmody yet?" Davey asked.

"Yesterday," Service said.

"He's the best."

"What are you doing here, Barry?"

"Gray wolf, endangered species."

"No shit, but you have field personnel and we enforce ESA for the wolves here. You don't send the boss on this sort of thing."

"Don't tell me how to do my job," Davey snapped.

Service was about to press Davey when a dark SUV pulled into the cluster of other vehicles and a man emerged, stumbling forward and shouting incomprehensibly. A Troop sergeant grabbed the man, pinned his arms, and stopped him.

Service watched as the sergeant talked quietly to Dr. Barton Brule, who began sobbing and collapsed. Two county cops helped the Troop move the lab director into the backseat of a cruiser with its engine running.

Service walked back to the building and watched the crime scene people erecting portable klieg lights. They wore FBI jackets. Two bodies were draped under dark plastic tarps. How the hell had the FBI gotten a team here before the state people from Negaunee? And why?

"Who're you?" an FBI technician challenged.

"Service, DNR."

The man grunted and turned away.

The lights erected in the remains of the lab showed that the bomb had been a powerful one. He looked at what remained of the ceiling and saw remnants of mounts for two video cameras. Were there cameras in the debris, and if so, what would the tapes show? He'd have to wait to find out.

Service rejoined Wink Rector at the coffee jug. The FBI men he'd seen earlier were talking in hushed tones, with their backs to Rector.

"You got leprosy?" Service asked under his breath.

Rector twisted his face into a pained grin. "I'm just hired help."

"Are there security cameras on the gatehouse?"

"It's a high-security facility."

"The cameras might show something."

Rector grunted and changed the subject. "You hear the weather forecast? They're calling for sixty degrees from midweek until Sunday. Talk about shitty conditions for deer hunting."

The FBI agent didn't even hunt deer, so why the weather forecast?

Service returned to the rubble of the building and nosed around, using his light. There were boot tracks everywhere. Whoever got to the site first had done a lousy job of preserving it. With all the foot traffic the ground was turning to mush, but away from the traffic he finally found two distinct paw prints, one of them extremely large. He tried to picture the animal that made it, remembering photographs he had once seen showing a couple of dead Canadian wolves said to be more than two hundred pounds.

Wolf tracks located, his job was done for the moment. He'd found sign of two of the animals, and there was no sense stumbling around in the dark all night. If two were out, all were probably out. They sure as hell wouldn't sit tight with so many people around. He didn't know much about wolves, but he did know that the smell of humans sent them running. Had the bomb been meant to free the wolves, or was their release a side effect? For that determination, they would have to wait for the technicians to complete their work.

Service walked the mile out to the gatehouse, nodded to the deputies at the roadblock, and studied the small cinder-block building for security cameras. There was one camera.

"Anybody know what the camera caught?"

"The Feebs took the cassette," one of the deputies said. "The state and feds are crawling all over the place. We don't even know why the hell we're here."

The usual jurisdictional squabbling, Service thought. "Where's Sheriff Lee?"

"On his way back from a meeting in Green Bay. He's gonna go ballistic when he sees all these feds."

Service knew the Chippewa County sheriff well, and the deputy was correct in his assessment. Sheriff Lee thought of the county as his personal domain.

Just as he decided to return to Rector, it dawned on him that he'd seen no tracks during his circuit around the perimeter. How had Kota approached the fence? Where had he come in from, and why not through the gate like everybody else? And why hadn't Kota shown up at the lab with the rest of the cops?

Service backtracked to the lab and sought out Barry Davey.

"You know DaWayne Kota?"

"The Bay Mills warden?"

Service nodded.

"I've met him."

"Have you seen him tonight?"

Davey looked irritated. "Why would *he* be here?"

Service had the same question, but said nothing about seeing Kota.

Pouring more coffee for him, Wink Rector said, "One of the vicks is the director's wife."

"I heard," Service said, accepting the cup of coffee. "Have there been any problems out here before?"

Rector said, "Not that I know of. The place is like Bumfuck, Nowhere. There's no publicity and no signs to indicate to the public that it's here, much less what it is."

Somebody knew, Service thought. "I need to talk to Brule."

"Now? He's in pretty rough shape."

"Best time to get info is right now."

"I'll have to ask permish," the resident agent said, not hiding the fact that he didn't like being reduced to lackeycom. Service didn't blame him. Wink was one of the good guys who worked a thankless job in the U.P. without complaint.

When he returned from talking to the other FBI men Rector said, "Five minutes is all you get, and I have to stick to you like Velcro." Rector looked unhappy about it. "That's a verfuckingbatim quote."

They approached the open door of the state police cruiser and handed the lab director a cup of steaming coffee. His eyes were puffy and red, his jowls sagging even more than Service remembered. The man looked devastated.

"Doctor Brule, I'm Grady Service."

"I remember you," the director said in a shaky voice.

"Doctor, did the wolves run loose in the compound or was there an internal holding pen?"

"Loose," Brule said. "So we could monitor behaviors."

Human or animal? Service wondered. "I don't remember how many animals were here."

"Five," the scientist said.

"Including a blue wolf?"

Brule answered immediately. "He was brought to us from Saskatchewan late last month. Not a pack animal, but we wanted to see how his introduction would affect the pack hierarchy."

"How did it?"

Brule stared at Service. "Is this necessary? My wife is dead."

"I'm sorry, sir, but somebody blew the fence. That could mean they were trying to release the animals." It could also mean that the bomber wanted a body count. "The thing that puzzles me is, why would they blow the fence at the building? Why not simply cut the fence where it can't be seen?"

"We have adequate camera coverage," Brule said.

"Around the entire perimeter?" Service asked.

"Yes," Brule said.

"Is there a central security facility?" Service asked.

"Landlines," Brule said, suddenly slumping forward in his seat and beginning to sob.

Rector pulled Service back from the vehicle.

Landlines. What did that mean? Were all the cameras hardwired into a central control room? If so, why had the camera at the gate held a cassette? Dial it down, he told himself. The feds were big believers in system redundancy and had the money to afford it.

"Is there a central control room, Wink?"

"Dunno," Rector said. "My first time out here."

"Wink, if you wanted to let the animals out, you could do it a lot quieter and smarter than this. Why use the *Queen Mary* when a tugboat will do the job?"

Rector whispered, "You are one suspicious sonuvabitch."

Peterson, the number two man in the Detroit office, walked over to them. "Get what you needed?"

"I've still got a lot of questions," Service said.

"Save them for morning," Peterson said. "A team is being formed, and you're to be part of it. We'll meet in the Soo at the state police post. Oh eight hundred."

"See you there," Service said to Wink Rector.

"Special Agent Rector will not be part of the team," Peterson said coolly. "He has other priorities."

Service said nothing. Why was Wink being left off the team? The U.P. was *his* territory, and he was connected and trusted everywhere. Hell, Wink was leading the bomb investigation at Tech which to his way of thinking that should have fallen to EATF. Maybe his superiors thought his plate was already full. Or maybe they were playing their usual turf games, despite claims to the contrary by the county's new attorney general.

"See you there," he told Peterson.

He grabbed Rector by the arm after Peterson went away. "What's the deal? This is your turf."

"I've already got Houghton and this one's above my pay grade."

"I don't understand," Service said.

"You will," Rector said, leaving him to walk back to the gate and his truck alone.

On his way back through Paradise, Service called Captain Grant and got him out of bed. It was just before 4 A.M.

He told the captain, "Two dead, both scientists, and one of them is the lab director's wife. Somebody blew the fence. There doesn't appear to be any wolves left in the compound, only why the hell blow it when you could just cut the fence quietly? This makes no sense to me This place is covered by video, so maybe we'll get lucky."

"You heard this isn't an isolated act?" Grant asked.

"Yes, but no injuries or fatalities in the other incidents, right?"

"That's my understanding," his captain said.

"I heard a mink farm was hit. Did they blow fences there?"

"No, they cut the wire cages and spray-painted the buildings."

"A bomb was used here but not elsewhere, a lousy choice on location and two dead. And no spray-painting here that I saw. That makes it an outlier, wouldn't you agree, Captain?"

Before his supervisor could answer, Service added, "The number two guy out of the Detroit Feeb office is here with a counterintelligence man from Washington, a team is being formed, and Wink Rector isn't going to be part of it. They asked me to sit in. First meeting is in the Soo at the Troop post at oh eight hundred. Do you want me on the team?"

Captain Grant was silent for a while. "Just keep me informed."

"Sir, Barry Davey is also here."

There was another pregnant pause. "Call me after your meeting in the morning."

"Yessir."

"What do you smell, Detective Service?"

"I don't know yet, sir."

"Well, keep that sniffer of yours working."

Service checked the clock on his dashboard. He was sixty miles from the Soo and he had a meeting in four hours. But he also wanted to see DaWayne Kota and he needed a short nap. As usual, more things to do than time to do them.

· 10 ·

The heavy fog was lifting slowly as Grady Service drove into the Bay Mills Indian Community. DaWayne Kota's behavior grated.

It was nearly 4:30 A.M. when he walked into the Tribal Police Station and asked for Kota's address. The female night dispatcher looked at him quizzically, but his badge gave him currency and produced the information he wanted.

Kota lived in a relatively new modular home not far from Monocle Lake. There was no vehicle in the driveway and no dry spot to indicate one might have been there recently. Service parked on the street and approached the house. Dogs began to bark from nearby dwellings. It took a long time for a response, but eventually a porch light came on. A woman came to the door and peeked out through a chain lock.

"I'm Grady Service, DNR," he said. "I'm sorry to wake you. Is DaWayne Kota here?"

"No, is there a problem?"

"I'm on my way to the Soo for a meeting and I wanted to talk to him. When will he be back?"

The woman was young and petite, a little plump, her hair twisted by pillows. Maybe she was Kota's daughter. She looked too young to be his wife. But you never knew. Maybe people said the same thing about Nantz and him.

"He got a call and had to leave. I don't know when he'll get back."

Had Kota gotten a call about Vermillion? He'd said he'd heard it on the police band radio. Had he lied? If so, why?

"Sorry to wake you."

"I don't mind," the woman said. "I'm used to it. Is there a message?"

Service gave her a business card. "Ask DaWayne to call me."

The woman studied the card. "The DNR has detectives?"

"It's a new job," he explained. "Again, I'm sorry."

The woman looked over his shoulder at the lingering mist. "Would you like me to make coffee?"

"Thanks, but I have to get to the Soo."

After the stops at Bay Mills, he drove to the house of Denny Ozman near Dafter and pulled into the long driveway, parking by the barn of the onetime hay farm. Ozman was a recently retired CO who now guided salmon fishermen on the St. Mary's River.

It was 5:45 A.M. and Service stretched out as best he could, hoping to catch a nap, but an insistent tapping on the window awakened him. He found Denny rubbing fog off the window with the back of his hand and peering in.

Service got out and stretched, feeling stiffness in the shoulder he had separated last summer. "Sorry, I needed a place for a quick nap."

"Youse coulda knocked on the friggin' door, eh? Sleepin' out here like some sort of bloody appleknocker. Geez. Jenny will be pissed."

An appleknocker was anybody not from the U.P., and Jenny was his wife. "No point waking you guys. I've got a meeting in the Soo at eight."

Denny grinned. "Let's get some coffee inta youse."

Service followed Ozman into the house.

The last time he'd visited, the old farmhouse had been a wreck inside. Now it looked like something out of a magazine.

As he looked around Ozman said proudly, "Jenny's da one with da taste, eh?"

Ozman made coffee and got out the cinnamon rolls. "I heard they made you a detective. How's she going?"

"Finding my way," Service said.

"Must be a bitch to have to work with others all the time."

Service nodded. "Den, do you know DaWayne Kota?"

Ozman brought the coffeepot and cups to the table. "Sure."

"Good warden?"

Ozman stretched. "I wun't want his job, I'll tell ya. Lotta young kids out there to Bay Mills and some old bucks used to doin' what they want. Tough to police that bunch, eh? All sorts of agitators telling them they can fish and hunt when they want, where they want. How're they supposed to know what they can legally do?" The retired CO slurped his coffee and looked across the table at Service. "Trouble with da Bay Mills crowd?"

"No, I just wondered about Kota."

"Good at his job, I think, but I retired before he was hired so I dunno firsthand. He seems to get it done and he don't take shit off nobody. Respects Indian ways, but he backs da law all da way."

Service changed the subject. "How's retirement?"

"Well, the money ain't grand, but it's okay. The guidin' business is growing, and the salmon runs are predictable so far. I can't complain. Even with da September shitstorm I was booked up all fall. Took a while for Jenny to get used to me being around so much, but now we got it worked out."

A female voice chimed in. "You betcha. I give him lists of stuff to do and he stays outten my hair." Jenny Oznan was short and wide with ruddy skin and a friendly smile that dominated her face. She looked half asleep as she poured coffee. "Did youse give 'im da good bakery or da junk you boughten on special?" she asked her husband. Service liked how the couple blended English and Yooperese. Like most I felong Yoopers they spoke so fast that they were sometimes difficult to follow. When he'd first returned to the U.P. after Vietnam and his Troop job downstate it had taken months to get his ear retuned.

"What's wrong with mine?" he asked.

"Not enough sugar."

"My job to be your sweet," he said and Jenny rolled her eyes and laughed out loud. Denny and Jenny made the sort of couple who had always seemed to belong with each other. Service wondered if Nantz and he would grow old together. The thought surprised him. Getting sentimental in his old age. Hell, he was already getting up there and he had nearly a twenty-year lead on Nantz.

At 7:30 A.M. Service pulled into the parking lot of the Cow Barn Bakery and saw a steady stream of truckers and people on their way to their jobs. There were hunters in pickups, in place before the opener to scout. They were dressed in jeans and plaid shirts. Most of them wore comer hats with the flaps sticking out like wings. They had on orange or red hunting coats that bulked them up. Some wore old-fashioned hunting tag holders pinned to the backs of their jackets.

A thirtyish woman pulled up in a pale blue Jeep with the rear left rocker panel caved in and giving way to pits of rust. A broken side window was held together with veins of gray duct tape. She had six young kids inside. He watched her lock them in, shake her finger at them, fluff up her hair, and run into the Barn. She came back quickly, balancing a tray with a hot drink and doughnuts. She was probably a regular with a standing order, on her way to drop the kids at day care. He could hear the kids shouting as she got in and began passing around the goodies.

More kids than seat belts, but he decided not to bother her. She had enough to keep her busy, and up here rules like the seat belt laws sometimes didn't make sense.

The Soo state police post was a nondescript one-story building made of cinder blocks painted tan. He was ushered into a small conference room fifteen minutes before the meeting was scheduled to begin. Davey was already seated, as were Peterson, the FBI counterterrorism man, and Phillips, Detroit's assistant special agent in charge. Service took a seat at the end of the table nearest the door. A state police lieutenant in a crisp blue uniform came in and sat to his left. Service didn't recognize him. His metal name tag said IVANHOE. Nobody spoke.

A man in a dark suit entered and took the chair next to the head of the table. Carson Vengstrom was the federal magistrate judge in Marquette, part of the federal Western District Court out of Grand Rapids. Vengstrom had held his position nearly fifteen years and was a nonentity. What was a federal judge doing here?

Freddy Bear Lee slid into the room behind the judge and looked around. Lee was the longtime sheriff of Chippewa County, an avid fly fisherman, president of the Chippewa County Chapter of Trout Unlimited, and a genetic Yooper. Lee had once been attacked by a black bear while he was fishing the Pine River. He had gotten a tree between him and the aggressive sow and driven the bear off by stabbing it in the nose dozens of times with his pocketknife. He had become Freddy Bear after that. He was not tall, but he was fit with short gray hair and a neatly trimmed brush mustache.

"Hey Grady," the sheriff said brightly, touching two fingers to the brim of a faded green Trout Unlimited baseball cap emblazoned with the words NO KILL.

The next person to arrive was Chick Reardon, Chippewa County's assistant prosecuting attorney, and right behind him came a short woman with highlighted hair and the tightest business suit Service had ever seen. She cruised confidently to the head of the table and sat down. Two more men in suits came into the room and took chairs against the wall behind Service. The two looked like Feebs and, if so, where was BATF in this thing? For Christ's sake, it *had* been a bomb.

The woman spoke, "Good morning, gentlemen. I'm Cassie Nevelev, assistant prosecuting attorney for the U.S. district court in Grand Rapids. After early-morning discussions with senior people in your organizations, this team has been assembled to oversee the investigation of the events at Vermillion and elsewhere."

Why was a federal prosecutor leading the team? Everybody knew that the FBI wouldn't be part of an interagency team unless it led the effort.

"I'm not a cop," Nevelev said, "but this case seems to offer the potential for jurisdictional confusion. It will be *my* job to help sort out who should be doing what."

Wink Rector was heading the investigation at Tech, not BATF, and now Justice was heading this fandango? Service knew too well that interagency cases could be problematic, but this was a double killing on federal property, which meant it belonged to the feds. Why did they need a referee? he wondered, looking at Peterson, who was rubbing his brown-and-gray beard. This thing was getting more twisted by the minute and all the time he was spending here took away from time on his poaching case.

"Lieutenant Ivanhoe?" Nevelev said.

The state police lieutenant opened a large notebook and began to talk. He was tall with longish black hair, a handsome man with an oversized head and little hands. His hair looked too dark to be natural, and with the thought of Ivanhoe dyeing his hair, Service fought back a smile.

"The investigation indicates a high-yield nonincendiary explosive device. The arson people believe it's unlikely that a problem in the gas lines or anything of that sort caused the blast. ATF investigators, of course, are doing additional work."

On what evidence? And where was the BATF rep? Service wondered why Ivanhoe was making the report. It had been the FBI's crime scene techs at Vermillion, not the Troops. Service expected Freddy Bear Lee to interject something, but the sheriff sat quietly studying his fingernails and the table in front of him.

"Special Agent Peterson, will you please bring us up to date?"

Peterson got to his feet. "Peterson, FBI counterterrorism. There were six attacks in the eastern and central Upper Peninsula last night and this morning. A McDonald's restaurant in St. Ignace and another in Marquette were struck. Nets on a fishing trawler were cut in Naubinway, breeding animals were released from a mink farm near Curtis, a veal processing plant was vandalized near Rudyard, and, of course, there was Vermillion, the only federal facility in the group and likely primary target of the attacks." Peterson paused to let the information sink in.

"Were there fatalities at the other sites?" Lee asked.

"There are no other known injuries."

"Were explosive devices used at any of the other venues?" the sheriff asked.

"If you'll bear with me and let me finish I think I can pull all this together."

Freddy Bear Lee nodded, folded his hands, and sat back.

"Evidence points to a coordinated terrorist attack by a group known as the Animal Freedom League. This is a shadowy, amorphous group held together by a shared political philosophy rather than a formal organization. The group has been active for many years in England, but has long been expected to strike targets in this country. That time seems to have arrived. This seems to be the year for terrorism," he added with a solemnity that Service found gratuitous.

Freddy Bear Lee spoke up again. "Why do you assume these events are all linked?"

Peterson looked unaccustomed to being challenged and seemed to bristle. "The AFL has traditionally struck multiple targets simultaneously, trying to overload emergency forces, but one target is always the primary. That's Vermillion in this case."

"But there was no painting, no slogans at Vermillion," Service said, unable to stay out of it.

"There's no need for paint when your signature is a bomb," Peterson said smugly.

Service argued back, "The bomb is a signature *only* if it's of a similar design with similar components to past bombs, right? Do we know this yet? Is the Vermillion device the same as those found at Tech or previous incidents attributed to the group? If they wanted publicity, they'd have gotten a helluva lot more if they blew their bombs at the college instead of at an isolated federal lab."

"That is under investigation," Peterson said, "but we are compelled to make an assumption in the interest of public safety. This morning we are issuing a warning bulletin to all potential targets and asking the media to tell the public to be alert for strangers around such facilities."

"Great," Service said, "with thousands of hunters in the woods, how long until they start blasting each other?"

Phillips, the Detroit ASAC, came to Peterson's assistance. "Granted, this is preliminary, but it's more than mere hypothesis."

"Based on what?" Service asked.

"We are aware of an individual living in this region who has been connected to the AFL in the past."

"Spit it out," Freddy Bear Lee said in a distinctly unpolite tone.

"Please," Peterson said. "As we saw in September and its aftermath, it's normal for acts of terrorism to create a wake of chaos. But we have dealt with this sort of thing before and we will deal with this."

"Yah, yah, the way youse hotshots dealt with Ruby Ridge, Waco, and Oklahoma City," Freddy Bear Lee said with a menacing growl. "Hell, it was one of our Michigan morons who killed those people in Oklahoma."

"Bickering is counterproductive," Lieutenant Ivanhoe said officiously in a slaughtered attempt to play peacemaker.

"Cram it, Eugene. I'm not bickering. This is my fucking county and I'm not going to be ordered around by a bunch of assholes who haven't got a clue."

"Gentlemen," Cassie Nevelev said, trying to regain control. "*Please!* That's enough. This team will honor dissenting opinions, but when we leave the room we will be in agreement, am I being clear?"

What Service understood was that Nevelev had already lost control. Not that anybody could rein in Freddy Bear Lee when he got up a head of steam.

"What role will each of us play on the team?" Service asked.

"We will collectively process information, share leads, coordinate investigations, and help analyze evidence. It's essential that nothing be held back. Follow your own investigative paths, but report back all details and findings."

Service thought about DaWayne Kota and kept quiet.

Peterson began to continue his briefing on the AFL, but Service's beeper hummed in his pocket. The message showed a number and the message CALL NOW. He excused himself, stepped outside the building, lit a cigarette, and called the number.

Pidge Carmody answered. "That was quick. I think we can work together."

"What do you want?"

"Just checking in, boyo. I've accommodations in Bessemer, purchased a rifle at Horns, and, as you predicted, they offered to grease me way into the gun club. Tiz always grand indeed how money talks so eloquently in the Land of the Free. I've purchased ten boxes of munitions, so I expect to be a busy boy at the club."

"Any sign of the Johns woman?"

"Not as yet."

"Let me know if you get contacted."

"Aye."

Carmody: Was he for real?

As Service came back into the conference room and slid into his seat beside the captain he heard Peterson say, "The suspect will be approached this afternoon."

"What suspect?" Service asked.

"For this room only," Cassie Nevelev said as a caution to the group.

"Her name is Summer Rose Genova," Peterson announced. "She lived in England some years ago and was arrested there several times at animal rights protests. She was present at a meat processing plant where a bomb was detonated."

"Was she charged?" Service asked.

"No," Peterson said. "You could say she was 'encouraged' to leave the country, and as soon as she departed, the violence from the AFL ceased. We have worked with Scotland Yard and Interpol to monitor her for years. She has been under our continuous surveillance since her return to the United States."

If so, that meant he had been seen visiting her. "I know SuRo Genova," Service said, making a preemptive disclosure. "She runs an animal rescue operation near Brevort. COs, cops, and animal control personnel work with her all the time, and I don't believe she would be involved in such a thing." On the other hand, he thought, the day he had met her she had roughed up two hunters and might well have shot them had he not happened along. Still, his gut said this was not SuRo's kind of thing. At heart she was a gentle, nonviolent soul. But she also had a hot temper and unbendable convictions, which made for a dangerous combination.

"Yes," said Peterson, "we're aware of your relationship and we were in fact just about to suggest that you be the one to interview her."

Peterson smiled maliciously from his place at the head of the table.

Service bristled. "I'll talk to her, but my way, and no damn team of black-suits running all over her property. If we barge in like the marines, she'll have a lawyer and we'll never get anywhere." Of this he was certain.

"Any objections?" Nevelev asked the group. There were none. "We stand adjourned and we will reassemble tomorrow morning, same place, same time."

Service walked outside to wait for Nevelev and muttered, "This is bullshit," his temper leaking out.

He fell into step with Nevelev as she walked toward her vehicle. "I may not be able to make every meeting," he said.

"I understand," she said dispassionately.

"No offense, but why isn't the FBI heading this up?"

"Do you always ask so many questions?' the prosecutor said, opening her door and getting in.

"Do you always answer questions with questions?" Service fired back at her.

Nevelev smiled, shut the door, started the engine, backed out, and drove away. Service used his cell phone to call his captain and related the meeting blow by blow.

When he was done, the captain said, "Keep going."

"No matter where my nose leads?"

Captain Grant said, "Within reason. You are more than able to hold your own with those people, Detective. I trust your judgment. Call me when you need heavier artillery."

Geez, Service thought.

I
t was early Saturday afternoon and en route to Brevort. Service telephoned DaWayne Kota's office at Bay Mills. A woman, presumably the dispatcher, told him Kota had called in and would be in the field all day. Doing what? Service wondered. And where?

Next he called Luticious Treebone, hoping to catch his old friend at home. They had graduated from college the same year, Service from Northern Michigan and Treebone cum laude from Wayne State, where he had lettered in football and baseball. They had joined the marines, met during training at Parris Island, and spent a year in the same long-range recon unit in Vietnam. The year had been hellacious and had included a high-risk mission into North Vietnam, but they had rarely talked about the war since their return. After the marines, they were in the same Michigan State Police Academy class and spent two years on patrol before seeking transfers to the DNR. Treebone had gotten fed up with chasing fish and game violators after a year on the job and transferred to the Detroit Metropolitan Police, where he was now a lieutenant in charge of vice. They saw each other several times a year and talked more often when problems arose or one of them needed support.

"Tree, Grady."

"S'up, bro?"

Service explained the situation, focusing on his suspicions about the behavior of the feds and their precipitous targeting of Summer Rose Genova.

"I know Peterson," Treebone said. "Wrapped tight as a mummy's johnson. The man can't count higher than number one."

"Why a federal prosecutor in charge of an investigation?"

" 'Member what the major used to tell us."

Their unit commander, Major Teddy Gates, had been a tough, fair leader who made good decisions for his men while acting like a dumb country boy from Mississippi, thereby hiding the fact that he had graduated fourteenth in his class at the Naval Academy. Gates and his two sergeants had formed a close bond in their time together.

Treebone said, "Swim in the swamp, you gotta expect some snakes."

Service laughed. "I need help—somebody with connections in the U.K. I need information about an American woman who was involved with animal rights activists there, eight, nine years ago. Her name is Summer Rose Genova."

"Spell that for me," his friend said. "Genova, okay man. I'll see what I can shake loose. Speaking of reptiles, we got us a new mayor in Motown and a new chief and you take care not to get yourself bit on the ass or find somebody else to suck out the poison. I got beaucoup snakes I gotta try not to step on down here. Back atchu, Semper Fi, bro."

"Semper Fi, my friend."

Talking to Tree always made him feel better, but it didn't change the fact that he was in a screwy situation—and this business with SuRo seemed ludicrous. He hoped she wouldn't try to chuck him out when he began asking questions. Seeing her was a waste of time, his gut told him. He had too many other questions he'd rather pursue. What was the exact security setup at Vermillion, and if there were tapes and the feds had them, when were they going to share?

And what exactly was a blue wolf? For that he would have to drive all the way to Crystal Falls and see Yogi Zambonet, the biologist who headed the state's wolf recovery program. Yogi had been born in Chassell, had gotten his Ph.D. from the University of Minnesota, and worked in Alaska and Idaho before returning home to Michigan, where he had developed into one of the most respected wolf biologists in the country.

Within the DNR Yogi was affectionately called Wolf Daddy. A tall gaunt man with a shaggy beard and long hair tied in a ponytail, the biologist tended to spend a lot of time alone in the field observing and tracking his animals, and catching up to him might prove difficult. Service radioed the district office in Crystal Falls, asked for the biologist, and was told he was not due in until the next morning. Service left a message that he needed to see him. He left his numbers for a call-back, and tried to shift his thoughts to Pidge Carmody and poachers.

But he was in no mood to think about work. Just outside St. Ignace he called Nantz's hotel and was put through to her room. "I'm sorry I had to bail out so fast, honey," he said.

"I'm glad you called, Grady. I've been worried. What happened at Vermillion?"

"There was an explosion," he said.

"But people were killed. Is this related to the stuff at Tech?"

"We don't know," he said. "You should see the vultures gathering: feds, state, county, everybody seems to be looking for a piece of the action."

"Maybe I should suggest Team 2001 get involved."

Service laughed. "Only if they send you."

"I have my first official meeting Monday morning."

"Really?"

"I have to meet with the cleaning service the state leases to clean these offices and give them a performance review," she said, groaning. "This sucks!" she added. "But I'm going to hang in there, Grady. I really am. We'll get through this, no matter what it takes. Where are you?"

"Heading into Iggy."

"God, and I could still be in Mack City. Be careful, babe. And call me?"

"Tomorrow for sure. I'll be in Crystal Falls."

"Mister Mileage," she said. "Any chance you can get down here?"

"I'll try."

"I could drive up to Mount Pleasant and we could have the night and I could be back here for work by morning," she suggested.

"We'll just have to see," he said.

He felt empty when he hung up. Being apart from Nantz was not as easy as he had anticipated, and busy as he was, the job did not satisfy him the way the old one had. Then he was almost always alone, finding his own way, not relying on so many different people from organizations he didn't understand or trust.

Service went through the usual ritual to gain entry to SuRo's sanctuary.

She met him at the door of her building.

"Didn't expect to see you again so soon, rockhead. Cuppa?"

"I've already had too much. You want a smoke?"

Genova eyed him suspiciously. "Do I need one?" she asked, opening the door for him.

"I don't know. Do you?"

He tossed a new pack to her and she looked at it before opening it. "This isn't a social visit."

"No," Service said. "Have you heard the news?"

She nodded. "Vermillion and all that."

"When I was here you mentioned a blue wolf, and the next thing I know the lab is bombed and the wolf has been released. That's the sort of coincidence that gives cops sour stomachs."

"Take Tagamet," she said sharply. "Is the wolf loose?"

"Five of them got out in the wake of the bomb."

"Were they hurt?"

He heard genuine concern in her voice. "We don't know. Why did you bring up the blue wolf?"

Before she could answer, he told her, "This morning I heard a story about you living in England and being linked to a group called the Animal Freedom League. The feds and state have been watching you since you came back into the country. Would you care to enlighten me?"

She sighed, but it was a sound of weariness, not sadness. "Yes, rockhead, I lived in England for eight years. That's where I met Howard. He came to London to lecture for a year, and we met at a party. I was arrested a couple of times. My alleged 'link' to the AFL was strictly that of unofficial spokesperson. I used to get anonymous calls warning of demonstrations and attacks, and I then passed these on to the authorities and the media. I have no idea who sent me the information. Did the feds suggest to you I was connected to AFL-linked deaths over there?"

He nodded.

"But they didn't tell you that I saved dozens of lives by reporting the information I had and keeping people away from places. Assholes!"

"I didn't tell them that you knew about the blue wolf at Vermillion. How did you know it was there?"

"If you will recall my words, rockhead, I said 'it's been said' there was a blue wolf up there. I was simply curious. You know me. I can't resist."

Service tried to read her voice.

"I kept our conversation quiet," he said.

"But now you're here to use your truncheon, make me take off my clothes and sit butt-nekkid under a glaring lightbulb?"

"Jesus, SuRo. Two people were killed. And a week ago bombs were found at the campus in Houghton, firebombs planted by ecoterrorists. I was sent here to talk to you because I know you."

"But not as well as you thought, eh? Are they coming after me?"

"Your background makes you a suspect, but they don't have shit and that reduces you for the moment to a convenient target."

"Do you *actually* think I could be involved in such a thing?"

"Truth? I don't think so, but I don't really know. You have a temper."

"And *that* makes me a bloody killer?"

"Dial down the hyperbole," he said. "This is serious, SuRo."

She crossed her arms defiantly. "What am I supposed to do?"

"Why the hell did you bring up the blue wolf?"

"I heard from a friend the night before I saw you. She heard Vermillion had a blue wolf. Blue wolves are pretty rare and people have a lot of funny ideas about them. Some cultures believe the wolves are thunderbolts sent by God to illuminate the possibilities of heaven. The Ojibwa claim the animals are sacred and can't be caged. There are all sorts of beliefs."

"What do *you* believe?"

She winced. "Verifiable facts, rockhead. Such wolves are rare, but they show up now and then as a recessive gene expresses itself. I don't attach magic to animals. I'm a doctor of veterinary medicine, not voodoo."

"What about all the other shit that happened?"

She said, "Mostly it seems to me that citizens are exercising their constitutional right to free speech. You're familiar with that?"

"By destroying property? The feds are calling it terrorism."

"When U of M students paint Sparty yellow in East Lansing they call it a prank. Paint can be cleaned up."

"This is more than paint, SuRo. Nets were cut, a veal processing plant broken into, mink released from a farm."

"Mink don't belong in cages, and if meat is disgusting, veal is magnitudes more so. I have no sympathy for these places, rockhead."

"What about for the people who did it?"

"I don't approve of killing, but I support citizens' rights to civil disobedience. This is America, not Afghanistan or China."

"Where were you yesterday after I left here?"

"Right here. That bobcat demands attention. Is there anything else?"

He couldn't think of anything. "No, I guess that does it, but you need to take this seriously. The state and feds have you at the top of their suspect list."

"I didn't do anything wrong. Do I need to call my lawyer?"

"That's up to you, SuRo."

Seeing him to the door, she asked, "How's your hotty?"

Still on slow burn, he thought. "Fine, thanks for asking." This conversation was going nowhere.

"I did nothing wrong, Grady Service, and that's the truth, not a semantic evasion."

He nodded and went out to his truck. His gut said to believe her, but the coincidence of her asking about the blue wolf remained as bothersome as DaWayne Kota's actions. It occurred to him that after all his years as a cop he was becoming paranoid and cynical. How would Nantz deal with *that* on a full-time basis?

· 12 ·

Jep Niemi was standing on the roof of Kira Lehto's veterinary clinic, holding a large black pail and chewing on a cigar stub. He looked down and nodded. Service wondered how long it would be until gossip started flying. Jep, the odd-job impresario of southern Marquette County, knew a lot of people and talked about all of them, even when he didn't know what he was talking about, which was more often than not.

Joamoni Christening, Kira's young door-guard receptionist, had never been one of his fans, and when he stood in front of her desk, she made her usual effort to stare through him. "Doctor is busy," she said curtly.

"Just here to fetch my critters," he told her. Joamoni waved him back to the kennel area with an exasperated sigh. He found Newf in a narrow dog run, wagging her tail and jumping up and down. The sight of his dog in a cage irritated him. Logically he knew she couldn't run loose among the other animals, but this wasn't right. He opened her cage and she jumped against his chest, knocking him off balance. She whined as she lapped his face. Where was Cat? He found her in a smaller cage in an area off the dog runs and she purred when he picked her up. Cat had always been independent, seldom sought attention, rarely purred, and never sucked up. Today even she seemed glad to see him.

Kira blocked his way as he started to leave.

"You weren't even going to talk to me?"

"Your gate guard said you were busy."

Lehto's face reddened. She waged a continuous war to make Joamoni more user-friendly. "That . . ."

"Thanks for taking care of them."

Kira said, "There's always a bed for you, Grady." She added quickly, "I meant for the animals. Are you headed home?"

Freudian slip or not, her message was clear. "Yes." He wasn't leaving them in jail another day.

"You look tired," she said.

"The ides of BOB," he said.

She flashed one of her professional smiles, one that she could turn on and off like a switch. "How's the detective job?" She had locked her eyes on his and kept touching his arm and it was making him nervous.

"Busy," he said.

"That should suit you just fine," she said flatly, her smile fading and her hand dropping away.

He was reaching for the door to his truck when Kira again intervened, placing herself in his way, and delicately took hold of his sleeve. "I'm sorry, Grady. I guess I still haven't gotten over us." His schedule as a CO—working all hours of days and nights without a vacation or real break—was the primary cause of their breakup. Looking back, he knew it never could have worked out with her.

Lehto touched his arm. "I talked to SuRo and she told me about your visit. You can't seriously believe she would be involved with fanatics like that."

"You know I can't talk about that, Kira," Service said. He also wished SuRo would keep her mouth shut.

Lehto placed the palm of her hand on his neck and pulled his head forward. On tiptoes she kissed his cheek then slid to his lips and nibbled, an old signal they had once had. She whispered, "Once you've slept with somebody, there're no secrets left to be kept."

"Thanks again," he said, as he pulled away and got into the truck with the animals.

Lehto folded her arms and looked irritated. A rapt Jep Niemi grinned from the roof and waved.

"Darn," Kira Lehto said without conviction. "You know how that Jep gossips."

Service understood her little game and bristled.

He got into the truck and opened his window and smiled at Kira. "If I had five minutes, I'd say jump in the truck and let's find a two-track, but I don't have five minutes." Kira had always been a frantic lover who got off at a speed between sound and light. It was a cheap shot, but she had asked for it.

The veterinarian's eyes gleamed with an emotional mix of desire and loathing. Kira Lehto was not used to being outdone.

Service looked at Newf and said, "I handled that pretty smoothly, didn't I?" The dog turned and looked out her window. "*She* did the kissing," he told the dog in his own defense.

The first order of business was to find someone to take care of the animals at Maridly's house in Gladstone. He called his friend Vince Vilardo, the Delta County medical examiner, and asked if he knew a high school kid who could look in on the animals and make sure they were fed.

The boy's name was Jimmy Crosbee and he showed up within forty minutes of the call to Vince. Crosbee was a junior at Escanaba High School and a football player who immediately made friends with Newf. Cat didn't attack him outright, which was as good a sign as was likely to come from that quarter. All the while the boy stared at Service's uniform.

"What do you have to do to be a CO?" the boy asked.

"First finish college."

"My old man says you only need a high school degree."

"That's the paper requirement. Nowadays most of the people we hire are college grads."

This didn't sit well with the kid. "I hate school."

"You've got your football. Maybe you can learn to use it to get what you want." He had used hockey to get his degree.

They quickly made arrangements for the boy to take care of the animals over the next two weeks. Service had no idea how long the Vermillion thing was going to go on, or where Pidge Carmody's efforts would take him, but with two active cases hundreds of miles apart and deer season looming, he guessed he was going to be on the move constantly. With the animals secure for two weeks, there was one less thing to worry about.

Yogi Zambonet called him just after 10 P.M. as he napped on the couch. "I got your message. I've got to check one of my kids up by Cable Lake in the morning. You want to meet me? We can talk while I work."

One of his kids. Service grinned. "Sure."

"Meet me at oh four hundred on CR Six Fifty-Seven where it T's for Cable Lake. The wolves get active early. Jesse Fulsik will be overhead. Most likely we'll sit right there all morning, but dress in layers. If we have to do any hiking, we'll have to cover some ground. I'll bring plenty of coffee and sandwiches. The temp's supposed to hit sixty tomorrow."

Service called the Troop post in the Soo to leave a message for Nevelev that he would not make the next meeting, and went up to Maridly's bed. Newf and Cat joined him. He took one of her sweatshirts from her dresser and draped it over his face so he could smell her, and was soon asleep.

Zambonet was already at the rendezvous drinking coffee, standing beside his battered truck, when Service arrived.

He parked behind the biologist and got out. It was in the high forties, but the temperature was going up fast, the air feeling almost balmy. The high this time of year was usually in the midthirties, with lows under twenty degrees.

"Some snow would make hunters happy," Service said.

"And wolves. Snow favors all predators," Zambonet said.

The biologist poured a cup of coffee for him. Service noticed that he wore faded jeans and nothing more than an unbuttoned flannel shirt over a T-shirt.

"You heard about Vermillion?"

Zambonet nodded. "Green fire. It was all over the news. Probably the first time most folks even knew the lab was there."

"Green fire?" Service asked.

The biologist grinned sheepishly. "The kind ignited by the animal rights and tree-hugging crowds."

"The wolves are loose," Service said.

"New blood for our packs."

"They'll fit in?"

"Eventually. We've got enough animals and packs now that sooner or later they'll find a place. If you go to enough bars late at night you can experience the same selection process."

Service laughed. "What are they doing at Vermillion?"

"Wolf research, whatever that means."

"You aren't familiar with Brule and his people?"

"Oh, I know Brule. He's on the other side of the great debate."

"What debate is that?"

"It's similar to the one that revolves around trout planting. Do you plant rubber trout in habitats that are marginal and unlikely to support reproduction, or do you focus on the habitat and food and let the fish choose where they'll establish themselves? The argument is wild fish versus planted fish. And it's similar for wolves. A grad student at Northern tried to transplant wolves in the seventies, but it didn't work. The idea and most of the money came from the Huron Mountain Club and the wolves were released there and all of them were dead in three months."

"The Huron Mountain Club?" The club was an exclusive enclave.

"Tree-huggers were all over their cases, and they were trying to jack up their image with the greenies. All the wolves here now came over from Wisconsin and Minnesota. Or across the ice from Ontario into the eastern Yoop. The point is that the animals have chosen to be here. They haven't been planted. They wouldn't be here if it wasn't right for them. Here's an interesting fact. When wolves disappeared from the state, they were last seen around Floodwood Lakes, north of Channing. And when they returned forty years later, they headed right for the same area."

"Why?"

"In the fifties the heaviest deer population in the U.P. happened to be north of Channing. To a wolf, deer equal food. When they came back, they went to the place where the best conditions had been before they left. We don't have a clue how this could be, but that's how it was. We found three wolves in 1989 and the first breeding pair a year later. I've been watching the packs grow ever since. There's so much we don't know about wolves that it boggles the mind."

"Brule is a proponent of transplants?"

"He believes a steady influx of transplants will keep the gene pool healthier."

"But you don't agree."

"No, his point is biologically sound, but it's irrelevant in our situation. We already have an infusion of genes from Wisconsin, Minnesota, and Ontario, so the real issue here is, how many animals can our prey population support? We're nowhere close to that limit yet, but if we begin to artificially introduce animals, we'll reach saturation faster, and saturation and a shrinking food population make predators turn strange. Wolves have come back here naturally. I'd like to see them hit their natural limit the same way."

"Does Brule have a lot of supporters?"

"Brule's irrelevant and he's full of shit, more politician than biologist. He's got the degrees, but his work . . ." Zambonet left the statement unfinished.

"Was he planning to release his animals?"

"I don't know and it doesn't really matter because he couldn't let them go without our permission and we weren't going to give it to him."

"Does he know that?"

"Damn right he knows."

"So he's basically spinning his wheels and wasting money. His facility is pretty elaborate."

"He talks about genetic improvements and all that, but I have the distinct feeling he wasn't preparing those animals for release, at least not here. He's got a lot of federal grant money, and what he built at Vermillion was learned at Yellowstone and applies only to a transplant program."

"The oval shape?"

"Right, no corners. Wolves know instinctively that man is dangerous. They're curious about us, but they don't like us. They pace all day long in an enclosure and they spook when they wind or hear the keepers. When you keep them impounded too long, their tempers get short. If you have corners, the alphas and elders end up tearing up the younger animals."

"So what's Vermillion's purpose?"

"I don't know," Zambonet said. "Brule doesn't talk about it. His idea of teamwork is him and another person in a two-person sailboat and he's the captain."

"Did you know there was a blue wolf in the compound?"

"I'd heard that, but I thought it was just bar talk. Wolves inspire a lot of fanciful things to be said, most of them wrong. Last week I had a guy at the Mill Town Inn in Foster City explaining to me how wolves take down prey by hamstringing them. I told the guy this wasn't true, that trying to grab a moose by the lower leg was inviting yourself to get the shit kicked out of you, but I don't think he believed me. Do you know that there is not one confirmed case in history in this country of a healthy wolf attacking a human being? Yet how often do you hear stories to the contrary? It drives me batty."

"Blues are the result of a recessive gene?"

"Probably. They come along now and then. I saw two while I was in Alaska, but they have way more animals up there."

"What about here?"

"We've got fewer than three hundred wolves spread over the entire area. Odds are we'll never get a blue."

"But there's one out there now. Does that create a problem?"

"Not biologically, but I'd think a blue wolf loose in deer season might find a tough road to hoe."

"As a trophy?"

The biologist nodded solemnly. "I'd think so. When you get something that occurs maybe once in ten thousand times, trophy hunters always take notice. Look at what happened to the deer in Marquette."

Presque Isle Park in Marquette had been home to several nearly tame albino deer, which somebody had shot. The case was still open.

Zambonet added, "If it's big or odd, man will kill it. That's what makes us the most dangerous predator of all. The wolves cull the young or the weak because they don't have the stamina to take down healthy animals except in rare circumstances. Wolves kill to eat and survive. But man doesn't need the food and we have the wherewithal to take the breeders and best specimens and we do. We kill for sport."

"How do you keep track of your animals?"

"Radio tracking collars, but we don't have the money to collar them all. We try to collar one in each pack to serve as a marker. The batteries last about three years. Our budget here has been about thirty grand a year, but even if we had more cash I doubt we'd collar more animals. We have what we need. Between the collars and our winter tracking surveys we have a pretty good fix on what's going on."

"Thirty thousand dollars? That's all?" He had to be joking. The money certainly didn't take into account the time COs spent handling depredation and nuisance calls from farmers and citizens. Few biologists factored CO time into their program costs.

Zambonet smiled. "It's enough if you're taking our approach. If you want to haul animals in from elsewhere, the price tag goes way up."

"Have you heard of the Animal Freedom League?"

"*Time* and *Newsweek* articles, that sort of thing. Some of my colleagues talk about them at symposia. But we don't worry about them here because we don't have captive animals."

But Vermillion did. "How easy is it to release wolves? Do you just open the gate?"

Zambonet laughed. "Wolves are creatures of habit and, like people, they're totally unpredictable. One time you open the doors and they fly out. The next group will stand inside for days, scared shitless to even approach the opening."

"What effect would a bomb have?"

Zambonet paused to weigh a response. "I would think the reaction could range from scaring them to death to making them run, but there's really no way to predict." The biologist looked at him. "Are you sure the Vermillion wolves are gone?"

The question caught Service by surprise. "I found tracks of two animals outside the enclosure."

"Two of five? You might want to be sure about the rest of them. Don't assume anything with wolves."

Service got his cell phone and called Joe Ketchum in Newberry.

Joe and his wife Kathy were COs in Luce County. She handled the southern part, and Joe's territory stretched north from Newberry to Grand Marais. He had been friends with the couple for years.

"Joe, this is Grady. Can you make a run for me over to Vermillion today?"

"Jesus, do you know what time it is? I thought you caught that case."

"Sorry, I did, but I can't get there right now. Do me a favor and take a look and let me know what you find."

"What am I looking *for*?"

"Are the wolves actually gone?"

Ketchum started to laugh but checked himself. "You're serious? The radio and TV stations are all jabbering about how that explosion freed them."

"It probably did, but I want to be sure."

"I'll be there in an hour."

Kathy came on the line, her voice filled with sleep. "Hi Grady. What're you and Maridly doing for Thanksgiving?"

"We plan to lock ourselves in the house and stay there three or four days until somebody hauls us out in cuffs."

Kathy laughed softly. "Try using the cuffs on each other," she said. "You'll like it."

A plane buzzed overhead in the darkness at 5 A.M. Service couldn't see its lights because of a low ceiling and wondered how the observer in the plane would see the ground.

Zambonet set his radio on the edge of the truck's bed and spoke to the pilot, Jesse Fulsik.

The biologist read coordinates off his handheld GPS unit. Fulsik repeated the coordinates and signed off, promising to check back.

"This pack likes the peninsula between Porier and Cable Lakes. This time of year they're in their rendezvous areas, the pups from last spring are up to fifty pounds and learning how to be pack members. This pack also dens around here and in late fall the deer begin to migrate south from the Superior shore into their winter yards down here. The wolves like to set up nearby to wait for heavier snow and easy hunting. They eat good here. Now we wait," Zambonet said, refilling his coffee.

They talked for a while about DNR problems and politics and Zambonet gave Service a perspective on a biologist's job. "Fewer and fewer of us trying to cover more and more, and as people retire, replacements are rarely authorized. I wouldn't be surprised if Clearcut tried to privatize the whole operation."

Service wouldn't put such a plan past Bozian, whose claim to fame centered on taking money and services away from people and labeling it progress. The governor harbored dreams of national political office and maybe he would be headed to Washington, but one thing Service knew and took solace in was that when Michigan's voters went to the polls next November Bozian would be finished. Whether a new governor could undo the damage Bozian had done was a different issue.

The radio suddenly came to life. Zambonet picked it up

"Got a pencil?" the pilot asked.

"In hand." Fulsik read off a series of coordinates. "I have a warbler at that location."

"Good reception?"

"Unfortunately."

"The numbers are solid?"

"Clean as your mama's underdrawers."

Zambonet reached into the bed of the truck and hoisted his pack, which looked massive to Service. "We're about four miles away. Ninety minutes max."

Service got his own pack out of his vehicle. "What's a warbler?"

"Mortality signal. If the sensors in the collar don't detect motion for four hours, the transmitter begins to speed up. We know something is wrong because wolves don't stay still for that long."

"What if the animal's sleeping?"

"You ever watch a dog sleep? They're constantly moving around, repositioning themselves, restless. Wolves are the same. When we get a warbler, we have a dead animal," he said through clenched teeth.

Newf never lay still for long, Service told himself.

Service took half of the sandwiches and one of the thermoses and placed them in his pack. The two men checked each other to make sure the packs were secure. Zambonet strode away, with Service struggling to get into step behind the long-legged biologist.

This was his first time in the area and Service was impressed with what he saw.

The biologist walked a hard pace, talking softly as he went, leading them over deadfalls, scurrying over logs, moving across boulders covered with lichen, always advancing in a straight line, letting nothing stop him.

Service considered himself to be in good shape, but the other man's pace was brutal. He wanted a cigarette and tried to get his mind off the nicotine his body was demanding.

"This is as close to wolf paradise as it gets," Zambonet explained as they hiked. "Impenetrable swamps, deciduous forests, aspen stands, high ground with good cover, hardwoods with heaps of mast crops for prey animals, a couple of small streams with healthy beaver populations, lots of springs and freshets, no roads, no people, no nearby farms with livestock to tempt the pack. How long this will last, I can't say, but right now it's got everything a wolf could want. This is home to the Net River Pack, which branched off the Nordic Pack. The Net River alpha male is a little guy as far as alphas go, but he's been an independent little shit since he was born. Natural leader type and all the ladies loved him. Most males leave their birth pack at two years, but this kid split at fourteen months."

"Is he collared?"

"Yeah," Zambonet said. "The little bugger went into Wisconsin two years ago and brought back a bride from the Bootjack Pack."

Along the way Service stopped twice to shed layers, which he stuffed in his pack before moving on. He had learned in the marines and early in his DNR career that anything you hung on the outside of a pack had a good chance of falling off, especially in rough terrain. If you wanted to keep what you had, you put it inside and buckled it down.

They stumbled nearly a mile across spongy, damp sphagnum, which was like walking on a loose trampoline. When they climbed onto rocky ground Service's calf muscles began to tighten. They headed into tamaracks so close together that they had to twist and wiggle their way between trunks. The scent of cedars filled his nose, and in the distance he heard ravens.

Zambonet stopped to let Service catch up. When he got to the base of a granite wall, he found the biologist on the radio with the pilot again.

"Ravens," Fulsik radioed. "Flocking."

"Same coordinates?" Zambonet asked.

"Virtually."

As they pushed up the hill past cedars into heavy white pines, the morning clouds began to separate, allowing the sun to peek through.

The searchers climbed cautiously down the hill into a swale packed with popples. Service saw the imprint of a two-track. Zambonet was studying the road and pointing off in the distance. "ATVs use this road in summer, snowmobiles in winter. They're not supposed to be in here at all, but that doesn't stop the bastards."

Service sucked in a deep breath trying to catch his wind. Even with two fewer layers he was sweating. Zambonet looked like he hadn't walked ten feet.

Service cursed the nature of his new job. Riding around in his vehicle all day making phone calls wasn't going to cut it. He was going to have to get his big feet back in the woods again, he told himself.

They followed the tote road for another mile and when they struck a low berm of balsams and boulders, Zambonet held up his handheld GPS receiver and stared at it. Then he took the tracking device off his back, flipped up the H-antenna, and turned it on. Service heard a fast clicking sound. The biologist said, "There were dens here last year. Probably will be again this year when they get down to making babies in January and February."

The two men moved deliberately. After fifteen minutes Zambonet knelt, his eyes fixed dead ahead and sniffing the air. The carcass of a wolf was nailed to the side of a tree with a spike. The animal had no head and no collar. The stomach had been sliced open and its entrails hung down to the ground. The warm weather had ripened the remains.

"*Fuck*," Zambonet said with a growl as he crawled slowly toward the dead animal. He felt its fur, held out its still legs, stared, continued to curse in a stream that made no sense and served only to release anger.

"Spiral out," he told Service. "The collar will be nearby."

It was fifty yards away, sitting on a flat rock. Zambonet used a stick to pick it up and deposit it in a plastic bag from his pack.

Service could see that the man was shaken.

"Who would do this?" Service asked.

"Some ignorant cocksucker who thinks wolves are sent by the devil to eat his deer," Zambonet said in exasperation.

Maybe, Service thought.

Zambonet looked at the detective and sucked in his cheeks. "I'm going to nail this motherfucker."

Service said, "*We* are." He knew that most violets who did this sort of thing couldn't keep their yaps shut. A determined CO from Iron River had doggedly tracked a wolf killer for two years and finally nailed a Wisconsin man for the crime. People who killed like this always talked to someone about it, either to make themselves look good or to rationalize what they had done.

"I'm going to pack the carcass out," Zambonet said. "I'll have it X-rayed for fragments, then send it down to Rose Lake for necropsy."

Service nodded. Zambonet took off his pack and took out a sandwich. "First we eat and have coffee. Out here we take care of us first."

Service had always found biologists oddly immune to the sickening odors of death. In college he had gone to a biology professor for help and while they sat in his office, the scientist dissected white rats, which he took one at a time out of a huge glass vacuum jar where they suffocated while he ate a sandwich with one hand and held a scalpel in the other. "Is it your alpha male?"

Zambonet nodded. "It's him," he said glumly.

"Cause of death?"

"Big-bore bullet. Probably went through, but I doubt we'll ever find it. I doubt he was killed here. It's almost impossible to get close to a wolf in this terrain. The shot would have to be a long one."

Service looked around, studying the crags and hills around them. Finally his eyes settled on a rocky promontory to the south. "How about from up there?"

"That's got to be three, four hundred yards," Zambonet said, shaking his head.

Service studied the hill. Four hundred yards was less than a half mile. In Vietnam snipers had often taken shots at a mile or more if they had the right weapon.

He put the remains of his sandwich in its plastic bag, walked back to where the carcass hung, and began looking around. Thirty yards west of the wolf he found spatters of blood on rocks and, using a balsam branch, carefully brushed a layer of leaves and pine needles away to find a splash of coagulated blood and tissue. He looked again at the rocky outcrop on the hill. "Yogi, you'd better take a look." The biologist studied the blood and got out a plastic bag, but Service grabbed his arm. "Let's not touch anything more. We can take the carcass after we get some of your people out here to help us. I think the animal was shot right here, which means the shooter mutilated him here. We might find evidence. Get on the radio and call for help. I'm going up that hill." Service pointed.

Zambonet was already on the radio when Service put on his pack.

"Ask your pilot to hang overhead for a while." The sun was out now, visibility good. "Tell him to overfly the hill, look for vehicle trails. From up there, they'll show up pretty clearly. He can also guide the others to us. I'll be back as quickly as I can."

Yogi Zambonet looked at him with a face that blended anger and hurt. Service understood. Biologists expended their energy preserving and encouraging the lives of wolves; it was law enforcement's job to deal with their unnatural deaths.

As he climbed, Service used Zambonet's handheld radio to talk to the pilot, who had spotted a trail on the back of the hill and a four-wheeler track farther down. When Service reached the crest an hour later he found the foot trail and a place on top the rocks where it ended. From the rocks he had a clear view of Yogi Zambonet and the kill site below. It was a shot that could be made, and the wolf would never know it was coming. Looking around, he found a single brass fifty-caliber cartridge stuck on a stick, which had been wedged into a crack in the gray rock, the brass gleaming in the sun. The rock was streaked reddish orange from iron deposits. Service suspected the brass had been left there to taunt them. The shooter was issuing a challenge.

Fulsik reported that he had traced the four-wheeler trail west from the hill to the Paint River; there appeared to be relatively fresh vehicle tracks on a two-track turnaround there.

By the time the biologist's technicians arrived to help secure the site, Zambonet and Service had marked off the area where the dead wolf had been found and the outcrop where the shot had come from. Service took photographs, but left the cartridge on the hill to be collected with the rest of the evidence.

It was four forty-five and dark when they returned to their vehicles. Service was tired and dirty. By then Fulsik was on the ground in Houghton. There was nothing further for Service to do that night. Yogi and his technicians headed back to the district office in Crystal Falls. Service called Simon del Olmo and asked if he could bunk in for the night.

Simon's small house was just off US 2, a mile or so from the gates of Bewabic State Park.

"Most exalted one," del Olmo greeted him at the door.

They shook hands. The younger CO handed him a Jack Daniel's with Diet Pepsi and a lemon wedge.

"Nurmanski happy out there in South Dakota?" del Olmo asked.

Nurmanski. He hadn't thought about Carmody, Nurmanski, or the poaching case all day. "I spent the day with Yogi Zambonet."

"Wolf Daddy. I think he can outwalk his wolves."

"We found a dead one today."

The young officer frowned and shook his head in disgust.

"Shot."

The younger CO said, "Forget work tonight. I'm making Cuban soul food. We drink, we eat, we sleep, go kick bad-guy asses tomorrow. How's your lady?"

"Still in Lansing."

"I guess your good friend the governor isn't done trying to stick the poker of power up your ass, *jeffe.*"

Service guessed that del Olmo was right. They dined on red beans and rice with habanero peppers and omelets made with a volcanic salsa.

Later in the evening a very weary Joe Ketchum called in on the cell phone. "You won't believe this. Three of the wolves were still in their little hidey-holes in the enclosure and a fourth one was hanging around like he was waiting for the others to come out. I got a vet over from Newberry and we got a tranq dart into number four."

"What color are the four?"

"Huh? Wolf colors."

"Is one of them blue?"

"No."

"Thanks, Joe. Great job. I owe you one."

"Grady, after we recovered the last wolf the Feebs swooped in on us and took control of the animals, said it was outside our jurisdiction. They acted like a bunch of Nazis. What the hell is going on at Vermillion?"

Service wished he knew.

When they finally got to bed, Service couldn't sleep. Zambonet had said something that didn't jibe. He got up and telephoned the biologist at home, got no answer, and tried him at the district office.

"Wha?" Zambonet answered.

"Service. How did you know the collar would be nearby today?"

" 'Cause it happe 'fore." The biologist's words were mingled with booze, maybe having his own wake for the dead male alpha.

"Same area?"

"Fuckin' fuckers," Zambonet said with slurred speech. "No, furder nort."

"Who caught the case?"

"Sheeeit. Sheena Grinda. Her idea, keep all details shuuuush."

Officer Elza Grinda was a thirty-something Swede who lived near Bruce Crossing in Ontonagon County, and had fashioned a record of getting the job done, but not one of willingly cooperating with other officers. She was a pathologically polite and reserved woman with wild, light brown hair that always looked windblown, and had many times successfully tangled hand-to-hand with troublemakers. In the DNR she was known as Sheena.

"Is the case still open?"

"Fuck should I know?" Zambonet said, snapping at him. "Grinda says she has a lead, you know—like somebody she thinks is the one—but didn't go nowhere. No evidence. Think you can do better? Huh?"

Service had a feeling about Grinda. He guessed her noncooperation was not because she wanted all the credit for herself, but because she didn't trust others to do the job as well as she could do it. He could sympathize.

"Good night, Yogi. I'm really sorry about the animal."

"Fuckin' fuckers!" Zambonet said as he dropped the phone.

Service immediately called the Baraga County Sheriff's office and got Grinda's home number, but was informed she was on duty. He got a radio patch through to her and arranged to meet her at 4 A.M. She told him how to find a place on Williams Road south of Haskins. He scribbled down the directions and tried to remember familiar landmarks in the area, but couldn't. She was on duty four nights before deer season began. He had no doubt she was out hunting for early shooters and jacklighters—which, he reminded himself as he settled down on the couch to sleep, is just what he used to be doing—and he missed it.

He toyed momentarily with leaving a message with Nevelev to let her know he was going to miss another meeting in the Soo, but decided to hell with her. Under Bozian, DNR law enforcement was down to 160 officers in the field, and they couldn't do their jobs *and* sit on their asses with interagency teams.

· 13 ·

Simon was up early with Service, the two of them stumbling around the kitchen like walking dead, making sandwiches and filling thermoses with pungent Colombian coffee. Neither of them had much to say. The firearm deer season would open at first light in three days and for two weeks after that there would be more work than the state's COs could handle. In some ways, the next few days could be the worst of all for violations and problems.

Driving north, Service saw trucks, vans, and cars tucked off the road. Most hunters would already be carping about the lack of tracking snow as they did their final scouting, spruced up their blinds, and replenished bait. A few of them would be poaching. And if any of them had brought their weapons along, either in their vehicles or carrying them, they could be ticketed for violation of the five-day quiet period that preceded the season. The law said firearms could be transported to camps, but had to remain there until the season opened. Otherwise, carrying a weapon would be construed as hunting out of season. There was no snow and none forecast until next Monday. The lack of snow meant that starting tomorrow, too many wounded animals would crawl off to die, a waste. It was disturbing how many hunters were lousy shots.

Service found a DNR truck where Grinda said it would be and snugged his own vehicle in behind it. No immediate sign of her. He got out, checked his watch, lit a cigarette, and stood against his truck, waiting.

A few moments after 4 A.M., a flashlight beam began to slash through the blackness of the woods. Service watched it drawing closer and heard an unhappy male voice. The voice was puffing, obviously straining and complaining vociferously.

"If I have to pay the fine *and* give up my rifle, why *shouldn't* I have the goddamn meat?" the man was demanding. "I'm sure as fuck gonna pay for it."

There was no answer.

The man didn't relent. "You think you can arrest everybody who shoots a little early? This is so much *bullshit!*"

"Yes," a woman's voice said. "Three days before the season is *not* a little early and you're right, it *is* bullshit."

Service grinned.

When the light beam emerged from the tree line, Service saw a man pulling a dead buck, a rope wound through substantial antlers. Elza Grinda walked behind the man, carrying a scoped hunting rifle and her Mag-Lite.

Ignoring Service, she opened her truck, picked up her radio, and called Station 20 in Lansing with a request to check the man's driver's license and Social Security number against the Law Enforcement Information Network computer for any outstanding warrants. Apparently he was clean on the LEIN. She used her dash lights to write a ticket, and supervised as the man huffed and strained to dump the dead animal in the bed of her truck. She put his unloaded rifle and clip in her cab and locked the door.

"You'll receive a summons," Grinda said, handing the citation to the man.

"I thought I just had to pay a ticket."

Grinda said, "You were hunting before the season and using an artificial light. I'm asking that your weapon be condemned and destroyed. A judge will decide."

"*Destroy* my gun? Are you fucking crazy, lady?"

For a moment, Service thought the man was going to unhinge, and he was ready to step in, but he sensed Grinda didn't need help. She looked like a beauty queen who belonged on a tropical beach with a drink with a colorful little umbrella in it instead of in a uniform in forty-degree weather in the north woods. Grinda simply held out the ticket until the man snatched it out of her hand and scowled.

"Do you need assistance finding your way back to your camp, sir?" she asked.

Ouch, Service thought, fighting a smile.

"Fuck you, Dickless Tracy! I was hunting these woods before some jerk shot his wad between your old lady's legs."

Grinda remained impassive but Service could sense her evaluating the man's state of mind.

The hunter was dressed in an orange camo snowmobile suit with new knee-high leather-top L.L. Bean boots. His face was flushed by emotion and physical strain, and he was perspiring heavily.

The man began to whine some more, thought better of it, looked at Service and shrugged. Before leaving, he stepped close to Service and said, "I wouldn't fuck that bitch with your dick." He stomped angrily down the shoulder of the road, kicking at anything that got in his way.

Service held out his thermos. Grinda took it and poured a cup. Despite the hour and having been on duty all night, she looked fresh.

"Early bird," Service said.

The conservation officer smiled grimly. "It's a beautiful nine-point. I don't condone it, but I understand his temptation. He had the animal staked out and baited with molasses, cabbage, corn, and salt. Said he hunted it all through bow season and he was afraid it would spook and run away before the opener and somebody else would get to it first. He was afraid to wait."

Service also understood. The best chance of killing a deer was the first morning of the first day of the gun season, when thousands of hunters were in the woods and moving around, shooting and pushing the animals. It was also the best time for a deer that a hunter had staked out to spook and get taken by another hunter. So it went: This was the luck part of the sport.

"Thanks for meeting me," he said.

She shrugged and locked her penetrating gray-green eyes on him.

"We had a wolf kill near Forier and Cable Lakes," he said. "A single fifty-cal round. The animal was beheaded and gutted, left spiked to a tree. Wolf Daddy says you had a similar case."

"When was this?" Grinda asked.

"We found it yesterday. Zambonet is sending it down to Rose Lake for a full workup, but we guesstimate it was shot the night before last."

"Close in?"

"No, it was a long shot—just under a half mile. We recovered brass, one round, left on a stick at the shooter's perch."

"Mine was similar," the woman said reluctantly. "High perch for the shooter, one round, fifty-cal, same mutilations. No brass, though. Think you'll get prints off yours?"

"I wouldn't bet on it," Service said, adding, "I never saw your wolf-kill in the reports." Each district filed a weekly report detailing the actions of its officers. Service had always carefully read the reports, knowing that things could tie together in unusual ways and that he could learn from other officers and their actions—both what to do and what not to do.

"It wasn't in there," she said. "Why advertise?" She folded her glove-less hands tightly around her thermos cup. In the dim lights of the truck Service saw that she had short, perfectly manicured fingernails. She added, "The reports are public domain, and they get reproduced by the media. Why give the perp coverage?"

"How about because it might have put some of the rest of us on alert?"

"It would also alert the shooter. It's my case, my judgment. My sergeant and lieutenant concurred."

"Yogi says you have a suspect."

"But no evidence."

"Maybe we can help each other."

"I haven't asked for help."

"I'm the one asking for help," he said, trying to read her. Was there room to negotiate? Her eyes betrayed nothing. He could try sugar or something more acidic and confrontational and decided on the latter.

"You have the rep of a good cop, but not a team player."

She bristled immediately. "Is this for real? *Grady Service* lecturing *me* on team play?"

"Especially me," he said. "I've been there."

"And now that you're a detective, *you* need help."

"I always needed help, Grinda. You do too, even if you don't recognize it."

The woman stood with clenched teeth.

"If you had this nailed, your suspect already would be in custody. Obviously you can't get this done alone, and now we have another dead wolf. I'm not trying to steal your case, Grinda. But you share and I share and let's see what we can get. Before the wolf, I had a bear taken with a fifty-cal near McMillan. We don't see many fifties outside of black powder season. It makes an impression. When I heard you had one too, I wished I had known, that's all. I know your case is your case, but if we have the same shooter, you can take the lead and the credit."

"It's already mine."

"Yeah, and you're sitting on your ass at the end of an evidentiary cul-de-sac."

The woman began to laugh, a deep, wracking cackle of demonic amusement.

Service let her laugh it out, standing silently, knowing she was laughing at him and not sure how to react.

"Jesus, Service. Is this what you call *salesmanship?*"

"I call it straight talk."

"Right, you get a new job and now you want the rest of us to bail you out."

Service sighed. Was her problem with the chain of command or with him?

"C'mon, what have you got, Grinda?"

The woman chugged the rest of her coffee. "I heard there was a single-shot fifty-cal being used by someone at the South Superior Rod and Gun Club. I looked into it. It was in the possession of a woman who claimed it was owned by her boyfriend who owns a gun shop and that she was just testing it, that it had been sold and would soon be gone."

"Wealthy Johns and Skelton Gitter," Service said, guessing and hoping.

Grinda looked startled. "How did you know?"

"I can't say."

She curled her lips in disgust. "One-way cooperation. I figured as much."

"No," he said. "It's not that way."

Grinda shook her head.

Service said, "Johns and Gitter are under the microscope. I'm tracking a cash-for-trophies operation and developing evidence suggests their involvement."

The conservation officer stared at him "You've got somebody inside?" She suddenly looked interested.

"Let me answer that question with a question. If you were undercover, would you want me revealing I had someone on the inside?"

Her eyes blazed hot. "No."

"Johns and Gitter, right?"

She nodded and said, "I know a guy who works there. He's always asking me out, so I took him up on it and as a favor I had him pull the paperwork on the fifty-cal. Gitter said he bought it from Harris Gunworks, but it was sold."

"To whom?" Service asked.

"A man named Mayhall in Mongo, Indiana. I had it checked out. I know an Indiana CO who owed me a favor. Mayhall actually lives and owns a business in Fort Wayne. He never bought the fifty, or any rifle.

He doesn't hunt, doesn't fish, and doesn't do the outdoors. In fact, he has a heart condition. Somebody used his name. He owns a cottage on the Pigeon River near Mongo, which is on the state border. He also has a place in the southern Porkies. He bought both places as investments, but never uses either of them. That weapon could be anywhere." Grinda's face was grim. "Why the hell are you involved in this, Service?"

"I thought I explained that. I had the bear case and I was with Zambonet when we found the animal yesterday. I told him I'd help. He told me about your case and now there's a potential link to another case I'm working." He didn't give her Nurmanski's name or any of the details and he did not tell her about Kaylin Joquist.

"What do you expect me to do?"

"Stay away from Gitter and Johns for now. Talk to Yogi, look at the evidence he gathered. Maybe you'll see something we missed."

"While you disappear into the mist?"

He gritted his teeth. "I'll get back to you. If we get enough for a bust, it'll be yours."

The woman stared at him, said, "I bet."

Service departed thinking she was pretty insecure, not nearly as confident as her performance suggested.

He wanted desperately to talk to Carmody, but under their agreement, Carmody was the only one who could ask for a meeting. He would have to wait. He opted instead to call Captain Grant.

As usual, no pleasantries were exchanged. The captain was all business.

Service began with a confession: "I missed the last two meetings in the Soo." When the captain didn't say anything, he said, "I asked Joe Ketchum to check the Vermillion compound. Four of the wolves were recovered yesterday. Three of them were still inside."

"Where were they when you were there?"

Service cringed. In other words, had he fucked up and not examined the premises as thoroughly as he should have? "I found the tracks of two animals outside the enclosure area, but the ground was pretty badly torn up. I should have gone inside, Cap'n, but with so many people around, I couldn't believe the animals would still be there." More to the point, the presence of so many agencies had broken his focus, but he kept this to himself. He hadn't done his job properly, and excuses wouldn't change this fact.

The captain paused before speaking. "I talked to Ms. Nevelev last night and she did not mention this, but she made a point of informing me of your absences." Was the captain perturbed? Grant was a proponent of sharing among officers and law enforcement agencies. Information was the lifeblood of the investigational process; unshared, it coagulated, dried up, and turned to dust. But why hadn't the captain made sure the force knew about Grinda's wolf? The man was impossible to read.

"Cap'n, if I have to be at every meeting, I can't do my job. Most of the people on the team are management types or from units where others can cover for them. I'm a working warden."

"I am not criticizing you, Detective. I am simply relating the conversation with Ms. Nevelev. I told you I trust your judgment, so let's not waste time on this. When I have a criticism, you can be assured you will be the first to know."

Service felt burned and duly chastised. He was thinking about himself and the captain was focused on the case.

"Nevelev has to be aware of the situation," Service said. "Joe called in a vet from Newberry to tranq one of the animals and afterward the Feebs moved in and took control of all the wolves. The Feebs told Joe it's not our jurisdiction. What the hell is going on, Captain?"

"Where were the animals found?" Grant asked, ignoring his detective's question.

"Three were still in the compound and one was nearby. I spent yesterday with Yogi Zambonet and he said releasing animals from captivity is a screwy business. He said the explosion might have sent them hauling or it might've hunkered them down; there's no way to predict wolf behavior. I asked Joe to see if I had missed something. I had."

"I see," Grant said. "The wolves stayed and Officer Ketchum found them, but the FBI took them. Why didn't the FBI find them if this is all theirs?"

Service kept quiet.

"I cannot understand why Ms. Nevelev didn't acknowledge this," the captain said. "Have you followed up with Warden Kota?"

The captain's formality grated at him. "Not yet, but he's on my list." For nearly twenty years he had done his job without having to keep an actual list, but maybe he needed to start keeping one, a thought he found irritating, though he couldn't pinpoint the exact source of his uneasiness. "Captain Grant, maybe there's a lot more going on here than we realize." This was a statement born not of knowledge but of intuition, and often Service contemplated how the gift of intuition could also be a curse. It was a gift you were born with and presumably had under your control, but once intuition took hold, it could overpower all logic. When this happened all you could do is hope that it held up.

If the captain heard, he kept his own counsel. Service decided enough had been said, enough fuel dumped on the captain's simmering fire.

"Yesterday Yogi and I found a wolf that had been shot. It turns out that this is the second one, both of them beheaded and mutilated and killed with a fifty-caliber. Brass was recovered with both bodies. All of this is a sicko message, probably to us. I just left Elza Grinda. She had the first kill and believes the weapon belongs to Skelton Gitter. It was placed at one time in the hands of his girlfriend."

"I see," the captain said, giving no indication he knew about Grinda's wolf or the decision to keep it out of the weekly report. "Officer Hjalmquist's grouse case pointed you to Mister Gitter and Ms. Johns, and Nurmanski pointed you into the same area, and now Grinda is focused there as well. Have you heard from your undercover?"

"Yes, he's in the area and getting established. I'll take in the team meeting tomorrow morning. Any further activity from 'terrorists'?" He pronounced the last word to leave no doubt that he doubted a conspiracy of the magnitude suggested by the feds.

"Nothing new—at least nothing Ms. Nevelev cared to mention," the captain said, sounding almost forlorn.

"I'll check in with you after tomorrow's meeting," Service said.

Service closed the cell phone and shook his head. Did the captain not know about Grinda's wolf? It seemed like every turn revealed new games. Service told himself if this was what detective work amounted to, they could have it. He'd rather be back in his old job in the Mosquito.

Nantz answered the telephone in her Lansing office, "Team 2001, Maridly Nantz."

Service said, "Do you fool around?"

Her voice brightened. "When I fool around, it's all business, buster. How *are* you, hon?"

They talked for a few minutes. He told her about arrangements he'd made for their animals and hoped she wouldn't ask about Lehto. How

long until Jep Niemi's rumor mill or her own network rolled something
to her?

"Maridly . . ."

She laughed. "God. Service. You're going to tell me you kissed
Lehto when you picked up our animals. I already know. That woman is
flat-out ballsy. She called me down here and told me she thought I deserved to know that she still has designs on you. She also made it clear
that you were the kissee and not the kisser, an honorable declaration. I
told her to go for it. Competition is good, right?"

He could hardly compute what he was hearing.

"Besides, she copped to the fact that she put the old smoocherooski
on you, but you drove off and left her standing with a hormone flash
flood in her wears." Nantz laughed. "Turning down a sure thing, Service. That's impressive."

He was speechless and tried to change directions "How did your
meeting go?"

"Dull, dull, and dull. What a life, giving a performance review to a
janitorial service. It took two minutes of face-time and twenty minutes of
damn paperwork. Grady, this is crazy to sit here doing nothing all day,
every day," she said. "I'm thinking I might visit Sam."

"It wouldn't be the first time," he said. She knew the governor and
last summer had confronted him about a case Service was working on.
Nantz's visit had forced him to back off. For the first time it struck him
that maybe the governor's target with this task force bullshit was actually
Nantz, not him. It would fit. He was petty enough to go after her. A feeling of shame began to creep over him. His ego needed reining in.

"You know I wouldn't really do it," she said. "I was just thinking out
loud." He wasn't so sure, but he didn't say so. "Where are you, hon?"

"Near Nisula, on my way back to the Soo."

"Please be careful, Grady. You wanna know what I told your horny
veterinarian?"

He was sure it was memorable.

"I said, 'Let the games begin.'"

All he could do was shake his head. His next call went to Bay Mills.
DaWayne Kota was still out of the office. After tomorrow's meeting in
the Soo, he'd drive out to Vermillion and see if he could locate the
never-there tribal game warden.

· 14 ·

He was driving east on US 41, nearing the Huron River–
Peshekee Grade Road that led north into the 17,000-acre Mc-
Cormick Wilderness, when drivers ahead of him began to
slam on their brakes. He flipped on his blue lights and eased into the left
lane. No traffic coming; everything had stopped in both directions. A
quarter mile ahead he saw a small bright yellow pickup truck on its side
in the middle of the highway and people standing around gawking. He
called the accident in to the Marquette County sheriff's dispatcher, gave
the location, and pulled onto the north shoulder. There was no room
around the wreck.

The nose of the tiny Toyota was pushed back, the engine block
jammed into the cabin. He looked at the car and saw steam, but no
sparks. Gas and other fluids were trickling onto the highway.

"Stay back," he told gawkers. "No smokes." Naturally he immediately wanted one.

Service eased up to the wreck and peeked into the cab No sign of a
driver or passengers. A large pink neon sticker in the spiderwebbed back
window declared, I HAVE PERSONALLY SEEN JESUS 13 TIMES! Service
hoped today wasn't number fourteen. He heard a siren within two minutes and saw a Marquette County cruiser coming from the east with its
light-bar flashing. People from stopped cars had moved over to the south
shoulder of the road and were staring down a steep incline. Service
joined them and saw a massive black body sprawled at the bottom. The
animal's forelegs were bent at obtuse angles, one of its hind legs still
twitching. Two human legs stuck out from under the moose. Service
fetched his emergency first-aid kit and box of disposable latex gloves
from the truck, asked people to move away, and slid down the embankment.

"Move your damn cars," he heard a familiar voice barking. He
looked up to see Deputy Sheriff Linsenman sliding down to join him.

Linsenman looked at the moose and said, "Holy shit, there's somebody under there."

"The moose is still alive," Service said.

Linsenman nodded, pulled out his nine-millimeter, and shot the animal in the head.

"Not anymore, he's not." The huge animal lurched once and lay still. Blood spattered the legs of the man pinned beneath and the surrounding grass.

The two law officers asked for help. Several people slid down the incline on their behinds to help shift the moose carcass so the officers could free the trapped man. Linsenman called 911 from the microphone hooked under his jacket epaulet while Service started a quick injury evaluation. The man's face was lacerated, an arm broken and bent at the wrist. He was unconscious, pale, his breathing labored. Shock for sure. Service snapped on a pair of latex gloves.

"Ambulance in fifteen minutes," Linsenman said, kneeling and gently tucking his coat under the injured man.

"He's shocky," Service said. "Tell them to step on it." Shock left untreated would kill. Even with treatment it could bring the same outcome.

Service took off his coat and laid it over the injured man. Linsenman put on gloves and held antiseptic gauze against the cut. They both knew not to move him. A thousand pounds on top of you was likely to cause severe internal injuries. There was nothing to do but keep pressure on cuts, keep the man warm and comfortable, and wait.

More sirens announced the arrival of additional help.

Twenty minutes later the injured man was strapped on a board, his head immobilized in a brace, and he was carried onto an ambulance that headed west toward L'Anse, which was closer than Marquette. Service and Linsenman stood outside the DNR truck, smoking and sharing coffee while two other deputies directed traffic and a wrecker hauled the Toyota away.

There was blood where the animal had been struck, but no tire marks. Could be the driver never saw the moose, Service thought. But the area was fairly open and this didn't seem likely, especially this time of year when most drivers had their eyes on the edges of the woods, fields, and swamps looking for deer.

The two lawmen asked people in the other vehicles what they had seen, and got as many stories as there were witnesses. Only two facts met agreement. The driver had been alone, and the man under the moose had been the driver. How he had ended up yards away, down the embankment and under the animal, was the subject of intense speculation.

"Not even Day One." Linsenman said.

Service nodded. "Day omega for the moose."

The deputy patted his sidearm. "Too bad it wasn't a bull."

"Too bad there's no moose season," Service said. Moose and wolves were under state protection.

Linsenman laughed. Service called the DNR office in Baraga and reported the dead animal. They'd collect it so biologists could do a necropsy. Unlike wolves, which had come back into the region on their own, moose had been transplanted, their numbers fluctuating ever since due to various parasites and diseases. As with the wolves, every moose death was taken seriously. Quite a few moose fell victim to vehicles every year. Service had once had a tourist ask where he could photograph a moose and told him, "Just drive east and west on the M-Twenty-Eight and try not to hit one."

Service was first on the scene, but Linsenman took on the task of piecing together the details of what had happened. He would talk to the driver if and when the man could talk, and issue a citation or not.

Service was five miles east of the scene when he got a cell phone call.

"Carmody. Where are ya, boyo?"

"Sixty miles east of you, give or take."

"Perfect. You know a place called Silver Mountain Lookout?"

"I know it."

"Get there as soon as you can."

The remains of the abandoned old fire tower on Silver Mountain sat on the northern perimeter of the Sturgeon River Wilderness. Sturgeon River Gorge lay about four miles to the southeast as the crow flies; between the two points, there were three-hundred-foot-deep canyons up to a mile wide. The dark, dense forests were thick with cedar and tamarack, hemlock, popple, sugar maple, basswood, aspen, and paper birch. The wilderness area was comprised of nearly fifteen thousand acres, and inside it there were few trails. It was a good deer-hunting country, but only the toughest and most competent hunters would tackle it. If the snows fell heavily when you were in such turf, you could have serious problems. It was one of those areas where a compass was mandatory and not a place Service relished chasing troublemakers.

The roads back to the small parking lot at the old fire tower were muddy, washboarded, and difficult to negotiate. Service took it slowly and kept both hands on the steering wheel. The ass end of his truck kept bouncing sideways, and the transmission was up to its usual tricks.

There were no other fresh tracks on the road, which struck Service as odd given that this was two days before the two-week deer season opened. There had seemed to be plenty of hunters coming north last Friday. Apparently not that many had come all the way over here, which showed how unknowledgeable some hunters could be. The bulk of the deer were here, not to the east. The lack of tracks also told him that either Carmody was yet to arrive, or would come in from the south and west. There was no sign of his undercover when he pulled into the gravel lot.

Service used his time alone to retrace the past few days. SuRo's non sequitur mention of the blue wolf at Vermillion bugged him. Her background, the feds insisted, made her a prime suspect. He didn't buy it. The facts of Vermillion were simple: a bomb and two bodies. What was the status of the autopsies? Were there security tapes? And what had DaWayne Kota been doing there? Why was Wink Rector not in the loop? Wink was FBI, he was competent, and it was a federal facility. Why had Wink been given the lead in Houghton? The BATF almost always took the lead when there was a bomb. What made the bombs in Houghton a lesser matter than Vermillion? Fatalities maybe, but there was something else and it bothered him to not be able to see it. Rector said BATF was all over Houghton, but they weren't even on the team in the Soo. Why had it taken Joe Ketchum to find that four of the five wolves were still there, and why had the FBI chased him off? He should have found them, he chided himself. Why had Nevelev not told his captain about the wolves being recovered? And who the hell gave the FBI the power to declare the wolves outside DNR's jurisdiction? He had so many questions about Vermillion that he didn't want to deal with the wolf case or Gitter and Johns. He would learn soon enough what Carmody wanted.

The undercover man didn't arrive for another ninety minutes and when he did, he looked muddy, disheveled, and tired. "Where's the bloody tower?" Carmody asked.

Service pointed. "That way, around the rocks and up."

"Let's climb," Carmody said, pushing past Service and trudging up to the tower.

"Why? We can talk here."

"Humor me," Carmody said.

Service followed and saw that Carmody was moving with great difficulty, limping slightly.

When they got to the top Carmody exhaled dramatically, pulled a flask from his coat and held it out.

"It's your meeting," Service said, waiting patiently. He didn't need a drink.

Carmody took a hit from the flask and said, "Sodding British," as he wiped his mouth with the back of his hand "Flat tire. Fooking jacks are worthless. I'd have a fag, if you'd be offering." Service handed him a pack of smokes and didn't tell him the Land Rover was probably assembled in the United States.

"Keep the pack. I've got more."

Carmody sucked smoke deep into his lungs and waited. "The grand mating dance has begun," he said.

"Johns?"

"Aye. I was sighting in the new long rifle and she came up and challenged me to a bituva shoot. Gorgeous creature, that. We had our contest and I let her win by a wee bit, you see. But make no mistake, the woman can shoot. Afterward she generously treated me to thin and tasteless American beer and invited me to lunch, where she plied me with Kentucky whiskey. After lunch and more than a few shots, we motored to her camp, had another whiskey or two, and she proposed another contest. Only this time she pulled out a fooking cannon of a rifle, a fifty-caliber behaymouth with a scope that would let you be countin' pubic hairs on a dwarf at two miles. We drove up a mountain called Ogidabik, which she said is local aborigine gibberish for 'on the rock.'"

Service listened.

"We each fired three rounds at plastic bottles hung from tree branches a good two kilometers distant. We both struck all three targets and repaired to her little hideaway in the forest. It's down a maze of logging roads east and north of your Presque Isle River. Bloody *awful* ground. We had a lovely evening, more whiskey, shooting pistols at everything in range, had a go in bed, drank more, had another go in bed, and I would be quick to point out I'm not referrin' to a quick slam-bam, doink-and-boink, but a marathon go. I had doubts I could keep up with her. This morning she makes an offer: a thousand dollars cash for the head of a deer with, and I quote, 'impressive horns.' To match her own, no doubt. I told her I needed neither the money nor the meat. She said it was a matter of sport. And what sport might that be? asks I. 'Gettin' away with it,' says she. And if I were to agree? She says she'll put me on to something even more lucrative. What constitutes impressive? I ask her. 'Use your judgment,' says she." Carmody shook his head.

"This is all pretty quick," Service said. "Whose camp did she take you to?"

"Gitter's methinks. The woman's bloody daft," Carmody said. "I've seen all kinds, mind you, but nothing such as the likes of Wealthy Johns." He added, "I told her I don't know the land, have had no opportunity to scout for animals. Says she: 'Think of it as a fine test of your resourcefulness.'"

Service waited.

"I find myself faced with wee problem. I need an 'impressive head.'"

Service immediately thought of the animal that Sheena Grinda had confiscated that morning. He said, "I have an idea."

They returned to the trucks, and he used his radio to call the Baraga office. He was told Grinda was "clear." He got her home telephone number and punched it into his cell phone.

"I have a favor to ask," he said when she answered.

"Service? You seem to ask for a lot."

"The buck you confiscated this morning. Where is it?"

"In my truck. I'll put it in the evidence locker tomorrow. Once it's checked in, we'll give it to somebody who can use the meat. If it doesn't spoil in this heat. I should've put it in the locker today."

"I want it," Service said.

"For what?"

"Bait."

Grinda grunted. "Bait for what?"

"Headhunters."

She didn't react right away. "The animal is evidence."

"Use your camera. I'll swear as a witness that I was there when you hauled the man out. I'll take responsibility."

"I think working with you is going to make me weary," she said.

He arranged to pick up the animal within two hours. Carmody would wait nearby, and Service would deliver the buck to him to take to his "employer."

"What do you think Johns has in mind?" Service asked.

"Dunno, but that bloody cannon seems to be the focal point."

Service had to agree, but would Johns be wielding it or would Carmody? She had already lied to Hjalmquist and Bois about the weapon's whereabouts.

The ambiguity of the whole thing left him uneasy, but he drove to Grinda's cabin seven miles north of Bruce Crossing while Carmody waited one mile north of her place.

A yard spotlight was on when he pulled his truck up to her cabin. Grinda came out wearing tights, running shoes, and an oversized green T-shirt with lettering that said WOODS COPPER. She opened the back of her truck and watched him transfer the dead animal. He used his knife to score an area below one of the tines.

"What are you doing?" Grinda asked.

"Leaving a return address," he said, not bothering to explain further.

"I'm treading water in my discomfort zone," she said.

"Lousy swimming, isn't it? Did you get your photos?"

"Right after you called."

"I'll get back to you," Service reminded her.

"We'll see," she said.

Carmody dumped the animal under a tarp in the back of his Land Rover and Service watched him drive south on US 45.

Service also headed south, but at Bruce Crossing he turned east on the M-28, facing a five-hour drive to the Soo and hoping neither weather nor circumstances interfered. He needed sleep.

By the time he reached Seney he had nodded off a half dozen times and knew it was too dangerous to push it any farther. He drove a few miles south on M-77 to the entrance of the Seney National Wildlife Refuge, pulled up the driveway, parked on the grass shoulder, reported himself clear to Station 20, and immediately went to sleep sitting up.

· 15 ·

Grady Service crawled out of his truck at 5 A.M. to stretch cramped muscles and take a leak. He was less than a hundred yards up the refuge's driveway from M-77 and it was quiet, the air motionless. He lingered to light his first cigarette of the day, enjoying the palpable silence. As soon as he got the cigarette in his mouth he heard a muted *thump* followed by screeching brakes and the sound of collapsing metal. He instinctively grabbed his oh-shit kit and ran down the driveway with his light.

To the south on his side of the road he saw the silhouette of something slumped on the shoulder; directly across the road from him a mini van was turtled on its roof in the cattails ten yards off the road. Shit-kicker music blared from the radio, something about friends in low places.

He ran to the lump on the shoulder and found a man, the fletching of an arrow sticking out of his chest. The man was on his back, writhing, gasping for air and choking, trying to move. One of the man's legs was bent ninety degrees to the side, and blood cascaded from his mouth. Service gently eased him onto his side, reached into his mouth with two fingers, and cleared the air passage. He wiped his hand on his jacket and saw the arrow protruding from the man's back and blood pooling on the gravel.

"Sir, it's going to be okay. Can you hear me?"

"Hurt," the man said, his voice a wet rattle.

Service felt for a pulse and fumbled to get on latex gloves, berating himself for having reached into the man's bloody mouth without protection. The man's pulse was racing and blood continued to pour out of his mouth, but the air passage was clear and he wasn't choking as badly.

"Fell, fell," the man said, his chest continuing to heave.

He didn't want to leave the man, but he needed to check the vehicle. He couldn't triage until he knew what he was dealing with. He got up and started to move toward the van when he heard another *thud* and the sound of shattering plastic and glass and looked back to see the lights of a car spinning crazily toward him like a malfunctioning top. He grasped the man by the collar and tried to judge where the spinning car would end up, preparing himself to haul the injured man out of the way. But the vehicle suddenly veered sharply to the east side and shot down into the cattails, stopping with a sudden and resounding sucking sound.

Service grabbed two flares from his emergency kit and lit them. One thing at a time, he told himself. Two vehicles and a pedestrian with an arrow in his chest. This had the makings of a giant cluster-fuck and he needed to get out warnings before it got worse.

He heard a door slam from the vehicle that had just gone into the ditch.

"Are you okay?" he yelled.

"B-bear," a woman shouted weakly.

Bear? He headed for the overturned van but saw the lights of another vehicle coming from the south and slowing as the driver spied the flares and the second vehicle in the cattails.

The logging truck stopped with its air brakes screaming. The truck was a double trailer loaded with pulpwood. The driver dropped down from his cab.

"Get on your radio, call for help. Get more flares out and check the car behind you," Service shouted at the trucker as he ran toward the van.

The mini van was on its roof, its engine still running. He got down on his knees in the cold muck, reached across the driver, and turned the key off. The driver was unconscious, strapped in, no air bag, pulse spotty. There was another person in the passenger seat, strapped in and hanging upside down and sideways.

He circled the vehicle and tugged on the door. It was jammed, but he managed to get it open a crack and wedge it wider using his thigh and hip. Booze fumes wafted out of the vehicle as two Old Turkey bottles and a couple of empty plastic schnapps pints tumbled out. The passenger was alive and bleeding profusely from a lacerated forehead. The man's stringy hair hung down, blood dripping from the strands. Fucking mess, Service told himself as he pressed a sterile gauze pad against the wound and held it there.

The truck driver came to the van, followed by a woman.

"What can I do?" the trucker asked.

"Pressure on this," Service said, worried about the man with the arrow in him.

The woman was behind the truck driver, shaking badly.

"Are you hurt?"

"S-s-scared," she said. "B-b-bear. Back there," she added, pointing.

He gave her the once-over. No visible blood. He sent her to his truck to get blankets and his extra flashlight. By the time she got back he was with the man on the shoulder of the road. He put one blanket on the man and then draped the other around the woman's shoulders.

The man on the ground was breathing, but it was shallow. Lots of blood on the ground where the arrow stuck through his back.

"Can you stay with him?" Service asked.

"I'm not trained," she said.

"Just talk to him, try to keep him calm, and don't let him move."

"What if h-h-he dies?"

"Stay with him, okay? He needs to hear someone close."

The trucker was where Service had left him.

"The driver's making weird sounds," the trucker said calmly. "Breathing problems."

Service went to the driver and felt no pulse.

He managed to get the man's seat belt released and supported him as he lowered him to the ground and pulled him a few feet up toward the road to get him out of the muck. He was still not breathing. Service knelt beside the driver, checked the airway clear, and began CPR. Nothing. He kept at it, getting the rhythm, trying to focus on the life in his hands.

The trucker said "Help's rolling from Seney—volunteer fire. There's a county mountie five minutes away, and a trooper in ten." Service cursed Bozian's budgets; night patrols in U.P. counties had been reduced to one county and one state car. He heard sirens coming south toward them. He kept breathing into the prone man's mouth and didn't stop until someone was beside him telling him in an authoritative voice to move over.

Service hurried back to the man with the arrow and found the woman holding his hand and talking gently to him.

The morning darkness was filled with blinking emergency lights. A man in a firefighter's coat was beside him, checking the man on the ground.

"We gotta roll with this guy," the fireman said. "He's bleeding out."

It felt like Vietnam, people bleeding all around him and everybody scared shitless and desperately trying to stay calm in order to do the right things. Service helped others shift the man onto a gurney. Somebody put an oxygen mask on his face.

"What the fuck is this?" someone asked, seeing the arrow.

"Don't touch it," a woman said. "Immobilize it."

"With what?"

"Your hand, asswipe. Just hold it steady until we get him loaded."

A Troop arrived at the same time as a Schoolcraft County deputy.

The Troop went to help at the van. The deputy took the woman from the other vehicle and walked her over to his patrol car.

Service sat down on the cold asphalt and leaned back, his adrenaline beginning to relent, but his heart still pounding. He sat there for several seconds, his mind unfocused, and was shocked back to reality by a woman screaming angrily.

"Goddammit, Ernie. Goddamn you!"

She trudged out of the woods on the far side of the road, stomping and splashing through cattails and muck.

Service went to her. When he tried to touch her arm, she pulled it away. "Where's my Ernie!"

Her eyes were wide with fear, emergency lights illuminating her face, her hair matted and askew. She wore sweatpants and a T-shirt and had thick black mud up to her thighs.

"Who's Ernie?" Service asked, trying to calm her.

"My husband."

Service grasped her arms firmly above the elbows and held her in place. "Ma'am! Please try to calm down and talk to me. Just calm down, okay? Take a deep breath."

The woman stopped trying to push toward the congestion of lights.

"Ma'am, where did you come from?"

She nodded her head to the east. It was all wildlife refuge land in that direction. "What's your name?"

"Barb, Mrs. Barbara Wildwood."

Service talked calmly and deliberately. "Okay, Barb. I'm Grady. We've got a lot of confusion out here right now, so I need for you to listen to me and help us, okay?"

She nodded.

"Where did you come from?"

"Allegan."

"I mean now, this morning."

"Camped."

"You're camped in the refuge?"

"Ernie says it's federal, our taxes pay for it. The truck's got one of those tents that fits in the bed. Ernie backed us up a two-track. We got here last night and celebrated. I thought Ernie would sleep in this morning, but he's got his mind set on a damn bear. He's been up here a couple of days every week, got a bear coming in to his baits Big bear. I told him, this time I'm going with you. Here we are married a year and he's gone hunting all the time. I wasn't going to stay home alone again."

"How far is your truck, Barb?"

"Don't know. Ten minutes, maybe fifteen."

"And you heard the commotion and walked out here?"

"I woke up and Ernie and his bow were gone and I went after him. He was too drunk last night to be up in a tree stand this morning.'

Frightened people were difficult to talk to. Service knew to guide gently, let the story come out at her pace in her way. "What does Ernie look like?"

"Forty-five, six foot, long hair. He wants to get it cut, but I tell him I like it long, makes him look younger."

"He wasn't in his tree blind?"

"I got turned around, couldn't find it," she said. "I heard the sirens and came to them. Have you seen my Ernie?" She looked at Service with lost eyes.

He put his arm around her shoulders and led her up the road to the emergency vehicles. One ambulance was already gone, the second one just pulling out, headed north.

Of all the places for an accident, he thought. There was no hospital closer than Newberry, Munising, and Maristique, none of them closer than forty-five minutes at emergency speed.

There was a man by a fire truck. Service left the woman in sweatpants by the county cruiser and walked over to him. His hard hat said DA CHIEF, the words hand-lettered.

"Service."

"Dino Halmarik. Real mess, dis."

"A woman just came out of the woods back there. She's looking for her husband. Name is Ernie and he was up in a tree stand."

The chief nodded. "Ernest Wildwood, the one wit da arrow. Dey're takin' him Newberry. But my people just call, say da guy is gone. You don't see dis every day, fella arrow in da gut. Think happen?"

"One thing at a time," Service said, which this time of year was rarely how it went.

He left the fire chief and went to the overturned van. A third ambulance had arrived; the passenger was on a gurney behind it

Service introduced himself to the Schoolcraft County deputy named Nighswaander.

"Driver in the ambulance?"

"He didn't make it."

Shit. "You talk to the passenger yet?"

"Nope. Thought I'd wait for you. Helluva mess."

Service nodded. Both men squeezed into the ambulance and knelt by the man on the gurney. His head was bandaged; someone had tried to wipe the blood off his face and left it streaked like warpaint. The man's shirt collar was wet and dark. Alcohol wafted off him.

"Uh-oh," the man said, staring up at the two police officers.

"What happened?" the deputy asked.

"Where's Yank?"

"Yank?"

"My brother, Yank Kranker."

"He's the driver?"

Service was impressed that Nighswaander avoided past tense.

"He's gone to the hospital in an ambulance. Who're you?"

"Reb Kranker, his brother."

"Yank and Reb," Nighswaander said.

"Our folks thought it was funny. Is my brother okay?"

"The hospital will take care of him," the deputy said. "Can you tell us what happened?"

"Some guy come stumbling up on the road. Yank and me was singing, headed for deer camp over to Eben. Yank cut hard to avoid the guy but I think maybe we nicked him."

"Where are you from, Mr. Kranker?"

"Hamtramck."

"How fast were you going, Mr. Kranker?"

"Yank was drivin' and I wasn't payin' attention. He does the speed limit. Yank don't speed."

"There were open intoxicants in the vehicle."

"I maybe had a few snorts," the man said.

"Was Yank drinking?"

"Yank don't drink. He used to, but he give it up. Is my brother okay?"

"He's headed for the hospital," the deputy said. "How many snorts did you have?"

"I wasn't driving so it don't matter, right? We were goin' to deer camp."

Nighswaander patted the man's leg. "Okay, Mr. Kranker, we're gonna let you head over to the hospital and get you checked out. I'll talk to you there later."

"What about the van—our *rifles?*"

"Let's just get you to the hospital and then we'll worry about the other stuff."

"Okay. You guys smoke? I'm out."

"You've got oxygen in here."

"Can't smoke nowhere anymore," the man said. "Are Yank and me gonna be on TV?"

Neither officer answered. They watched the ambulance drive north.

"Poor bastard," Nighswaander said. "His brother's dead."

"So's the man they hit," Service said.

"The one with the arrow?" The deputy shook his head, made a clucking sound. "You first on the scene?"

Service pointed at the refuge driveway. "On my way to the Soo for a meeting. Pulled in there to get some sleep. I heard the impact." He explained what he had heard, seen, done.

"You come outta there couple of minutes later you mighta been smack in the middle of it. You fellas don't get much sleep this time a year, do ya?"

Service looked at his watch: 6:42 A.M. "You guys do?"

Nighswaander laughed. "Not much."

"The wife of the deceased pedestrian is in your patrol car."

The deputy nodded. "She know the score yet?"

"No."

"I'll tell her. Who's the other woman?"

"She was in the car back there." Service pointed. "She said something about a bear."

The deputy went to the new widow. Service got coffee for the other woman and walked her back to her PT Cruiser, which was mired in muck on the side of the road. The grill was smashed in, hood popped and crumpled, a piece of plastic hanging off at a strange angle, one headlight gone.

"I'm sorry," the woman said. "I'm afraid I got a little emotional. I'm Lorelei Timms, Lori."

The name seemed vaguely familiar. "Grady Service. Can you tell me what happened?"

"I was headed to Marquette to meet my husband, Whit. We've got a place near Big Bay. I was driving along, no traffic, and suddenly this black thing came out of nowhere. Ran right under me and I was flying and spinning all over the place. I thought I was going to roll, but it stayed up and I went into the swamp. I was hanging on, not steering. Scared the hell out of me."

"Thanks for getting the blankets and light."

She smiled. "That was smart, getting me to do something to get my mind off me. How did that man get the arrow in him?"

"I don't know."

"He died, didn't he?"

"Yes ma'am."

"My God," she said. "You're a conservation officer, yes?"

"Yes."

"Do you handle this sort of thing often?"

"Never one quite like this."

"How will you sort it out?"

"I don't know yet," he admitted. It had all happened at once.

She nodded. "I'm sorry that man died. What about the man you were giving mouth-to-mouth?"

"He didn't make it either."

"My God," she said in a whisper.

The volunteer fire chief came back to them and said, "Senator Timms, anything we can do for youse?"

"If a wrecker can pull me out, we'll see if it'll start and I can be on my way—if you're done with me." She looked at Service.

"That thing ain't gonna run," the chief said. "Somebody we can call for you?"

"My husband," she said, giving the chief a phone number, which he wrote down on a pad.

Senator Timms: That's why the name was familiar. She was a state senator from Petoskey, Charlevoix, someplace north of Traverse City. He'd heard her name before, but couldn't remember the context.

"Glad you're running for governor," the fire chief said. "You can't do no worse den Sam Bozian comes to da folks up here."

She said gently, "I haven't announced yet. Is that an endorsement, Chief?"

"It's on da radio youse gonna run, eh? You'll get my vote," he said, not catching her irony.

Service left the senator and walked along the highway with his light on, looking for the bear. He found it on the west side of the road, sprawled on its side, its stomach burst, intestines shining blue under his light beam. It was a big female, close to four hundred pounds, shiny black fur thickened for winter. He could see a substantial layer of yellow fat she had accumulated to see her through hibernation.

"That's a shame," he heard the senator say from behind him. "I didn't see it. It just came charging across and then it was under me."

"The way it usually happens with bears," he said. "When they decide to cross, they just go."

"Like some politicians," the senator said.

He saw the blood trail that ended at the carcass and started back-tracking. He stepped off sixty-three yards. There was an elliptical splash at point of impact and twenty yards of intestine strewn around from the impact point forward.

The senator was right behind him. "What're you looking for?"

"You dragged it."

"I thought for a second it was under me, and then I was spinning."

"Lucky you didn't go over." PT Cruisers could be death traps.

"Officer, do you mind if I follow you around for a while?"

"Why?"

"I want to watch you do your job."

He checked his watch. He still had to figure out what happened with Ernie and his tree blind and there was no way to make the Soo meeting. The county or state could handle the accident report on the van. He'd make out the report on the senator and her bear.

"Let's get some coffee first."

She was a quiet woman. When the sun began to lighten the eastern sky he got a good look at her. Tall, a little heavy, intense eyes, medium-length hair streaked with gray. She wore an untucked flannel shirt, jeans, and boots that had gotten a lot of wear.

"Your husband going deer hunting?"

She smiled easily. "No, I'm the hunter. Walt doesn't hunt, but he likes to be along and I like having him. When I'm in Lansing, he's usually back in Petoskey with the kids, so this is our vacation. How's the herd this year?"

"Not good up your way. It's never good close to the Superior water-shed and we had a tough winter last year. Where's your camp?"

"Huron Mountains," she said.

He studied her for a moment. "The Club?"

"Yes, Cabin Fifty-Two, Tamarack Lodge. It's the newest one, built in 1989 to celebrate the club's centennial. My family's been in the club since the beginning."

The exclusive Huron Mountain Club was located north of Big Bay and had been shrouded in mystery and mystique throughout its history. The founders had been local power brokers, but they soon brought in members from all over the Midwest. In the early going they all had one thing in common: money. Bentley, McCormick, Dodge, Ford, Alger, Washburn, Shite, McMillan—these were the names that stuck in Service's head, but few facts about any of them except a vague memory of Henry Ford being initially rejected for membership.

What stuck most in his mind was what Yogi Zambonet had told him, that the club had been involved in the failed experiment to transplant wolves in 1974.

If Timms was part of the Huron Mountain bunch, she came from deep roots of power and influence. Club people were used to getting their way.

"I'd think the hunting might be okay at the club," he said, knowing the club had its own wildlife manager.

They walked back up to Nighswaander's cruiser to see Barbara Wildwood. She was standing by the car with a vacant look on her face but stared at him when he approached.

"I'm sorry for your loss," he said.

She had red, swollen eyes. "Thank you. They took Ernie to Newberry. I guess I ought to be with him."

"Mrs. Wildwood, I know this is a difficult time, but where is your truck? I need to look around, see if we can figure out what happened."

"There's a two-track down that way a tich," she said, pointing. "I need to get the truck anyway."

Service didn't want her to move the vehicle until he could examine the camp. Her husband had said something about falling, and his wife said he'd been drunk. He had a pretty good idea what might have happened, but he needed to see it, understand it, be certain.

"I can drive you there."

She said, "Thanks."

He went to get his truck and the senator trailed along. "Got room for me?"

"It'll be a tight squeeze," he said, wishing she'd go away, but she was a senator and it wouldn't do to get on her wrong side. One politician after his scalp was enough.

Fifteen minutes later they were parked on a two-track near the Wildwoods' truck.

There was an empty Jack Daniel's bottle on the floor of the tent in the truck's bed and two plastic glasses.

"Where's your husband's blind?"

The woman pointed. "Through the tag alders, Ernie said. There's supposed to be some big beeches somewhere in there."

Service looked at the senator. "Could you help her pack up?"

The senator raised an eyebrow. "Sure."

He followed a game trail through dead ferns, saw where Ernie had gone in, and eventually came to the white pine near a pocket of mature beech trees. The blind looked new, installed twenty feet up in the white pine. The man hadn't set it up last night; it had been there for a while. Wildwood's name, address, and phone number were painted on the bottom of the platform.

There was a reeking bait pile twenty feet out from the tree, and at the base of the tree a broken compound bow lay on the ground, with a crushed quiver and several bent arrows strewn around. Heavy blood. It looked like the man had fallen and landed on his own arrow. The blood trail started back toward the truck camp, but began to drift right until it was headed for the highway. Service thought he could read the signs: Ernie had been losing blood, trying to get back to his truck, but gradually lost his ability to think and drifted off course to the west. The blood trail led out to the road and Service saw that the bleeding hunter had stumbled in front of the oncoming van and been hit. He wondered which had killed him—the arrow or the collision.

He guessed that the hunter or the crash had also spooked the bear onto the road, a marriage of bad karmas.

The women had loaded the truck by the time he got back to them.

"I think your husband fell from his stand onto the arrow. I think he tried to get back to you, Barb, but he lost too much blood and got lost." He didn't tell her about the mini van. Such details could come after the autopsy. Right now she needed something positive to hold on to.

The widow grimaced. "He should never have been out there."

Service didn't ask how much the man had to drink

"Can I go to Ernie now?" the woman asked.

Service gave her a business card and told her to call him if she had any questions.

Senator Timms stood next to him watching the woman drive away. "Do I get a ticket?" she asked. "I might've been going a little faster than fifty-five."

"Your speed didn't cause your problem," he said.

"Well, I doubt I'll be going over fifty-five up here at night again."

"These things happen," he said.

"You didn't know who I was until the chief came along."

"My mind was sort of occupied."

The senator smiled. "You heard I'm running for governor?"

"Not until this morning."

"I'll make the formal announcement in Marquette this afternoon, then I'm going hunting. What is the DNR looking for in a governor?"

Service knew not to unload on Bozian. "I don't speak for the DNR."

"Let me rephrase that. What are *you* looking for?"

"Somebody who cares about what we have."

"What does your leadership want?"

"I don't talk for my leadership."

She smiled. "You don't like politics."

"Somebody has to do the jobs," he said. "I couldn't."

She said, "You're a diplomat, Officer Service, and I'm sorry that people died this morning and that I killed that poor bear, but strange as it seems, I am glad to have had this experience. Do you have another card?"

He dug one out. It was streaked with dirt and dried blood.

The woman studied it. "Perfect," she said, extending her hand and shaking his firmly. She took a card out of her purse and held it out to him. "If you ever need anything, you call me. Do you mind if I call you from time to time?"

"I can't get into politics, Senator," he said.

"It's Lori, and I understand that, Officer, and I wouldn't put you in that position, but from time to time I may need an objective viewpoint on certain issues."

"You've got my number, Senator."

"Indeed I do," she said. "What will you do now?"

"Do the paperwork on your accident, help get you back on the road, assist the county to make sure the road's clear of debris, get the dead animal off the road, and head for our district office in Newberry to write my report."

She got into the passenger seat of his truck. "What's the computer for?"

"Mostly the Automatic Vehicle Locator." He turned on the computer and showed her, telescoping the electronic maps down to their present location, then up in scale to show her the vehicles of three other officers in neighboring counties.

"You can find each other this way."

"And Lansing can find us, too," he said.

She smiled. "Does it work?"

"It does what we need it to do."

"You really *are* a diplomat," she said.

"That's not a universally held opinion," he admitted.

She reached over and patted his arm. "When you're a woman and direct, you're a bitch or power hungry. I expect it's pretty much the same for police officers."

He got to Newberry at noon and found Lisette McKower eating at her desk.

"Is that blood all over you?" she said, looking up from her salad.

"Personal injury accident in Seney."

She looked him in the eye. "What were you doing *there?*"

"I pulled into the refuge to catch a nap. I was headed for a meeting in the Soo this morning. I heard the thing happen."

"What are you doing here?"

"I missed my meeting in the Soo, figured I'd get the paperwork done and catch tomorrow's meeting."

"Why don't you stay with Jack and me tonight. The girls would love to see you."

"Thanks, but I think I'll bunk right here and head out early."

"You always have to do things your way."

He was working on the bear accident report when McKower came into the conference room and turned on the radio.

"*Sam Bozian has done no favors for our state. This morning I was involved in a tragic incident and I saw firsthand the selflessness and professionalism of our emergency and law enforcement personnel. We rarely think about conservation officers, but this morning I met an officer named*

Grady Service who handled a situation that would have crushed most of us. He gave aid to the injured and reassured the living with a selfless humanity I've rarely encountered. When I asked him what he wanted in a governor, he said, 'Someone who cares about what we have.' Someone who cares about what we have. I think that I am one of those people, and when I am elected I will do my utmost to uphold the high standards of public service that I was privileged to experience this morning on a lonely stretch of highway in the middle of nowhere. Thank you all for coming. I'll take a few questions and then I'm going hunting."

McKower turned off the radio. "Do you have some sort of magnet for governors?"

"She's a state senator, not the governor."

"If Lorelei Timms has decided she wants the job, the competition better strap on their armor. What did you do?"

"My job," he said, thinking that for the first time since Labor Day he had felt useful and productive.

"Selfless humanity and sensitivity," McKower said, smiling. "You did good, Grady Service."

"Two people died," he said.

"I'm sorry Grady, but some things are beyond control—even for you."

· 16 ·

It was 5 A.M., less than ninety minutes before nimrods could start blazing away at high-speed beef. Service had slept at the Newberry office, showered, and was headed to the Soo. He had just crossed the Soo Line tracks where they intersected M-28, his mind somewhere in the mists of Never-Never, poring over his cases, yesterday's bizarre events, and Nantz's circumstances, when the radio crackled and snapped him back to reality. "Officer needs assistance."

The call came from the Chippewa County police dispatcher. Service pulled over to the side of the road, eased the transmission into neutral, lifted the cover of his black laptop, and punched up the AVL mapping system. He checked in on the radio, got the exact location, checked it against the computer map, saw he was close, and told the county dispatcher he was responding.

He switched off his lights as he turned north off the highway onto a two-track that showed it had seen a lot of recent traffic. Running dark, except for the glow of his computer, he eased his way north through the woods toward the Hendrie River, glancing at the running map as he went. The system was relatively new to the force, and despite his initial skepticism he had to admit that the amount of detail it provided, and its tie to the GPS system, made it a useful tool for finding his way on unfamiliar ground. When it worked. There were only two techs in the U.P. to do repairs. Today it was working.

A mile or so in he saw flashlights and the headlights of cars and trucks illuminating a clearing. Several black buggies were parked on the sides of the road, their horses tied, feeding from canvas buckets. He also saw a DNR truck. He parked and waded the rest of the way through calf-deep slush.

Two groups of bearded men in black and gray clothing were all yelling and gesturing at each other with considerable animation. Service approached quietly and saw CO Bryan Jefferies at the center of the storm. When the towering Jefferies saw him, he stepped away from the groups, which quickly jacked up the verbal assaults. Jefferies and Service had once taken PPCT training together. The Pressure Point Control

Tactics system had been a hybrid of martial arts and dirty street fighting and the younger CO had manhandled him that day, politely excusing himself each time he threw Service to the ground or immobilized him with a pressure hold. It had been a long day. PPCT had since been replaced with a new hybrid program, and Service was glad.

"Good," Jefferies said. "A friendly face."

The crowd was growing louder. Some shoving was starting.

Jefferies pivoted and shouted, "Everybody knock it off and stay where you are!"

Turning back to Service, he said, "Here's the deal. There are two groups here. Mennonites and Amish. Both groups had a group hunt under way."

"Early," Service said.

Jefferies sighed with exasperation. "I know, I know, and using spotlights, and no hunter orange."

"Maybe God gave them permission," Service said, grinning.

"Maybe that same God will smite you with lightning for that remark," the young CO said.

"If he's all his fans claim, he knows where to find me," Service said.

Jefferies continued, "One of the Mennonite drivers spotted a buck and fired his shotgun. Some of the double-ought buckshot hit a rock and ricocheted, smacking one of the Amish men in the knee. The rock slowed down the pellet, but the leg's probably broken. It could have been worse. An ambulance is supposed to be on the way to haul the vick to Newberry."

The officer went on. "The Amish crowd took umbrage and claim they also fired at a deer, only their bullet hit one of the Mennonite trucks, putting a hole in the grille and engine block. The Mennonites claim the Amish shot was intended to insult their religious beliefs. The Mennonites retaliated by shooting an Amish horse. I've been here thirty minutes trying to sort it out. Hunting season hasn't even opened. Can you believe this shit?"

Jefferies was thirtyish with a menacing thick mustache, inordinately tall, and held a degree in human physiology from a small college. He was built like a power lifter. "All they want to do is argue."

The first light of day was showing lavender and orange in the eastern sky, the temperature rising. Service had a meeting to get to and no time for a drawn-out verbal group grope. He approached the groups and stood silently so they could all see him, saying nothing.

The bickering men quieted and stared.

"Shame on you," he said when he finally spoke.

Mouths dropped and heads bowed.

"I'm Service and we have a problem here. Either we sort it out here and now, or Officer Jefferies and I will arrest the whole lot of you and let you explain to a judge and your own communities what happened out here. It's not yet legal to shoot and lights are illegal. You ought to know that." Which didn't guarantee they did.

"We've got an injured man, which at best is incompetent discharge of a firearm. I won't even talk about worst case. We can arrest the lot of you, or, the shooters can step forward and take responsibility. Somebody shot a man in the leg. Somebody blew the window out of a truck. And somebody shot a horse. I am not assigning guilt. You know who you are and we need to talk to you to get this thing sorted out. Accidents happen, but when you lose your cool, God probably doesn't look kindly on it." After a theatrical pause he added, "What will it be?"

The two groups began to mumble and talk among each other and eventually one man stepped forward from each group. "We organized the hunts and we did the shooting," one of the men said. Service doubted this was the truth, but he admired the effort at leadership.

"Okay, you two step aside." To the others he said, 'Leave the horse and truck and the rest of you get out of here. There better not be any more trouble."

It took fifteen minutes for the groups to disperse. By then there was fairly good light and the ambulance had arrived to transport the injured man.

The dead horse was still hitched to a black buggy.

The two men glared at each other.

"Hunting licenses," Service said. The two men handed their licenses to him. "We're writing both of you up for the incompetent discharge of a firearm. We could also charge you for shooting early and not wearing hunter orange, not to mention reckless discharge and not exercising safety, but we'll overlook most of this. I would think that God would expect you both to settle this peacefully. To forgive is divine, right?"

The men nodded.

Jefferies pulled Service aside and asked, "What the hell is 'incompetent discharge'?"

"I'm making this up as we go along. Just flow with it," Service said, returning his attention to the men.

"Who owns the truck?" Service asked.

"My brother," one of the men said.

"Give your keys to Officer Jefferies. Bryan, see if you can start it."

Jefferies got into the truck and began trying to turn over the motor.

"Did you shoot the vehicle?" Service asked the other man.

"I didn't intend to," the Amish man said.

"But you hit it."

The man nodded.

"Who owns the horse?"

"My nephew," the Amish elder said.

"Who shot the horse?" he asked the Mennonite, who confirmed culpability with a peremptory nod.

Jefferies called over to them, "The truck's kaputsky."

"Is the truck your primary transportation?"

"It is," the Mennonite said.

"Is the horse your nephew's primary transportation?" Service asked the other man.

"Yes," the Amish man said.

"Okay," Service said, "three shots, two accidents, two primary means of transport equally out of commission. You're both being cited for incompetent discharge, the damages look equal to me and that's it, end of discussion and dispute. Ask God to tell you what he thinks about your behavior today."

The men stared at Service.

"Officer Jefferies will bring your citations to you and you pay the fines in Newberry."

The men didn't move. Service stepped toward them and waved his hands at them. "Shoo!"

The men trudged down the road, one on each side, not looking at each other.

Jefferies leaned against his truck and started laughing. "*Incompetent discharge?*"

"Visit them tonight and tell them the charges are dropped. God intervened. I'll explain to McKower what went down."

"Yes, Your Detectiveness," the CO said with a grin. "What a job, eh?"

This time they were lucky. Sometimes things like this resulted in loss of life and then there was no joke. He'd seen enough dead recently.

Service arrived at District 4 Headquarters as Lieutenant Lisette McKower was climbing out of her vehicle. "Just back from Star-Range

Golf Course," she said wearily. "The manager called to complain about trespassers and shots fired. I drove out there and found two bozoids in camo ghillie outfits lying on a dead doe in a damn sand trap! The county hauled them in. God, every year the opener draws out the magnum morons. I thought you went to the Soo?" she concluded.

"I'm on my way."

They got coffee from a pot in a small conference room and went into McKower's office. Service told her about the near religious war and by the time he finished, she had spit coffee on her blotter, laughing.

Recovering, she said, "We can't ignore a shooting."

"Leave it be, Lis," he said.

Suddenly she looked at him harshly. "What were you doing out there with Bryan?"

"He called for backup and I was closest. Am I supposed to ignore calls like that?"

"Of course not," she said.

"Lis, tell me about Captain Grant."

She looked alarmed. "Is there a problem?"

"No problem. I like working for him, but I never know what he's thinking."

"Sort of like working with you?" she said, hinting at a smile.

"Did you know he was going to move me to Marquette?" he asked.

"No," she said. "Grady, he's a reserved gentleman. I think he feels deeply but he seldom shows it. Maybe he can't show his emotions, but I know one thing: He won't accept incompetence and he'll never back off supporting those who can do the job."

"Can he handle the politics?"

She squinted inquisitively in his direction and he told her about Vermillion, some of which she knew and most of which she didn't.

"Grady, if the Feebs—or any other agency—try a power play that the captain thinks compromises his people or our mission, he will cut their balls off."

Service wondered. He finished his coffee and began to edge toward the door. "Thanks for backing me for this job," he said.

She smiled. "You like it?"

"The old job was better," he said. "I knew what I was doing. But this—"

She stopped him short. "Good," she said. "Keeping you off balance might just keep you out of trouble."

"I'm not complaining but when I got this job the plan was for me to report to you *and* the captain. What happened?"

"His call."

"One more thing?"

She shrugged.

"Sheena Grinda. What's her story?"

"The ice queen," McKower said. "Damn good officer. She was up for the job you got, but the captain selected you."

Up for the same job? This could explain some of her attitude. "I got the job thanks to you," he said.

McKower shook her head. "The captain came to me, Grady. It was his idea. All I did was agree. He wanted *you*."

This was news and he wasn't sure how to take it. If the captain had handpicked him, he had to have had a good reason. Now he would worry about letting the captain down. Life had been a lot simpler as a CO in a plain brown wrapper.

Service had his second shower of the day in the locker room at the Sault Ste. Marie Troop post, put on the fresh uniform he kept in the truck, and was ready for the meeting five minutes before it was scheduled to begin. The same cast as last time filed in. Judge Vengstrom from Marquette, Sheriff Freddy Bear Lee, Barry Davey, the two Feebs, the hulking Lieutenant Ivanhoe from the MSP, the same two guys in dark suits slouched in chairs in back. No sign of the county prosecutor. Cassie Nevelev was last to arrive, sweeping in with an air of being so busy she could barely squeeze in the meeting. She wore a chic black suit and high heels that sounded like she was pounding the tile floor with a ball-peen hammer.

"We've missed you, Detective Service," she said, looking over at him. "Have you interviewed Ms. Genova?"

"If she's under surveillance, you already know the answer." He was in no mood for games.

"Yes," Nevelev said. "Of course we know you were there, but we have been patiently awaiting your presence to receive your report. I'm asking specifically about the content of that discussion. An oral report will suffice for now."

"She's not part of this . . . thing," he said groping for a noun.

Nevelev rubbed an eyebrow with her finger. "Would you care to enlighten us with regard to how you reached this conclusion?"

"No," Service said. "I wouldn't. What I would like to know is why it took a CO to find four of the five wolves at Vermillion—with three of the four still inside the compound. I also want to know why you didn't disclose this to my captain, and why FBI personnel at Vermillion told Officer Ketchum it was not in the DNR's jurisdiction. These are just for starters," he said, pushing his chair back. Freddy Bear Lee tapped his leg and grinned supportively.

Nevelev looked amused, enjoying the leverage her position gave her. "You were at Vermillion the night of the explosion, Detective. Why didn't you find the wolves? The animals were your only reason for being there. You have not answered the question about the suspect, Detective."

She had hit him in a tender place. Service leaned forward and stared at the woman. "Hey, if *you're* going to withhold information, why not me? We all know the steps to *that* dance."

Judge Vengstrom coughed, suggesting he might speak, but he kept quiet.

It was Lieutenant Ivanhoe who jumped in. "This is unprofessional," he said indignantly.

Service knew from experience that when rank started attacking and jawing about professionalism, they were feeling discomfort, and he was not about to let up.

"Yes," he replied. "Thank you, Lieutenant. That's precisely the point I'm trying to make. If this is a team, fine, but the concept of sharing cuts all directions. If not, then maybe we should forget all this window dressing and save the taxpayers their money."

"I'm for that," the sheriff said, siding with Service. "We're not getting a bloody thing from you people. Homicides in my county are *my* business."

Service watched Ivanhoe and the others looking nervously at each other and trying to do it inconspicuously.

"When there is relevant information to share, I can assure you it will be shared," Nevelev said.

Service said, "Genova was never part of the AFL. She was used as a conduit. She got anonymous warnings, which she passed on to government agencies. She saved lives."

Peterson, the FBI counterterrorism expert, rolled his eyes. "You believe *her?*"

"Give me evidence to show me differently," Service snapped, tapping the table for emphasis. "It's innocent until proven guilty, or is that rule down the toilet?"

Peterson reddened, but made no comeback. Nevelev audibly sucked in a breath.

"What the hell is going on at Vermillion?" Service asked. "What's the status of autopsies, where is the crime scene report? Do we have a cause of death? Where are the wolves now? And again, why was one of my colleagues told that Vermillion is outside our jurisdiction?"

Nevelev looked at Barry Davey, who said calmly, "The animals have been relocated to a secure location."

"Where?"

"To a safe place," Davey said evasively.

"What about the fifth animal?"

"It will be recovered," Davey said.

"How, by whom?"

"We have resources," the USF&WS man said.

For the next hour Service and the sheriff pressed the others for information, getting nothing but evasive and general responses. It took a great deal of willpower not to storm out of the room.

Freddy Bear Lee intercepted Service in the parking lot after the meeting. "This is bullshit, but we've put those assholes on notice," the sheriff said.

"I should have found those animals," Service said.

"Never mind the mea culpa. How much do you know about what they were doing at Vermillion?"

"Not much. I went there once to meet the director."

"Did you see the animals?"

"No." It had struck him as odd then, but the director had explained they were shy and couldn't be approached by strangers because it upset them.

"What did they tell you they were doing?"

"Wolf research." He clearly remembered that the director had not been specific and that he had not pressed him because the meeting was strictly a fill-the-square visit at the behest of his captain.

"Did you see all the facilities?"

"I saw the main office and laboratory."

"I mean *all* the facilities."

There were more? "I don't know."

"Maybe it's something different than they say it is, eh?"

Service looked at his friend and thought about it 'What do you know, Fred?"

"I know when they built that sonuvabitch that it was classified Usually the feds have to file a plan so the state and county can look at the general design. Even the feds have to abide by local building codes and ordinances, eh? All we got was a plan that showed the outline of the area—no buildings, no nothing. The county raised hell, but the feds talked to the state, who said that's just how she is—national security. Now what in the hell do wolves have to do with national security? Makes ya wonder, eh?"

This just added to his questions. "What about the autopsies?"

"The feds brought in their own people and closed the proceedings and the records."

"They can't do that," Service said.

"We've got a federal judge and prosecutor on our so-called team. I think they can bloody well do what they want. You know the old saw, it's easier to ask for forgiveness than permission." The sheriff paused. "Look, Grady, one of my people heard from somebody who heard the crime scene team picked up footprints in the dust near the bodies and the footprints don't fit either of the vicks or the techies."

"Somebody went inside *after* the explosion?"

"That's the way the feds see it."

The conversation with Freddy Bear Lee haunted Service during the short drive to Bay Mills.

DaWayne Kota was not in his office. Service was directed again to his house, and when he arrived the tribal CO was outside, standing on his driveway.

"Been looking for you, DaWayne."

"I heard," the tribal CO said.

"What were you doing at Vermillion that night?"

"I already said."

"You didn't say shit. *Nind apenindimin*, we will trust each other. We have to."

Kota chewed his bottom lip for a moment and nodded. "*Geget*, truly. You want to drive?"

They drove to Vermillion but were stopped a half mile short of the security gate by men wearing FBI windbreakers. Both men presented their badges but were told it was a federal security area; they were not authorized to enter.

"They've sealed 'er off," DaWayne Kota said as they drove back down Vermillion Road. "Stop here."

Service stopped and Kota pulled out a piece of paper. The crude drawing showed the oval wolf compound, the lab building, the small security gate, and two other small buildings, both of them located near the area designated as protected for piping plovers.

Kota took a pencil and made some marks inside the oval. "I don't know this for sure, but when I was in the army I worked with dogs and it looks to me like that compound is equipped for that kind of training."

Service let the man's words sink in. "They told me it was there to let the wolves get adjusted before they're released." Although Yogi Zambonet insisted the state would never allow such a release.

"Could be," Kota said, his tone implying he didn't believe it.

"Goddammit, DaWayne. What the hell were you doing out there?"

"Kids," Kota said, shaking his head. 'I heard some of our kids from Bay Mills were planning some pranks, going to shake up white hunters coming north."

"A *bomb?* That's your idea of a prank?"

"No kids did that, especially *these* kids. They can't put air in the tires of their bikes and pickups, but I heard there was a problem out here and I thought I'd better have a look just in case. You never know, right?"

Service didn't respond. A cop's gut was his compass.

Kota said, "After we met that night I looked through the compound. It looked to me like they were training animals in there. I don't know for what. I also looked in the lab. Those people were shot. Service. There was a bomb, but they were also shot."

The detective stared at his colleague. Something Freddy Bear Lee had told him suddenly registered.

"How'd you get in?"

"I walked in while the rest of you were jabbering, and before the crime scene people got set up. They were around, not paying attention. They're used to dealing with the dead, not the rest of us. It was easy."

"You left footprints," Service said.

Kota shrugged.

"There were two security camera mounts inside the lab," Service said.

"Yah, one camera was blown all to hell "

"And the second one?"

"I wanted to have a look, make sure it wasn't them kids."

"You took it?"

Kota nodded.

"What did it show?"

"Not kids," Kota said, evading the question.

"Where's the camera now?"

"I have the tape."

"Jesus, DaWayne."

"Things happened so fast. I have it and I don't know what to do with it."

"You could've dumped it."

Kota shook his head. "Couldn't do that. It shows something."

Service let him simmer. "You could give it to the FBI."

"Don't trust feds, and then I'd have to explain why I was out there. I could give it to you."

Service felt a chill. "We're withholding evidence."

"Givin' it to you makes it your call what you do with it," Kota said.

"Where is it?"

"Safe," Kota said.

"Keep it that way."

"You don't want it?" Kota asked, showing a rare flash of emotion.

"Not yet. Tell me about the kids you were concerned about."

"They didn't do anything."

"What caught your attention?"

"They were making noise about Indian land and all that treaty stuff."

"And?"

"I heard they were gonna paint some stuff, let hunters know this is their land."

It didn't seem likely that kids defending their traditional hunting grounds and rights would be painting anti-meat slogans.

"Talk to them, DaWayne. Be damn certain."

"I have talked to them. That mean you'll take the tape?"

"Yes, but not yet." He needed to talk to McKower, find out exactly what legal swamp he was wading into.

He wasn't sure why he was avoiding the tape, except that the intuition thing was working again, and it was telling him there was more to this than homicides; if he accepted the tape, he might be drawn into something too big for him to handle.

Service drove back to Bay Mills, delivered Kota to his house, got on the radio, and arranged to meet Joe Ketchum, who was working with Kathy, checking hunting camps several miles west of Hulbert Lake. He wondered if someday he and Nantz would be working together. It was a nice thought.

The Ketchums met him at a crossroads COs called Dodge City. The couple looked tired.

Service brought cinnamon rolls he grabbed on the fly from a roadside Stop-and-Rob, and fresh coffee, all of which the couple attacked voraciously.

"Must be nice not catching this duty," Kathy said.

Service shrugged and turned to Joe. "Did you get a good look at the grounds at Vermillion—inside the compound?"

"I took my sweet time. I found the three wolves near a shelter inside the fenced area. The shelters were low, two-by-fours covered with a spruce roof."

"They weren't inside the shelter?"

"Nope, right out in the open. Like dogs."

"Spooky?"

"Wary but I wouldn't say spooked. Usually a wolf takes a look and he's outta there. But they seemed comfortable enough long as I didn't try to get too close."

"What else did you see?"

"Funny you should ask. It looked to me like there had been other structures that had been moved. You know, outlines in the mud and drag marks, like from a Bobcat or something. I suppose they have to do maintenance in there, or after the bomb they needed to move something."

"You followed the tracks?"

"I was too busy looking for the animals. The fourth one was maybe a hundred yards outside, lying on a sand berm. Looked like she was waiting for the others to come out."

"Was she spooked?"

Joe Ketchum pursed his lips and thought. "She scooted away when she saw me, but not too far. I got the feeling she didn't want to leave the others. Pack mentality, maybe. When I got the vet we found her pretty much where I first saw her. We baited her in and got a dart in her no problem. I couldn't believe how easy it was. It was like she's used to people."

"Did you notice anything else?"

"When I first went in I didn't advertise myself. There were several trucks in the area, guys loading stuff from that main building. Nobody challenged me."

"Markings on the trucks?"

"None."

"But they didn't run you off until after the wolves were captured."

"Right."

"They've moved the security gate south across the marsh," Service said. "I was out there today and they wouldn't let me in."

"What's going on, Grady?"

"I wish I knew." Service tried to piece it all together, but couldn't. He finished his coffee, got back in his truck, and called Kota.

"That night we met at Vermillion. How did you get in?"

"I came through the swamp east of Marsh Lake. You take the last two-track before Whitefish Point and follow it west along the shore. A few miles in, the road takes a switchback to the south. Snowbugs use the trail in winter, but you can get a truck through if you're careful and have the clearance. I left the truck at the bend and walked in along the creek."

"I never saw your prints."

"Spruced my way in and out."

Meaning he used something to obliterate his tracks. Service had done similar things. "How far from your truck to the lab area?"

"Two miles, all bad ground."

The road was virtually impassable, but the trick in mud was to maintain your momentum. Eventually Service bumped his way to the switchback where Kota said he had left his truck and started walking with his pack and emergency gear, knowing he was not going to be back until after dark.

The ground was muskeg and it took nearly an hour to get to the area, which was illuminated by low-intensity lights. He advanced cautiously and was almost to the main building before realizing that all of the steel fencing was gone. The place was being stripped clean. There were six large trucks and a bulldozer on a flatbed trailer. He didn't want to use a light. Trying to remember the drawing Kota had sketched, he made his way westward toward the abandoned lifesaving station. The frame of an original clapboard building stood near some new buildings being erected by the Piping Plover Pals Conservancy, which now had title to the land. There were trucks in the low marsh between the barrier dunes and the shoreline, roughly where Kota's drawing showed federal facilities. This was a half mile from the wolf facility. As he watched, there was a sharp concussion to his right. A cloud of dust leaped into the air, and bits of stone and sand rained down fifty yards from where he was hidden. An explosive charge had been set off.

He reversed direction and walked back through where the wolf pen had been, past the empty lab building and trucks, and veered westward toward the original security gate, which was unattended. The Feebs had set their security farther south—where he and Keta had encountered them earlier that day. He carefully slid into the abandoned gate building, put the red cover on his light, and looked around. Wires and coaxial cables drooped from the wall, cut clean, some stripped out of metal conduits. At this rate it wouldn't be long before Vermillion no longer existed.

It was after 10 P.M. when he got back to his truck. By habit, he waited nearly fifteen minutes to make sure he was alone.

He called McKower as he entered Paradise.

"McKower," she answered.

"It's Grady, Lis. I need help."

"Are you hurt?" He heard concern in her voice.

"No. I'm headed for Newberry. Meet me at the office?"

"I'll be there in ten minutes."

"It'll take me longer," he said, stepping on the accelerator and not caring that the onboard computer would tell watchers at Station 20 in Lansing that he was speeding without having declared an emergency.

McKower wore faded jeans and a sweatshirt that proclaimed DAMN NEAR RUSSIAN. The department's most frequent critics claimed that the DNR acted like the KGB, and this had become a joke in the law enforcement division. Lis had given all District 4 personnel a shirt when she got promoted. Now similar shirts had popped up in all the twelve districts around the state, and the brass in Lansing was sending out weekly reminders that nonuniformed personnel should adhere to all departmental dress regulations.

She wore no makeup and there were bags under her eyes. She offered coffee, but he refused. He had so much in his system it would take a week to get rid of it.

"What's wrong?" she asked.

"The feds are tearing down Vermillion and it's off limits to us. In a few days it will be back to nature."

McKower studied him. "You witnessed this demolition?"

"I snuck in on foot tonight."

"You trespassed?"

"Goddammit, it's not trespassing. It's my case and I belong there. The feds are really uptight about this thing, Lis. They're not talking, not sharing. They withheld information from the captain. They have a federal judge and federal prosecutor from Marquette on the team," he said. "The night of the bombing I ran into DaWayne Kota at Vermillion. He said he had heard about the problem out there and came out to take a look."

"Not in his purview," she said.

"I know. It struck me as odd and I've spent days trying to find him. I learned after the team meeting this morning that the crime scene team picked up footprints in the dust near the bodies in the lab building. I confronted Kota today and he said he had been inside looking around and that the two vicks had been shot. Today he and I drove out to Vermillion, but the Feebs wouldn't let us in. Kota says the bodies were torn up by the explosion, but he insists they were also shot. There's been no mention of this to the team, and the feds won't talk about autopsies—you know the usual runaround about how it takes time and like that. The footprints weren't disclosed to the team either. The wolves that Joe Ketchum found have been moved by USF&WS, and Barry Davey refuses to say where. This whole thing sucks."

McKower looked at him. "Where are you going with this, Grady?"

He wished he knew. "I was in the lab building the night of the explosion and saw the bodies but the techs were setting up and I didn't want to foul up their work. What I did see were mounts for two security cameras. I didn't see cameras and I asked Kota about them. He said one was destroyed and one wasn't."

"And?" she asked.

"He's got a tape."

The lieutenant's eyebrow lifted. "What does it show?"

"He won't say. He wanted me to take it."

"Did you?"

"I'm not sure what to do. If I take possession, I'm obligated to turn it in and say where it came from, right?"

The lieutenant looked dead serious. "That depends," she said. "If you *found a tape*, that would take care of that. A found tape wouldn't have anything to do with Vermillion until you saw what was on it. And while I agree that we're obligated to turn over evidence, we don't have to do that until we have a look at it, *know* that it's evidence, and maybe make a dupe. I mean, if the tape was *found*, we'd look at it, right? We wouldn't know who it belonged to until we looked at it and we'd want to know, maybe so we could return it to its rightful owner. It's not evidence until we see it. Maybe it's just a cartoon or a skin flick."

Service sat back in his chair and studied his friend. She had always been so straight and by the book it was hard to believe what she was proposing.

"What do we tell the captain?"

"Let's see the tape first. Just make sure the tape is *found*, are we clear on that?"

"Very."

Service called DaWayne Kota from his truck and explained the plan. The tribal CO didn't ask any questions, which confirmed that the tape was something he would be glad to be rid of. The question was, did Service want it?

The plan was simple. Service asked Kota to leave the tape in a paper bag in the middle of the road that crossed Naomikong Creek. It was isolated and not particularly good deer country, which meant the likelihood of bumping into hunters was remote.

Kota was to park beside the creek, face his truck west, lights out, and wait until Service approached. Service would flash his blue light a half mile from the site. As soon as Kota saw the light, he was to pull away with his lights out and not turn them on again until he could no longer see Service's headlights. This way, Service would not have seen who dropped the tape and he could testify to this truthfully.

The pickup went as planned; Service found the bag with the tape in it. He wore latex gloves to pick it up and when he got into the truck, he wiped the plastic cover of the videotape clean. There might be prints other than Kota's on it, but at this point that was unimportant. Whatever the tape showed would dictate what had to be done next.

Less than two hours after he saw her at the office, Service called McKower at home. "I found something."

"You want to meet at the office?"

"Be there as quick as I can," he said.

"You could stay with us tonight."

"No thanks, I just want to see what we have and be done with it."

"Take it easy," she said.

Less than ten minutes north of Newberry, his cell phone sounded. It was Freddy Bear Lee and he sounded excited. "Better hustle your ass down to Trout Lake."

"I'll give you a bounce five minutes out," Service said, hitting his blue light and mashing down the accelerator. He telephoned McKower as he flew past the district office.

"I'm headed for Trout Lake," he said, not bothering to explain before he hung up.

· 18 ·

Five minutes out of Trout Lake, a town born during the logging boom in the 1880s, Service radioed Fred Lee to get directions. When he reached the road that led to Frenchman Lake, he turned onto Woofs-R-Good Trail and, a few hundred yards farther on, saw a knot of emergency lights and police vehicles.

Freddy Bear Lee was waiting and greeted him grimly. "I thought you'd better be here for this."

Service followed his friend down a grassy path to a cedar-log lodge with a gaudy sign in red, white, and green that read RICCI'S UPNORTH RESORT. The place had been rumored for decades to be a summer camp for Mafiosi from Detroit and Cleveland, a place where mobsters brought girlfriends, not families. The building was lit by ground spots.

Signboards were strewn along the path and lawn. EATING MEAT IS IMMORAL. HUNTING IS MURDER, DON'T KILL BAMBI. HUNTERS: BE A DEAR & HELP THE DEER HERD GROW—SHOOT YOURSELF. Service glanced at the signs and shook his head, thinking there was no bigger pain in the ass than an American with a cause. The two men clomped up the steps to a sprawling veranda, where three Chippewa County deputies and a state police trooper were talking quietly.

Sheriff Lee opened the door, and Service walked inside. There were nearly fifty people stuffed into the towering great room. It stank of sweat, blood, and wet clothes. The room was illuminated by a chandelier made of deer antlers. The people ranged in age from twenties to sixties and older, all of them with cuts, visible bruises, and torn clothing. No Chippewa, Service observed as Lee tugged on his arm and led him to a side room with a deputy stationed at the door. The man gave way as the sheriff pushed the door open. Service stepped inside and closed it. There sat Summer Rose Genova, one of her eyes swollen and closing, her hair fouled and tangled, her lower lip split. She had streaks of dry blood on her cheek and chin.

Freddy Bear Lee remained outside

SuRo said wearily, "You missed all the fun, rockhead."

"Are you all right?"

"You ought to see the other guys," she said, wincing when she tried to smile.

"What the hell is going on, SuRo?"

"I want my attorney." She pushed a card across the table and Service picked it up.

"I'll call him for you."

"The law entitles *me* to the call," she said.

"You don't want me to call for you, that's *fine*. You gave me his card." Her actions and comments seemed irrational. "Are you sure you're okay?"

She glowered at him and waved her hand, a signal of dismissal or telling him to make the call. He decided it was the latter.

Service stepped outside the room. Freddy Bear Lee shrugged. "This could've been a lot worse. The rainbow people moved in around midnight to set up for this morning. They were going to demonstrate to disrupt hunters, but some of the lodge's guests found 'em before they could get organized and all hell broke loose. Joey Ricci did a helluva job stopping the mayhem and called us." Joey Ricci was forty-something. He had inherited the lodge from his late father Carlo, who founded the operation in the 1940s. Joey had grown up in the U.P. and from all reports had nothing to do with the mob other than providing them a place to play.

"Genova organized the whole deal," Lee said.

"What charges?"

"Well," the sheriff said, "they aren't carrying firearms or lights so we can't say they were hunting or shining after or before legal hours. And nobody else was hunting at the time so they weren't harassing anyone. Best we can do for now is trespass, disturbing the peace, and maybe some assault and resisting arrest charges, though as I understand it, Ricci's guests were the aggressors. As scraps go, this was pretty much the Peanuts gang versus Delta Force."

"SuRo looks like she got roughed up pretty bad," Service said.

"If so, she brought it on herself. The woman is quick with her dukes, eh? Got a punch like the Old Brown Bomber himself. It took four of my people to subdue her. One other thing," the sheriff said. "Nevelev called me and told me that autopsies show that the victims at Vermillion were shot. They took .380 slugs out of the stiffs. The case is being classified a homicide."

"It was already a homicide," Service said. But bullets might point toward a different motive, he thought, and confirmed what DaWayne Kota had observed.

Service started to move away, but Lee caught him by the arm. "Nevelev says they got a search warrant, entered Genova's compound, and found a nickel-plated .380 Walther PPK. They're doing ballistics as we speak."

Service went to get coffee from an urn. An older man with long gray hair and a scraggly beard glowered at him and said, "Yo, pig."

"Get back in your time machine, Gramps. The sixties ended thirty years ago," Service said, suppressing a grin.

Service used Ricci's phone to call the name on the card. He had met S. Montgomery "Wiggy" Wiggins at SuRo's. He was her attorney.

Wiggins had once been a high-profile plaintiff's attorney out of Aspen. He had retired in his late forties to become a fishing guide on the Au Sable. Since then he had been dabbling in high-profile cases as a defense attorney. He had never lost a case on either side.

"This is Detective Grady Service, DNR."

"SuRo's woods cop," Wiggins said. "How's it going?"

"Not good. SuRo has been arrested in Trout Lake. The county is still trying to sort out charges, but right now it looks like inciting to riot, trespass, disturbing the peace, and resisting arrest. More important, she's also a suspect in a murder case." Service quickly briefed the lawyer on Vermillion, the shootings, and the finding of SuRo's Walther at her compound.

Wiggins grunted. "Is she okay?"

"She's bent but not broken. She'll be arraigned in the Soo."

"When?"

"Maybe today if the county can get its act together. They've got at least fifty people to transport."

"Can I talk to her when she gets to the Soo?"

"Absolutely."

"Miranda yet?"

"In a couple of minutes."

"Okay. Tell her to keep that big yap of hers shut until I get up there. I'll meet her at the jail."

Service took two mugs of coffee into the room with SuRo, set one in front of her, and sat down. "Wiggy will meet you in the Soo. He asked me to tell you to keep your big yap shut until you can meet with him."

Genova sat with her arms crossed. "When do I get advised of my rights?"

"Feeling pretty smug?" Service asked.

"Did it hurt all those big men in uniforms to have to do their duty?"

Service stared at her. "SuRo, the two people who died at Vermillion were shot with a .380. A search warrant was executed on your place this morning and your .380 Walther was found. The lab will do a ballistics comparison. I told Wiggy about this."

"Like that's the only .380 in existence, rockhead?"

"Can the bravado, SuRo. The feds have you in their sights and they aren't going to let up until they take you down. Why are they so set on getting you?"

The veterinarian looked across the table at him. "I want to talk to my attorney," she said.

Service got out a Miranda card and read her her rights. When he was done, he added, "That formality out of the way, you don't have to say anything to me. Wiggy will meet you in the Soo before the arraignment, but maybe you'd do better to talk to me. Once the attorneys wade into this thing, both sides are going to become strict constructionists."

"Do you *honestly* think I would kill someone?" she asked.

Service thought for a minute. *Could* or *would*, one letter difference in words, and miles of difference in meaning and intent. When he had first met her she had seemed on the verge of doing just that—with what he assumed was the same Walther that was now being tested. "In anger, yes. In cold blood, no."

"I didn't kill anyone, Grady."

"Sometimes drawing a line in the sand too early isn't the way to go," he said. "What's your relationship to that zoo parade in the other room?"

"I'm their leader," she said.

He felt his neck heat up. "You said you weren't part of that stuff in England."

"This isn't England and I said I had nothing to do with killing anybody in the U.K. I never denied being an activist."

"You'd better hope the ballistics come back negative."

"You know bloody well the feds can make things come out the way they want," she said angrily. "I have no more to say, rockhead," adding, "Nothing personal, okay?"

Genova was seething and Service couldn't quite read her. Usually her temper was open for all to see and pale before, but this morning it was under the surface and intense. Maybe not enough sleep. He could identify with that.

After getting his thermos from his truck and filling it with coffee, he said good-bye to the sheriff and drove north, headed back to Newberry to meet McKower and look at Kota's tape. It was just after 4 A.M. He decided he'd bunk at the district office and get with Lis in the morning.

His cell phone rang five miles north of Trout Lake.

It was Nantz. "Grady, I am going to see the governor today and I'm going to give that insufferable dickhead a piece of my mind."

"I'm coming to Lansing," he said, the decision made and announced before he could think about it. "Don't do anything until I get there."

"I'm really pissed, Grady. I'm sick of being treated like a fucking pawn by a bunch of suits."

"I know," he said weakly.

"We're gonna do something about this, right?"

"I'll be there, five hours max," he said.

She slammed the phone down.

Service pulled over to the shoulder to think. Carmody was working the case in the west and he had Kota's tape, which he had not had time to look at and didn't want to look at until he and Lis could view it together. He hadn't checked in with the captain since yesterday, or was it the day before? And he was going to miss another meeting in the Soo. Time was losing context. Logic and duty told him to stay in the U.P., but Nantz was hurting and he was going south. There was no real decision to be made: Maridly came first.

He called McKower. "I'm going to Lansing."

"You what?"

"You heard me."

"Is Maridly okay?"

"No," he said, hanging up.

Two hours later he was passing Indian River on I-75 when he got another call on the cell phone. "Detective Service? This is Lorne O'Driscoll. Maridly Nantz has just been admitted to Sparrow Hospital."

"What happened? Is she okay?"

"I'll meet you at the hospital," the chief said, abruptly ending the conversation. The chief had called him about Nantz? This wasn't good. Service flipped on his blue lights and accelerated. The computer in Lansing was tied into the GPS system and would detect that he was exceeding ninety and the chief would know why he was barreling south.

Around Mount Pleasant he got a call from Treebone.

"Grady, Tree. I've got someone you need to meet."

"Tree," Service said, interrupting his friend. "Nantz is in Sparrow Hospital. I'm headed there now."

"What's wrong?"

"I don't know. I'll call you."

19

The parking lots of Lansing's Sparrow Hospital were jammed. Service beached his vehicle at the front entrance and hurried inside. A blue-haired woman sat at the reception desk. "Maridly Nantz," he said.

The woman smiled insipidly. "What a beautiful name. Is that a man or a woman?"

He was tempted to reach over and grab her by the throat. "She was brought here this morning."

"Let me check." The woman awkwardly punched some numbers into the computer console. "The machine's dreadfully slow this morning. Aren't you glad the snow hasn't come yet? I can't wait to get to Palm Springs."

Service wished she were there now. He left her fumbling with the computer and went back to Emergency Services. The seats in the hallway were filled with pale people, some with fresh bandages, some with tissues pressed to their faces.

He grabbed a doctor by the arm. "I'm looking for Maridly Nantz."

"Ask there," the doctor said, pointing at a window.

The young woman inside looked exhausted. "Maridly Nantz," Service said.

The woman's eyes narrowed. "ICU," she said.

Service found his way without asking for directions and found Chief O'Driscoll sitting in a waiting room with his hands folded in his lap.

"Chief?"

O'Driscoll looked up. "Detective, I want you to take a deep breath. Maridly has had a rough time. It appears she was attacked."

Attacked? Service felt his blood boil. "Where is she?"

"They've done some surgery and she's under heavy sedation."

"Goddammit, Chief!"

"We don't know what happened, Grady. She was found in the hallway at her hotel."

"This wouldn't have happened if she was still at the academy," Service said. He was on the verge of exploding, realizing that this had happened *after* he had talked to her. "When was she found?"

"About an hour before I called you. Why were you headed to Lansing?"

"Nantz got it in her mind to go visit the governor."

O'Driscoll looked concerned.

"She called me about 4 A.M. and I decided I'd better get down here. What happened?"

"We don't know yet. There was an anonymous call to nine-one-one. The Lansing police and hotel personnel found her. The police said the door to her room was open."

Service had to fight to keep his temper in check. "How bad is it?"

O'Driscoll shook his head. "We'd better wait for the doctor."

Service sat unmoving for twenty minutes. Above him was a NO SMOKING sign. He ignored it, took out a pack, and tapped out a cigarette. Chief O'Driscoll stared at him, glanced at the sign, and said, "Got an extra one?"

The doctor finally showed a half hour later. He looked to Service like an undernourished high school student—a sophomore, not a senior.

"I'm Doctor Caple." The diminutive man faced Chief O'Driscoll. "Ms. Nantz is stable. Her sixth and seventh ribs are severely fractured in the rectus abdominus area. Her clavicle has been shattered between the trapezius and sternocleidomastoid. She has a spiral fracture of the upper radius."

Neither Service nor O'Driscoll spoke.

"I'm not a forensic specialist," the doctor said. "I'm a surgeon—a mechanic—but it looks to me like Ms. Nantz was struck forcefully on the clavicle, perhaps to deny her use of her arms. Blows were then delivered to her ribs, and her arm was brutally twisted to produce the fracture of the radius."

"Somebody beat the shit out of her," Service said.

"Yes," the doctor replied, "but I don't think he counted on her fighting back. Her knuckles are lacerated and we have recovered flesh samples from under her fingernails. You find who did this and you are likely to find some deep scratches and horrendous bruising. She fought hard, despite the pain that must have radiated from the clavicle. Ms. Nantz must have a very high threshold for pain."

O'Driscoll surreptitiously squeezed Service's arm to calm him.

The doctor said, "I've inserted a pin in her clavicle. It will be there a while, and then we'll take it out. We've also pinned the radius More surgery may be needed. We won't know that for a while."

"Permanent damage?" the chief asked.

"Probably not," the doctor said. "She's fit and seems to be a resilient young woman." The doctor put his hand on Service's shoulder. "There was no sexual assault."

Service wrenched away. "I want to see her."

"She's sleeping," the doctor said.

"I don't give a fuck," Service said with a menacing growl.

The doctor led him into the business end of the ICU cube farm and showed him to the one marked 14–3. Service sucked in a breath when he saw the tubes and monitors attached to her. He sat down beside the high-tech table-bed and held her hand and felt tears welling in his eyes.

The doctor and the chief were talking quietly when he emerged from her room. "I'll take one of your smokes," the doctor said. "To hell with the rules."

Service offered his pack.

"Doctor Caple thinks she'll recover just fine, Grady."

"But I do have a concern," the doctor said. "Her X rays concern me. We'll do some tests, but Ms. Nantz appears to be lacking bone mass, which could presage injuries in the future. What does she do for a living?"

The chief spoke before Service could. "She's a conservation officer."

The doctor nodded. "Physically strenuous and dangerous. I want to do more tests."

"Some people have thin bones," Service said in his girlfriend's defense.

"It's not that simple. Probably we have nothing to worry about, but if she has thinning bone mass, we will want to find out why and take the appropriate steps. You can't be physically confronting people if your bones are going to break easily, right?"

Service tried to wrap his mind around the concept of Nantz and thin bones and couldn't. "How long will she be in the hospital?"

"Three days, four max. We want to guard against clots If all goes well, she'll be released from ICU recovery after twenty-four hours."

At that moment Service saw someone at the end of the hall who made his blood pressure skyrocket. Governor Samuel Adams Bozian was waddling down the hall, an overcoat draped over his shoulders and flapping as he walked, making him look like an obese vampire.

Service clenched his fists, but O'Driscoll's hand held him in place.

"Officer Service," the governor said with his most concerned political stump-face. "I am so sorry about Maridly. I heard about the accident when I reached my office and came right over. How *is* she?" Two of the governor's bodyguards hovered down the hallway. "Chief O'Driscoll," the governor added coolly.

"Governor," the chief said in a low and threatening voice. "This is the *last* place you should be."

"It wasn't an accident," Service said.

Bozian ignored Service and talked to O'Driscoll. "Maridly's father was my friend. I've known her since she was a wee one."

Service was shaking, but his chief held on. The chief said, "Governor, there was no accident. All the evidence points to an assault, and Governor, we are going to use every law enforcement resource in the state to find out who did this and then we are going to put the coward so deep into lockup he'll never crawl out. Him and anybody else involved."

The implied threat in the chief's voice was clear. The governor took a step back.

"Good God, Lorne. I know my people and your people have had some political and philosophical differences, but you can't seriously think I'm responsible for this."

The chief did not back off. "You ordered Nantz out of training, Governor. You stuck her in a bogus task force in an empty office with nothing to do and left her there. You have a personal problem with Detective Service, Sam, but you don't have the balls to go after him head-to-head. You picked on Nantz and now she's in ICU. How would *you* read it?"

"What are you talking about?" Bozian asked, stammering. "Lorne, do you honestly think—"

"I only know what I know," the DNR law enforcement chief said, cutting off the governor. "And right now I don't like what I know."

"I'll get to the bottom of this," Michigan's governor said, jerking a tiny cell phone out of his suit pocket and launching his massive body back down the hallway, the bodyguards falling into step beside him.

Chief O'Driscoll released his grip on Service's arm.

"If that bastard had anything to do with this, he's dead," Service said.

"If that turns out to be the case, we will do our jobs and use the system the way it is designed to be used. There will be no vigilante effort, am I understood?"

Service nodded, but thought, We'll see. He toyed with telling the chief that Bozian may have targeted Nantz because of what she had done last summer to help him, but decided the chief didn't need to look at the situation from a new angle. O'Driscoll was pissed and Bozian deserved to sweat.

"Grady, there's nothing you can do here now."

"I'm going to be here when she wakes up."

"All right, but after that you will let Fae and me worry about Maridly. We have plenty of space. When Maridly is released from the hospital, she'll come home with us. If she finds you hanging around all the time, she may start wondering if the doctors have told her the whole truth. She'll be fine with us. When did you last eat?"

Service shook his head. He couldn't remember.

"I want you to go down to the cafeteria and get some food in you. Then come back and wait for your lady to wake up."

Service ate a toasted bagel with veggie cream cheese in the cafeteria and went out to the parking lot to have a cigarette. He called Treebone, but his office said he was on the way to Lansing. He wasn't surprised. If it were Kalina in the hospital, he'd be there for Tree.

Grady Service went back up to Nantz's room, pulled a chair next to the bed, and sat there. "As soon as you can speak, Nantz, I am asking you to marry me and you'd better say yes."

20

T reebone called on the cell phone while Service was out for a smoke break.

"ETA in ten, where you at? How's Nantz?"

"I'm in the parking lot in front of the entrance. She's still sedated."

Treebone arrived in a black van and when he removed his massive frame from the vehicle, it rocked in relief. A woman got out of the passenger side and followed behind him.

The two men embraced briefly. "What's the story?" Treebone asked.

"Somebody attacked her."

Treebone sucked in a deep breath and chewed his inner cheek. "They get the perp?"

"She was found in the hallway outside her room at the hotel where she's been staying. But she fought back. There was skin under her nails and her knuckles are torn up."

"Hotel where she's staying? She's at the academy, Grady."

"I'll explain later," Service said.

The woman joined them. She was tall, her skin the color of obsidian, henna-colored hair cropped short. "Shamekia Cilyopus-Woofswshecom, meet Grady Service," Treebone said solemnly.

The woman's handshake was firm enough to let him know she was strong, but pliant enough to communicate the greeting.

"You won't believe it man, but Shamekia and I were once an item back in our college days. She went on to law school. Smart lady."

The woman smiled and nudged Treebone with an elbow. "Luticious has an overdeveloped fantasy life and a terrible memory. He and Kalina have been an item since way back. I ought to know. I tried to move in, but Kalina . . . that sister's *baaad* when it comes to her property, know what I'm saying?" she said, her eyes flashing.

Kalina was Treebone's wife of almost twenty-five years. Service had been their best man. "Kalina's prayin' for Nantz," Treebone added. "I want to see her."

Shamekia Cilyopus-Woofswshecom said, "I'm going to get a cup of coffee. I'll be in the cafeteria."

"It's in the basement," Service said.

"Naturally," the woman said as she glided away.

"Who is she?" Service asked as they walked the halls.

"The brightest lawyer I've ever met. She was with the FBI, special agent in the Office of Liaison and International Affairs. She had three years in the London Legat before she got retired."

"*Got?*"

"Yo," his old friend said. "You listen good for a white-boy woods cop. She sued the Bureau for discrimination, so they pulled her bodacious bootie out of Washington and put her in London. S'posed to be a prize assignment. Hoped they'd buy her off, but it didn't work. Shamekia gets outraged, only way to settle it is to make it right, dig? They settled big. She's back in Detroit six months, partner in Fogner, Qualls, Grismer and Pillis. Tight-ass old Wasp firm. They brought her in because the woman is connected, see? You want dope on Brits, she can bring it on most quick. You want to throw shovels of dirt on the Feebs, she'll be even quicker."

Treebone stared at Nantz in the bed and shook his head. "Mother-fuckers," was all he said. On their way to the cafeteria Service explained what had happened, including the whole Task Force 2001 business and Bozian's unexpected appearance at the hospital.

Treebone stopped Service and looked at him. "I know you and the governor got bad blood, but Bozian's no fool, Grady. This can't be the Man's work. Our governor-man wants to be You-Ass-of-A's main man and he ain't dumpin' that for no pissant woods cop."

"I know," Service said. After his initial anger, he had reasoned his way to the same conclusion. Besides, he was pretty sure that Nantz, despite her vehement opposition to the governor's political views, had a soft spot for him.

The two men got coffee and joined the former FBI agent at a table.

"Call me Shamekia," she said with a smile that showed perfect teeth. "No one can pronounce the rest of it. Do you mind if I take notes? I don't trust tape recorders. Too long with the Bureau, I guess. They're only now moving to online reports."

Service nodded and began. "There's a woman named Summer Rose Genova. She's a veterinarian who runs the Vegan Animal Rescue and Reclamation Service in Brevort. That's just west of St. Ignace. She's been there about eight years. You've probably seen media reports about animal activist stunts in the U.P.?"

"I saw," the woman said grimly. "Green fire. Two dead, which is odd in the United States. Animal rights activists rarely kill people here."

Green fire. That term again. "Right, but I have my doubts about animal activists at Vermillion. The rest, I don't know about. They're not my business. The FBI moved in on Vermillion almost before the dust cleared. They took over the wolf research lab where the deaths occurred and started dismantling it. The vicks were shot rather than killed in the explosion. The Feebs moved in with a federal prosecutor and judge and they have a state police lieutenant in their pocket. The federal prosecutor is heading the investigation."

"Not the Bureau?" she asked.

"No. First thing they did was seal off the site and create a team. The resident agent from Marquette isn't even on the team. I'm part of it, only it's not a real team. We're spoon-fed what they want us to have, which so far isn't much," he said, stopping to let her catch up with her notes.

"Right out of the gate they announced that Genova was a prime suspect in the Vermillion incident and they cited her history in England, which was where she was before she returned to the States. They claim she was a member and the spokesperson for an animal rights group that killed people. Early this morning she was arrested at an antihunting demonstration in Trout Lake. She denies the allegations about the U.K., but freely admits to organizing and leading the demonstration. She's proud of it."

Service paused. "This morning I learned that the victims at Vermillion were shot with a .380. The Feebs got a warrant and found the same caliber weapon at Genova's place. They're now doing ballistics. SuRo thinks they're stacking things against her."

"What do you think?"

"The jury's still out," he said. "I want to believe her. What bothers me is how quickly they fixed on her as a suspect. They claim she's been under continuous surveillance since she returned to the States."

"Surveillance for eight years? As in twenty-four seven?" the lawyer asked skeptically.

"That's what they claim."

"What do you want to know?" the former agent asked.

"Everything about SuRo, starting with what actually happened in England. Have the Feebs really had her under surveillance since she returned to the States and if so, why? If she's guilty, fine. If not, I don't want to be pushed where evidence doesn't lead."

"Please excuse this question, but why is a woods cop worried about this?"

"The man has an overdeveloped sense of justice," Treebone chimed in. "Nearly got our asses shot off more than once."

"My concern is the wolves."

"What will you say if the ballistics match?" Shamekia asked.

"That would bother me, but that alone won't mean she was the shooter. She's obnoxious and opinionated, but I just don't buy what the Feebs are trying to sell. It feels to me like they landed with a case already made, and that gives me the willies."

"Where is the BATF in all this?" the former agent asked.

"Basically MIA," he said. "I saw an agent at the crime site the night of the explosions, but there's no BATF rep on the team."

"And the Bureau's resident agent is out of the loop?"

"Way out, but he's running the investigation of the bomb incident at Tech, so maybe I'm reading more into this than I should. When I asked him why he wasn't part of the Vermillion team he said it was 'above his pay grade.'"

"Did he? Above his pay grade," the lawyer said, pushing her chair back. "There are some very nasty people in the animal rights movement," she added. "You should see the psychos in Europe."

"SuRo may be a zealot, but she's not a psycho."

"The Bureau's swooping in like Mighty Mouse to take control and put together an investigative team, that's standard operating procedure. But a federal prosecutor leading the investigative team—that's not standard."

Her voice told Service she had doubts. "And?"

"Let's just say I wouldn't accept what they're dishing out at face value. As you know, Hoover took the Bureau into a lot of places it didn't belong and despite the best efforts by some leaders since, the organization has a way of backsliding to old habits, especially in times of stress," she said. "Tearing down the facility with such haste is unusual—to say the least."

"Can you work through the Bureau?"

The lawyer laughed. "The only way I talk to them is with a judge as referee. No, I know people in the U.K. and they will be considerably more forthcoming than my former colleagues. I would think you're pressed for time."

"Definitely," he said.

"I'm sorry about your friend," she said.

Service nodded.

"Now, I'm going to leave you gentlemen and get on back to Detroit and do what I do best."

Service didn't understand. "I thought you rode with Tree."

"I did so we could talk, but my car and driver were right behind us," she said. "She'll be waiting."

The two men stood as she excused herself and departed.

"Is she for real?" Service said.

"Ain't no act, brother," Treebone replied. "When that woman mosey down the Cass, pit bulls be looking to hide in their masters' assholes."

Nantz awoke twenty hours after surgery. Service saw her eyes flicker as fear and confusion flooded into them. He immediately punched the call button for a nurse and one came barreling in, followed soon thereafter by Dr. Caple. Service stepped outside while they examined Maricly. He found Treebone in a subdued conference with a short, muscular man in a double-breasted black blazer over a purple shirt and gray sharkskin slacks.

Treebone turned to his friend. "S'up?"

"She's awake."

"I like it when God pays attention to Kalina's prayers," Treebone said, turning to the man in the blazer. "Detective Johnelvis McMann, meet Detective Grady Service."

McMann stuck out his hand. "Your lady okay?"

"She's awake."

"I just told Lieutenant Treebone we've got her assailant."

"Where?"

"Right here. He was brought in a couple of hours ago. He's been incapacitated by pain, vomiting, in and out of consciousness, the whole deal. His old lady panicked and called nine-one-one. He's being prepped for surgery."

"Are you sure?"

Detective McMann nodded and motioned for them to follow him.

There was a uniform guarding the door to a private room of the surgical pre-op area. McMann pushed open the door and motioned Service and Treebone inside. The man in the bed had long deep cuts and scratches all over his face. "We'll do a DNA workup," McMann said, "but this looks like our man. He works for the cleaning service that takes care of the office where Ms. Nantz works. He apparently met her there and decided he'd like to see if she was friendly. He told one of his asshole buddies at work about it. Obviously your lady didn't take to his advances. He has a crushed testicle and he is one sick puppy."

Service stared at the man, torn between anger and relief, ashamed of his paranoia. The attack had nothing to do with the governor.

"Get on back up to your woman," Treebone said, pushing him toward the door.

He found her alone, propped up in bed, awake, but not entirely alert, looking small and drained of her spark.

"Grady?" she said with a raspy voice. "I hurt, honey."

He sat down on the bed and held her hand tenderly. "You're going to be okay."

Her eyes welled with tears, but she fought them back. "I really hurt," she said.

"It's going to be all right," he repeated, patting her hand.

"Why?" she asked. It was not a question he could answer.

Minutes later Service heard shouting in the hallway and left her to ask for quiet. Treebone was being angrily dressed down by the Lansing detective, who was a head shorter than his friend, but pressed against his chest like an attack dog.

"It was *you*, goddammit!" McMann said angrily.

Tree held up his huge hands and shook his head. "I don't know nothin', man."

"Sonuvabitch," McMann said.

"Keep it down," Service said.

"Your pal here assaulted the assailant."

"Motherfucker's gone woo tang," Treebone said, holding up his hands again.

Service waited for an explanation.

McMann supplied it. "We left right after you, but your pal said he forgot something in the room. I let him go back in alone. Then, when we get back here, my uniform calls and says the nurses found the perp writhing in pain and they rushed him into surgery. His other nut's crushed. Jesus."

Service looked at Treebone, who tried to look innocent, but he knew his friend and he had no doubt that McMann was right. Tree liked to make out that Service was the one who believed in justice, but Treebone was the devout hard-liner when it came to paybacks.

The Lansing detective started to shake his finger at Treebone, stopped, shook his head in disgust, and stalked away.

"Tree?"

"Fuckwad don't deserve even one nut, man. I'd a lopped off his johnson and stuck it in his mouth if there'd been time."

Service saw a vicious grin begin to form on his friend's face. "We're supposed to enforce the law, Tree."

"I did, man. Eye for an eye, an' like that. Don't go preachin' righteous on me, Grady. It don't mean nothin'."

Service shook his head, walked back into Nantz's room, sat on the edge of the bed, and rested his hand on the pillow beside her battered and swollen face.

"Grady," she said in a whisper.

"What, hon?" he asked.

"I heard what you said."

"What I said?"

"You know," she said, tugging feebly at his fingers.

He shook his head. What was she talking about?

"I've heard everything," she said. "I just couldn't talk."

He stared at her as a tiny smile formed. Then he understood.

"The answer is yes," she said. "But not today, okay honey? The honeymoon would *really* suck." Her eyes flickered and closed and Service sat staring at her, fighting back the urge to shout. Out of trepidation or happiness, he wasn't quite sure.

Chief O'Driscoll came to the hospital with his wife, Fae, after lunch, his normal cop-in-charge attitude back "I talked to Doctor Caple." he announced to Service. "They're going to do tests tomorrow and release her forty-eight hours after that. The doctor says to anticipate a recovery of sixty to one hundred and twenty days."

She'll lose her place at the academy, Service immediately thought.

Fae O'Driscoll chimed in, "We've made up the spare room for her. Everything will be fine."

Service's genetic default did not lean toward optimism—or toward accepting help, especially from the top woods cop in the state.

Later his cell phone rang. It was Freddy Bear Lee.

"The ballistics match. Geneva's Walther is the murder weapon," the Chippewa County sheriff said. "She's been arrested on an open murder charge and is being housed here. The feds went to transfer and arraign her in federal court in Grand Rapids. Homicide on federal property is a capital offense. I think the feds are going to push for the death penalty. Her lawyer will plead her not guilty. He's fighting the move to GR. He can probably delay it for a few days, but when the feds want something, they usually get it. Nevelev is pushing to deny bail. The feds want to take custody."

Service rubbed his eyes. Death penalty? Freddy Bear didn't understand Wiggy's tenacity or skill. If Wiggins was fighting the move to GR, she probably wouldn't be going. How could he have been wrong about SuRo? Death penalty? Why were the feds so obsessed with her?

"Word's out on your girlfriend," Lee added. "Is she okay?"

"She will be," Service said, hoping the doctor was right, but knowing that saying something over and over had no influence on fate.

"I'm heading back soon," Service said.

"When?"

"Soon," Service said. "You can have my vote on the team."

"Yah," his friend said. "Thanks heaps, chum."

· 21 ·

Service remained in Lansing until Nantz was released on Tuesday. He had gotten a couple of pages from Carmody but had no timely way to get back to him, and the pages had gone unanswered. He thought about looking at Kota's tape, but left it alone. Better to be ignorant than to discover something he would have to deal with. Right now his sole focus was Maridly's welfare.

Chief O'Driscoll came to the hospital every day to eat lunch with him in the cafeteria and check on Nantz. On Monday the chief said, "Nantz's assignment to Task Force 2001 is over. She can return to the academy as soon as she gets the medical green light." The chief looked across the table at him. "Given the medical prognosis I think we should slide her to the next class."

"That's not until next fall," Service said.

"She needs time to heal, Detective. There are pins in her collarbone and arm, and concerns about bone density."

The chief's logic was unassailable, but Service did not want to make Maridly's decisions for her. "Nantz will decide," he said.

"Counsel her," the chief said. "She's going to be a good one and we want her to have the full academy experience."

Who was "we"? Service wondered. "I'll talk to her," he said.

The chief nodded and left to return to his office in the Mason Building.

Throughout Nantz's stay in the hospital, Service slept in a chair beside her bed, ate his meals in the room on trays from the cafeteria, and left her side only to smoke.

Monday morning he had called Captain Grant.

"I'm missing meetings and my contacts with my undercover," he confessed.

"Your priorities are in order," the captain said.

He'd also called McKower, who'd said much the same thing. "You, running to your lady's side. God, if this may not be the real thing, Service."

"Shut up, Lis."

That afternoon Sheriff Lee called to let him know that Genova had tried to incite a riot at the jail. "Are you sure she's sane?" Freddy Bear asked.

"What's her beef?"

Freddy Bear laughed. "Exactly. No vegetarian meals. She's threatening a hunger strike."

"Believe her," Service said. "Can you arrange something?"

"It's already taken care of, pal, but she's still pissed."

On Tuesday morning he walked beside an orderly who took Nantz to the lobby in a wheelchair and helped her into his truck. They followed Chief O'Driscoll to his house on Northlawn in East Lansing. Fae O'Driscoll greeted them at the door and quickly pointed out that a late neighbor had been one of the scriptwriters of *Top Gun* and that Duffy Daugherty, the legendary MSU coach, had also lived nearby. "Biggie Munn, too," she added. "This used to be the center of the university community, but now all the coaches are building palaces elsewhere." Fae seemed less than pleased about the geocultural shift.

O'Driscoll's house looked small from the outside but turned out to be spacious. Service supported Nantz as she walked through the back door and helped her onto a blue couch. There were potted plants everywhere. The spare room was built off the back of the ground floor. It had lavender walls and purple accents.

"Chicken soup for lunch?" Fae asked, leaving without waiting for an answer.

After lunch, Service helped Maridly to her bed and hovered. Finally she said, "Grady, I'm going to be fine. You have to get back to work, darlin'."

He didn't want to go. "You'll call me when the test results come back?"

She smiled.

He turned to leave, but couldn't.

"It's good this happened," she said.

"This is good?"

"I have a confession to make, Grady. When I went to the academy, I didn't know if I could hurt another person. I mean I had real doubts about being able to use a gun. But if I'd had one at the hotel, I would have shot that bastard without hesitation," she said. "Now I know I can handle the job."

"I never had any doubts," he said. She would learn that in reality the use of a weapon was never an easy decision.

"You would have if you'd been inside my brain. Now go on, honey."

He bent down and kissed her gently on the lips. As he stood in the doorway to the bedroom, Nantz smiled and whispered, "When I get better, I want you inside more than my brain." She winked and raised an eyebrow.

He dragged his feet leaving. The chief told him repeatedly not to worry and eventually he surrendered, got into his truck, called central dispatch to let them know he was back on the air, and headed north on US 127.

Driving north he wondered what Carmody was doing. He called McKower to update her on Nantz's status and called Treebone and thanked him for being with him. He tried to reach Shamekia Cilyopus-Woofswshecom, but was told she was not available. He left a message for a call-back in her voice mail and continued north.

By the time he got to Mount Pleasant, an hour north of Lansing, he was obsessing and fretting about Nantz and called O'Driscoll's house. Fae told him Maridly was asleep and he decided it wouldn't be right to wake her. Get it together, he chided himself.

He switched to an AM radio station out of Grayling and shook his head at what he heard. A reporter was talking about "incontrovertible evidence" from some foundation that there were mountain lions on both peninsulas of the state. An unidentified DNR spokesman was said to have responded by saying that the department believed that there were undoubtedly cougars and that they were being seen, but that all of them were former illegal pets either escaped from or turned loose by their owners. The spokesman insisted that there was no incontrovertible evidence of breeding pairs. If and when evidence showed breeding pairs, he said, the DNR would put together a plan to manage and protect the animals.

A plan that would require COs to do all the dirty work of enforcement, Service reflected. The state didn't need another rare and endangered animal to worry about. Wolves were enough.

At some point, he reminded himself, he needed to look at the security tape from Vermillion and find out where Carmody was, but first he wanted to stop at the Chippewa County Jail to talk to SuRo Genova.

Mountain lions? "Gimme a break," he said out loud.

Genova's scrapes had scabbed over and her bruises were fading to purple and green with yellow auras, but her eyes looked as clear and uncompromising as ever. There was a scowl on her face.

She was escorted into an interrogation room and sat down without acknowledging him.

"I don't like being played with," Service said.

Genova stared daggers at him.

"Your Walther is the murder weapon. What the hell is going on?"

"I didn't shoot anybody," she said.

"Your gun did."

"To quote the NRA: Guns don't kill. People do. I repeat: I . . . did . . . not . . . kill . . . anybody. Was that slow enough for you to follow?"

"I hope Wiggins is up to this."

"Don't you worry about Wiggy," she said coolly.

"Federal charges, SuRo. Homicide on federal property is a capital crime."

Genova crossed her arms and sat defiantly.

One of the jailers stepped into the room behind Service. "You've got a call."

Service left Genova in the interrogation room and went out to an office where a phone was lying on a soiled blotter filled with doodles of breasts and curvaceous women with featureless faces.

"Service," he said, picking up the receiver.

"This is Shamekia. I'm sorry this has taken so long."

"I've got Genova in the interrogation room right now."

"I'm not sure where to begin," the former FBI agent said.

"Start with what makes sense to you."

"Mrs. Genova was apparently a very controversial figure. Her maiden name was Billows. My contacts across the pond say that for quite some time they were pretty sure she was part of the Animal Freedom League. She claimed to have no connection to them other than to share their views on vivisection and meat eating."

"How long is 'quite some time'?"

"Years. Eventually they arrested a senior official in the AFL and he traded testimony for leniency. He swore the group used Genova simply to point them away from others. Genova was so eloquent and outspoken that the authorities were misled for a long time."

"But she wasn't part of the group?"

"Only as a sympathizer and unwitting victim in her own right. She was involved in various demonstrations, but not as a member of the AFL or another violent group."

"She claims she prevented people from being killed."

"She's telling the truth. She was religious about calling the authorities whenever she got a communiqué from the AFL. When the Brits determined she wasn't an insider, they tried to convince her to help them, allowing phone taps and putting a tracer into her computer, but she refused."

"Was she forced out of the country?"

"Not in the way you mean. I think she got fed up with badgering from the government. She married an American physician and a year later they relocated to the United States."

"If the Brits are certain she wasn't part of the AFL, why is the FBI so convinced that she is?"

"That's not at all clear to me," the former agent said. "Apparently Genova had a longtime boyfriend who was part of the AFL. Maybe she knew, maybe not. The Brits don't think so. But the boyfriend was a very, very bad boy. The Brits say he was also a longtime member of CARP— that's Catholics Against Religious Persecution, a small group of extremists loosely affiliated with the IRA. The Brits call it a contract unit for wet work."

"Assassinations?"

"Right. The boyfriend was one of their deadliest operators, but the RUC learned his identity and he had to split. He ended up in England and got involved with the AFL."

"From Irish rights to animal rights?"

"His only interest was killing Englishmen or those who sided with them. It took them a while, but the Brits connected him to several operations that targeted English companies with subsidiaries in Northern Ireland. There was no hard evidence of a strategy or an end game, but there was a clear trend and it made sense that this guy was involved."

"So he kept fighting the war under the banner of animal rights. What happened to him?"

"He faded away. Rumors have put him in Libya or Angola, but no-body knows. Interpol has issued bulletins on him, but he's basically been off the radar for eight years," she said. "I suggested to my contacts that he must've had some sort of official government assistance in order to drop out of sight the way he did. My contacts concede that this theory has some merit, but they also say that they have thoroughly infiltrated virtu-ally all the major warring factions in Northern Ireland and little happens up there that they don't get a whiff of sooner or later."

"Do they have a name or a photo?"

"No photo, but his name is Mouse Minnis."

"Mouse?"

"Right, and that's not a nickname. There's no photograph, not even a sketch. The man has little background and no face."

Service took out his notebook and had her spell the name as he wrote it down. "Minnis was Genova's boyfriend?"

"According to my sources."

"Before she married?"

"And afterward," Shamekia said. "She married Howard Genova and continued to see Minnis until she left the next year."

Interesting, Service thought, immediately wondering if the attrac-tion was such that he might have followed her to the United States. Which was not uncharacteristic of how his mind worked.

"How do these people know about the boyfriend?"

"A woman named Bridget Galway came over from one of the Catholic groups—not CARP. She claimed that the group had put a price on her head and she wanted out before they killed her."

"The Brits accommodated her?"

"They debriefed her and gave her a new identity. She told them about Minnis."

"But not his identity?"

"Only his name and that he had used the AFL as a cover while re-maining active in CARP, taking special assignments outside Northern Ireland. This led them to see that he had been hitting people with links to the North. Do you want me to go further with this?"

"Where else is there to go?"

"You pointed out that the Bureau seemed dead set on getting to Genova, and that makes me wonder why. They rarely do anything with-out a reason."

"Genova's pistol was the one used in the killings here."

"That doesn't mean she used it," the former agent said.

"I know." This was exactly what SuRo had said.

"Let me get back to you," Shamekia Cilyopus-Woofswshecom said. "Not everybody in the Bureau is an asshole."

When Service rejoined Genova he tossed a pack of cigarettes on the table. She pounced on it. "SuRo, let's assume for a minute that I buy what you're telling me."

"It's your money," she said. "Spend it how you like."

"I'm trying to help."

She sneered. "Didn't sound that way a while ago."

"I was pissed."

"Okay," Genova said. "I'll play along."

"We're not playing, SuRo."

"Life is a game, rockhead."

"I checked your version of events in England."

"And?"

"British sources side with you."

"You talked to them?"

He ignored her question. "I'd like to know about your boyfriend."

Summer Rose Genova nearly dropped her cigarette and looked on the verge of panic, but quickly regained control. Service read the reaction clearly.

"I knew a lot of men in England. Biblically, if that's your meaning."

"This one was with the AFL and before that an outfit called CARP. His name was Mouse Minnis. He's no longer in England. A woman came over to the Brits and fingered him. Minnis disappeared. You were seeing him after you were married to Howard. Did you ever see him again?"

Genova sat very still and mashed out her cigarette. "Wiggy doesn't want me talking to cops," she said, abruptly standing up.

"I can't help you if you don't help me," Service said.

"Help yourself, rockhead. That should be a big enough challenge for you."

"Who else had access to your weapon?" he asked.

"Nobody. I keep it locked up," she said over her shoulder, heading for the door.

Service lit another cigarette after she was gone. Sometimes when you were talking to suspects your mind arced across a gap. There was no logic, just a sudden spark of intuition or something that left you looking at everything from a new perspective. He was certain SuRo had seen Minnis since leaving the U.K. The question was when and where and who he was now. And did it matter?

After a moment, he decided there was no point in letting his imagination run wild.

As he walked out to his truck, Freddy Bear Lee joined him. "She say anything?"

"She insists she didn't do it."

"They all say that," the sheriff said.

"Sometimes they're telling the truth."

"How's Maridly?"

Service looked over at the sheriff. He had never met Nantz. How did he know her name? "Hurting, but she'll heal." Soon, he hoped. She would not like losing most of the year waiting for the next academy class.

"There's a team meeting tomorrow," Lee said. "Why don't you bunk at my place tonight?"

Freddy Bear lived with his eldest daughter, Velma, who taught French at Soo High. She was short and plump and seemed destined for spinsterhood. Grady was too tired to argue and he didn't want to impose on the Ozmans again.

Velma was out with friends. The two men whipped up a dinner of eggs scrambled with Italian peppers and onions from a jar. They ate a half pound of bacon with the eggs and half a loaf of rye bread toasted dark.

Dishes stacked in the dishwasher, they went into the sheriff's study. Freddy Bear opened a bottle of cheap Spanish cream sherry and offered a Dominican cigar to Grady, who declined. Freddy Bear lit one for himself.

"The Genova woman isn't stupid," Lee said. "If she used her Walther to pop those folks, I'd think she'd be smart enough to get rid of it."

Service nodded agreement and let the sherry curl warmly down his throat. "But if somebody else used it . . ." he said, not finishing the sentence.

"Then that somebody put it back where it could be found to set her up," Lee said, finishing the thought. "You believe her?"

"I want to," Service said. "When did the ballistics come back?"

"I called you as soon as I heard. Nevelev announced results at the team meeting and passed around the test photos. No question it was the weapon."

"Fingerprints?"

"Just Genova's," the sheriff said after a pause.

"But?"

Lee puckered like he was thinking. "Well, there were no prints on the grip or the trigger or its guard. Just on the barrel and clip."

"So she tried to wipe it down."

"Why wipe it down? Wouldn't dumping it be better? Besides, she's a veterinarian, and if she wanted to wipe it clean, she'd do that."

Grady Service took a sip of his sherry and nodded. "Maybe she was shook up."

"Does she strike you as the sort to get flummoxed?"

Service shook his head. For a hothead, SuRo was as cool as you were likely to encounter.

"So how come you wipe down half a gun?"

Either to set up someone or to make it look like you were framed, Service thought. Was SuRo this devious? She had been an activist in the U.K. and was still one.

"Do you know her husband?" Freddy Bear asked.

"I met him once."

"What sort of a fella is he?"

"Surgeon. Sort of quiet, dignified."

"The kind to have a jealous streak?"

"I don't know. Why?"

"If Genova didn't pull the trigger, who did? I'm looking for motives. She's married and lives alone. Is she the kind to step out on him?"

Service didn't tell his friend about SuRo's carnal escapades in England, or his suspicions about the United States. "Maybe."

"Huh," the sheriff said.

"Freddy, where the hell are you going with this?"

"I don't exactly know. I overheard one of the Feebs say something to Nevelev about Genova having a gentleman visitor."

"At her compound?"

"Location wasn't specified. All that was said was that she had a pretty high libido for her age."

Service felt weary. "The Feebs would know if they have her under continuous surveillance."

Service felt the sherry blooming in his stomach. Continuous surveillance, he thought, and sat bolt upright in his chair.

"Has Nevelev mentioned surveillance or security tapes?" he asked, suddenly remembering that he had one from Vermillion that he had not yet looked at.

"No mention of tapes, but the word is they were on her around the clock so wherever she goes, they must go."

Service looked at his friend. "If she drove up to Vermillion and shot those people, her tail would be a witness, or at least knew she was there, right?"

"I suppose."

Grady Service went out to his truck and retrieved the tape from the paper bag Kota had left it in. When he came back into Freddy Bear's office, he said, "You got a VCR?"

Lee looked at the tape and said, "It ain't a DVD. You want me to fire it up?"

Service shoved the tape into the VCR, queued it up, and turned around to look at the sheriff. "I'm not sure you want to see this, Freddy."

The sheriff looked puzzled.

"I found this tape on a road out by Naomikong Creek. I don't know who it belongs to. I meant to look at it earlier to see if I could identify the owner, but I sorta got caught up in other things."

Sheriff Lee smiled impishly. "Let me get this straight. You found a tape in the middle of bloody nowhere and at this very moment you think we ought to look at it?"

"You don't have to see this, Fred. Consider this a legal advisory."

Freddy Bear Lee took another cigar out of its wrapper, rolled the cigar across his lips, snipped off the end, and lit it. "In for a dime, in for a dollar, eh," the sheriff said. "Roll that sucker."

Service inserted the tape in the VCR and hit PLAY. The tape had been rewound. Did that mean Kota had looked at the whole thing? The picture wasn't all that clear, but there was a clock on the bottom of the screen, ticking off real time. The real-time clock showed 1801. How long were the tapes, four hours, six, eight? He hit STOP and FAST FORWARD, and let it run to the end. The time showed 2400, a six-hour tape.

Why hadn't Nevelev said anything about security tapes? Service wondered.

He had gotten the call from Captain Grant just after midnight, Service remembered, reaching to rewind the tape to its start. "Did they fix a time of death?" he asked his friend.

"Three-hour block before midnight. That's prelim, but they don't think it will change much."

Service selected SLOW FORWARD and watched the tape roll until it hit 2130.

A man and a woman were working in the lab. They came and went through the same door, a door that seemed to open into the wolf pen. Once the woman came leaping through the door, looking shook and gesturing wildly. The man tried to calm her and then they were both laughing hysterically. The woman was Larola Brule.

It finally hit Service that he didn't know anything about the other victim.

"What do we know about the biologist who died with Brule?" he asked his colleague.

"Lanceford Singleton."

"Is that him?"

"I never met the man, but he looks like the ID photo I saw."

Service kept moving the tape forward. Suddenly the angle of the tape changed. It had been above, looking down and now it was lower, perhaps head-high.

"The camera's been moved," Service said, keeping his finger on FORWARD.

As it flashed through a scene, Freddy Bear said, "Ooh boy." Service stopped the tape and hit PLAY.

The man and woman were undressed. She was sitting on a lab counter, her legs wrapped around him. The two men watched in silence as the couple moved around the lab engaging in various sexual acts. They seemed to take pains to stay in sight and range of the camera. A little show for the camera? If so, for whom?

Nearly thirty minutes after the sex session began the camera picked up a silhouette coming through a door behind him.

The figure had a pistol in both hands, held out in front. The face seemed bare, but too far back in shadows to make out details. The figure fired without saying anything, and the camera caught the violent and spasmodic reactions of the two people as they were struck and flew out of view. Service saw two fast muzzle flashes and wisps of smoke.

The figure then whirled and stalked through the door.

Nothing moved in the laboratory.

"Bloody hell," Lee said through clenched teeth.

Service backed up the tape and replayed the shootings. The woman had been shot first, then the man. He made a mental note.

"Brutal," Freddy Bear Lee said. "Just walked in and whacked them, eh? No hesitation. Ya don't see that shit every day."

Service had made the same observation. Cool, efficient, ruthless. All these said *professional* and *experienced*. He kept these conclusions to himself. A professional hit, and the woman got it first. What did these facts add up to?

"What do we know about the vicks?"

Lee blew a smoke ring. "A helluva lot more than we knew before, eh? I heard rumors that Singleton was a cocksman, which last I knew wasn't against the law. I guess we can put that in the known column now. He was boffing Brule's wife."

"Jealousy?" Service asked.

"Wouldn't be the first time we seen that."

"Have you talked to Brule?"

Lee shook his head. "Still in quote, 'seclusion,' unquote."

Did Brule know about his wife and Singleton? Had Singleton been involved with other women? Service lit a cigarette and sat down. "I hate this shit. Homicide's your line, Freddy, not mine."

"You did just fine last summer and we both wear badges," the sheriff said. "Your mind's not going anywhere mine's not. Let's just keep noodling this, eh?"

"The video resolution's bad," Service told his friend. "Too dark, too much shadow, can't see the shooter's face."

"We got a guy up to Lake State does techie stuff for the county. He might could give us a better picture, maybe blow up the frames," the sheriff said.

Service turned to his friend. "Should we turn this over to the Feebs?"

"Are you loco?" Lee replied. "We'd never see it again."

"It's evidence, Freddy."

"Listen, Grady, these shits are withholding from us. Ask me, I say we follow our own leads and use our own resources, see what we come up with. Then we share. We show them ours, they show us theirs, and like that."

"You mean a trade."

"Whatever," Lee said, exhaling a ragged smoke ring.

"We're crossing a line," Service said.

"I've crossed 'er so many times before I've worn a path," the sheriff said. "You have, too."

"Facts," Service said. "The shooter didn't hesitate. Demeanor suggests a professional hit. He killed the woman first. She was the main target."

"I agree."

"I'd like to see the tape enhanced," Service said, "but if the techie screws up, we've lost evidence. We don't need that on our heads."

"How about I make a copy and let him work from that."

"Will that work?"

Lee got on the phone. "Hey, Shamper, Sheriff Lee. We've got a tape we'd like to get juiced up, stills enlarged, clean up the video, all that good stuff. But you're gonna have to work off a copy, not the original. Can do?"

The sheriff hung up the phone. "Well, he whined and said the original would be better, but he thinks he can do something with the copy and maybe that will convince us to give him the original."

"Can he keep his mouth shut?"

"Well, the man's a born gossip and a bituva flake, but I'll pull him aside and get the ground rules clear. He won't be a problem."

The sheriff then got out a blank tape and copied the surveillance tape. He put the original in a safe under a carpet in his floor. "She'll be fine right there."

"We need to talk to Brule," Service said, "and we need to know if the feds know about his wife and Singleton."

He also needed to know what SuRo's tail had seen if he had followed her when she left her compound. If she was the shooter, the feds would know she had gone to Vermillion and the tape, once enhanced, might prove it. Why were the feds dancing on this one? He wished he could get back to his real job.

Service slept fitfully on a couch, alternating between weird dreams about Maridly and the blue wolf.

· 23 ·

Service was still asking himself what they were doing parked in front of a house on Vairo Street in St. Ignace at five in the morning. Freddy Bear had awakened him and nearly dragged him out to his Jeep. They were halfway to Iggy before his mind cleared enough to ask what his friend was up to.

"Just follow my lead," the sheriff said cryptically.

At 5:15 A.M. a light came on in front of a white bungalow. Lieutenant Eugene Ivanhoe came out to the porch in workout clothes and started doing stretches.

"Dumb fucker believes his body is a temple," Lee said. "If so, his only worshipers are half-wits," he added, quietly opening his door.

Ivanhoe came down the steps to find a flashlight in his face.

"You fucking moron," Lee said with a growl. "You're a peace officer about to go running in the dark and you aren't even carrying a piece. Geez oh Pete, how'd you get promoted, Eugene?"

Ivanhoe held his hand up to block the light and Lee turned it off. "Sheriff Lee?"

"You betcha."

Ivanhoe looked perplexed, lost somewhere between confusion and anger.

"We've got a team meeting this morning," the state police lieutenant said.

"We'll get to that later," the sheriff said. "Some of us are getting tired of being treated like mushrooms—kept in the dark and covered with shit. You forgettin' who you are, son?"

Ivanhoe mumbled something, but the sheriff lit into him before he could respond coherently. "I knew your folks, son, and I know you just got posted back up here, but you're a Yooper so start actin' like one of us or we're gonna make your life so hard that freeway patrol in Benton Harlem will be a step up."

No county sheriff had official hold over the state police, Service knew, but a smart sheriff with an agenda had innumerable ways of making a Troop's life miserable.

"I don't understand."

"That's pretty fucking clear, ya bloody nitwit. You ever go to the circus?"

Ivanhoe said, "Sure, when I was a kid."

"You remember how the elephants paraded through town and after they passed, along come a bunch of rowsers pushing brooms and shoveling up pachyderm shit? Those fellows are called gafooneys and that's what the Feebs have made you. The U.P.'s ours and they're piling shit on your shovel."

"I don't think so."

"You don't think, Eugene. Don't you smell anything funny here, son?"

The state police officer didn't answer.

"You feel like the feds are leveling with you?"

"Of course," Ivanhoe said with a defensive shrug.

"Okay, let's test that," Freddy Bear said. "Genova was under constant surveillance, is that right?"

"That's what they said."

"So how come they didn't know right away that Genova had done it? I mean, her tail should have been with her if she drove up to Vermillion and popped those people. If so, why didn't the tail stop her right there? Or, if he saw her there, how come we haven't heard that?"

"They're being cautious."

"Hello!" the sheriff roared. "What about security tapes?"

"What about them?"

"They show them to you?"

"No."

"They show you the one that shows the shooter?"

Ivanhoe began to stammer. "I, I . . ."

"Aye aye? Is that a yes?"

"No."

"I didn't think so. Did the feds explain why they're tearin' down the facility at Vermillion?"

"Public safety hazard," Ivanhoe said weakly. "Too expensive to replace."

"In the middle of the boonies with winter about ready to make camp?"

"Snowmobiles can reach it."

"Are you telling us you couldn't secure that place if it were up to you?"

"Of course not, but it's not my decision."

"Exactly. *They're* making all the damn decisions, Eugene."

"National security," Ivanhoe said.

"Whose, theirs?"

"I don't know."

"That's the point, son. You think they've taken you into their confidence, but you don't know a weasel-dick more than we do, and they haven't told us shit. They've treated us all like we ride the short bus."

"It's good procedure to compartmentalize."

"Not if you create an interagency team, for Christ's sake."

"What do you want?" Ivanhoe asked, finally mustering some defense.

"For you to do your *job*. You look real pretty in front of a mirror, but take a closer look and you'll see there's nothing there. You could be a fucking vampire, Eugene. There's no there, there. You following me?"

"No."

Lee said, "Grady?"

"Where's Brule?" Service asked.

"Transferred," Ivanhoe said. "Convalescent leave."

"Where to?" Lee wanted to know.

"National security."

Service said, "Did they tell you Brule's wife was banging Singleton?"

"She was?" The trooper's tone was one of total surprise.

Service intervened. "Did they tell you the wolf lab wasn't there to transplant wolves?"

"What's it for?"

"We don't know, but we ought to, don't you agree?"

"Yes," Ivanhoe said, after considering the question for a moment.

"Have your people interviewed Vermillion employees?"

"No, the feds are doing that."

"*Really?* Have you seen the interview reports?"

"Not yet."

"You betcha, and you're never gonna," Lee said. "Look," he went on, softening his tone, "the feds are good at this divide-and-conquer shit. They barge in, make a lot of noise, talk about cooperation, and do what they bloody well want. It's like phone sex, all talk and nothing left but sticky hands when it's over."

Ivanhoe's heavy brow pushed out over bugged-out eyes.

"Me and Grady know for a fact that Genova didn't shoot those people. It was her gun, but not her pulling the trigger."

Service knew this wasn't completely accurate. The video showed the shooter but not clearly enough to make an ID, but he took his cue and joined in. "And we know that Genova told the truth about what happened in England. She wasn't responsible for deaths, and she wasn't part of the AFL. The FBI knows this, so why are they lying to us?"

Ivanhoe looked crestfallen.

Sheriff Lee asked, "Do you have a list of Vermillion employees?"

Ivanhoe nodded.

"How come we don't?" Lee asked.

Ivanhoe said nothing.

"We need a copy of that list, Eugene. Are you with us or are you siding with that buncha liars?"

"I need to think about this," the state policeman said.

"Well, don't think too long, son, or all this will be swept under a great big federal carpet and that will be the end of 'er. And maybe your career too."

Back in the Jeep, Freddy Bear said, "Ivanhoe grew up in Iggy. His old man worked bridge security. Eugene's probably okay, but he's a tight-ass more concerned about politics and appearance than getting the bloody job done."

There was a different air in the meeting room in the Soo when the team convened.

Cassie Nevelev wore a black jacket over a deep blue turtleneck and had multiple strands of silver and jade draped around her neck. Judge Vengstrom wasn't there. Neither was the Chippewa County prosecutor. Ivanhoe sat to the federal prosecutor's left, his uniform so crisp and wrinkle-free it looked like he had been teleported directly from the dry cleaner to the meeting room. Phillips, the ASAC from the Detroit FBI office, wore the standard Feeb uniform, a black suit with a dark tie and a starched white button-down shirt.

Barry Davey was unshaven and wore blaze-orange camo clothing.

Nevelev eyed Service before speaking. "We're sorry about Ms. Nantz," she said.

Did everybody know about Nantz and him?

"Where's Doctor Brule?" Freddy Bear Lee asked with the same hard edge he had employed earlier with Ivanhoe. The Chippewa County sheriff had hardly spoken during the ride back to the Soo.

Nevelev raised an eyebrow. "He's on convalescent leave and will be reassigned when he's recovered."

"On leave from which agency?" Lee asked gruffly.

"U.S. Fish and Wildlife," Nevelev said.

"How is it that you know he's on administrative leave?"

"I'm in charge of the team," she said.

"I forgot," Lee said. "With all due respect, there are several of us here this morning who'd like answers to some questions."

"Such as?"

"Such as why Vermillion's been demolished."

"An engineering assessment showed that the cost of repairs would be excessive. It was a simple economic decision."

"So what happens to the so-called project they had out there? You got four of the five wolves back," Lee said.

"That's Fish and Wildlife's call," Nevelev said.

"Is it now?" the sheriff said sarcastically. "When do we see a report of interviews with employees of the lab?"

"The team is being provided with all relevant information."

"Relevant to what, the federal government's private agenda?"

Nevelev's face reddened. "Did we have a bad sleep night, Sheriff?"

"I haven't slept for shit since this whole thing began, and the longer it goes the less sleep I get. I don't like it when I don't get my sleep."

"Perhaps you should consult your physician," Nevelev said.

Service had no idea where his friend intended to take his line of questioning, but the whole thing was deteriorating. "When will Genova be arraigned?" Service asked.

"This afternoon," Nevelev said.

"In the Soo?"

"Yes, in the Soo."

Which meant Wiggins had prevailed. "Do you have a motive?" He emphasized the pronoun deliberately.

"She leads a terrorist group," Nevelev said.

"We saw the terrorists," Service said. "College kids and aging hip-pies."

"Don't underestimate their capacity for violence."

"Nor will I overestimate it," Service said. "Again, what was her motive?"

"Not hers alone," Nevelev said. "The Animal Freedom League's."

"Based on what?"

"I have no idea how such people justify their agendas."

"A lot of that going around," Freddy Bear Lee said, chiming in.

Service kept pressing. "You said earlier that Genova has been under continuous surveillance."

"Yes," Nevelev said. "That's correct."

"Explain to the team why her surveillance tail didn't intervene when she allegedly entered the Vermillion facility and shot two people? Or at least why she wasn't detained after the explosion? Or that she was even seen at Vermillion?"

"I'm not at liberty to discuss surveillance procedures."

"There's not a lot of liberty for anyone to discuss anything," the sheriff said.

Service continued, "How do your forensics people account for the odd pattern of wiping on the murder weapon? Prints only on the barrel and clip. Why would she wipe down only half of it?"

"I cannot account for the inconsistency of human criminal behavior," Nevelev said sharply.

Service kept going. In a fight you rarely knocked out an opponent with a single punch. The trick was to hammer home lots of punches to get the brain reeling. Knockouts were gotten by the accumulation of sharp, well-aimed blows.

"The night of the explosion I talked briefly to Doctor Brule, and he said something about the security system and landlines. I assume this means the cameras were hardwired to a central facility and that there are tapes. Will the team get to see them?"

"The tapes are under review and analysis," the FBI's Phillips said haughtily.

"*All* of them?"

"Yes."

Bullshit, Service thought. "We haven't seen them," he said. "And we have had no description of the security system there. Why does the system blend hardwiring and cassettes? We can't participate unless we have a full picture."

Nevelev and Phillips traded glances. "There are national security issues here and these make it necessary for us to walk a fine line."

"A fine line or a bloody plank?" Sheriff Lee said.

Service watched Barry Davey and saw that he was doing his best to look inconspicuous.

The meeting was over in less than twenty-five minutes. When Nevelev had left the room, Ivanhoe walked over to Sheriff Lee, dropped an envelope on the table, nodded, and left the room without a word.

The envelope contained a list of names and addresses of employees of the Vermillion lab.

Lee slid it over to Service and said, "Now we can start to dig. Use my office?"

At the sheriff's office downtown, Service got a phone call from DaWayne Kota.

"You find anything interesting lately?" the tribal CO asked.

"Yep. Did you?"

"The blue wolf has been spotted."

"Where?"

"South of Munising."

"By whom?"

"A trapper from Covington saw the animal last Friday."

"You're sure it's the same one?"

"Our people wouldn't mistake a blue wolf for anything else. A wolf can make fifty miles a day easy. So the animal hasn't gone that far, given the time he's had."

"Meaning what?"

"I thought you'd want to know."

The call made no sense to Service. Was Kota trying to tell him something?

Shortly after the Kota call, Barry Davey called Service and asked him to meet for coffee. They went to a shop called the Cemetery Cafe, which was just down the hill from Lake Superior State's campus.

"Has Carmody concluded his mission yet?" Davey asked.

"No. Why?"

Davey swallowed loudly. "I may have to pull him out. Something else has arisen."

"You told me I could have him until this thing's concluded."

"Shit happens," Davey said.

"If you pull him out now, I may have to start all over."

"It can't be helped."

"It's set so that I can't call him. He has to call me."

"I know the contact protocol for undercovers. Next time he calls, tell him to get in touch with me."

"Do I get to be part of that discussion?"

"When it's time," Davey said. "I'll try to arrange a replacement for you."

Service got stiffed with the bill for two coffees and cranberry scones and bristled at the inflated prices.

He called McKower from Lee's office. "I found something," he said. "It shows the shooter."

A long silence ensued. "What's the next step?"

"Freddy Bear Lee has seen it. We've duped the tape and we're getting a copy enhanced. We can't see the shooter's face in the original, but maybe a photo whiz can clarify it."

"Do I want to see this?"

"It shows the two vicks going at it before they're shot."

"I see," she said. "Before the explosion?"

"Yes."

"I'm here when you need me. Do you want me to call the captain?"

"No, I'll take care of it. Thanks, Lis."

Service looked at the sheriff. "Let's look at the tape again."

"Why?"

"We need to pinpoint the time of the explosion."

It didn't take long to learn that the shooting took place at 2202 and the explosion at 2205:30. The shootings took place three and a half minutes before the bomb went off, so what was the purpose of the bomb and how had it been detonated? An attempt to cover the shootings, or to release the wolves?

Freddy stared at the VCR. "The shooter's either the luckiest bastard in the world, or he triggered the bomb from a safe distance."

If true, Service thought, the bomb had nothing to do with releasing wolves.

That afternoon, Service and Sheriff Lee drove to Paradise to meet with Jacki Laval. There were thirty names on the Vermillion employee list. "Why are we starting with her?" he asked Sheriff Lee.

"Grapevine," the sheriff said, not bothering to amplify.

Laval lived in a prefab house on a small land parcel about a mile from Water Tank Lake and the entrance to Tahquamenon State Park.

There was a relatively new Dodge mini van parked by the trailer and two snowmobiles on a trailer near a small metal pole barn.

Sheriff Lee banged on the door. After a while a tall, thin woman with a horsey face opened the door and stared warily at them. It was afternoon, but she looked like she had been asleep. "Jacki Laval?"

She nodded.

"You work at Vermillion?"

"Worked. I guess that's done now. At least, that's what we're all hearing. Nobody's bothered to talk to us directly."

"You haven't been interviewed by the FBI?"

She shook her head.

"Can we come in?" Lee asked.

The woman pulled the door open. "You fellas want some coffee? Won't take but a minute to make with my Krups." She pointed proudly to a new coffeemaker.

Lee accepted and the woman showed them to a round table, where they sat down. Service looked around the room. Only a leather recliner looked new. There were some photographs on the walls, including a couple of Laval in a uniform Service recognized.

"You worked at Kincheloe?" The air force base had been decommissioned by the feds and converted by the state into a series of minimum- and maximum-security prison units.

"Until I got the job at Vermillion. Pay's about the same, but the conditions are a lot better. In prison it's one hassle after another."

When the coffee was ready, she filled three cups and brought them to the table.

"Do you work security at Vermillion?" the sheriff asked.

"No, I was a day maintenance supervisor. Been there about a year."

"Surprised you're not in security."

"Too much competition. I took the maintenance job to get my foot in the door. Like I said, I spent enough time in prisons."

"Did maintenance include working with the animals?" Grady Service asked.

"No," the woman said. "The biologists and their techs insisted on doing anything that got close to the animals. I guess the wolves get kind of goofy around people."

"Did you do maintenance on the security cameras?" the sheriff asked.

"No, security took care of that. My people cleaned the lab and the outbuildings."

"Did you have much contact with Doctor Brule or his researchers?" the sheriff asked.

"Not really. They had their own thing. People with educations like that tend to stick to their own kind."

Service noticed the woman rubbing her hands together.

Freddy Bear took a long swig of coffee and smacked his lips. "It's been said you had some contact with Doctor Singleton."

The woman tried to hide her surprise. "I knew him," she said softly.

"It's been said that maybe you knew him pretty good. This is official business, Ms. Laval."

Service thought Freddy Bear was bluffing, but the woman flushed and began to tear up. "Maybe," she said.

The sheriff's voice softened. "We're not here to hassle you, Jacki. We're just doing our jobs. We aren't making a value judgment, eh? We're just looking for facts to help us find out who did this."

Jacki Laval took a deep breath. "Yes, I knew the bastard in the way you mean."

"Intimately?"

The woman nodded.

"Long time?"

Laval shook her head. "More of a fling, eh? We were together a few times over two or three weeks. My friends all told me to stay away from him, but I wouldn't listen. Stupid me."

"You broke it off?"

Her mouth formed a leer. "More like he got what he wanted and moved on to get it somewhere else."

"That honk you off?"

The woman looked alarmed. "You don't think . . ."

"Just answer the questions, Jacki. You aren't a suspect, but we'd like to know more about Singleton. Was he mixed up with other women at the lab?"

"Maybe all of them," she said bitterly.

"He come here with you?"

"No way," she said sharply. "My old man would kill me. We met at his place."

Service wondered if the husband would kill Singleton.

"In Paradise?" the sheriff asked.

"No, not there. Too many snoopy eyes in town. He rents a camp over to Bearpen Creek."

"Do a lot of people know about it?"

She shrugged.

"And the FBI never talked to you about this?"

"Nobody talked to any of us about anything. My husband won't find out about this, right?"

"No, it's just between us, and thanks," the sheriff said. "You want to show us on a map where that camp is?"

"You didn't pick Laval by accident," Service said when they got in the sheriff's vehicle.

"You must be a detective," his friend said with a grin. "Doncha wonder what we're gonna find?" he asked Service as they drove south to look for the researcher's rented camp. It was late afternoon, overcast and darkening quickly.

The road down to the camp was two muddy gravel tracks with a grassy high center and cedar and tamarack swamp closing in on both sides, not the place to encounter a vehicle coming the other direction. Because it was hunting season, there were plenty of tracks on the road— ATVs, SUVs, and trucks.

According to Laval, they were looking for a single-story, cedar-shingle bungalow, set on the north side of the road, across from Bearpen Creek. Laval had no idea how far the camp was, only that the road was rough and that sometimes it seemed like it took forever to get to it.

The distance turned out to be just a shade less than five miles, and set back as it was, they nearly missed it. Only the faint outlines of a driveway told them there was a cabin set back from the road. It was dark under the trees. Lee pulled the Jeep up the track and parked with his headlights illuminating the front porch of the cabin.

"Your regular love nest in the swamp," Freddy Bear Lee said.

The two of them were cautious entering. In a hard plastic holder beside the front door, a card listed the owner's name and telephone number in Rudyard. The sheriff used his cell phone to call the owner and ask permission to enter. The owner wasn't there, but his wife was and she said, "Go for it."

As with many camps in the U.P., the doors weren't locked. Service went in first, shining his flashlight around until he found a light switch.

The sudden light made them squint as they tugged on latex gloves and looked around without moving. Service saw nothing particularly interesting.

Lee moved back toward the two bedrooms and Service walked around the living room. It was a cozy but basic place, a little fancier than most hunting camps, but still rustic. The floor had a few thin carpets on top of a wooden floor that looked like it had been cut from a gymnasium. There was a combination TV–video player and a stereo that would take disks and tapes.

The Chippewa County sheriff emerged from the first bedroom holding a videotape between his thumb and forefinger. "Whole box of 'em in a closet. No labels." He turned on the video player and inserted the tape. "Too bad we don't have popcorn," he quipped.

The first tape showed Larola Brule dancing with her clothes off. "Not too subtle," the sheriff said.

Farther into the tape, Brule and Singleton were engaged in the same contortions they had seen on the security tape. "Enthusiastic gal," the sheriff remarked.

They watched two more tapes and found Singleton engaged with a different woman on each of them. One of them was Jacki Laval.

"Talk about enthusiasm," Lee said. "I guess we ought to look at the rest of them," he added. "Old Singleton was quite the pike, eh?"

"Now what?" Service asked.

"We gotta look at 'em all, get an ID on the women, find out if they're married or whatever, get photos of their men, run backgrounds, and try to match them to your video."

"How many tapes?" Service asked.

"Thirteen and a couple of shoe boxes filled with Polaroids."

Service had no interest in watching videos of Singleton screwing various women. More important, he doubted the killer was related to any of the other women. Larola Brule had been killed first, and it had looked like a professional hit. Still, in police work you had to fill in all the blanks, go through the motions, leave nothing undone. "I'll leave the tapes and IDs to you."

"Okay, I'll put them in the Jeep."

They spent another two hours methodically going through the place, but finding nothing extraordinary other than a glass bowl filled with condoms. "Hey, at least Singleton practiced safe sex," Sheriff Lee said.

On the way back to the Soo, Service called East Lansing from Lee's cell phone and got Fae O'Driscoll. "Can I talk to Maridly? How's she doing?"

"She's doing fine, Grady. I'll take the cordless to her."

Service heard the chief grumbling about something in the background. Then there were clunking sounds and Maridly's sleepy voice asking, "Wha?"

"It's Grady," Fae announced.

"Honey?" Maridly said.

"Sorry to wake you," he said, not meaning it.

"I'm *glad* you called." He could hear longing in her voice.

"Are you all right?"

"Sore and kinda dopey. I told Fae and Lorne I don't think I should stay here. I have to see the doctor early next week and then I want to come home. You think you could come fetch your woman?"

Service's heart raced. "You just say when."

"I heard what Tree did to the asshole who did this to me," she said. "I'm gonna give him a big kiss when I see him."

Service thought about denying Treebone had done anything, but decided against it.

"Where are you?" Nantz asked.

"Watching fuck-flicks with a sheriff."

She giggled. "Get real."

There was nothing he wanted more. "Seriously," he said

"*Good* ones?"

"Strictly amateur."

"You sound tired," she said.

"That time of year," he said. "I'd better let you get back to sleep."

"Okay," she said. "Grady?"

"Uh-huh?"

"I love you."

"Uh-huh," he replied.

"God, I love your eloquence," she said with a soft giggle. "You're not alone?"

"Right."

"Well, I'd talk dirty to you, but it would hurt too much. Be careful, honey."

"Looks to me like you got it bad," Freddy Bear Lee said.

"Got what?"

The sheriff laughed out loud.

Service fetched his truck from the sheriff's house and called Lisette McKower.

"McKower," she answered sleepily.

"Larola Brule wasn't the only female the male vick was duking."

"You think there's a jealous husband?"

"Freddy will look into that."

"Your voice says you think it's something else."

"I don't know, Lis," he said. Whatever it was, it was unlike any case he'd ever handled before. Or wanted to handle again.

Heading west, he got as far as Seney and felt himself nodding off. He pulled into the wildlife refuge driveway again for a nap and fell into deep sleep.

He awoke with gray light creeping through his passenger window and drizzle tapping a tattoo on the roof and running down the hood.

He grabbed his cell phone and checked his voice mail.

Carmody's voice roared, "We need ta meet, ya daft shite, but I can't reach ya. I'll try again tonight at half-nine. Be by your phone."

"Goddammit," Service said out loud. He had slept through a page. That had never happened before and it bothered him.

· 24 ·

After a breakfast pasty and coffee at the Golden Ladle in Seney, Service called ahead to Captain Grant at his Marquette office. "I'm very pleased to know you're still on the planet, Detective. How's Ms. Nantz and where are you?" This was about as close to sentimental as the captain got.

"She's on the mend," Service said. "I'm just leaving Seney and I need to see you, Cap'n. I'll be there in ninety minutes."

An hour later the captain called him back.

"I'm feeling a tad purk today," Grant said. "I was just about to head for home. Why don't you meet me there? You know how to find it?"

"Yessir."

The captain lived in a geodesic dome house built on the banks of the Dead River. Service had never been inside, but he had driven past it.

Captain Ware Grant greeted him at the front door, wearing a gray cardigan sweater with leather elbow patches and pale moleskin pants. Service followed the captain through a living room packed with antiques to a glassed-in sunporch. There were strung bamboo fly rods standing in a rack on the floor and a fly-tying bench in the corner. Unlike some benches Service had seen—say, Shark Wetelainen's—materials were not strewn around. The captain was a meticulous man in all things. The Dead River sparkled as it tumbled over a hundred-yard-long riffle below the house.

To the Ojibwa the mists spawned by the many cascades and small falls on the river were spirits departing for the unknown. They had called the river *djibis-manitou-sibi*, River of the Spirits of the Dead. Europeans shortened this to Dead River because iron, gold, and silver mines leeched pollution from their upstream locations, but the river was far from dead and there were stretches with great trout fishing. The captain's house overlooked one of the most productive areas.

"You could use a shave," the captain said. "What would you drink?"

"I'm on duty, sir."

The captain smirked. "Technically we both are. We'll let it be our secret. I like a glass with my lunch."

Lunch? It was barely 10 A.M.

Grant left the porch and came back with two glasses of amber liquid. "Single-malt Scotch," he said, offering a glass to his detective.

The Scotch burned smoothly and it struck Service that for a man feeling a "tad punk" his captain seemed just fine—and that his departure from the office might be more playing hooky than being under the weather. This possibility made him look at his superior through new eyes.

"This is your meeting," the captain said.

Service wasn't sure where to begin.

"How's Ms. Nantz?"

"She'll recover," Service said.

"The advantages of youth," Grant said wistfully. "I understand she gave a fine account of herself in abhorrent circumstances."

"Yessir."

"And your comrade, Lieutenant Treebone. I don't agree with what he did, but neither can I condemn him." How did the captain know about Tree? He decided to let it drop, but the captain had more to say. "What the lieutenant did was unprofessional," Grant said. "And thoroughly human. When friends are involved, it's sometimes difficult to maintain professional objectivity."

"Yessir."

"You're uneasy about the Vermillion situation."

"Yes," Service said, wondering if the old man was a mind reader and whose meeting this really was.

"Like most Americans, you harbor an innate distrust of the federal government."

"I'd prefer to think of it as healthy skepticism."

"Are you experiencing continuing obstruction by the federals?"

"Yes, but we're beginning to make inroads. The FBI seems set on pinning the two killings on Genova, but I'm not buying it. Captain, I'm fairly certain that Larola Brule was the primary target of the killing. She was shot first, and it looked to me to be an efficient, professional hit."

"I see," Grant said. "You have experience with professional hits?"

"No sir, but the shooting is on one of the Vermillion security video tapes."

The captain leaned against the back of his chair. "What does the team think?"

"They haven't seen the tape. I found it."

The captain nodded ponderously. "You *found* a tape? Dare I ask the circumstances?"

He knew it sounded ludicrous, but the find couldn't be disproven. "It was in a paper bag on a road."

"I see," the captain said, taking a sip of Scotch.

"I haven't turned the tape over to the team. I don't trust them."

The captain sat back. "What's your objective in this case, Detective?"

"To find who exploded the bomb at the lab and released the animals."

"And the homicides?"

"They're part of the solution."

"Are the bomb and shootings separate events?"

"I don't know that yet."

"Are you playing at homicide detective?" the captain asked.

"Sheriff Lee and I are working together, and the homicides are his business."

The captain nodded approvingly. "Sheriff Lee is a professional and an exception. Elected law enforcement officials are often less than efficient or professional. You both realize that not sharing the tape puts you on questionable legal footing."

"We both think this is the right thing to do for the moment. The tape shows the shooter, Captain. The lab was still intact when the killings took place. The bomb went off three and a half minutes after the shootings. The tape shows the shooter, but the image is poor. Still, from what I can see, the body type doesn't look like Genova. Sheriff Lee is trying to get the tape enhanced. The hooker in this is that Genova was arrested leading an antihunting demonstration in Trout Lake and the FBI has recovered a .380 Walther PPK from her compound. Ballistics show that it is the murder weapon."

The captain studied him. "Her weapon, but not necessarily her using it."

Service nodded. He was tired of going over the same ground and getting nowhere.

Grant said, "The fact that the two victims were shot prior to the explosion does not automatically eliminate the bombing as intended to release the animals. It is possible that the bomb was intended to obscure the shootings, but it is also possible that the bomb was intended to release the animals and that shooting was more a matter of opportunity.

Still," he added contemplatively, "knowing the timing aids the investigation. Why do you think the FBI is so focused on Genova? The focus on her came before the discovery of the weapon, correct?"

"Yes, and that's the puzzler. All I know is that the Feebs tell one story about her activities in the U.K. and allege she was part of the Animal Freedom League, and she tells a diametrically opposed story. I have reason to believe her version."

"Evidence?"

"The British do not concur with the FBI."

"You've talked to them?"

"Through an intermediary."

"I see," the captain said. "Hearsay."

"Sir, my contact is a former FBI agent who served in England and maintains her contacts with British intelligence."

"Former?"

"She sued the Bureau for discrimination and won. She's now a lawyer in Detroit."

"A lawyer with her own ax to grind against her former employer?"

"There's no love lost, that's for sure, but I don't think she has an ax to grind. She won big in her case and I trust her. My point is that if the British are correct, then the feds are lying to us, or holding something back. At this point it's impossible to tell."

"And therefore you are not showing them all your cards—so to speak."

"Yessir."

The captain gazed out the window for a while. "There are just as many dedicated men and women in federal service as in the DNR," he said. "Are you familiar with my background?"

"Military intelligence?" He had never heard the captain talk about his life before joining the DNR. Nobody had.

"Not military," the captain said without further clarification.

Service wondered if it was CIA or one of the many shadowy agencies that comprised the country's intelligence network.

He went on, "Despite dedicated people, organizations sometimes go astray and lose perspective. The engine of intelligence is politics. It was not designed this way, but it has evolved to this. Interagency and interjurisdictional cases can be very frustrating. Do you know why you were selected for your position?"

"So you could keep an eye on me?"

The captain flashed a rare smile. "Our Lieutenant McKower has a sense of humor. I picked you because you have a complex mind and a facility for complex cases. Despite rubbing against conflicts with jurisdictions, you have always seemed to find a way to the right solution, for the case and for continuing relations. This is a rare quality in an officer."

"I haven't always handled things smoothly."

"Only cretins seek smoothness, Detective. Professionals seek answers and will go to any length to get them. Sometimes this entails unreasonable risks and the stretching of established protocol. Are you feeling uneasy right now?"

Service admitted that he was.

"You sense that the feds are masking something."

"At the very least they are not telling us the whole truth."

"Are they claiming national security interests?"

"Yes."

The captain's beard danced a couple of times. "That's often a sign of obfuscation."

"Sir, they've essentially razed the Vermillion facility. The lab's director is not reachable and they are pushing hard on Genova, whom they claim to have had under continuous surveillance for eight years. If so, why didn't their surveillance people apprehend her at the crime scene or stop her in the act?"

"Do you have a theory to offer? Much of the science of investigation is art, and sometimes we have to create a less-than-compelling theory to provide a starting point in the search for truth."

He hadn't really thought of it in those terms. "They act like they've been caught with their hand in a cookie jar and somehow Genova represents a threat to them. But I can't figure out what the cookie jar is. It's possible that Vermillion was designed more for animal training and conditioning than for temporary housing of transplants, which Yogi Zambonet says the state would have blocked. And he said he had informed Brule that the animals could not be released. If Brule knew this, what were they really doing at Vermillion? If we assume their stated mission isn't the real one, I still don't understand why the feds are so intent on Genova."

"Perhaps Ms. Genova's involvement is tangential to something else."

This comment caught Service short.

"Is it possible that you have misjudged the motives of our federal colleagues? September eleventh has created a lot of choppy water in the law enforcement and intelligence communities. Nobody wants to be saddled with another failure, and no doubt some individuals will seek to use the wake of this disaster to pursue personal agendas and advancement. It has always been so."

Was this an allusion to something in Grant's past? "Captain, I don't know what their motives are. All I can see are their actions, and these aren't sitting well with me."

"What do you propose to do next?"

Grady Service shook his head. "Wait for Sheriff Lee to have the tape enhanced. We have the original, but we made a copy."

"There are far better federal resources for such technical matters."

"I don't feel I can trust them."

"A terrible conundrum," the captain agreed.

"The sheriff and I finally managed to get a list of Vermillion employees. We know now that Doctor Singleton was involved with several women at the facility, including Doctor Brule's wife."

"This raises the specter of jealousy as a motive."

"We certainly can't rule it out yet. But why would Brule destroy his own laboratory and project?"

"Jealousy is never a rational emotion."

"Still, in the brief conversation I had with the doctor the night of the explosion he seemed genuinely devastated by his wife's death."

"Why do you think the doctor is unavailable?"

"The feds say he's convalescing and will be reassigned, and that the lab was razed as a prudent fiscal decision; rebuilding would cost too much. These seem like reasonable explanations, but I just can't buy into their convenience in the wake of what happened."

There was a moment of silence. "What progress on the poaching case?" the captain asked in a sudden shift of topic.

"I think we're getting close, but there's a catch."

The captain looked at him attentively.

"Barry Davey's threatening to pull our undercover."

"Did Special Agent Davey offer a rationale?"

"Changing priorities, which sounds to me like different words for national security. Davey is part of the Soo team and I have a suspicion he's trying to punish me by pulling his man out."

"Would you like for me to talk to Davey or his superiors?"

"No sir, not at this point. I think Carmody is close to bringing the case to a conclusion and I want to keep him engaged. Davey has instructed me to have Carmody call him, but I have a meeting with the man and I want to see where we are. If he's not close, I'll have no choice but to tell him to call Davey." Actually what Davey said was that Carmody should get back to him. He didn't specify that the contact be by phone, or ask for precise timing, all of which gave him room to maneuver, Service tried to assure himself.

"And if the man is close to resolving the case?"

"I'll deliver Davey's message when it suits us."

The captain grasped his knees and leaned toward Service. "Has it occurred to you that you may be making the same sort of decision that the federals are faced with?"

Service didn't understand. "We need the undercover, sir."

"Perhaps the FBI and Fish and Wildlife have needs they must satisfy as well."

"Are you suggesting that I tell the undercover to contact Davey?"

"I am suggesting only that another man's motives can sometimes appear dubious. Think about what's gone on from their perspective, Detective. Whatever you decide, I will support, but think it through, and whatever you decide, bear in mind what it is that we are all trying to accomplish."

The captain made sandwiches of Finnish bread slathered with butter and stacked with sweet onions and cheese. "I have elevated cholesterol," he said as he set a crock of pickles beside the sandwiches. "My doctors would object if they saw this repast, but they aren't here, are they?"

Service nodded, wondering if this was some sort of veiled message to him.

Later in the afternoon he stopped at the house in Gladstone to check on the animals and rest before heading west to be nearer to Carmody when the call came through tonight. Newf was all over him, while Cat gave herself a bath, but she did so sitting on the end of the couch where she could see him. "You don't fool me, you misanthrope," he said to the cat. "You missed me." Cat ignored him.

N antz telephoned at 4 P.M. with deep concern in her voice.
"Honey. What did you do for Thanksgiving?"
Service said, "Thanksgiving?"

"Today? You know . . . the holiday?"

He had completely forgotten. "I had lunch with the captain," he said.

"Did you have turkey?"

"We had onion and cheese sandwiches."

"Good God," she said.

"And Scotch," he added. Thinking back on it, the sandwiches did seem like a pretty poor Thanksgiving dinner, but they were what the captain wanted. What kind of life did Ware Grant lead away from work?

"I've got great news. The doctors say my bone density is normal." she said.

"You were able to talk to a doctor on Thanksgiving?" he said.

"Fae invited Robbie to dinner and he brought me the test results."

"Robbie?"

"Doctor Caple."

"Oh." The chief's wife invited another man to Thanksgiving dinner with his girlfriend? He felt a surge of jealousy, which he immediately tried to ignore. "How do you feel?"

"Achy and sore, but it's getting better. I have even better news! I've been relieved of duty with Task Force 2001 and returned to the DNR for training. I can start back at the academy as soon as I get medical release. Robbie is going to send my records to Vince so he can monitor me. This means I can come home, honey!"

Vince Vilardo was an internist and the appointed part-time medical examiner for Delta County. Vince and his wife, Rose, had been Grady's friends for years and since summer had taken to Nantz almost like adoptive parents.

"Vince is a good doctor," Service said. "How long are they giving you?"

"A month if I need it. It'll be great to be home and together, won't it, hon?"

One month, with two pins still to be removed? This wasn't the time frame the chief had talked to him about. She was being overly optimistic, and he decided to let her think what she wanted until he had time to talk to her about the realities. It would be good to be normal again, even for a month.

"When do I pick you up?"

"Robbie's already given me the test results, so I don't need the appointment Monday. Isn't that great?"

"Do you want me to come get you now?" He wished she'd stop calling the punk doctor by his first name.

"Can you?"

"I'll be there," he said.

"You'd better, Detective." Her voice sounded husky and playful, back to normal. No woman's voice had ever had the effect on him that Nantz's did. She added, "Get this. Sam sent me a personal note apologizing for the task force thing. He said it was a clerical error."

Typical government, Service thought, to blame things on people at the bottom of the totem pole. "That's good." He had no doubt that the original order had come from Bozian. The action and note were no more than ass-covering, and Service knew he owed Lorne O'Driscoll for confronting the governor at the hospital. It seemed that he was suddenly accumulating debts to people—Captain Grant, O'Driscoll, Freddy Bear Lee.

"I'm glad all this happened," Nantz said.

"You are?"

"It's a test, honey. The things we want most always require us to pass a test."

"Does that include us?" he asked. Was Robbie part of his test? he wondered.

She laughed her infectious laugh. "God, Service. Don't be so thick. We *are* the test!"

Her voice suddenly dropped an octave. "Remember what you said when you thought I was out of it . . ."

"I remember."

"I'm holding you to it, Service."

"Just holding me will be enough," he said.

"You betcha. I'd better go. I'm helping Fae tonight. We're taking turkeys down to some gospel mission. I love you."

"See you tomorrow," he said, thinking he needed to get gas and call the captain. He hoped Carmody wouldn't want a meeting tonight.

"I'll be as nervous as a lifelong virgin before her wedding night. Take care of yourself, hon."

Nantz. She was a live wire and he still didn't understand what she saw in him.

An hour later she was on the phone again. "Never mind picking me up," she said.

"What?"

"I tried to get a commercial flight but on such short notice I couldn't work it out."

"That's okay. I can drive."

"You don't need to drive all the way down here, hon. I talked to a friend, Tucker Gates. He's ferrying a bird down to Lansing for Big Bear Air on Saturday. He'll deliver that bird and he'll fly me back in mine. Pretty good, huh? I can get a rental car for the time I'm home and leave my truck here. Tuck will pick me up Saturday morning and we'll be back by dinnertime, which is probably a good thing. The forecast is calling for some nasty weather swinging down from Alberta on Sunday. Heaps of snow!"

"Is this Gates guy safe?" Big Bear Air was a small contract outfit based at the Delta County Airport near Escanaba.

"He's an old boyfriend, Grady, and the best pilot I've ever known. He flies Warthogs for the air guard out of Battle Creek."

Service pictured a swaggering fighter pilot, full of himself. "How did you meet this guy?"

"Are you jealous, Service?"

"Just asking."

"He's done contract work for the department and he really wants to get on full time. We went out a few times years ago. He's a great guy. Don't worry, okay?"

"I'm not worried." Shaken up, irritated maybe, but not worried.

"I love you, Grady Service. I can't wait to see you."

God, life could be complicated, he thought.

       *   *   *

At 5:30 P.M. it was beginning to rain as Service aimed his truck northwest up the M 69, thinking it would help to get closer to Carmody when he called.

Between Felch and Foster City a deer suddenly bounded out of the heavy brush on the side of the road. Service knew from long experience not to swerve. The deer had sealed its own fate and struck the Laramie nearly dead center of the steel deer guard. He felt the animal dragging beneath the truck and braked to pull to the side of the road just past where the road passed over Quarry Creek.

He left the motor running as he got out and shone his flashlight under the vehicle. The animal was still alive, its sides heaving and breath forming clouds. He decided to take some time to let the small button buck settle and got back into the cab. If the deer wasn't hurt badly it would recover and crawl out on its own. If the blow were lethal, it would die. He had no desire to get kicked trying to extract an injured animal from beneath the truck. He lit a cigarette, turned on his flashers, and checked his watch. It was just after 6:30 P.M.

Listening to the motor, he reminded himself to get more gas up the road.

All he could do now was wait for nature to take its course. Nantz was coming home. He reminded himself that she was hurt and would need to take it easy. The rain turned to snow.

Fifteen minutes later a slow-rolling truck came up behind him, passed, and immediately pulled over and parked on the shoulder just ahead of him.

A figure shuffled back toward Service's truck and stood just beyond the reach of his headlights. The figure wore a ratty long coat with a hood. When the man got close, he knelt and looked under the truck, then struggled back to his feet. Service got out.

"Cheaper to shoot 'em," the figure said with a familiar croaky voice.

It was Limpy Allerdyce, the poacher who had once shot him and served seven years in prison because of it. The previous summer Service had solved the mystery of the murder of Allerdyce's son. The old man was the leader of a clan of poachers and lawbreakers who lived in a primitive compound in the most extreme reaches of southwest Marquette County. Allerdyce had known Service's father and claimed to have had an "arrangement" with him, implying he had been one of his father's informants.

"Just like your old man," Allerdyce said "Always in a pickle, eh? You want me to take this critter off your hands?"

"Might be the first legal one you ever took," Service said.

"Old farts grow wise," Allerdyce croaked back. "They all eat good, eh?"

Service knew Allerdyce would never change, and he had forged a truce with the miscreant; for the moment he wasn't interested in knowing why the old man was out in his truck in the rain. Not that he couldn't guess. Probably road hunting at night, but Service wasn't going to press it. By law the Michigan State Police could issue a permit to allow motorists to harvest a deer killed by a vehicle. Service doubted Allerdyce would bother with such a formality. The old man had pretty much ignored all laws all of his life.

The buck struggled momentarily beneath the truck and Service knew it was still alive.

"Poor thing's done in." Allerdyce said.

Service thought for a minute and decided.

"Take it," he said.

Allerdyce looked frail, but he immediately dropped to his knees and rooted around beneath the truck. Then he shuffled back to his truck and backed it up. He left the motor running and came back with a rope.

The animal made no more sounds.

Allerdyce ducked under the truck again. got up, and began pulling against the dead weight of the animal, which he hauled to the rear of his pickup. He opened the top half of the gate on the cap, reached down, hoisted the deer, and pushed it in. It landed with a loud *plop*.

"You're a good man, Sonny. Your old man he woulda been proud. I guess both of us is gettin' wiser, eh?" Allerdyce let loose a little cackle.

Service shone his flashlight into the bed of Allerdyce's truck. There were two small bucks inside, plus the one the old man had just loaded. The throat of the newest addition had been cut.

"All of them hit by vehicles?" Service said.

"Youse bet. She's a bad night for da deers oot on da blacktop. eh. And a good night for da supper table."

Service knew he could cite the old man; probably there would be a rifle in the cab, uncased and loaded. As a paroled felon, Allerdyce was not allowed to handle firearms of any kind for any purpose, but the animal was out from under his truck and Service thought it a fair trade, given the circumstances.

Allerdyce stood still, waiting to see what Service would do.

"Thanks, Limpy."

Allerdyce cackled. "Just like his old man." The poacher started to move toward his cab, but stopped. "You hear inna-ting 'boot a blue wolf runnin' over to da Skeeto?"

Service tensed. *Skeeto* was Limpy's term for the Mosquito Wilderness Tract. "A blue wolf?" Service answered. If there was a blue wolf in the Mosquito, McCants would have told him.

Allerdyce chuckled. "Yep, a blue one. Just thought youse might like to hear what's passin' mouth ta ear, eh."

With that, the poacher was on his way with three deer in the bed of his truck. Sometimes you had to look the other way, Service told himself, grimacing at his sudden pragmatism. Maybe age was catching up to him. Compromise at any age amounted to surrender, pure and simple, and Service was never comfortable with surrendering to anyone over anything. Except for Nantz.

And a blue wolf in the Mosquito? Doubtful, but possible. If anyone knew, it would be Allerdyce. The old man was a sociopath, but he knew his craft. Still, why had he brought it up?

The snow kept coming. Service was parked in the hamlet of Alberta by 9 P.M. There were lights on in most of the small houses and a few vehicles coming and going. Henry Ford had built the town during the depression, and it had become a lumber camp during World War II. Little had changed in the village since then.

The call came precisely at 9:30 P.M.

"Service."

"Finally at your post, boyo. I haven't long to chat, but the lady has put out a reward for anybody who can find a blue wolf—not to bag it, but to find it. Once it's found, I'll be going along with her to do the business."

"When?"

"She's just gotten word that the animal has been seen in a place called the Mosquito. We'll be moving over there in a day or so."

"There are no wolves in the Mosquito," Service said.

"There, elsewhere, it doesn't matter," Carmody said. "Sooner or later her finders will locate it."

"It's not that simple," Service said. "Her finders?"

"It's the lady's plan, not mine."

"Is her other half involved?"

"Couldn't really say yet. Me gut says it's her show, but I couldn't swear to it."

"You need evidence."

"I know my job, Service."

Grady Service decided not to relay Barry Davey's message. He needed Carmody to finish before the end of deer season, when most of the heavy poaching would stop. It was now or never "When will we meet?"

"When I decide," Carmody said in an almost amused tone. "Worried, are you?"

"I'm not comfortable being out of touch so long."

"Welcome to the shadow world. Time I run. I'll be in touch."

"Call if you change locations."

"Aye, wouldn't do otherwise, bucko."

With those words, Carmody hung up and Service stared at his cell phone.

It was a pain in the ass to work cases at opposite ends of the U.P. and he decided he would return home and sleep in his own bed—or rather, Maridly's bed. The concept of a bed made him laugh out loud. A far cry from his old setup on footlockers. Your life's changing, he told himself as he made a tight U-turn to return to Gladstone.

The snow was steady. As he passed the old Narenta railroad crossing on US 2 near Hyde, his headlights caught a flash of something large and dark soaring low over the truck toward the Highland Golf Club course on the south side of the highway. Service instinctively put on his brakes and squinted to see what it was, but the snow was heavy and there was nothing to see but gossamer curtains. It damn sure wasn't a bird, he told himself.

He knew the Delta County Airport lay six or seven miles directly to the east. If what he had seen had been an aircraft, it was precariously low and ominously silent. He parked his truck on the shoulder turned on his flashers, grabbed his emergency pack and compass, pulled on his Gore-Tex coat, pulled the hood over his baseball cap, and started walking in the direction the shape had seemed to travel.

The golf course was flat with only a hint of rises. After ten minutes he was ready to give up and return to his truck, but there was a tree line ahead and he decided to walk that far before turning back. The snow turned to rain again as he approached the tree line, and with his flashlight he saw a couple of large white pine branches lying in the rough near the fairway. He shone his light into the treetops and saw that something had sheered off the tops of some trees. He immediately keyed the microphone of his eight-hundred-megahertz handheld radio, called the Delta County dispatcher, identified himself and his location, and asked for assistance. "Possible aircraft down," he said as he shuffled on, returning the radio to its carrying case and plunging into the trees.

There was no fire ahead of him, but one hundred yards into the forest his light picked up a glint of metal.

He hurried toward the reflection and saw a small plane nose-down, one wing lying on the ground close to the wreck and the other wing torn, but caught in a tree and propping up the aircraft at an awkward angle. He pulled out his radio again and confirmed his location and the facts that an aircraft was indeed down and he was at the wreckage.

He eased toward the wreckage through twisted strips of aluminum and aimed his light into the cockpit. The pilot was slumped against his yoke, held in place by his shoulder harness. Service had to stand on tiptoes to see. He could smell fumes.

Service used his flashlight to search the ground for something to stand on and finally located a substantial piece of deadwood in the shape of a Y. He dragged it to the aircraft and propped it up. Using the wood as a foot stand, he pulled himself up to the cockpit window. It was closed. He tapped on the window, but got no response from the pilot. He tried to slide the window open, but it was jammed. There were fumes in the air. He heard sirens in the distance and deliberated waiting but he was here now. He knew that moving a severely injured person could sometimes make injuries worse, but the fumes were definitely intensifying, and he was still smarting from the two deaths at Seney. Probably a leak from the tank. Would the rain and snow evaporate the fuel? He didn't know and he wasn't going to wait to find out.

Operating in total darkness, he took off his hat, pulled his sidearm from its holster, and wrapped it in the hat to avoid making sparks. It took a half dozen sharp whacks to crack the window, but when it went, it shattered into pellets. He felt his perch wobbling and grabbed the window frame to brace himself, reached inside, and felt the pilot's neck for a pulse. Still alive. He stretched his arm inside and found the door latch and released it. The door didn't open.

The sirens were closer now, but he hurried to get the pilot out. There was nothing worse than to get close to a save only to have fate jerk it away from you at the last moment. He pulled and pulled on the door, but it refused to give. No choice, he told himself, his mind racing. The pilot looked pretty small. It would be a tight fit but he would have to pull him through the window. He reached in and tried to release the safety harness, but the mechanism refused to budge. Shit. He found the parachute cord knife he had carried since Vietnam, opened the hooked blade, and slashed his way through the nylon webbing with one hand while bracing himself against the fuselage with his leg and holding the pilot's collar with his other hand.

When the harness was cut away, the pilot's weight sagged forward and to the side. Service dropped his knife onto the ground behind him, got both arms around the man, and began to pull. Something on the man's jacket caught on the window, but Service kept tugging. His perch was slipping and with a final surge, he pulled the man through, and clutched him as they tumbled face-to-face.

They hit cold muddy ground hard. Service fought to regain his breath, eased the pilot onto the ground beside him, and rolled him over to take a look. His big flashlight was gone, but he carried a small one attached to the zipper of his jacket. He illuminated the man's face and found himself staring at the wizened features of Joe Flap.

"Jesus Christ, Pranger!"

Joe Flap was an old-time CO, a horseblanket who, until retiring a few years back, had been one of the few contemporaries of his father still on the force. Until this past fall Joe still flew occasional missions for the DNR, but he had been grounded in October, and Service couldn't imagine what he would be doing up on a night like this. Or flying at all.

"Jesus, Joe." Flap had crashed so many times and had so many close calls that other pilots and COs called him Pranger. *Prang* was pilot slang for a crash.

Service felt for a pulse. The little man was unconscious, but his pulse was steady.

People were yelling from the edge of the woods and Service answered them, guiding them to him. He saw lights slashing through the woods from the fairway to the north of him.

A fireman was first on the scene, followed closely by two EMTs from Escanaba Ramparts.

The fireman flashed his light around and grunted. 'Fumes. Let's move him outta here."

Service helped the men carry Joe Flap to the edge of the golf course as more help arrived.

They put the injured pilot down on the fairway while an ambulance fishtailed across the golf course toward them. Service stood back while the EMTs worked on Joe and followed the gurney as it was rolled over to the waiting ambulance. Just before loading him, a female EMT said, "He's back." Service stepped forward and looked at his old friend. "Pranger?"

"Jeezo-peto, Grady, I gone and done 'er again."

"You're gonna be okay, Joe."

"Yah, I know da drill," Pranger said weakly. He grasped Service's sleeve. "How close was I?"

"I don't know," Service said. "Five, six miles from the runway."

"Goddamn shoulda made 'er. I had da tailwind. I shoulda made 'er," the old man said with a groan that was part anger, part anguish.

Service watched as the ambulance sped away with its lights flashing. A fire truck rambled across the golf course toward the crash site. Service followed along to fetch his pack, flashlight, and parachute knife.

There was growing activity at the wreck site.

"You first on the scene?" a fireman asked.

"Yah."

"You see it go down?"

"I saw something cross over the road and thought I'd better take a look."

"There's no fuel in the tanks. She's bone-fucking dry," the fireman said, shaking his head.

When Service got to Sisters of the Third Order of St. Francis Hospital, Joe Flap was in surgery. Vince Vilardo was in the hallway just outside the emergency waiting room. "I was up checking on a patient when I heard they brought Joe in and that you were first on the scene."

Service wasn't surprised. Information moved on the Yooper grapevine faster than on the Internet, and was often more accurate.

"How is he?" Service asked.

Vince said, "Per Wahl's working on him."

Service didn't know a doctor named Wahl. "He just started in September," Vilardo said. "Per knows what he's doing. How 'bout I grab us some coffee."

Service found a seat and slumped into it. Too much time in hospitals lately. First Maridly, now Pranger.

Vince brought coffee in paper cups. "I put sugar in it, eh? Three lumps. You look like you could use the jolt."

Service took the coffee and drank, not tasting it.

Just over an hour later a doctor in blood-streaked green scrubs came out and Vince stood up. "Per," he said.

Service glanced up at the doctor, who looked even younger than the one who had tended Maridly in Lansing. Suddenly everybody was looking too young.

"I'm Service."

The doctor looked tired. "I thought he'd make it," he said. "He was busted up pretty bad and there was internal bleeding, but we got in there with clamps and started getting it under control. Then his heart gave out. Nothing we could do," the young surgeon apologized. "We tried everything. I'm sorry."

Sorry? Joe Flap had been the last Korean War veteran in the force and now he was on the verge of becoming the last man from Vietnam. Was this his fate too?

"I can't believe a man his age was still flying," the doctor said to Vince Vilardo.

"He wasn't supposed to be flying," Vince said. "He was grounded in October. He didn't pass the FAA physical."

Service stared up at his old friend. "What the hell was he doing up there at all?"

Vince shook his head. "You know how he was, Grady. The government could take away his papers, but he still had that bloody plane."

Vilardo put his hand on Service's neck and rubbed. "Let's get out of here. Come to the house. Rose and I will get you something to eat and open a bottle of red."

Grady Service felt numb, but followed his friend out to his house on the shore of Lake Michigan. A small stream ran by the house; every fall it was filled with spawning coho salmon, and in the spring the steelhead came in for their ritual. He'd met Vince when he and Rose had once offered the DNR use of their house to catch poachers. That had been too many years back to think about.

Rose Vilardo hugged Service when he entered the house. As usual they all made straight for the kitchen, which was the command post for all action in the Vilardo household. Vince broke open a bottle of Amarone and poured healthy portions. Rose sat with Service while Vince grabbed his apron and started shuttling around the kitchen. Soon the air filled with the smell of garlic and basil as sauce makings sautéed. When the pasta was done, Vince dumped it all into a strainer and from there into a big bowl, mixed in olive oil, and plopped the bowl on the table with a fresh loaf of Italian bread.

"Joe was just over to dinner last week," Rose said.

"I grounded him," Vince said. "I had no choice. I passed word to the department, but you know Joe, he wasn't one to hold grudges. Still, he seemed pretty lost without flying. I saw him up a couple of times this fall, but the weather was good then. But tonight, I can't understand it," he said sadly, shaking his head.

Service didn't understand it either, but he had an idea. "Once you get really good at something, it's hard to give it up," he said simply.

Vince stared at him and nodded slowly.

Grady Service called Maridly at two in the morning. Fae O'Driscoll grumbled in her gentle way as she took the phone to Nantz.

"Grady?" He heard concern in her voice.

"I'm okay," he said. "Joe Flap crashed tonight. He didn't make it."

"Oh my God," Nantz said, quickly adding, "Are you afraid of me flying today?"

His mind was on Flap and himself. "He shouldn't have been up there," Service said, feeling tears beginning to leak out. He had known Joe was grounded, and he should have been looking in on him, but his new job took up all his time. In his old job this wouldn't have happened, he told himself. "I could have prevented this," he said, breaking down.

"It's not your fault, honey."

He could sense Nantz's gentle and soothing tone, but not her exact words as he wept not just for his friend Joe Flap but for all horseblankets who did their duty anonymously and slid into oblivion.

· 26 ·

I t took only one glass of wine for the strain of too little sleep and the emotions of recent events to overwhelm him. Service conked out sitting in a chair in Vince's living room, and awoke the next morning with one of Rose's afghans over him and only a vague recollection of the details of last night's conversation with Maridly. The main memory that lingered was the unwavering beam of emotional support of her voice coming through the earpiece. It was one thing to want a particular woman and another thing entirely to need her. He had never before needed anyone, and to his surprise he wasn't uncomfortable with it.

Vince and Rose offered breakfast, but Service settled for coffee and one piece of dry rye toast from Carmello's Fantastico Paremporium in Gladstone.

Vince said, "I meant to tell you last night that I talked to a Doctor Caple at Sparrow and he shared Maridly's situation with me. It sounds like she'll come out of this all right. It will do her good to be home.'

Service nodded. Nantz would be in competent hands with Vince, but his mind was torn between anticipating her return and the loss of Joe Flap. Pranger had no surviving relatives; the DNR had been his family. Service had called the captain and McKower last night on his way to the hospital to let them know about the crash, and he knew that the word would be moving out through the DNR with lightning speed. He guessed Joe's burial would be soon and a small affair, with a memorial service to follow later, when deer season was over and officers could get away to attend.

"Theoretically she can get back into this session of the academy, but the chief wants me to convince her to skip this one and start new in the fall when she's fully recovered," Service said.

"Maridly will listen to you," Rose Vilardo said.

Joe Flap might have listened to him too — if he had made time for him. The thought brought bile into his throat.

"Are you feeling all right?" Vince Vilardo asked. "You sort of dropped off last night."

"Just thinking about Joe."

"He shouldn't have been up there."

Service had thought about this all night. "Maybe, but I can't imagine a better way for an old pilot to go." Joe had been close too many times to count, but this time was his time and there it was. He also recognized that maybe he was rationalizing his own failure.

Vince got up to pour more coffee and said over his shoulder, "Grady, how many years have you got in?"

Service looked up at his friend. "Why?"

"Just asking. Rose and I are talking about packing it in."

"To become a couple of snowbirds playing bocce in Florida in winter?"

Rose laughed. "Heavens, no. We'd die without snow!"

Vince signaled for Rose to hush. "You need to plan these things, Grady. We've been talking about retiring for a while now. You have to think ahead."

Service did the mental math. Four years in the marines and two with the state police counted, plus his twenty with DNR law enforcement. "I've got twenty-six years."

Vince raised a bushy eyebrow. "You could go now. You know what they say in the department about people who stay longer than twenty-five."

He knew. Pensions were frozen in value at twenty-five years and didn't grow after that. Those who stayed were said to be addicted to the work or on power trips. He put himself in the addict category. Service grinned. "I'm still having fun."

Vince gave him a questioning look, but the Vilardos said no more about it. Service went out to his truck, called in to let Lansing know he was on duty, and called Candace McCants to ask her to meet him on the north perimeter of the Mosquito Wilderness. He caught McCants on her way out to patrol. She said she had plenty of coffee to share. Proud officers crowed that they bled green, but Service knew that most of what coursed through them was coffee.

McCants was sitting in her truck at the rendezvous point, poring over a topographical map, when he parked beside her and got inside her truck, taking his coffee mug with him. He helped himself to her thermos. "You hear about Joe?" He held out his cigarettes and she took one. They both lit up.

"Got a call last night," she said, folding the map. "You found him?"

"He fluttered over me and into the trees At first I thought I was hallucinating, but figured I'd better check. I didn't know it was Joe until I had him out of the bird."

McCants gave a sympathetic cluck. "You think we'll do a memorial at the howl?"

Howls were end-of-deer-season parties where large numbers of active and retired COs came together to relive the just-past season, drink, eat venison, and hang out.

"Dunno," Service said. "Maybe." The Lansing hierarchy didn't approve of howls and had sent down orders for years that such gatherings should end. Despite orders, COs still got together surreptitiously, only in smaller groups. Joe's memory deserved a statewide howl; Service wondered if that was even possible and decided it wasn't. Lansing would never leave the field uncovered, even for a day.

"You know about Vermillion?" he asked her.

"I've heard some things," she said. "Two homicides."

"Yah, and one of their wolves is still loose. We got four of five back, but the last one is a blue wolf and he's traveling."

McCants listened attentively.

"I ran into Limpy Allerdyce last night before the crash and he said the blue's been seen out here."

"A blue?" his colleague said. "I think they're pretty rare. How's Limpy?"

"Don't ask," he said, remembering the three dead deer in the bed of the old poacher's truck. "A wolf's a tasty target for hunters, endangered or not."

McCants nodded. "I haven't seen any sign of wolves here, Grady—blue or otherwise—but I keep thinking they'll push in here sooner or later. They'd have plenty to eat."

"Keep an eye out," he said.

"Do you miss this?" she asked.

"I spend all my time sitting on my ass in the vehicle and making phone calls. I miss the feel of dirt under my boots."

"Anytime you need to get out in the dirt, c'mon down and join me," McCants said with a grin.

"You like it?" he asked.

"I'm still trying to learn my away around. It's a *huge* chunk of territory—and it's intimidating to follow your act."

"You can handle it," he said. Service understood her awe for the area. He had been in and around the Mosquito most of his life, and just last summer had learned some things about it he had not previously known. The Mosquito was one of those places that was always surprising you. "If you hear anything about the blue, or any wolf in here, call me."

McCants was smart and flashed a wry grin. "Have you got something going down?"

"Could be," he said.

"I'll call," she said.

After McCants drove away, he called Sheriff Lee.

"I was just gonna call you," the sheriff said. "That asshole Shamper bollixed up the tape job. I thought he could handle it, but now I'm wondering. He keeps pissing and moaning about his equipment."

Service thought about his meeting with the captain. The FBI had some of the best photo technology in the country, but he couldn't bring himself to turn over the tape to Peterson and Nevelev. It occurred to him there was another way. "Freddy, can you make another copy of the tape?"

"Sure, what for?"

"I'll call you later and explain."

Their conversation done, Service grabbed Shamekia Cilyopus-Woofswshecom's business card out of the folder where he stored cards and called her office.

A woman answered, "Fogner, Qualls, Grismer and Pillis, Shamekia's office."

Service smiled. Even her secretary couldn't pronounce her last name. "This is Detective Service. Is she in?"

"One moment, Detective."

"Grady?" the former FBI agent said when she picked up.

"I was afraid you'd have a four-day weekend. I have a favor to ask."

"Managing partners don't get four-day weekends," she said.

"I've got a tape that needs to be technically enhanced, stills, clarity, the whole thing. It's a copy, not the original. I figured you might know somebody who can handle this on a very confidential basis."

"Indeed I do," she said. "What's on the tape?"

"Look at it when you get it. The key moment is 10:02 P.M. You'll understand."

"I'll take care of it. What do you want me to do when the work is done?"

"Fax the photos to Sheriff Fred Lee in Chippewa County. His card will be with the package."

"When will the tape get here?"

"I'm going to have it couriered to you today." He asked for directions and wrote them down. "Thanks, Shamekia."

"Look," she said. "On that other matter?"

"Yes?"

"I can't verify this yet, but I am beginning to get a very strong sense that the Bureau may have been involved in Minnis's sudden disappearance from England."

Service hesitated. "Gave him a new home, brought him in from the cold maybe?"

"That's a very real possibility."

Mouse Minnis had been Genova's boyfriend, and the Feebs had to know she had never been part of the Animal Freedom League. Yet they were trying to put her away for murders she didn't commit. The tape seemed to show this. What had his captain said, that perhaps Genova was tangential? It was an interesting notion.

"The Bureau's obsession with Genova continues to bug me."

"I hope to know more about that by Monday," Shamekia said.

"The tape will be there tonight," Service said.

"I'll stay in my office until it's in hand."

"Thanks, Shamekia. Say hi to Tree."

The woman laughed huskily. "I'm havin' brunch with Tree and Kalina tomorrow. You ever notice how subdued the big man is in his wife's presence?"

Service laughed out loud. The five-foot-tall Kalina ruled her six-five husband with absolute authority.

His next call went to Freddy Bear Lee. "Can you send somebody to Detroit with the new copy? I've got someone down there who can get it cleaned for us."

"I'll send Altina Lodner," said Lee.

Service gave him Shamekia's name, address, and phone number. "Put a business card with the tape. She'll wait at her office until it arrives and she'll fax stills when they're ready."

Lodner was a good choice. She was all business and wouldn't need to be told how important the delivery was. Less experienced deputies might see the trip to Detroit as a lark.

"Thanks, Freddy." He didn't tell the sheriff about Minnis and the FBI. Maybe the captain was right; sometimes you kept information to yourself that might be shared because your gut told you to hold it close. Maybe it was holier-than-thou thinking, but he had a hunch the FBI's actions were something more than simple prudence.

When he called Yogi Zambonet, the biologist seemed distracted and irritated.

"This is Service. The Vermillion blue is still loose. Is there a way to trap it and put a collar on him?"

"You might want to get over here," Zambonet said, ignoring Service's question. "We've got a real green fire ready to break out." There was palpable concern in the biologist's voice.

"Your office?"

"Yah, like posthaste."

Service checked his watch. It was just after 10 A.M. and Maridly said she would be home by dinner. He guessed he had enough time to get to Crystal Falls and back, but the idea of making the drive was a pain in the ass. Nantz would be arriving in Escanaba this evening and he wanted to be there when she came in. What the hell did the biologist mean by a green fire? More agitation by environmentalists?

Service walked into the District 3 office through the front entrance. Margie, the district's dispatcher-secretary-receptionist, was in a hushed debate with two men in flannel shirts about property lines. She waved at him and smiled as he passed.

The biologist sat on a stool in his cubicle, staring at a poster of two wolves barely visible in a snowstorm. Zambonet's office was cluttered with wolf posters and photographs, black radio collars, and several stainless-steel leghold traps.

"Where's the fire?" Service asked. Zambonet swiveled slowly around on his stool. He groaned as he got to his feet, took Service by the arm, and led him quickly past several small cubicles to where they could see the small waiting area on the Division of Environmental Quality's side of the building.

A woman in a black business suit and black pumps was talking quietly to a man in a faded brown corduroy suit. The woman's back was to them. Both had black hair. Indians, he guessed, dressed for business.

"*That's* the fire," Zambonet said. "Or the accelerant," he added.

Service watched the two visitors and when the woman turned around, he sucked in a breath.

"They're here to talk about the blue wolf," Zambonet said. "They want to know what plan we have to protect it."

Service wasn't listening to the biologist. His eyes were still on the woman in the black suit. "What did you tell them?" he asked, the biologist's words barely registering.

"Shit-all, so far. I'm glad you're here."

"Let's talk to them," Service said, stepping into a small conference room.

The biologist fetched the guests.

Service stood when they walked in. The woman's dark eyes were fixed on him.

Zambonet held business cards and read from them. "Ms. Natalie Namegoss and Mr. Gaylord LiBourne, this is Detective Grady Service of the Wildlife Resource Protection Unit. Would you folks like a cup of coffee? We drink a lot of it this time of year."

"Thank you, black for me," LiBourne said. "Is there a rest room handy?"

"Also black," Namegoss said.

Zambonet and LiBourne left together, and Grady Service and the woman eyed each other across the table. It had been twelve or thirteen years, Service thought. She had a streak of gray now, almost a stripe, but she was still stunning. "*Ahh-neen*, Nena."

The woman smiled. "*Ahh-neen, petcha*," she said. "You were in the news last summer."

"Seems like you're always in the news," he said, which drew a shrug and a smile.

He had met Namegoss while she was a law student at University of Oklahoma, on an internship with the American Indian Movement, and in the Upper Peninsula on a fact-finding tour to prepare a briefing on treaty rights. Her rental car had run out of gas between Munising and Marquette and he had been on his way to a predawn patrol of fishermen on an Alger County river where poachers often operated. He had taken her into Munising to a gas station, gotten her coffee and a can of gas, returned her to her vehicle, and put her back on the road.

It had not been an auspicious beginning. It was dark, well before sunrise, and she had seemed wary of getting into his vehicle. On the way back with gas and coffee she had said, "I was told *wa-bish* lawmen look down on Nish-naw-be women." *Wa-bish* was Ojibwa for "white."

"Not all *wa-bish* are racists," he said. "Just as all *Nish-naw-be* are not racists."

"You speak the language?"

"Just a few words. I can barely speak English."

She let go of a nervous, but pleased chuckle. "Woods cop," she said. "Game warden."

"Woods cop works for me."

Before getting her back on the road, he had given her one of his business cards. "If you have more problems, call me."

He never expected to see her again.

Two days later his sergeant had called to tell him a complaint had been lodged against him. "What kind of complaint?"

"Chippewa woman," his sergeant whispered. "Said you were anti-social."

Service knew who it was. "Did she call in?"

"She's standing right here," the sergeant said.

"Give her the phone."

Service didn't wait for her to talk. "I don't know what your problem is, miss, but I don't appreciate bullshit calls. I stopped in the middle of the night, got you gas, coffee, and put you back on the road. What's your problem?"

"My name is Natalie Namegoss and you didn't even ask me my name, Officer," she said.

"I didn't need your name."

"Oh, but you do, Officer. I didn't thank you properly that night."

His anger ebbed, her tone of voice puzzling. "You don't need to thank me."

"Oh, but I do. I was remiss. I would like to take you to dinner—as a thank-you."

Service had stared at the phone. "I'm working nights."

"How about lunch? You do eat lunch?"

"Yes."

"Yes you accept or yes you eat lunch?"

"Both," he said.

"You aren't a conversationalist, are you?"

"When I have reason to be."

She laughed teasingly. "Well, I will just have to find a good reason for you to talk, won't I? Lunch tomorrow. Where's good for you?"

He had to see the county prosecutor in Marquette in the morning. "Marquette, Scipio's Pizza. Noon?"

"Noon is fine. Do we need reservations?" she asked.

"For pizza?" It was his turn to laugh.

"Good, noon it is, Officer Service."

His sergeant came back on the phone. "What the hell was that all about?"

"Beats hell out of me," Service said.

Two days after their lunch they were wading the Yellow Dog River south of Big Bay and he was teaching her to fly fish. He learned that she had been born in the Soo, the daughter of full-blood Chippewas, a doctor and a teacher. Her parents had moved to Columbus, Ohio, so that their only child could get a better education.

Over the next month they were nearly inseparable, both of them neglecting some of their duties in favor of more enjoyable pursuits. She tried to teach him more of the Ojibwa language and in time she became *ne-nan-ing,* meaning "five times each time," and he began to call her Nena instead of Natalie. He became *petcha* which means "lasts long." It had been a month of sheer lust with no promises implied or asked for, but she had made an impression on him. She was smart, adventurous, independent, and focused almost solely on the life ahead of her. The last thing he had read about her placed her with the American Indian Movement, living in Denver.

Now her card said INDIGENOUS PEOPLES' RED-GREEN CIRCLE.

"What's this?" he asked, pointing to the symbol on her card.

"Native Americans dedicated to environmentalism. Red and green."

"How're your parents?" Service asked.

"My father retired. He was in the running for surgeon general in the first Clinton administration, but he got out-politicked. I thought he'd move into a small practice to keep active in medicine, but he hasn't. He fishes and shoots photographs. I think he's happy."

"Your mother?"

Namegoss shook her head. "She met an Athabascan lawyer from Juneau and decided to move on. He was twenty years younger. She passed away last year."

"I'm sorry," Service said.

"Live for today," Namegoss said. "We can't get yesterday back and there's no way to predict tomorrow. You still working nights?"

He smiled. "Some."

"I was thinking along the lines of lunch. How's the pizza around here?"

"I thought we couldn't get yesterday back."

Namegoss gave him a look. "I'm talking about today, now."

He was more than flattered; something definitely stirred in him. Their month had been one to remember. He was relieved when he said, "I'm seeing someone."

She raised an eyebrow. "Seeing as in we saw each other, or seeing as in love?"

He didn't answer.

Namegoss raised her eyebrow again and let forth a soft whistle. "I'd like to meet *that* woman."

Zambonet came back with coffee with LiBourne trailing close behind him.

Namegoss was first to speak. "We're aware that a blue wolf was released from Vermillion," she began. "We're here to find out what the Michigan Department of Natural Resources plans to do to protect the animal. All wolves are sacred to our people. We believe that what happens to the wolf will happen to man and vice versa. The wolf was nearly extinct, but now it is returning. Native Americans were similarly hunted and persecuted for the purpose of extermination. By watching the wolf we can learn to live a more natural way. And to survive." Namegoss took a deep breath and her voice hardened.

"That's the philosophical spin. We're not here to make nice. The facts are these: The blue wolf was part of an American government experiment to use wolves for military surveillance. We have indisputable evidence of this and we suspect that the state is not party to such federal bullshit, so we believe we can be allies in this."

Her black eyes lasered into Zambonet, who sat impassively. Service felt the lanky biologist's leg bouncing anxiously under the conference table.

"Let's cut to the chase," Service said. "What is it that you want?"

"We want what we want for all our brothers," LiBourne said. He had a soft, almost musical voice. "We want our brother to remain free, not to be returned to captivity."

"There's no plan to recapture the wolf," Yogi said, suddenly joining in. "Now that he's out, he'll disperse as any other redundant pack animal would do."

"Disperse?" LiBourne asked.

"He'll travel around until he finds a female to mate with and then they'll start their own pack. Or he'll continue to have conflicts with existing packs. More wolves are killed by other wolves than by humans or vehicles."

LiBourne received the information passively and said, "But some of our brothers have been killed," he said politely.

Zambonet looked over at Service, who said, "Yes."

"What's being done about it?" Namegoss asked.

"It's under investigation," Service said.

"The classic federal bromide," Namegoss shot back.

"We're not feds," Service said.

"Your words are the same," she countered.

"Our blue brother would be a trophy for some," LiBourne said.

Service agreed. "The law doesn't differentiate a blue wolf from other gray wolves. The penalties are the same and the blue runs the same risks that other wolves run. The Endangered Species Act classifies them as endangered. There are stiff fines and jail time for killing or harassing."

"How many wolves have been shot?" Namegoss asked. "Not since the animals decided to return on their own, but this fall."

"Three," Zambonet said.

Service felt his neck turn hot. Three? Had Yogi held back on him? Sonuvabitch.

"The same shooter?" Namegoss said.

Service put his arm in front of the biologist. "It's under investigation."

"Yes," Namegoss said. "We've heard that Three of our brothers are dead and the blue wolf is out there, and what do you plan to do to protect him?"

How did you protect something you couldn't find? "Is there anything else?" Service asked to end the discussion and the meeting.

Namegoss and LiBourne picked up their briefcases.

LiBourne followed Zambonet out the door, but Namegoss held back.

"*Petcha* is a fine quality in sex," she said, "but not in finding a killer."

"Sometimes it takes sheer endurance to get to any destination. It's under investigation," he repeated.

"You would make a fine politician," Namegoss said with an admiring smile. "You are skilled in the art of saying something that is nothing." She put another of her business cards on the table. "We're at the Verdigris Inn in Iron River. The invitation to lunch stands."

"Lunch?" he said.

"Lunch," she repeated in a monotone.

Their visitors gone, Service launched into the biologist.

"You *asshole! Three* wolves. It's not enough we've got Sheena Grinda playing Lone Ranger. *Three?* Jesus Christ."

"Calm down, for Pete's sake, *chill!* The third one was found last night. Just before you walked in I got a call from Gus Turnage in Houghton."

"Gus found it?"

"He said some Finn named Wetelainen found it."

Service nodded and changed tone. "Yalmer Wetelainen, the Shark. He found it near the Firesteel River."

Zambonet looked confused. "I thought you didn't know. Thirty seconds ago you were ready to rip off my head."

Wetelainen managed the Yooper Court Motel, two miles from the campus of Michigan Tech in Houghton, and worked only to pay for his hunting and fly-fishing obsessions. He was forty, bald, thin, short, and partial to beer, especially his homemade brew, which he made and consumed in copious quantities, mostly because it was cheap. Despite drinking beer and straight vodka in alarming amounts, Wetelainen never showed a single symptom of inebriation. And despite eating and drinking like a pig, he never gained weight. Service and Gus had decided their friend's unique metabolism fit no known human physiological profile and because of this, they had named him Shark.

"Shark is a friend. He has a camp on the Firesteel. Last summer he showed me a female and four pups in that area. Is the dead one a female?"

The biologist shook his head. "Gus is bringing the body down for necropsy. It's a male."

Service felt relieved. Since seeing the wolves last summer he had thought often of them and hoped the day would come when wolves would settle in the Mosquito.

"Last night?" he asked Zambonet. He had talked to Carmody last night, and the undercover had said nothing about another wolf. What did this mean?

Gus arrived an hour after the Red-Green Circle people departed, dragging the carcass in a black plastic garbage bag and hoisting it up to a table with a stainless-steel top. The animal had dark fur, nearly black, which the office's fluorescent lighting turned a dark blue.

"Where's the head, Gus?" Service asked.

"This is all we found," Turnage said.

Service and Turnage talked while Zambonet measured the body. Service helped him load it on the scale for weighing.

"Have you seen Wink Rector?" Service asked.

Gus said, "Yah sure, he's around town all the time nowadays."

Which could offer a rational explanation for his not being part of the Soo team.

"BATF there?"

"Yah sure. They'll be gathering evidence for months."

BATF was visible in Houghton, but not at Vermillion. Why?

Yogi estimated the animal's age at three years. The carcass minus the head weighed seventy-one pounds. "Nice big fella," the biologist said sadly.

"He looks blue," Service said.

"Trick of the lighting in here. This fella's pure black. Not common, but not rare like a blue. You see a blue in the bush and you'll understand what I mean. It's not something you'll soon forget."

"What blue?" Gus asked.

Service quickly briefed him on the events at Vermillion, the escaped blue wolf, and the two previous wolf shootings.

"I heard something about Grinda's wolf," Gus said. He dropped a black plastic garbage bag on the table and opened it. Inside was a shirt that looked like a CO's uniform top.

"What the hell is this?" Service asked. "You gonna do your laundry while you're here?"

"The animal had been gutted, and this shirt was hanging on the carcass. That happen with the other two?" Turnage asked.

Service gave him a look. "No. It looks like this one is an even more direct message to us."

Turnage said with a grunt, "Like a six-foot-long middle finger standin' straight up."

"You recover brass?" Service asked.

Turnage took out a small, clear evidence bag and placed it on the table. "This was at the shooter's perch, stuck on a stick. I brushed it for prints, but it's clean."

Service saw Wolf Daddy look over at him and cringe. Every wolf kill was a stab at the biologist's passion.

"I wish I had known about Grinda's wolf earlier," Service said.

Turnage shrugged and said deadpan, "What can I say, we working wardens don't like talking to you paper-pushing pukes."

The biologist grinned at the put-down and Service bristled momentarily, but his mind was too engaged in the wolf situation to take real umbrage.

"Can I ask a theoretical question?" he asked Zambonet.

"Uh-oh," Turnage muttered as an aside.

"Ask," the biologist said, raising an eyebrow.

"Theoretically you could capture a wolf to put a collar on it."

"That's not theoretical. We do it all the time," Zambonet said seriously.

"I mean a specific wolf."

Zambonet paused before answering. "Theoretically, if you have the manpower, the know-how, and some luck. You have to identify the animal and its travel routes and habits, then put down a heap of traps and check them once or twice a day to make sure the animal isn't injured when the traps are sprung. When a wolf learns about traps he's usually too damn smart to fall for it again. We think the older ones teach the younger ones, so when you have a pack, you usually have some knowledge and wariness of traps being passed along. The challenge is to trick the target animal into stepping in a sixteen-square-inch space inside a territory that can be up to one hundred square miles."

"Granted it's a challenge," Service said, "but you still manage to trap and collar them."

"We do."

"What about the blue wolf?"

"You mean trap and collar him? You gotta be smokin' wacky weed."

"We're having a theoretical discussion here," Service reminded him.

Zambonet issued a sort of gasp of exasperation. "*Theoretically*, sure. The first order of business is to identify where he is. Next we send out our trackers to narrow it down. Then we put out the traps, bait them, and stand by."

"The blue is in the Mosquito," Service announced.

Zambonet jerked his head around to stare at the detective. "Says who?"

"Limpy Allerdyce."

"Jesus Christ," Zambonet said. "That asshole!" Everybody in the DNR knew Allerdyce.

"Who better to know where animals are?" Service countered.

"Allerdyce tells you there're wolves in the Mosquito so you get sucked over there and he goes elsewhere," Zambonet argued.

"Limpy won't shoot wolves, and if he says the blue wolf is in the Mosquito, then that's where the blue is." Service hoped. He was thinking out loud, trying to work something out and not entirely clear on what he was looking for.

Zambonet flashed a skeptical look.

Gus Turnage said, "If Limpy told Grady this, I'd tend to believe him. He didn't get to be what he is without knowing his business."

The biologist shot back, "It also seems to me that his business includes misleading you people."

Service didn't tell them that he and Allerdyce had a sort of understanding. Service had learned that Allerdyce had been one of his father's informants and that because of this, Allerdyce never poached in the Mosquito. Now they had a similar relationship, or at least a start at one.

"What I don't understand," Service said, "is why the blue would head down there. If he's looking for a mate, there are no wolves in the Mosquito."

"Sure there is," Zambonet said. "I trapped and collared one there in September."

"In the Mosquito?"

"It was in the northeast quadrant by Mosquito River headwaters," the biologist said.

Service said, "McCants should have been informed."

"Listen," Zambonet said, "a few years back we had a handful of wolves. Now I've got at least sixty packs and dispersers are moving and setting up house all over the place. I can't be telling every bloody grayshirt when a wolf pops up somewhere."

Service disagreed, but this wasn't the time to argue the point.

"This is the first wolf in the tract?"

"First I've confirmed," Zambonet said. "Three-year-old female."

"Already collared, right?"

"I said that."

"Why's it taken so long for the wolves to move into the Mosquito? Is there something wrong with the habitat?"

"No way, it's great, lots of deer and beaver. It's like a chow line, but it's also a bituva scoot inland from the main migration corridors over from Wisconsin and Minnesota. We know so little about wolves. Fifty years ago when they were last in the Yoop they were north of Channing in the Floodwood Lakes district. In those days that's where the largest deer concentration was. Forty years after they disappeared from the U.P. the first wolves came straight back to Floodwood and their pups dispersed from there. We don't know how they knew to go back there. Maybe there's some sort of genetic memory chip at work, but the point is, they didn't spread all over the place. They went to the place that used to have the most prey animals and settled there first, then spread out. The people who came over the Aleutian land bridge didn't all run right down to San Francisco or Topeka, eh? It takes time for men and animals to spread out, but now that she's there she's got cherry territory."

"Why would the blue be there?" Service asked.

"Pussy," Zambonet and Turnage said simultaneously, and all of them laughed.

Gus added, "You're so tight with Maridly now you don't remember when you prowled around like a wolf looking for company."

"I never prowled."

"Right, and Shark don't drink too much."

"Why wouldn't he just be passing through? I mean, how easy can it be for one wolf to find another?"

"Not easy," Zambonet said, "but not as daunting as you'd think. We had a predation case in Baraga County in September, couple of sheep killed. Bobber trapped the whole pack and relocated them more than a hundred miles north into Houghton County, in the Misery Bay country. We released the six animals separately, more than ten miles apart. In twenty-four hours the pack had reunited. Wolves seem to be able to find each other when they want to." Bobber was Bobber Canot, the state's lead tracker and Zambonet's primary assistant.

"You never had any problems," Turnage quipped.

Service ignored Gus. "But he could be headed elsewhere."

"Of course. It's not like he's dialed a destination into his NavStar and followed an electronic map. He's doing what any single male would do, looking for food, shelter, and a lady, and right now, the lady is probably his primo interest."

"*Any* lady?"

"Like I said, he's just another single male. Think of the forest as a bar and mating season as last call."

"But wolves mate for life," Service said.

Zambonet grinned. "Eventually, but they only get to fuck a few days a year, so he's not gonna be choosy if a four-legged opportunity sashays into view."

"But he could be homing in on this female?"

"Could be. Probably he's smelled her and heard her. Even lone wolves howl, though we aren't sure why. But you could also be right. He may just be passing through. If you find them together, then you'll know."

"That's the only way?"

Zambonet thought for a moment. "No, if I had several reliable sightings in the area, I'd think maybe he's there for a reason."

"Several reliable sightings?"

"Reliable, meaning not from some asshole poacher."

"Let me get this straight. First you get multiple reports of sightings, and you assume he's staying in the area and that the female is the magnet. Then you set traps to capture him and attach the collar, right?"

"Theoretically," Yogi said.

"Understood," Service said. "Let's forget the theoretical. What if the wolf was declared a national security concern and the president ordered you to capture the animal. Would that change your tactics?"

Zambonet dropped an implement into a stainless-steel tray, where it clattered like a broken tuning fork. "What the fuck is going on?"

"We're having an intellectual discussion," Service said.

The biologist sneered. "This is about as intellectual as a Letterman stunt."

"Humor me," Service said.

"Dubya doesn't give a shit about wolves. He's got enough on his plate these days—even for a Texan."

"Okay, Mother Teresa."

Gus Turnage intervened. "She croaked."

Service ignored his friend. "Yogi? C'mon, talk to me."

"Okay, if the future of the world depended on it . . ."

"That's the spirit," Service said.

"If that was the case we'd start flying surveillance on the female, lay in some traps to see how her boyfriend handled them, and once we had him pinpointed running together with her, we'd take a chopper in and run him until we could pop him with a tranq dart."

Service said, "I think maybe we have a plan."

The biologist flushed. "A plan! Jesus Christ, Service. We're talking theoreticals here and pure theory is usually half bullshit. If you run a wolf hard, you can kill him. Or he can react to the tranq after that kind of pursuit. Do you want to kill the wolf in order to save him?"

Service grinned. "Nah, we already tried that in Vietnam. Let's forget the theoretical and talk reality. That wolf is loose and somebody is going to kill him, sooner or later. The best chance we have to keep this animal alive is to get a collar on him and to be able to move with him and stay close."

"The three wolf kills so far haven't been any place near the Mosquito," Yogi Zambonet reminded him. "I can't believe a Yooper would kill a wolf," he added under his breath.

"A Yooper farmer would kill one," Service said, "and there're lots of flatlanders and nonresidents in the woods right now. There is *somebody* out there hunting the animal," Service said. "Not just a wolf. *This* wolf."

Zambonet started to argue, but Gus Turnage stopped him. "Pay attention, Yogi. Grady just told us in veiled fashion that he has somebody working the case and he *knows* this wolf is being hunted."

The biologist's mouth hung open. "For real?"

"Theoretically," Service said. Good old Gus. Service added another wrinkle to the discussion. "Even if there wasn't a theoretical targeting of the animal, what happens if our visitors today get pissed and run to the media and start blabbing about a rare blue wolf running around the woods in the U.P.?"

"I'd hate to think," Zambonet said with a shudder.

"Exactly, we can't allow that to happen. We need to find a way to appease those folks so that we can do what we have to do. Let's get practical about this. You start organizing what we need, and I want Shark Wetelainen brought in."

"I don't know him," Zambonet complained.

"*We* do and you will," Service said with a glance at Turnage.

"I'm supposed to drop everything and get ready for this . . . stunt. What are you going to do?" the biologist asked.

"I'm going to *do* lunch," Service said, thinking the last time he had a lunch with Natalie Namegoss it had turned out to be a lot more.

"Lunch?" Gus said.

"Yah, I'm gonna play *Let's Make a Deal*." Or some form of *Survivor*.

Natalie Namegoss sat across from Grady Service, scanning the dining room, which was painted a blinding white. "Petto's Pine Box?" she said. "It's a bit sterile."

"It used to have a different function. Up here businesses tank but buildings live on." Like the aftermath of a neutron bomb, he thought.

A waitress came for their drink orders. Service asked for coffee and Namegoss studied him. "Coffee, just like last time," she said. "You were on duty that day, too. A glass of Merlot for me." she told the waitress.

When the waitress left them, Service said, "This is business."

"I'm glad you came, Grady" she said. "It really *is* good to see you. I just wish the circumstances were different."

"*Nin babi-miwi-da-di-min,*" he said, struggling with the language he had studied intermittently since his childhood. Not sure of his skills, he translated to English, "We have patience with each other."

"There was a time," she said, her eyes locked on him.

"*Pag-a-man-i-mad,*" he said. "A strong wind is coming up."

"*Nin jog-an-as-tum,* you can use English," she said. "I'm duly impressed. Am I the strong wind?"

"You might be," Service said. "I won't even ask how you know about the wolf shootings or what was going on at Vermillion."

"Ve haff owa zawzes," she said in a mock German accent.

"The blue wolf is a problem," he said.

Namegoss cocked her head. "And?"

"I think we want the same thing, but we aren't going to get it if we don't work together."

"Handsome *wa-bish* extends the olive branch," she said. "Or is it the Trojan horse?"

"An olive branch is better than finding another wolf carcass," he replied sharply. "Zambonet tried to explain today that focusing on a single wolf is difficult, but we think we have an opportunity."

Namegoss listened attentively as he talked about the Mosquito Wilderness, the female wolf, the sightings of the blue wolf, and what the DNR proposed to do to catch, collar, and follow the animal.

"And with all this," he concluded, "we still may fail."

"That would be tragic," she said. "What do you want from us?"

"We'll keep you tuned in all along the way, but you can't go to the media. If word of the wolf gets out, we'll have a lot of crazies out there looking to take a shot."

Namegoss nodded solemnly but said nothing as she processed what she had heard. "Is your investigation of the shootings focused on an individual?"

"Yes," he said.

After another pregnant pause, she nodded and said, "All right. We keep quiet while you try to collar the wolf, but there's one condition."

Service felt himself tensing and he fought to control it. "What?"

"We want to be part of the effort. With one of our people."

"Who?"

"DaWayne Kota," she said.

"DaWayne?" Had Kota called in the heavy artillery? "I didn't know he was political."

"He's not," she said. "He's a fine tracker."

Service nodded.

"And," she added with a self-deprecating laugh, "he's my cousin, several times removed. I won't try to talk you through the genealogy because I'm not sure I understand it myself."

"DaWayne will be welcome," he said. "Is that it?"

She cocked her head again. "No, now let's have lunch and talk about what, as you put it—comes next."

He looked her in the eye. "I'm sorry, Natalie, but no lunch for me. If we're going to do this thing, we have to get after it now. Try the D.C. pizza," he added.

"As in Washington, D.C.?"

"As in Death Certificate. This place was a funeral home for forty years."

Namegoss made a face and began laughing. When he pushed back from the table, she looked up at him and said, "You really must introduce me to your woman sometime."

Outside, he lit a cigarette with a shaking hand and sucked the smoke deep into his lungs.

He called the house in Gladstone from his cell phone in the truck and got his own voice on the answering machine. She wasn't home yet.

He left a message: "Hey you," he said. "I'm sorry I couldn't be at the airport but I wanted you to know that I wouldn't trade you—"

Suddenly Nantz's voice cut in. "In a *minute*, Newf!" she said with her mischievous laugh. "Service, you romantic dog. You trying to get in my wears? Why don't you save the schmooze for face-time. *Bundolo, Kreegah!*" she shouted into the phone.

"What the hell is that?"

"I don't have a clue, but Tarzan used to say it all the time in the comics."

"You aren't supposed to be back until dinnertime," he said.

"I know. Tuck pushed it up and I was game. I couldn't wait to get back. Whoa," she said. "Am I hearing a man complain because his woman is *early?*"

"I just wanted to be there to meet you. I'll be there as quick as I can."

"I'll try not to start without you," she said with a lecherous laugh and hung up.

He was about to pull away from the restaurant when he saw DaWayne Kota ambling toward him. Service rolled down the window. "*Ahh-neen*, DaWayne, coincidental presence?'

"*Bojo*, Twinkie Man. Did you talk to Natalie?"

"You're in," Service said with a nod. "You got wheels?"

The Bay Mills game warden nodded, but Service said, "Leave them here and jump in. We're going back to the district office. I'll fill you in on what we're putting together."

Ten minutes from the office, the taciturn Kota said, "You want to see a picture?"

He handed a snapshot to Service. It was in color, taken in low light, probably just before sunset. The wolf in it was not just blue, but a shimmering electric blue.

"Where is this?"

"North of the Mosquito, three days ago," Kota said. "He's been followed since he left the compound."

"By whom?"

"Who do you think invented the concept of networking?" Kota said, obviously pleased with himself.

Service grinned and speeded up.

"One thing," Service said as he turned into the DNR District 3 office parking lot. "If you're in, you're all the way in. No freelancing. We agree on a plan and then we all stick with it. The time to disagree is before we make a decision. After it's made, that's it. Do I make myself clear?" Not so long ago Cassie Nevelev had given a similar speech to another team. The irony soured his stomach.

"Who makes these decisions?" Kota asked.

"I do," Service said. Limpy reported the blue in the Mosquito. Carmody indicated that Wealthy Johns believed it was headed for the same area. And now Kota had a photo. That should be enough to convince Yogi.

"Whatever you say, *petcha*."

Service looked over at Kota and found him grinning.

"Helluva network," Service mumbled.

Kota smirked and stared straight ahead.

· 28 ·

Gus Turnage was helping to inventory gear in Zambonet's office. Black patent-leather radio collars were side by side on a table next to a black six-foot-long metal poke-stick with an opaque syringe attached to the tip. A pale blue Tupperware cup held several red plastic ear tags. The biologist's field drug kit was in a marked bag on the floor and Yogi Zambonet was putting ice packs into it.

Service introduced Kota to the two men, who nodded and shook hands.

"Where do we go?" Turnage asked.

"I'll call you on that," Service said. He knew he was being less than forthcoming, the captain's words about selective disclosure echoing in his ears. "Just be ready," he told them. He put the photographs on the table and said, "Near the Mosquito, three days ago."

Zambonet said, "Bobber's on the way." Service was relieved. He admired Canot's skills, and they needed an expert on wolves. His own skills were adequate for most things, but his real strength was in tracking his own species.

"Gus, can you call Shark and get him down here?"

"No prob," his friend said. "He'll come a-running. It'll beat heck outta tying flies while the Techineers from the college screw themselves senseless at the motel."

"I don't like this," Zambonet said with muted petulance.

Service said wearily, "Just get the gear and team together and be ready to move."

"Can I put a flying ear up to find the female? If the blue's wooing the lady, finding her will lead us to him."

"Do whatever it takes," Service said. "I'll get back to you." He didn't want to answer a lot of questions. He had a difficult drive ahead of him, and the sooner he got that done with the sooner he could get home to Nantz.

"When?" Zambonet asked.

"When I get back to you," Service snapped. He couldn't blame Yogi for being prickly. Wolf Daddy was used to running his own show. But this was about dead wolves, not live ones, and at least for now that shifted responsibility to law enforcement.

During his drive he called Gus Turnage. "Did you put out the word on the CO shirt you found with the wolf?"

"Yep," Gus said. "Know where we're going yet?"

"Soon." Service wished he could be more specific, but he needed to talk to Limpy Allerdyce. This left him questioning his sanity as he drove along, wondering how the third wolf shot with the fifty fit in. If Carmody was with the woman and hadn't mentioned it, did that mean her roommate Skelton Gitter was part of the deal too? This was something to think about, and he had the time.

The poacher's camp was a difficult seventy miles away, most of it on roads with dented signs that announced SEASONAL ROAD: NOT PLOWED IN WINTER. For once he was glad winter had not yet arrived.

Allerdyce and his clan lived in a ramshackle compound in southwestern Marquette County, which was the largest county east of the Mississippi River and bigger than the state of Rhode Island. The camp was built on a narrow peninsula between North and South Beaverkill Lakes, a long way from civilization. The site had been carefully selected, and was the sort of place you were unlikely to stumble across unless you were another poacher, which would be a serious mistake. With water on two sides and swamps on both ends, it was difficult to get to. There was a two-track from a U.S. Forest Service road down to the compound's parking area, and then a half-mile walk along a twisting trail under a conifer canopy to the camp. The surrounding area was thick with cedars, hemlocks, and tamaracks. In terms of isolation, it was a fortress. And there was no way to call ahead because Limpy didn't believe in telephones. He had no choice but to make his way to the camp and march in, the reality of which gave him a sharp chill.

It was after dark and he had lost an hour to the time-zone change, which lay just west of Marquette County, putting the western U.P. in the central time zone and the rest of the Yoop in the eastern zone. He parked the truck, quietly closed the door and locked it, taking his handheld radio and Mag-Lite with him. The light took the place of a baton, which always felt to him like a riding crop, making it a prop, not a weapon or a tool. About halfway to the camp Service heard several rifle shots from a small-caliber rifle, a .222 or a .223. The timing of the shots suggested somebody plinking at targets in the dark. It was against the law to shoot after dark during deer season, but this was Limpy's camp and Allerdyce, the lifelong outlaw, had been an effective poacher because he had rules for the clan. He would not tolerate poor shooting by his people. Multiple shots meant wasted ammo and an increased chance of detection by patrolling COs. Limpy's people were expected to make one round count. And if most poaching was done at night, that's when practice needed to be done. Service doubted there was much game left in the immediate vicinity of the camp. Limpy and his people poached for both cash and sustenance, pretty much killing everything they encountered.

Service sucked in a deep breath and moved on toward the camp. He was pretty sure that he could trust Limpy would talk to him but how the rest of his people would welcome him was a separate issue. It seemed unlikely that the old man had admitted to them that he was cooperating with law enforcement.

The camp was dark and locked abandoned, but Service sniffed a faint hint of smoke lingering in the crisp air. No one could remember a deer season like this: It had been in the low sixties the entire first week, and now on the ninth day of the season the air finally seemed to be cooling back toward normal.

Service went to the cabin where he had seen Limpy last summer. Somewhere behind him he heard someone quietly rack a round into the chamber of a shotgun.

"Youse lookin' for Limpy?" a familiar female voice asked from the cabin's porch. Honeypat was the widow of Limpy's late son Jerry, but long before being widowed she'd been consorting with her father-in-law and countless others. It had been her dalliance with Limpy that allowed Service to arrest the poacher and send him to prison for seven years. The old man had been released from Jacktown last summer, and Honeypat had immediately taken up with him again. It was tough to differentiate between habits and addictions.

"He sure ain't here for pussy." Limpy Allerdyce squawked with his irritating cackle from the darkness. Service heard Limpy smack the woman's behind. Honeypat laughed out loud and an unusually jovial Allerdyce said, "How ya doin', Sonny? Youse come about da wolf, didjas? Would youse break bread wit us or take a sip? Honeypat brewed up some dandy cider."

"Cider's good."

A door cracked open, but little light escaped. "Watch da steps," Allerdyce cautioned and Service stepped gingerly, crossing the porch into the dim light ahead. The door closed quietly behind him and a wooden match sparked, emitting a puff of sulfur; a kerosene lantern rattled in the dark, and a familiar hiss began to push dim yellow light across the room. Service smelled wood smoke, kerosene, meat cooking, earthy mold, stale sweat, other scents, not identifiable.

Limpy sat in a creaky rocking chair, motioning for Service to sit across from him in an upholstered chair darkened with stains, the batting protruding like hairs from the ears of an old man. Honeypat rattled dishes and cups off somewhere in the dark. He was startled when her hand suddenly thrust a cup into the light in front of him. The cider smelled of apples, nutmeg, mint, and orange. She moved to Limpy's side and stood in the light, fully dressed. Service was taken by surprise. Over the years he had rarely seen Honeypat dressed; he had seen her in the buff so many times that she seemed most natural that way. In the dim light Service thought she looked younger and less haggard than the last time he had seen her. More likely it was a trick of the lighting.

"Looks good, don't she?" Limpy said. "Just her and me now, eh gal?"

Honeypat beamed a proud smile at Service that left him feeling queasy. The idea of Honeypat and Limpy settling down as a couple was unimaginable.

Service said, "The wolf."

"Yah, over to da Skeeto."

"You've seen it?"

"Onna my grandkittles seen it," Limpy said.

Grandkittles? Allerdyce had his own language.

"Which one was it seen it?" Limpy asked, rolling his eyes up at Honeypat.

"Aldo," she said, "Corona's youngest pup."

Service had no idea who Corona was, much less Aldo. He thought about the word *pup*, a member of Limpy's pack. The term fit, the clan operating like a pack, killing together, preying on the weaknesses of law enforcement, which didn't have enough people to cover all the possible areas, each pack member aggressively protecting the others. The clan numbered in the hundreds and grew continuously. One raid some years back had netted seventy people, and that time Limpy had said that half the clan wasn't there. If there were a Fortune 500 for poaching operations, Limpy's clan would be in the top ten and a Standard & Poachers blue chip at that. What they did was wrong, but they did it well, and Service grudgingly appreciated their skill.

"Aldo," Limpy repeated. "Dat lil shit's gonna be a good un, mebbe. Got da nose of fox."

"And fucks like a snowshoe buck," Honeypat said with a leer and raised eyebrow. "Like his granpa," she added.

Service had no interest in a catalog of clan traits. "What was he doing in the Mosquito?"

"Not whachouse think, eh?" Limpy said firmly. "You know my kin don't work da Skeeto. But Aldo, he likes da look-sees. Been fuckin' an Ojib from L'Anse and dat Injun pussy got his head all fulled up with wolf talk and Injun bullshit."

"Aldo saw the blue?"

"Been followin' it."

"Is he here?"

"He's in the Skeeto wit da wolf and da squaw," Honeypat said.

"Why's he tracking the blue?"

Limpy said, "Heard him mebbe some likker-talk mebbe a flat-lander wants to pop da blue. Aldo ain't gonna be lettin' dat happen, mebbe."

There was pride in Limpy's voice. "I don't work da Skeeto and if I don't, my people don't. Dat was da deal wit yer ole man, Sonny. Now it's da deal wit you. Limpy gives da word, he keeps it. Limpy makes da law, his people keep it doncha know."

One for all and all for one, Service thought. "We're going to trap the blue, put a radio collar on him," Service said, not sure he could finish what he had to say with Honeypat standing here.

Allerdyce squinted at him. "Ole Honeypat knows da deal. Dey all know, eh? We got no secrets in da bed or da clan." Limpy rubbed her left thigh. "Say what it is you want."

Service sipped the cider. Did Limpy mean there were no secrets in his bed with Honeypat or in all the beds he shared? This was not the Limpy he knew, and his suspicions were immediately aroused. Lifelong violets didn't change. The cider was sweet and loaded with alcohol. "I'd like your help."

"You want an old man out dere wit youse young bucks?"

"He ain't old," Honeypat said in quick defense of her man.

Limpy grinned up at her and cackled. "Not in dat way I ain't." He looked over at Service. "When we hunt?"

"The blue's following a collared female. We're putting an airplane up to find her."

"Da blue's up tord da nort Fish Creek Section," Limpy said. "If Mr. Blue wants pussy, she'll be up dere too. Dat's da way it is, eh. Womans can get herselves some worked up over a male wit da wants. Gets 'em goin' it does."

Allerdyce was a Freudian: All life reduced to sex. "Aldo is at Fish Creek?"

"I'd say," Limpy said.

"Meet me there, tomorrow at noon."

"You want Aldo?" the old poacher asked. "Da boy's odd and don't much like peoples. Just squaws. But he'd be a help."

In for a dime, Service thought. "Bring him."

"Don't nobody bring Aldo. He'll see and hear and he'll come in. Or he won't," the poacher said with a chuckle. "It's da Allerdyce blood."

Service couldn't wait to escape the stinking confines of the poacher's cabin. "I've got to get to Gladstone tonight."

Limpy winked at Honeypat. "Sonny-boy's pussy come home taday."

Honeypat smiled lasciviously, and Service wondered how Limpy knew. The old man was always knocking Service off balance.

"You better get," Honeypat said. "Man's gotta take care of business."

An allusion to her marriage to Jerry who had strayed far and often? Never mind that she did, too.

"You heard 'er," Limpy said. "Ole Honeypat knows."

Allerdyce led him to the front porch. "Use your light goin' out. Everybody knows youse here, eh."

The two men stepped outside. The camp was still dark with no sign of life, and the temperature was plummeting.

Limpy sniffed the air. "Snow," he said. "Big blow. She'll be crawling in 'boot mornin', goin' like da wildcat by sundown."

Service didn't question the poacher's meteorological forecast. Pain in his shoulder and joints was broadcasting the same forecast. The season's first Alberta clipper was sailing in on the jet stream.

Small ice pellets were spitting halfheartedly as he pulled up the long driveway to the house. Muted lights were on inside. Service opened the unlocked front door and expected Newf to be all over him, but she did not come. He made his way down the hall to the kitchen. There were candles in the kitchen and fresh flowers in a vase. Another bouquet in green tissue was on the counter. There were snipped stem tips in the sink. Nantz's bags were on the floor in the kitchen, abandoned there. A bottle of champagne was in an ice bucket on the counter. He used a towel to pop the cork, filled two flutes and walked into the living room. The red power light was illuminated on the stereo, but there was no music. Nantz always had her tunes on.

He saw her curled up on the couch in the den, a blanket half on her. Newf was at the end of the couch and looked up at him, her heavy tail thumping twice. Cat was perched on Maridly's hip, sound asleep.

He fumbled with the sound and smiled when he heard the voice of Peggy Lee singing "Waiting for the Train to Come In."

Nantz stirred on the couch, smacking her lips with sleep.

He sat on the floor and massaged her neck.

"I'm sorry, honey," she whispered. "I ran out of gas. What time is it?"

His answer was a kiss. When she tried to loop an arm around his neck her cast whacked him in the side of the head.

"I'm sorry," she said.

He carried her upstairs, pulled back the covers, gently lowered her to the bed, and covered her.

He showered, dried himself quickly, and slid under the covers beside her.

She was snoring lightly. He pressed his body against hers and her hand came back to his hip and squeezed lovingly. He kissed her on the neck and settled his head on the pillow to sleep, feeling whole for the first time in a long time.

The phone rang at 4 A.M. It was Yogi Zambonet. Not wanting to disturb Maridly, Service took the phone downstairs.

"We've got a signal," the biologist said.

"Fish Creek Section?"

"How the hell did you know *that?*" the surprised biologist asked.

"It's my job. How's the weather?"

"Turning sucky and the forecasts aren't good. We may not have air cover if the storm settles in."

"Let's get everybody out to the area, meet at noon."

"We're bringing shelters," Zambonet said. "We may be out there for a while."

"See you there." Service went out to the garage, got his minus-twenty mummy bag, camp pack, and showshoes, and packed everything in the backseat of his truck. It took thirty minutes to load his four-wheeler into the bed of the truck and get his snowmobile trailer hooked up. The snow was still only in the spit phase, but farther north it would be heavier. Probably the four-wheeler would handle it, but if the storm turned serious, he would need the sled.

When he got back into the kitchen he found a groggy Nantz with her eyes half closed.

She took his hand and led him to the couch. He tried to hold back and be gentle, but she kept urging him on. When they were done she grinned and said, "See, I won't break. I've got aches, but that won't stop our loving. Understand, Detective?"

He made Basque omelets and enough coffee to fill two large thermoses.

"What were you doing in the garage?" Nantz asked.

"We're going to try to collar a wolf," he said. He told her the story of the blue wolf, the three dead wolves and the fifty, the suspicious behaviors of the feds, the meeting with Namegoss and LiBourne, his two meetings with Limpy, what the collaring entailed and why it was necessary. When he told her about the undercover operation, he omitted Carmody's name, but she shuddered visibly. He didn't plan to tell her about his past with Natalie Namegoss but the phrase *selective disclosure* popped into his mind and he thought, not with Nantz.

He said, "Natalie Namegoss?" Nantz looked at him. "We had a thing a long time ago."

"A thing?"

He nodded.

"As good as us?"

"No."

Nantz hugged his arm and grinned. "Thank you for telling me, but your past is yours, Grady. There's no need for secrets. Whatever we did before helped make us into who we are now. I don't freak out over that stuff, okay?"

Which made her the first woman he'd ever known to adopt such an attitude.

"Even Kira?"

She flashed a mock frown. "That's different. We overlapped and she still has designs on you." She broke into a smile to let him know she was kidding. "I want to go with you," she added.

"Go?"

"To help trap the blue wolf."

"I don't think that's a good idea. You're on medical leave."

"I'm going," she said firmly. "You guys take ride-alongs all the time, and you have VCOs. I can do that. Hell, I've *done* it."

"You didn't have a broken arm and a pin in your collarbone last summer." He was tempted to talk about her return to the academy, but decided this was the wrong time.

Out of the blue she said, "I had a long talk with the chief. He wants me back in the academy, but in the fall class. The pin in my arm might not come out for six weeks, maybe longer. The collarbone pin comes out in two weeks. I didn't like what the chief proposed, but he talked straight to me, Grady, and I said okay. I didn't want to, but he was making sense. That means you're stuck with me until fall!"

"Great," he said, in part because the chief had talked to her. "But you can't come with me. You've got a cast, pins, bruises."

"I can do this, Grady." Her tone told him she had made up her mind and once set, she was not likely to back off. The snow was getting heavy, and her cast was a problem, but if she was game, he thought he could help her manage it.

"Let's get you packed." Like him, she had all the necessary gear and kept it organized.

She threw her good arm around his neck and kissed him hard. He wasn't sure if it was her cast banging his head earlier or this particular kiss that left him seeing little specks of colored light.

Service and Nantz reached the meeting site before the others and drank coffee while they waited. There was already three inches of fresh snow on the ground and more falling in large wet flakes. "Good thing we have the sled," she said.

"You won't be doing much riding on the sled in your condition. After a few years of winter patrols most of us have bad backs."

He noticed that she didn't argue with him.

Zambonet arrived just before noon. Shark Wetelainen and DaWayne Kota were in a second truck with Gus Turnage. Bobber Canot drove a third truck. All three vehicles pulled snowmobiles and four-wheelers on trailers.

There was no sign of Limpy Allerdyce.

They met by the trucks, their breath forming clouds as they talked. The temperature was right at freezing. Zambonet shook hands with Nantz. Kota nodded. Shark and Gus hugged her and Service saw that she didn't cringe or pull away. Shark's hug was that of a bear and it had to hurt, but she betrayed no pain.

They all got cups of coffee and Zambonet took out his charts. They were sheathed in acetate and backed with stiff cardboard.

"Jesse put the wolf here late yesterday," he said, tapping the map with his grease pencil.

Service studied the map. Fulsik's position put the animal on the south edge of the Fish Creek Section, about a mile from where they were parked. Service kept glancing down the road, wondering where Allerdyce was.

"We takin' da sleds?" Shark asked.

"No," the biologist said. "We'll drive the trucks in as close as we can get and make camp. If we tranq the blue, we'll want to be close."

"The animal could have moved on by now," Service said, scanning the area for Allerdyce again.

"She'll be around here," Zambonet said. "This snow will help the wolves hunt."

"But if she's moved?"

"Jesse's gonna be upstairs in an hour or so," Zambonet said. "If he can get off the ground. Houghton's gettin' pounded by heavy lake-effect snow."

"And if he can't take off?"

"We still could get lucky,"

"If she hasn't moved," Service said.

"Right."

Nantz spoke up. "If your pilot can get out of Houghton he can land in Escanaba and operate from there. The snow down there is always lighter. There's a better chance of Delta County staying open than Houghton."

The biologist seemed to ponder what she said. "That makes sense. We have a second bird down there equipped for the mission. If Jesse has mechanical problems, he'll have a backup there. Swede Pahlberg's our contract pilot in Escanaba. I'd call him, but he took his family to Tennessee for Thanksgiving. He won't be back until Tuesday night."

Nantz nudged Service. "What about Tucker Gates?"

"I don't know him."

"He flew me back from Lansing," she said. "He's a great stick. He used to fly fires for me. I'm sure he'd do it." Her face flushed as she talked.

Zambonet studied her. "There's no time to train a new pilot."

She said, "Train me and I'll fly with him. It's just ADF and GPS, right? Direction and sound?"

"Basically," the biologist said.

"We can do that," she said brightly. "I'll call him."

Service followed her to the truck and lit a cigarette while she used the cell phone. As the number rang she held out her hand and mouthed, "Smoke." He fumbled as he handed her a cigarette and tried to light it for her. He'd never seen her smoke, so what was this about? She exhaled a ragged cloud of smoke. Obviously she had not been smoking regularly.

"Tuck? Maridly. The DNR needs a pilot to fly a wolf. How's the weather over there?" She laughed and said, "Cool. They'll walk me through procedures and I'll meet you at the airport. Let's shoot for a fifteen-thirty takeoff." She nodded several times. "I'll be there soon as." She looked at Service, holding the phone against her chest. "Can you ask Zambonet where the bird is and if he can get it serviced?"

Service left her and asked the biologist where the plane was, and who would prep it. He also told him that Nantz and Gates were looking at a 3:30 P.M. takeoff. Zambonet said the bird was at Markham's Air Service and he'd make sure it was ready, adding, "No way I can train them for a takeoff today. Besides, they fly *only* if Jesse can't get out of Houghton."

Walking back to his truck Service saw Limpy and another figure on the edge of some cedars fifty yards away. They were dressed in white camo, standing there like ghosts. Even at fifty yards Service recognized the camo suits as Pinclidotis, top-of-the-line gear from the Italian sporting goods manufacturer. It was difficult to lock on to the notion of Yooper poachers buying thousand-dollar hunting suits, but Allerdyce was not the average poacher, and he knew Limpy's army never went wanting for reliable equipment and tools. The clan might live and act like savages, but their gear was second to none. Which made him wonder who among the clan was responsible for researching such things. He made a mental note to think more about poachers and technology later.

Pushing his curiosity aside, he relayed to Nantz what Zambonet said, and she passed the word to Gates, said, 'See ya, bye," and abruptly snapped the cell phone shut.

"Yogi says he can't train you for a takeoff today. There's not enough time."

"Baloney," she said. "I have to drive back to Escanaba. He can talk to me on the cell phone while I drive. It will save time. We're gonna be on the radio when we fly, so we can get used to talking to each other. I can do this, Grady."

He didn't want to argue with her. "*Only* if Fulsik can't get out of Houghton. If Jesse gets out, he flies and you and your friend support, okay?"

"Yes dear," she said, rolling her eyes like a kid.

Service left her in the truck and walked toward Allerdyce. The boy with him was under twenty, a little over six feet, cadaverous, his face ruddy from the cold. "This here's Aldo," Limpy said. Allerdyce looked at the boy. "Tell 'im."

"The she-wolf's joined up with the blue," he said. "They're about two miles off, where Fish Creek flows into the Mosquito." The boy spoke distinctly with no hint of his clan's idiosyncratic approach to language.

"How close can we get our vehicles?" Service asked.

"Close if you're cautious," the boy said. "There are a couple of old tote roads back that way. It's pretty uneven, but you can get through. There's no water over the road."

Could this boy really be related to Limpy?

"Got da squaw along?" Limpy asked the boy.

The boy nodded toward the cedar forest to the south of them. "She's with the wolves."

"Youse hump 'er in da woods do ya?" Limpy cackled.

"Grampa," the boy said with obvious discomfort.

There might be hope for the kid, Service thought. "Let's go meet the team."

Limpy said, "Aldo will go on ahead."

The boy faded into the trees and was gone. Limpy watched him go. " 'Fraid that boy won't make it with us," he said. "Got too many pineapples. How do youse tink dat happened eh?"

Service blinked. Pineapples?

"Mebbe some stranger got into Corona back den. Dat one, he went to da high school Republic and did good. Now he's talkin' college." The old man cackled. "An Allerdyce at da college." He shook his head in disbelief.

Zambonet was already briefing Nantz. The wolf collar had a preset frequency and the plane had an antenna mounted on each wing. The idea was to keep flying the signal until it got louder, then went silent, which would mean the collared wolf was below. Something about turning off one antenna at a time and sometimes both and Service couldn't follow the biologist, but Nantz nodded attentively, asking questions. When they hit silence, she was to toggle the GPS and relay the coordinates to the ground team. There were more details, but Nantz wanted to get going, and she and the biologist arranged to talk by cell phone during her drive.

Everything was happening too fast for Service.

"The blue has joined the female," he told Zambonet.

The biologist looked over at Allerdyce and frowned. "Opinion of the resident *expert?*"

Allerdyce laughed and said to Service. "I *like* dis one."

Zambonet's expression suggested the sudden affection would remain unrequited.

"The wolfies're near where da Fish and da Mosquito gets tagedder," Limpy said. "Boot two miles over to da sowt." He pointed.

"We can drive the trucks in," Service added.

Gus and Shark had already unhooked the trailer with Service's snowmobile and were transferring his gear to Gus Turnage's truck. Nantz's face was bright red, her skin shiny.

"Maridly?" he said. She did not look well

"I'm fine," she said with an edge to her voice. "After sitting on my ass all this time, I'm glad to be useful again. I'm sorry to steal your wheels," she said.

"You fly only if Fulsik can't."

"I know."

He walked her to the truck and kissed her She handed him his cell phone and charger. "I've got my own," she said. "You'll need yours." He watched her drive away, the truck fishtailing on the rutted road.

Bobber Canot was huddled with Allerdyce, who was using a stick to make a map in the snow. Canot was nodding, asking questions in hushed tones. They acted familiar with each other.

"Shall we put the show on the road?" Service asked.

Canot said, "Limpy's shown me the way. I'll lead and he'll ride with me."

Kota would ride with Zambonet. Shark and Gus would follow. Service would bring up the tail on his sled.

Before the convoy headed out, Service pulled Canot aside. "Do you know Allerdyce?"

"People out in the woods as much as us tend to cross paths. I don't condone what he does for a living, but Limpy knows his way around out here. That's for sure."

"Do you trust him?"

Bobber Canot grinned. "That old man always has an angle and from what I know, it somehow always reduces to money."

Always reduces to money, Service repeated silently as he wriggled into his snowmobile suit, pushed down his helmet, got his machine off the trailer, and started it up. Where was the money for Limpy in this?

As the convoy began to move he pulled down his face shield and locked it. A biologist and his tracker, a fanatic fly fisherman, an Indian game warden, a straight-arrow CO, two generations of poachers, a Chippewa woman, Nantz, a pilot he didn't know, and him. One more and they'd be the dirty dozen.

J esse Fulsik was grounded in Houghton by heavy lake-effect snow, and Nantz was being prepped by Yogi Zambonet via cell phone as she drove to Escanaba to meet Tucker Gates.

Service was antsy about her flying and listened to snippets of one side of the cell phone tutorial as he worked with the others to put up the tent and settle the camp. Shark Wetelainen, ever attuned to the weather and environment, had brought along a military-surplus wall tent, sixteen by twenty feet, and it took most of the group nearly thirty minutes just to scrape snow so that the canvas floor would be on relatively clear ground. It took another hour with all of them working together to erect the unwieldy frame and clumsy canvas shelter, staked and roped into place.

It was Limpy who pointed out the site for the tent, a suggestion that all but Service and Bobber Canot questioned, but after much discussion the group grudgingly agreed that Limpy's site was the best and set about to get it ready. The tent had a small woodstove in the corner and straight metal pipe to vent smoke. All of them but Limpy gathered dry wood and broke it or cut it into pieces to fit the stove. They started a woodpile inside the shelter while Limpy drank coffee and offered directions like a supervisor.

All the while, Yogi was on the phone with Nantz.

"Right, right," Yogi said. "There's an H-style antenna on each strut. You have a radio monitor and the GPS. You have the collar freq, right? You fly volume and sound. You want to make course corrections to keep the sound steady and loud. Keep both antennae engaged until you establish a rough location—within a quarter mile. Then shut down one antenna and listen. If you have a weak signal, bank into a turn and fly the signal to maintain volume. If the signal fades, switch the first antenna off and turn on the other one. You may end up flying a corkscrew course. The bird has a stall package to let you go low and slow. Keep altering course until you get a steady, strong signal. Then you fly the heading that keeps the signal beeping like this: *click-click-click, zip*. When you get *nada*, hit your GPS to mark the spot. That means you just passed over the animal. Got it? *Click-click-click*, silence, fix the coordinates. When you think you've got the animal pinpointed, switch on both antennae and fly directly over the animal. Same deal: *click-click-click*, silence. Hit your GPS again and relay *these* coordinates to me. These are the numbers we need down here. Usually the pilot gives us visual landmarks to mark the spot, but with this cloud cover, you're not going to be able to do that."

Zambonet paused to listen. "A couple of hundred yards, but don't worry about that. You find her and we'll take it from here. Make radio contact when you get to the area."

The biologist grinned weakly and looked at Service. "She asks good questions. I hope they can do this. It isn't easy. Usually I test my pilots by putting a collar in the woods and seeing how close they can come. Two hundred yards is what we need. If a pilot can't pass the test, they don't fly for me. With the velocity of the plane, two hundred yards is about as close as they can get from the air. We usually want a clear sky to do this, but we won't have that in our favor today. It's really, really not easy," Zambonet said, shaking his head.

Service grinned. Nantz could do it. He wondered how she was holding up. "What's the Escanaba weather?"

"Flyable, so far," the biologist said.

It was just before 4 P.M. when Service heard the single-engine Cessna 182. He heard the pitch of the engine changing sharply, almost like it was sputtering, and instinctively looked skyward into the snow. He didn't like the sound, but got Zambonet's attention and jerked a thumb upward.

Zambonet got on the radio and began trying to raise the plane. "DNR Wolf Air One, this is Wolf Ground One." He repeated the call several times.

Finally there was a garbled reply. "Wolf . . . Gr . . . Air, ov'r."

"DNR Wolf Air One, you are breaking up. We've got poor atmospherics. Go to backup freq, copy?"

Service heard the biologist's receiver click twice, a signal that the aircraft had heard the instruction.

Then Nantz's voice came through clear and strong. "Wolf Ground One, Wolf Air One is on backup freq, how do you read me?"

"Five-by-five," Yogi said. "We're gonna be out of light soon. You hearing anything up there?" To Service he said, "Not that the light we have down here is worth squat." Service studied the sky. There was a faint glow backdropping the falling snow. He could make out the silhouette of treetops, but not easily. Official sunset would be in less than twenty minutes. At ground level it was already dark.

"That's a roger, Ground One." Nantz sounded relaxed, confident, in control.

"Say altitude, Air One."

"Angels are ground plus five hundred feet," Nantz radioed.

"Careful," Zambonet said, rubbing his hands together.

"Roger that," Nantz said. "Our charts show no vertical obstacles in this area. We can drop a bit lower if you want us to."

"Negative," Zambonet said. "Negative descent, maintain current altitude. Let's play the cards we're dealt."

"Tuck thinks he can get under the clouds," Nantz said.

Zambonet's response was immediate and clipped. "Negative, negative. *Maintain* current altitude. Copy?"

"Wolf Air copies. It's a bit bumpy up here. It might be smoother lower down. Can you give us a short hold-down?" Nantz asked.

Service could hear Nantz pressing to get every edge she could. In her shoes, he'd do the same thing.

"*Maintain altitude*, transmitting now," Zambonet said, depressing a switch on the radio, and looked at Service. "ADF. Their receiver will pick up on our signal, give them a heading to us." He got back on the radio and read off the camp's coordinates from his GPS.

"Roger, Ground One, we've got you and we also have a collar signal and we are commencing runs."

Nantz sounded calm. The biologist looked at Service and raised an eyebrow in admiration. Service felt a surge of pride.

"Wolf Ground One, DNR Air One, we have aural null." Nantz read off the GPS coordinates. "She's a cool one," Zambonet said to nobody in particular. Seeing Service's puzzled expression, he added, "Aural null, no sound, cone of silence. It means they're directly over the radio collar."

Zambonet checked the chart in his lap and made a dot with his grease pencil. "I've got the position. Can you run a north–south check and then east–west? Let's get a cross-reference. Then do your two-antenna flyover."

"Roger, Air One out."

The bearded biologist took a small apple out of his coat pocket. It made a crisp popping sound when he bit into it.

Service smelled coffee brewing on the woodstove and tried to imagine Nantz in the cramped cockpit overhead. Less than half an hour later she called with a set of coordinates. The biologist made another mark on his chart and grinned. "Looks good, Air One. The plots are on top of each other. Great job. You can RTB. We'd like you back just after first light in the morning, copy?"

"We'll try," Nantz said, "but the weather in Escanaba isn't looking good for morning."

"Roger," Zambonet said. "Bump us on the cell phone if you can't get up and keep us posted on the weather."

"Roger," Nantz said. "DNR Air Wolf One is clear."

The biologist looked at Service. "She's a pilot," he said perceptively. "Radio discipline always tells."

"Do we need them in the morning?" he asked the biologist.

"Only if the animal moves tonight."

Shark Wetelainen set up a gas grill and began cooking venison steaks.

Service hated waiting around and pulled Limpy Allerdyce aside. "How far away is Aldo?"

"Not too. Why?"

"Let's go see him."

"Eats first," Limpy said.

Service watched as the poacher took small portions, sampling salt and pepper on the palm of his hand before sprinkling his meat, which he cut a piece at a time, eating one before he cut the next, acting remarkably civilized. What was it about Limpy that had made his father trust him? Or was this all a lie from Limpy? Down deep he didn't trust Allerdyce. Probably never would, he told himself as he got a steak for himself and began shoveling it down.

"Should mebbe slow down, Sonny," Limpy rasped. "Chew, not healty ta wolf down da eats."

Gus Turnage snickered, trying to stifle a laugh. Service scowled at Gus.

They were plowing through ankle-deep snow. The wind was picking up, pushing the tumbling snow sideways.

"Have you been to Aldo's camp?"

"I smell da smoke," Allerdyce said.

Service sniffed the air, but the wind prevented him from smelling anything. He had always considered himself Limpy's equal in fieldcraft, but maybe that was more ego and wishful thinking than reality. It was not a comforting thought.

Thirty minutes into the trek, Limpy began to mumble and Service craned to listen. Talking to himself? Service shone his small flashlight at the poacher and saw a thin wire curling down into his collar from an ear bud. The old bastard was using a radio.

"Not dat far now," he muttered over his shoulder.

Limpy refused to have telephones at his camp, but he was using a radio, probably one that operated on Family Radio Service frequencies. FRS had a limited range but required no FCC license to operate. More and more poachers had electronics that matched their pursuers: police scanners, vehicle radars, night-vision scopes, motion detectors, radios of all kinds. Obviously Allerdyce was keeping up with the competition, an observation that suggested the old man had not abandoned his lawbreaking ways.

Depending on brand, terrain, and weather, FRS radios had a range of two to five miles. "What's your radio range?" Service asked. The forest was thick around them.

"Don't need no radio to talk Aldo," Limpy said. Limpy might be along to help, but he wasn't going to willingly surrender professional secrets. If he wasn't talking to Aldo, then who?

The old man led them up a small hill, stopped, and urged Service to angle to the right.

"You want a light?" Service asked him.

"What for?" Limpy said with a chuckle. 'I can see good." Service didn't like the inference, but kept his mouth shut.

When they stopped walking Limpy said, "We're here."

Service saw nothing. Limpy reached forward, his hand causing something plastic to crackle. He pulled a cover aside to reveal a flickering interior light. Service ducked inside and Limpy followed.

Aldo was sitting in front of a tiny fire ringed by blackened rocks the size of softballs. Two sleeping bags were in stuff sacks along a wall. The pit had seen lots of use, and Service wondered by whom. The shelter was a shallow cave. Service looked up. What little smoke there was curled up into an opening in the rocks above them, a natural chimney. The spot was well chosen.

They were in the northern reaches of the Mosquito and he had never seen the cave before. DNR scientists and techies were forever debating the half-life of knowledge, how long it took for half of what they knew to become obsolete, and Service wondered how long it would take before he lost half of what he knew about the Mosquito.

Service squatted. Limpy's grandson looked young, relaxed, at home in his cave.

"Where's da squaw?" Limpy asked his grandson.

"With her brother and sister," Aldo said.

"We got a radio signal on the female today," Service said.

"She's not far from here," Aldo said. "The male's with her."

"You've seen them?"

"Daysi's with them."

"Injun hokum-pokum," Limpy muttered. "Buildin' casinos to fleece da white man."

"The wolves aren't afraid of her," Aldo said, ignoring his grandfather's muted complaint. He held up a black FRS radio. "She's got one of these. If they move, she'll let us know and leave signs to help us follow."

Had Limpy radioed ahead to Aldo?

"The weather's getting bad in Escanaba," Service said. "We may not have air cover in the morning."

The boy shrugged and said confidently, "Daysi can follow them."

Service said, "Your grandfather can call you on the radio when we're ready to move in. Tomorrow at first light if the snow lets up. If not, later." Aldo didn't answer, but Service saw him sneak a puzzled side glance at Limpy.

They were on their way back to the main camp. "How old is Aldo?" Service asked.

The poacher shrugged. "Eighteen mebbe. Da squaw's older, I tink. Claims she can talk to da wolves, but Injuns claim all sorts a stuff, eh?"

Back in the tent Limpy zipped his coat, lay down on the frigid canvas floor, and immediately went off to sleep, no sleeping bag, no blanket, no pillow, nothing but the clothes and boots he wore. The group stared at him like he was an animal, but Service understood. Limpy was focused on what they were doing—or what *he* was doing—and nothing else mattered. You slept when it was time to sleep, or when there was opportunity, and you ate when you needed fuel, hungry or not. Life in the bush always reduced to basics.

Service didn't tell the others about Daysi and the wolves.

The wind howled and battered the heavy canvas walls throughout the night.

They were all awake at 4 A.M., stoking the fire and readying breakfast. Nantz called Service's cell phone at 5 A.M. "Weather's marginal," she told him. "Tucker's willing to try, but we might not be able to get back in here. We've got strong winds and blowing snow. We can use Menominee as our alternate. The snow's lighter down there."

"Stay on the ground," Service said. "We have the animals located."

"Call you later, okay? I do," she added, her two-word code for she loved him.

"No flight this morning," Service told the group. "Nantz will keep us posted on the weather."

"Won't let up twenty-four hours," Allerdyce said, stretching and getting up off the floor. "Worse tonight den last night."

Zambonet grimaced. "The National Weather Service says it will start to tail off later today."

"Twenty-four hours," Allerdyce repeated. "You'll see. What's for breakfast? We got bakery?"

Service grabbed the poacher's arm. "Call Aldo, tell him it won't be this morning."

"I'll walk over dere later," Limpy said, watching Shark scramble eggs. Limpy had a radio. Why wouldn't he call his grandson?

Zambonet spent the early morning checking his equipment and talking them through what would take place once they had the wolf in a leghold trap. He took a radio collar out of a box It looked different from the ones Service had seen in the biologist's office.

"Built-in GPS," Zambonet said. "If we can get this on the male, we'll be able to track him precisely. This collar's accurate to three feet."

"You use these all the time?"

"Nope. I bought this with my own money Been saving it. This *is* a matter of national security, right?"

Service grinned. Yogi was on board.

After eggs, hash browns, and venison chops, Shark began assembling the makings of hunter's stew for lunch. The others went out to collect more wood, each coming back with his clothes caked with snow. Limpy disappeared. To Aldo's camp, Service assumed. The old reprobate was not going to admit to having a radio.

Service probed the snow with a stick, estimated nine or ten inches and still accumulating. Jesse Fulsik called in from Houghton with a weather update from there. "Clear and still," he told Zambonet. "Clear up to our asses and still snowin'." The Keweenaw had twenty inches on the ground and counting. Zambonet wanted his equipment within fifty yards of the capture site. Service knew they couldn't get a truck to Aldo's camp and decided they would have to use the snowmobiles to carry the gear. He explained the situation to Zambonet, and together they transferred equipment to two of the snow machines.

Carmody called at 3 P.M. "This has to be quick," he said, his voice barely audible. "We're in the Mosquito."

"Where in the Mosquito?"

"No clue, lad. She's gone steely-eyed and tight-lipped. I'll give you a shout."

"Another wolf was shot the other night when you called."

Carmody grunted. "Not us, lad. She had hold of a gun that night, but not the fifty."

"Is the fifty with you?"

"I can't say. She holds information tight. I'll be in touch."

If Wealthy Johns didn't shoot the third wolf, who did?

There was a lot to think about before Carmody got to the area. He wished Shamekia would call today, but knew she wouldn't.

Freddy Bear Lee called at 7 P.M. As Limpy predicted, the snow had intensified throughout the day, sagging the roof of the tent. Shark and Gus and DaWayne Kota went outside periodically to scrape it off.

"Service, Fred."

"Yah."

"I got the fax. The shooter was a woman, Grady."

The message caught him short. "SuRo?"

"Your friend got the video cleaned and it's still a bit of a blur, eh, but you can make out the face and it's definootely not Genova. I talked to your friend about an hour ago and she's running the photo through the Interpol and FBI computer databases of mug shots to see what pops up. She's also talking to somebody in London."

At least SuRo would be clear. "Have you informed Cassie Nevelev?"

"Hell no, but the feds and Feebs still have a lot to explain about why they're on Genova's ass so hard. Where you at?" Service told him. "Middle of the bloody wilderness, eh," his friend said.

The word made him smile. He remembered reading a recent Jim Harrison description of the U.P. as "undistinguished and slovenly, a wilderness by default," spared development only because there was little of value to the rest of the state. He had long admired the writer's work, but Harrison might sing a different tune if he saw the Mosquito.

"You want to see the photos?" the Chippewa County sheriff asked.

"How?"

"I'll bring 'em to youse. She's only a baby blizzard, eh?"

Service gave him directions and GPS coordinates to where he had left his trailer, and another GPS fix for the camp.

"Be there sometime tomorrow," the sheriff said.

"Bring your sled," Service said.

"I never leave home without it."

Two hours later the cell phone rang again. It was McKower. "Grady, I'm at Marquette General. The captain had a stroke this afternoon. He was shoveling snow and passed out. When he came to, he managed to call nine-one-one. I just talked to his doctor. The captain's left side is paralyzed, but this may pass. They're going to run tests, try to determine if there's permanent damage." Lis sounded deflated. "Where are you?"

"In the northern Mosquito, near Fish Creek. We're trying to put a radio collar on the blue wolf."

He imagined the gears turning in her mind. What the hell was he doing in the Mosquito? The turf now belonged to McCants. But she didn't challenge him. "They don't think he'll die," she said after the long pause. "I'll keep you informed."

"We got the video enhanced," he said, 'and a clear photo of the shooter. It's a woman."

"Genova?"

"Freddy Bear says no. FEMUNSUB at this point." FBI jargon for "female unidentified subject." "You want to see the pics? Freddy's bringing a set to me. I can have him drop a set to you along the way. Does the chief know about the cap'n?"

"I just got off the phone with him. He's going to fly up, but right now all air traffic is grounded. The storm has socked in everything north of Cadillac. He'll probably be here early tomorrow. I would like to see those pictures."

"Freddy will bring them. Tell the cap'n I'll be there as soon as I can."

"Just do your job," she said. "That's what he'll want."

He called Freddy Bear Lee on the cellular and asked him to drop a set of photos to McKower at Marquette General. Then he called Nantz.

"Hi," she said, sounding tired.

"Captain Grant had a stroke. He's in Marquette General."

"How bad?" she asked, her voice a whisper.

"Lis says he'll live, but they don't know yet if there's permanent damage."

"I'm so sorry. Is Lis with him?"

"Yes."

"I could drive up there."

"Let Lis handle it, hon."

"We're not getting shit done here," she said. "I loathe sitting on my ass, Grady. Tucker and I are sleeping in the hangar. No way are we getting airborne in the morning. The snow's letting up a bit, but the winds are still brutal and with this drifting it's going to be a battle to get the runway cleared."

"Don't take a chance," he said. "Stay on the ground until it's safe. The wolves will wait."

"Okay, babe. Bad over there?"

"It's always bad when we're in different places."

"Ooh, Service. Did I hear an unsolicited romantic, loving thought? You big old love-puppy!"

He felt a blush coming over him and changed the subject. "Genova didn't shoot those people at Vermillion."

"Well, duh," she said. "Who did?"

He didn't know, but he was determined to find out. "Talk to you later," he said.

He immediately called Candace McCants. McKower hadn't brought it up, but this *was* Candi's territory now and she deserved to know what was going on. He remembered Sheena Grinda laughing at his lecture on teamwork and shook his head. Just like his old man, the do-as-I-say, not do-as-I-do school. He felt like a jerk.

"What?" McCants answered in the wary deer-season voice that all COs developed for two weeks each year when every time you picked up the phone there could be anything on the other end.

"This is Grady. I'm in the Mosquito near Fish Creek. I've got Zambonet, Gus, Shark, Bobber Canot, DaWayne Kota, and Limpy with me."

"Allerdyce?" she said. "It sounds like Armegeddon."

"The Mosquito is yours. You want to join us?"

She laughed out loud. "I wouldn't miss this to do squat jumps on Russell Crowe. I take it you have something going down."

"Soon," he said, leaving it at that. He gave her the coordinates and promised to explain further when she arrived. Next he called Sheena Grinda.

"I thought you passed away," she said, digging him.

He cut her off. "I told you if we made a case, the best would be yours." He gave her directions and a list of equipment to bring and prepared to hang up, but her voice stopped him.

"Service?"

"What?"

"Thanks."

All the calls left him questioning everything. This job required him to keep too goddamn many people in the loop. He was separated from Maridly, who was flying hurt in bad weather with some old beau. Joe Flap was dead and the captain was on his back in the hospital. He had an explosion first assumed to be intended to release the wolves, but now looking more like a murder cover-up. He had the feds and FBI playing some kind of game that made no sense, and Natalie Namegoss and her Native American greenies threatening public pressure on the department. On top of all this, the damn blue wolf was still loose and snow was coming down by the dumpster load; last week it had been in the sixties.

Instead of settling into a funk, he suddenly felt alert and energized. Nantz had said to him one night that he was the sort of man who was born to ride a roller coaster, not a merry-go-round. She was right. But how often did roller coasters come off their tracks?

He came out of his reverie to find a grinning Limpy Allerdyce standing next to him.

"Kinda hard ta untie all da knots in da ole noggin sometimes, eh?" The old poacher handed him a cup of coffee and they went outside to have a smoke. When they got outside, Limpy took out a small flask and tipped some whiskey into Service's coffee. "Java, hooch, smokes, whatever it takes in our line of work, eh?"

Our line of work indeed, Service thought. They touched cups together and stood in the howling storm, poacher and guardian, side by side, joined for the moment in mutual pursuit. Grady's ex-wife had accused him of having a death wish, but she had been wrong. He wanted to live big and hard on the roller coaster, to live like this, where scores got kept and nothing but unknowns loomed ahead.

· 30 ·

The group drove their snowmobiles to Aldo's cave-camp and found him outside and waiting for them. Had Limpy radioed ahead? Service wondered.

"They haven't moved," Aldo announced.

"What's he talking about?" Zambonet asked.

"You'll see," Service said.

Service, Zambonet, Limpy, and Canot followed Aldo on foot across a low-slung hill into a shallow valley lined by raked tamaracks.

A small woman was standing in the lee of dark, dense cedar slash. She wore knee-high mukluks over deerskin breeches dyed dark green. A black bearskin anorak stretched to midthigh. Her hood was down, her long black hair whipping in the wind, ice clots glistening. She was short and wide, with a long face and prominent cheekbones. She smelled heavily of castor oil and held Aldo's hand while he introduced her.

"This is Daysi," Aldo said. "She'll show you."

She tugged on Aldo's sleeve, stretched up, and whispered to him. Aldo spoke for her. "Just two, Daysi says. Otherwise, too much scent. Wolves don't like how people smell."

Canot and Zambonet followed the girl into the cedar slash.

Limpy stared at his grandson, who ignored him. Service poked Limpy and led him back to the snowmobiles. Thermoses were taken out, coffee poured. No cigarettes were lit. DaWayne Kota offered a tin of chewing tobacco. They waited silently while the wind whistled harmonics through the rocky terrain and tree branches rubbed like fingernails dragged down blackboards, leafless limbs rattling like drumsticks in a grating cacophony.

When the lookers returned with Aldo and Daysi, Yogi Zambonet looked both elated and confused. Canot was grinning like he had just scraped clean a winning instant lottery ticket.

Zambonet let Bobber Canot explain. "There's a series of drumlins and the animals have been in the popples. Good vegetation in there, grasses layered underneath the snow, maybe the result of an old fire, definitely not cutover regrowth. It looks like a rendezvous site, but not quite, and it's too early for dens. I can't figure out why they're here like this."

Service saw Daysi start her whispering routine again, but he said, "Daysi?" before Aldo could serve as her spokesman.

"I know where they'll den," she said shyly.

"Too early," Zambonet said. "Way too early."

"Maybe it's her first time," Daysi offered, avoiding the biologist's gaze.

"They're animals," Yogi said.

DaWayne Kota spoke up. "I think she means maybe this will be the female's first pups and she wants to have things just right."

"They don't think like humans," Yogi said.

"Sometimes they just act like us," Aldo said.

Zambonet nodded and turned to Bobber Canot. "Will the traps hold?"

The tracker looked at the others. "Our traps are designed to hold bears, but last year we trapped a ninety-pound male gray wolf that straightened out the drag chains."

"That kinda stuff happens," Shark said. He had been trapping and hunting most of his life.

"Three-quarter-inch steel?" Canot countered.

Wetelainen shook his head and stared off into the distance.

"That one last year had five-inch tracks. This fella's bigger. *Heaps* bigger. Seven-inchers," he said. "Like pie tins."

"My kids don't get that large," Zambonet said.

"This animal was trapped in Saskatchewan," Service reminded the biologist.

"They get bigger up there, but this . . ." He didn't finish the sentence.

"The traps'll hold," Bobber Canot said. "I think I can get down some decent sets. I took a good look at this fella's tracks. He follows the female, and their moves around obstacles are predictable. I'd like to give it a try. I'd sure like to see this big fella," he said with relish.

Zambonet thought for a moment. "Can you get your sets down by dark?"

"Sure." Canot looked at Wetelainen. "You wanna help?"

"You betcha," Shark said, his eyes flashing.

It took ten minutes to get their traps and scents. Canot held up a trap. It was black. "The MB seven fifty," he said. "It goes five, six pounds, and it's strong enough to hold a big bear. Leghold type with double underspring, offset jaws; we grind the jaws smooth to prevent injury, boil the traps in alder bark to knock off the metallic sheen, and set them flat on the ground, which makes them easier to hide. Each trap has two drag chains." He rattled the huge chains.

"What about bait?" Shark asked.

Canot dug several plastic bottles out of a pack. "Castor oil and 'Just Mice.' You ever see that movie *Cry Wolf?* About a cockamamie wolf researcher up in the Arctic? He s'posedly lived with the wolves and discovered they lived exclusively on rodents. Was a buncha bull mostly, them eatin' just mice, but they sure seem to like the smell of 'em just fine."

Service watched the two men heft their packs and head out. Shark and Bobber were a lot alike, he decided, happiest when they were stomping around the bush.

Zambonet exhaled, his breath dissipating in the wind. "We need to be closer to the wolf, but we'll have to wait until they actually get him in the trap. When Bobber has him we'll take the sleds in and use one of them as a table to do what has to be done. Our first concern is the safety of the animal. We've got about one hour from the time we drug him. We'll need to move fast. I'll use the poke-stick to immobilize him. I'll hit him first with ketamine, one cc per ten pounds of estimated weight, followed by xylazine. He'll be awake the whole time, but unable to move."

He quickly checked off what had to be done. "As soon as we start on him, I'll install a head shroud so he can't see, insert a digital rectal thermometer, and tag his left ear." Zambonet showed the approximate location on his own ear. "Red for Michigan, yellow for Wisconsin, green for Minnesota. The tags let us see at a distance if a tagged animal is ours. He won't be able to see, but he'll hear everything we do, and this will jack up his heart rate. When his heart rate increases, so does his temperature. We measure pulse and temp. The two give us a measure of stress. His temperature is *critical.* We don't want it to exceed one-oh-six. When we're done, I'll stick him with yohimbine and then we'll carry him back to the trap site and monitor him to make sure he's gonna come out of it all right." Zambonet looked at the others to see if they were listening.

Daysi said, "Can these drugs hurt him?"

Zambonet didn't pull his punches. "The muscle relaxants can cause problems — even kill an animal — but that's never happened to one of my kids, and it's only rarely happened in Alaska where they do this a lot. The relative risk-to-benefit ratio is good. The other shots will protect against parvovirus and other canid diseases. We have to knock him down to help him, but he won't feel any pain," the biologist said.

Daysi said, "If you want, Aldo and me want to help."

The biologist nodded his assent. "First we measure length and girth, and weigh him. I'll take a skin scraping to check for mange. After that, we inoculate with ivermectin and penicillin. Last we apply eye ointment."

Zambonet took his two new assistants aside to teach them procedures and get his gear ready.

Limpy sat on a log watching and smiling at everyone like an imbecile. Everything about Allerdyce's behavior bugged Service, but he had other things to think about now.

Kota, Service, and Gus Turnage went to explore.

When they got out of earshot of the others Service told them, "There's a wolf killer headed here. We need to look at where the animals have been moving, see if we can find places where a long shot might be possible."

"Why a long shot?" Kota asked.

"Single-round fifty cal," Service said.

Kota nodded.

They followed drifted-over wolf tracks through the wind, sometimes losing their way, but Kota and Service always managed to refind the tracks. After considerable hiking and looking around they squatted under a tree and talked.

There was a relatively clear area in front of them, at least a hundred yards long, but narrow. The wolf tracks passed diagonally across the area into dense balsams on the side of a low rise to the west.

Service looked at Kota. "They go through here to get to where the woman has been watching them. Wolves are like people. They like trails and shortcuts. They follow the same paths."

Kota scanned the surrounding ridges. "It could be a killing field," he said grimly.

"Okay, let's take a look," Service said. "No radios."

He sent Gus up one ridge and Kota up another. From below he used hand signals to guide them to locations that looked like good shooting perches. They were to approach each site carefully, not leaving tracks in the immediate areas they were scouting. After ninety minutes of looking, Service motioned for them to rejoin him.

"Goin' from or to their area, I'd want to get me a quartering side shot from up there," Kota said, pointing at his ridge. "Good shot from there," he added.

"My shot would be more north–south and longitudinal on the body," Gus reported. "If you want a trophy, you'd want a side shot to make sure you had the best angle on vitals."

And less chance of ruining the head, Service thought. The wolf killer always took the head, and he wondered why.

"Okay, let's get back to the others and clear the area. The animals may start to move around when it gets dark." Which wouldn't be long.

Service told Gus, "McCants and Grinda are joining us. They'll cover one perch and we'll take the other. We'll get the tac plan worked out tonight."

The others were on their machines and waiting for them. "Traps set?"

"Let's hope," Canot said as they cranked up and headed back to camp. Aldo and the girl remained behind. Limpy looked back at Daysi from his sled in a way that made Service's skin crawl.

McCants and Grinda were waiting in the tent, gear unloaded, sleeping bags laid out, snowmobiles ready. Grinda was cleaning her forty-caliber SIG. She nodded when she saw Service. McCants high-fived him and smiled.

While dinner cooked, Limpy went outside to smoke. Service joined him.

"You ought not look at the girl like that," Service said.

Limpy cackled. "Da womens want da same ting, Sonny. All of 'em da same, you mark my words."

Nantz called that night. "Weather's lifting tomorrow morning. We can fly."

Service passed the phone to Zambonet, who said, "That'll help. We want you to fly the female. When we get the male collared, he'll become primary. Good luck." He handed the phone back to Service and left to talk to Canot.

Nantz said, "I talked to McKower today. She said the captain's resting comfortably, complaining about being in the hospital. You men."

"The chief there yet?"

"Tonight, Lis says."

"How're you?"

"Ready to fly," she said. "What's going on there?"

"We have traps down. Now we wait."

"I hate waiting," she said. "For anything."

He understood.

There was a noon message from Shamekia on the cell and he called up the number and punched it in.

She answered her own telephone. "You're late at the office," he said.

"I needed to talk to you. A message wouldn't do. The shooter's name is Kitty Haloran. You remember the discussion we had about Minnis?"

Service searched his memory. "A couple of women came over and blew his identity. Minnis disappeared."

"Haloran was the second CARP person to come out, and not a defector. My sources say she was sent to find and kill Bridget Galway, whom you know as Larola Brule."

"Brule was IRA?"

"Affiliated group, not CARP, and a low-level functionary but with a grudge and she gave the Brits invaluable information."

"And ended up with Fish and Wildlife?"

"As did Minnis. He's known now as Carmody."

Service sucked in a breath and let it out slowly. "Fish and Wildlife doesn't deal with this kind of thing."

"They do if they owe favors to other government agencies. And Minnis was effective. You would be amazed at the sins agencies will forgive in the interests of finding competent people."

"Why would Fish and Wildlife need a killer?"

"They don't. They needed somebody fearless, and Carmody is that. Since he's been here his record has been exemplary. With one exception."

"Genova?"

"Right on. FBI surveillance has seen him several times over the past eight years."

"Why didn't they pick him up?"

"The Feebs on the scene probably don't know his background. To them he's just a Fish and Wildlife special agent with a taste for the lady."

"Bullshit. They've put the hot lights on SuRo since the get-go. Why?"

"That one I can't answer."

"Where's the Haloran woman?" Service asked.

"Disappeared."

"New identity?"

"Nobody knows anything. She's still wanted. Do you want me to turn all this over to the feds?"

"No, we'll let it play for a while." He would tell Freddy and let him carry the information back when it made sense to do so.

The sheriff arrived just before midnight, cursing and covered with snow. "Tipped my bloody snowbug over," he said. "Piece of shit. I'm gonna have to get outriggers," he said with a grimace. "Twisted the shit out of my wrist." He handed an envelope to Service. "A lot bloody quicker than U.S. Postal snail mail and a good deal cheaper. I saw your captain. He doesn't look so good."

Service talked his friend through the information Shamekia had passed along as they looked at the photograph of Kitty Haloran. "A real looker," Freddy Bear Lee said. "You wouldn't look past that face. You want me to hang with you or talk to our illustrious team leader?"

"Stay. I'll ask Shamekia to fax the photos to Nevelev, and give her Haloran's identity and leave it at that."

"What about your boy?"

"He's somewhere in the area now and close to finishing our case. We're trying to trap the blue as we speak."

"If Haloran came for a payback to Larola Brule, she's probably back in a hole in Europe by now."

"Could be," Service said. Right now his only interest was the blue wolf and Pidge Carmody. What a mess: a blue wolf in a green fire.

31

When the cell phone buzzed in the middle of the night Service quickly wriggled out of his sleeping bag and went outside.

"Get your wolf trapped?" Carmody asked in a low, roily voice.

Service blinked in the dark and swallowed hard. He had said nothing to the USF&WS man about trapping a wolf. "What was that?"

"Fookin' amateur," Carmody whined. "You heard me, boy. You're trappin' a wolf. *The* wolf. Down the darker stairs, where blue is darkened on blueness," the undercover man mumbled. "That from the distinguished D. H. Himself, ever mindful of all things carnal and what's more carnal than the takin' of life?"

"What're you talking about?"

"Bloody fookin' amateur," Carmody whispered. "You've a rat in your knickers, man, down there chewin' off yer fookin' manhood and passin' information to the lady here as coolly as one of Auntie's readers."

Service's mind raced. Allerdyce had pointed him at the blue. Then Carmody reported that Johns had a finder who had pointed her into the Mosquito. And he had seen Limpy using the FRS radio. The conclusion was inescapable: Allerdyce was the rat!

"What's this rat's angle?"

"Ah, the angle, asks he. Tiz the oldest of all, man: punts, pence, pounds, pennies, coin-a-the-realm, euros—a finder's fee if ye will, and so to speak."

Could this be true? There was no doubt that Allerdyce was motivated by money, but the old man had sworn repeatedly that he would never poach in the Mosquito, that the arrangement he had agreed to with Service's father also applied to the son. If Limpy was working with Wealthy Johns, why had he tipped him about the blue and then volunteered to help? The rat *had* to be Limpy, but what the hell was his game? The man was a lawbreaker, but he wasn't stupid. There had to be an angle he wasn't seeing.

"Where are you?"

"Well ye should ask. Me lady's acquired a caravan, the best money can buy. All the comforts, ye might say, hot water, a loo, her succulent and ondulatin' self."

"Where?"

"A boundless vision visits upon us, an untamed peninsula, vast wastes of forest verdure. It surroundeth in silence and ice. A bit foggy on the origin of that paraphrase."

"That's a bit on the ambiguous side."

"Sorry, boyo. I'm a bit turned about, you see. But the lady insists we reside within stalking distance."

"Describe the place."

"Would, I swear, but it's dark as the woman's soul and I've not been free of conjoinment until now."

"When will she move?"

"Ah, the question of the day. Soon, if ebullience be an indicator. Mad as the hatter, she is, lubricated with wantonness all day, and this very moment she's dancin' about the caravan with her body painted red as blood, a veritable Boadicea. She's been talking of taking the animal from under your noses, you see."

"Has she," Service said in clipped words.

"That's the spirit, boyo. A spurt in the old competitive juices heightens the game, yes?"

Carmody's words were increasingly slurred. "Are you drunk?"

"By your standards or mine?"

"Jesus."

"Jaysus, indeed. Took a bit more than anticipated to tumble the lady's gyroscope, but tumble it and her I did. Would you be wantin' me to pinch her now?"

Service quickly reviewed the case. With Carmody's testimony, they would have Wealthy Johns paying for an illegally killed deer, and for conspiracy, but she had done nothing more they could clearly nail her with. She had lied about the fifty-caliber's sale, but he wanted evidence of the poaching case in cement. Three wolves and a bear had been shot so far. How much more and who else was involved?

"We need that fifty and her in the act," Service said.

"Aye and have it ye shall. Now I must return to duty—to kneel at the lady's tiny feet, you might say!"

"I don't want her to take a shot," Service said. "Carmody?"

"Aye, I'm a shade pissed, not deaf. Professional to professional, can ye imagine another way for the likes of us to live, Grady-boy?"

Moments ago he had been an amateur.

"Relax, boyo. Carmody has things under control."

Service immediately went into the tent and looked for Limpy, but he was gone. What exactly could he have told the killer? That they were going to trap and collar the blue wolf? How many people he had with him? This was the limit. She would know they were following the blue, but not their plan. All he knew was their location and he had known that without all the trouble they had gone through. A finder's fee, Carmody said. And what was that comment Carmody had made earlier, about the woman having finders? Shit. No wonder Limpy was being helpful. What warped game was the old bastard playing this time? Whatever it was, he would pay, Service promised himself.

The group was assembled before first light near Aldo's cave. Daysi reported she had been near the wolves all night and had heard sounds. "He was in pain," she said, her voice cracking.

Service went with Canot, Shark Wetelainen, Aldo, and Daysi to check the traps.

The woman steered them to where she had heard the animals.

Service snapped the red cover over his Mag-Lite and pointed it into the aspens, near a fallen log. The animal was a dark mass against the white snow, prone and pointed toward them, its front left paw caught in the trap. The snow and ground around the wolf had been torn up.

"He didn't much like it," Canot said softly. "Don't blame him," adding, "Drag chain."

Service shifted the light and saw that one of the thick steel chains had been straightened like a piece of taffy stretched to breaking. The second chain seemed to be holding, but the wolf wasn't really struggling. It lay still, its breath coming in short, furious bursts, its sides heaving. Its eyes were red slits under the flashlight beam, its ears flat, nostrils flared. Snow melted on its thick blue fur.

The size was difficult to comprehend. "Bigger'n a by-God swamp buck," Shark said in awe.

"Fetch Yogi," the tracker said, and Wetelainen loped away to get the biologist. The first hint of morning light was spreading across the eastern sky. The snow was still falling in dense dry flakes.

Daysi knelt in the snow, five feet from the wolf, speaking to it in a quiet voice. Service couldn't make out what she was saying.

The color of the wolf's pelt left Service reeling. It was bright blue in the rising light.

"Your grandfather's gone," Service said to Aldo.

"He was here."

"Did he call you on the radio?"

The boy looked at him. "No. Just Daysi and I have radios."

Limpy had a radio. If he wasn't talking to Aldo, then it had to be Wealthy Johns. Service felt his temper rising. "Did you talk to him?"

The boy's face hardened. "No, he made a grab at Daysi."

"A grab?"

"You know how he is," Aldo said, his voice dripping disgust.

"Is she all right?"

"She won't talk about it."

"Daysi?" Service whispered.

"Not now," she said, pleading. "Our brother is frightened."

Service looked at the girl and the wolf and backed away. Fucking Allerdyce.

Zambonet hardly paused when he reached the wolf. He carried his black poke-stick and looked at the animal. "One twenty?" he asked Canot.

"More."

"One thirty?"

"Heavier still."

"Jesus, Bobber."

"One forty—at least," the tracker said.

Zambonet shook his head, took a vial out of his drug bag, and filled the syringe, checking the level several times before he was satisfied. "This is a load," he told Canot.

"So's this fella," the trapper said with a nod at the wolf.

"Okay, let's get this show on the road," the biologist said, circling the animal.

The wolf kept its eyes on Daysi, who kept talking. The animal showed neither fear nor anger, seemed resigned to its fate.

Zambonet braced a knee on the log, reached out with the poke-stick, and injected the animal in the haunch. It flinched but otherwise didn't react.

They all stood and watched. "Clock started," Bobber Canot said, checking his wristwatch.

When the animal looked incapacitated. Zambonet touched it with the blunt end of the poke-stick and got no response. He passed the stick to Aldo, knelt beside the wolf, took its scruff in one hand, slid his other arm under the massive animal's back haunches, and tried to lift but couldn't stand up. Canot joined him in supporting the animal's rear and helped the biologist lift the animal. Service walked behind the two men as they stumbled under the animal's weight through the snow toward the snowmobile, leaving tracks that resembled the twisting pattern of DNA.

It was lighter this morning than yesterday, but still snowing. The wolf was placed on green canvas on the long, narrow seat of the snow-mobile. Zambonet worked quietly, sliding on the head shroud, inserting the rectal thermometer, and installing the ear tag.

"Temperature?" he asked Aldo.

"One-oh-three."

"Okay, that's good. Let's try to keep it right there," he added, patting the animal's head.

Aldo and Bobber helped him attach the scale to the canvas cover and lift the wolf. All of them strained under the weight.

"One-four-eight," Zambonet said. "We should have gone with another cc of ketamine," he mumbled to nobody in particular.

"You want to give him a boost?" Canot asked.

"What's his temp?"

"One-oh-four," Aldo said.

"He's doing fine," the biologist said. "Let's just get it done. Better for the animal to be underdosed than overdosed."

"A hundred and forty-eight pounds," Canot said, adding a low whistle. "That's thirty-four pounds more than our biggest one."

"And this one is still growing," Zambonet said, peeling open its mouth to examine its teeth. "He'd be four, max."

Canot whistled. "Talk about pumping up the gene pool."

Zambonet used another syringe to draw blood and spun it down with the battery-powered device he carried in his wolf kit. He gave the sample to Daysi to store in a plastic bag.

"Temp?"

"One-oh-three," Aldo said.

"Good, great. Atta boy, almost done, big boy. Almost done."

Service felt a surge of respect for the biologist. These animals were much more than a job for the man. Yogi's heart was in his wolves the way his own heart was in the Mosquito. Bobber Canot used a camera to snap photo after photo and Service thought about how some officers bitched about tracking down missing or dead wolves or taking complaints from the bird hunter or farmer who had lost a dog or calf. He decided he would never bitch about wolves. The animals were special and deserved all the support he could muster.

The biologist took a skin scrape and administered two quick therapeutic injections, then squirted ointment into the wolf's eyes. They carried the animal back to the trap site and set it down gently, where Zambonet immediately injected the animal again.

"Yohimbine," he said, not looking up. "It counters the ketamine."

Everything done, they backed away to wait and observe.

At thirteen minutes the animal swished its tail and lifted its head. Two minutes later it used its massive front paws to push itself into a wobbly sitting position.

Zambonet announced, "He's gonna be just fine. Let's go, let's go."

They reassembled in camp. Zambonet and Shark would remain, Zambonet to handle radios and air cover, Wetelainen to cook and pitch in where needed.

Service took Aldo and Daysi aside and looked the boy in the eye. "You have to keep Daysi away from your grandfather."

The boy nodded solemnly. "She can't go to her people," he said.

"They don't like Aldo," Daysi said, clutching the boy's arm. "He's *wa-bish.*"

Because he was white, or because he was an Allerdyce? Service wondered. Limpy had never been a friend of Indians.

Service talked to DaWayne Kota, who said the girl could go to his sister's place in Bay Mills and made a call to arrange it.

"Aldo, your grandfather is working with a poacher who wants to kill the blue wolf."

The boy looked furious, but said nothing.

Service, McCants, Turnage, Grinda, Kota, and Lee had spent a good portion of the previous evening working out their tactical plan. With the addition of the sheriff, Service altered the makeup of the teams. Grinda would join Gus and him. Lee, McCants, and Kota would comprise the second unit. After much discussion he decided it would be best if the surveillance teams stayed in place until they had contact or he decided it was not going to happen. Moving back and forth to camps in shifts for hot food and warmth would only increase their comfort and their chances of detection. They were just going to have to sit tight and endure.

It was still snowing, but the temperature was not dipping below the low twenties at night and they had the gear and clothing needed to stay warm and to sit tight for an extended period. They packed food and water in their packs for three days, but would have to go without hot food. Last night he had talked around the specifics of the mission, but now he laid out the details.

He told them about Wealthy Johns and Carmody, the fifty-cal, the three wolves, and the bear. Carmody was his undercover and would step in to seize the weapon before she could get off the shot; they were there in the role of observers and as backup for the federal agent, but if something went wrong, they would intervene. He did not reveal Allerdyce's betrayal or Carmody's background. He would deal with these on his own terms, in his own time.

"Once we get into our hides, we stay put," he said. "Let's get it done," was his final instruction.

They were settled in by 10 A.M. Each team had a handheld radio, but was to maintain radio silence except for hourly check-ins, which were to consist solely of clicks. One click from him at nine minutes after every hour was to be followed one minute later by a two-click response from the other team. If and when it became apparent that the surveillance was a waste, he would use voice to pull the teams out.

The temperature was just above freezing, the snow wet again and still falling hard, though he saw that it was beginning to come in waves, which suggested a break in the offing. He wished it would make up its mind.

Service sat three or four yards from Gus. Grinda was a bit above them, watching a likely trail up the back of the ridge. She had picked a spot that allowed her a good sight line. By leaning slightly back she could see Service and give a hand signal. If she saw or heard something coming up the trail after dark she would flash a tiny red light attached to the zipper of her jacket. The beam would not carry, but could be seen by him.

For the first hour he thought about Carmody and his background and shuddered to think he was depending on a former IRA thug to uphold the law. McKower had told him when he had been promoted that he had been put in the job because his cases always seemed to become inescapably complex. Well, she couldn't blame the developments in this one on him. He was simply riding this wave.

Gus Turnage had a white Hudson's Bay blanket draped over his legs. Now and then he waggled a finger at Service to let him know he was alert. He and Gus had sat many a time and he had no doubts about his friend's ability to stay focused and alert, but Grinda worried him because he hadn't worked with her.

It was dark before 4:30 P.M., the snow finally relenting. Service saw patches opening in the cloud cover to reveal an indigo sky and a few early stars. His eyes went to Orion the hunter, the three stars of the constellation's belt standing out like a beacon.

Around 9 P.M. Nantz checked in by cell phone.

"The weather's cleared up over here and Yogi wants us to fly. He wants a fix on the male."

"Roger," he whispered. "One fix and outta here, okay?"

Click-click, she answered.

They briefly heard the Cessna pass overhead in the snow clouds an hour later.

Nantz called back at 11 P.M.

"Our bird's back in the barn," she said. "The male is stationary, about three hundred yards southwest of where you collared him," she said, adding, "I do," and hung up.

Three hundred yards southwest: Shouldn't the animals be moving? Or was the effect of the ketamine lingering?

By 2 A.M. the cold was creeping up his legs through his boots, and he kept flexing his toes to maintain circulation. Twenty years ago he would have ignored the weather. Hell, five years ago.

There was a clear sky with stars by 4:30 A.M., suggesting the sun would be bright in the morning. As the air warmed, there would be the sound of melting snow and falling ice.

Another aircraft passed overhead moments after sunrise. Service tried to see it, but couldn't. Probably Jesse Fulsik down from Houghton. Nantz would have called if it had been her.

At 7:30 A.M. the top of the sun was a bright orange disk against a lavender-and-blue sky. The temperature seemed to drop several degrees after the sun came up.

Thirty minutes after sunrise, Gus Turnage gave him a hand signal, pointing to the clearing below them. Service turned and saw the two wolves loping through the snow, plowing a trail with their chests, following the same path they had previously used.

By midmorning the sun was warming everything, and the tallest, widest trees were beginning to noisily shed their snow.

At 12:30 P.M. Service heard a gunshot behind the hill. It was difficult to judge a precise direction or distance from their position, but he had heard one distinct *pop*, a handgun, not a rifle.

Grinda peered down at him and cupped a hand to her ear. He nodded.

Gus gave a similar signal.

At 1 P.M. Grinda gave another hand signal, pointing to the back slope of their hill. She then touched forked fingers to her eyes. She had seen someone or something. Service got Gus's attention and relayed the message to him.

A small figure in white camo slithered onto the outcrop below them and unfolded the tripod attached to the barrel of the black fifty-caliber weapon that looked taller than the figure. Service kept watching for Carmody, but there was no sign of him. The figure spread out an insulated ground cloth. Johns, Service told himself as she slid a single round into the breach, sighted the long-barrel weapon down into the clearing toward the wolf tracks, wriggled around to get comfortable, and spread her legs apart for balance. Where the hell was Carmody?

The weapon was adequate reason to take her, but he waited for the undercover to show. It was not safe to move until he knew where everybody was.

At 2:30 P.M. the woman pulled back the hood to her parka, rolled onto her left side, peeled off her balaclava, shook her head, and lay back. She had short black hair. Using binoculars, Service got a good look at her face and stared, dumbfounded, his heart pounding. Wealthy Johns was Kitty Haloran! Where was Carmody?

Just before dark Service's cell phone vibrated quietly in his pocket. He fumbled to get it out and snap it open.

"Don't say a word, boyo. I've had a bit of a setback here. The woman's all yours."

A setback? Carmody's voice was strained and weak. "Carmody?"

"Ach, I told ya not to talk, ya daft Yank."

"There was a shot."

"I won't be dancin' again."

Service heard the pain in the man's voice. "I never saw it comin'. So who's the amateur?" Carmody said with a grim laugh.

"Where are you?"

"Never you mind, keep your head in the job, lad," Carmody said, hanging up.

Service knew he had to get someone to the man. Carmody would be bleeding, and if the wounds were even moderate, shock and exposure could kill him. Grinda was in the best position to move over the back of the hill and backtrack, but he knew Gus could move silently and leave no sign. He crawled over to his friend.

"Carmody's been shot," he whispered. "Backtrack her trail and find him. If she starts to come down, we'll stop her. Try to get him back to camp and call for help."

Gus nodded. Service watched his friend work his way up to Grinda, who immediately slid down to Gus's abandoned position. "That woman killed two people at Vermillion," Service whispered to her. "She's shot our undercover. Gus will find him and get help. We'll stay with her."

"Take her now?" she asked softly.

Service looked at the sky. "Not yet. I want Gus to get to Carmody and I want her to make a move on the wolves. If we get into darkness, we'll have to wait for first light."

"If she stays in place."

"She'll stay," Service said. She wanted the blue wolf. "Got on your long johns?"

Grinda smiled. "Long janes," she whispered.

Night fell, the wolves did not come, and there was no word from Gus. The woman lay motionless on her perch, her weapon pointed into the clearing below. Service was impressed with her discipline. Only a trained sniper or a psycho could endure this.

A partial moon threw slivers of light across the hills and valley below.

Sometime during the night Service saw a glint from where the woman lay, and then the brief red flash of a dot of light on the snow below. He bit his lower lip. She had a laser sight attached to the scope on the rifle. If that dot touched a target, it was going to be dead when she pulled the trigger.

He had his night-vision device along but couldn't risk scoping the field below. The slightest glint would give them away, and a shootout in the dark was too dangerous.

Maybe the wolves would not come back until morning.

His gut was tight.

At 6 A.M. he heard the Cessna again.

It came in low over the hill, passing close to McCants and her team, and fluttered along the length of the valley before banking to the north, climbing and disappearing, its running lights blinking red and green as it disappeared out of sight. Were the wolves moving back? Was it Nantz or Fulsik? It would be useful to know if they had picked up a signal, but he didn't dare use the radio right now.

He started to lean toward Grinda when he heard voices shouting below them.

"Ya fookin' cunt!" Carmody roared in pain and fury.

"Yer a bloody obstinate man, Mr. Carmody," the woman said in a thick brogue. "Ye've wasted the walk," she added icily.

Grinda was suddenly beside him. "It's going south," she whispered, her voice calm.

A handgun suddenly barked below, belching a muzzle flash.

Grinda said, "SIG."

Her own weapon was already in her hand and she was standing up.

"I'm tough to hit, eh Minnis!" the woman shouted.

Grinda was immediately on her feet and shouted, 'DNR!" as Service tried to unholster his weapon, stand up, and move a couple of paces to her left to give them separation.

There were three more shots all at nearly the same instant, and a grunt as Grinda collapsed beside him and slid down into the snow, coming to rest at his feet.

One muzzle flash from below, two from beside him. He moved his eyes left and right trying to sharpen rod-and-cone night vision.

"I'm okay, I'm okay," Grinda grunted from his feet, her breath coming fast. He felt her writhing around against his leg and groaning.

Snow suddenly crashed behind Service and he swiveled to face the sound. "It's Gus, it's *me*," his friend said. "That fucking cocksucker, that fucking cocksucker, he took my weapon, the cocksucker."

Service kept his eyes on the area below. "Shut up, Gus," he whispered. "Check Sheena."

"I *hate* that name," Grinda complained.

"Grady?" a voice crackled over the handheld. It was McCants.

"We've got two down," Service said. "Hold your position until we can see. Stay off the radio."

Click-click.

Two shots from Grinda, why? At night you were trained to use a muzzle flash as your aiming point, the theory being that the shooter would be directly in line with the flash, which was the source of the most pressing threat.

C'mon sun, he told himself, trying to will it above the trees to the east.

"No blood," Gus whispered.

Service peeked down at where Haloran had been, but she seemed to be gone. He heard Gus tell Grinda to relax and stop squirming.

As the sky began to lighten, Service could see the snowy shelf below. A body was stretched out on its back under some small spruces away from the lip of the area. Carmody? Where was the woman?

No sign of the fifty-cal or Haloran. He took out his radio. "Candi, we have two down and the subject and weapon are gone."

"You want us to come to you?"

"No, hold your position and keep your heads down."

Click-click. She didn't ask if anybody was dead. In the midst of shitstorm you had enough distractions without worrying about the fate of others.

Service knelt beside Grinda and began to examine her. "Copping a feel?" she said through clenched teeth and a pained grin. "The vest stopped it," she said breathlessly. "Middle of my solar plexus. God, it *hurts.*"

He felt. "There?"

She winced. "I wonder what it feels like without a vest."

"You don't wanna know," he said.

He looked over at Gus, whose head was covered in blood.

"Gus?"

"I found the cocksucker and put a tourniquet above his knee. He belted me when I was trying to help him! Took my piece. There's no gratitude in this line of work."

Grinda tried to sit up but Service pressed down on her shoulder. "Stay down. She's gone and so is her weapon."

Service got on the radio.

"Candi?"

"Here."

"Any sign?"

"I think there's a set of fresh tracks cutting across to the slash on the other side of the opening," she said. "I can sort of make out a path. The snow was disturbed where someone came down the hill. It looks like a rough landing."

"Fell?"

"Sorry, I'm too far to read it."

Service got out his binoculars and eased into a place between two small boulders where he could see and have some protection. He scanned the clearing and saw the tracks. Had she fallen or had she slid down intentionally? He tried to find a blood trail, but couldn't. Assume no blood, he told himself. He debated calling for backup, but by the time help could arrive, Haloran could be long gone. Six against one should be enough. Except for the damn fifty. If she could get up high, she might be able to pick them off one at a time. But there was no high ground where she had gone; his people held the best ground.

He keyed in his mike. "Candi, stay where you are."

"What if she runs?"

"We'll deal with that as it comes. She's got a fifty and she can use it." *Click-click.*

"The light will help us," Grinda said.

Service slid down to the terraced area below and went directly to Carmody. His pulse was weak. The tourniquet had loosened. Service retightened it and opened the man's coat to find a plume of blood spreading down the chest.

He looked up above and said, "Gus."

His friend came sliding down behind him

Service cut open Carmody's shirt. The entry wound was in the high belly. He looked at Gus, who was opening their first-aid pack and pulling out gauze. "All we can do is pack it and maintain pressure," Service said as he broke open a space blanket and began to work it around Carmody.

"We've got to get EMS in here," Gus said.

Service got on the radio and called the Delta County sheriff's department dispatcher, gave their location, and told her they had shots fired and two down, one of them dicey. They needed EMS and backup and they needed them to run silent. He gave the dispatcher their location, and asked her for a read-back to make sure she had it right. She did, and promised help was rolling.

"Are you under fire?" the dispatcher asked.

"Not at the moment."

Service tried to think fast as Gus touched his hand to his head and stared at the blood.

"She's not gonna be all that mobile with that big fifty," Service said. "We need to push her, keep her moving, not give her a chance to set up. I'm going to go down the back of the hill and circle around. You stay with Carmody." Service climbed back up to Grinda, who had struggled into a sitting position and winced as she reached for her rifle case and began to slide out her weapon.

Service looked at her.

"We've gone way south of south," she said with a look of resignation.

Service knew she was right, but they had limited options. He could use Kota to come in below and help him, but Kota's authority didn't extend off the reserve. Besides, it was too dangerous. If he went alone, he had only to worry about Haloran. Trying to hook up with Kota would add to the danger and present a potential distraction.

He slid Gus's rifle case down the incline to where his friend was still working on Carmody.

"Take the radio," Grinda said.

"No. If I go down, that cuts commo for you and Gus."

Grinda nodded and Service helped her over to a rock where she could make a rest for her rifle. He gave her his night-vision equipment. "If this thing stretches into darkness, use it."

He had moved quickly down the back of the hill and circled wide of the clearing, approaching from the east. He had been at it all day, taking it slowly and deliberately, and still had not cut Haloran's trail. He was within a hundred yards of the clearing. Had she set up in the woods on the edge so that she could shoot upward? Possible. Assume nothing, he cautioned himself.

Service didn't need to check his watch to know that he had about thirty minutes of light remaining. He had gotten into the cedars on the far side of the clearing and was cautiously crawling forward, checking for movement and taking it slow. Maybe Haloran had fled, but he doubted it. In her circumstances he would find a hidey-hole and wait for an enemy to come to him, take him out, and then move to the next target. When you were outnumbered, the best tactic was to whittle down the odds one at a time until you could get into a superior position. Right now it was purely one on one, and Haloran had the edge because he was in the position of trying to find her. All she had to do was sit tight and wait and he had already seen that she was up to it

In the waning light he was about to resign himself to another cold night, but movement to his right caught his attention. He froze, moving only his eyes, and saw a cedar limb shudder slightly, spilling snow. Below it protruded the barrel of the fifty-caliber rifle pointed toward him. The bore looked big enough to shoot a round the size of a walnut.

The fact that it was pointed in his direction didn't mean she had seen him. It was too hard to swing such a heavy weapon around. More likely she had it pointed in a general direction. She wouldn't aim until she had a target to shoot at. He suddenly thought of the red laser and cringed. Assume the worst.

He lay still, watching the barrel, hoping to see movement.

"There ya be," a voice said from behind him.

Service didn't move.

"I wanted the bloody wolf, but you'll have to do," Haloran said. "Gracious of you to come alone," she added. "But I've always loved an audience."

He tried to quickly assess the situation. She was behind him, how far he couldn't judge. He had heard no sound from a weapon, which meant she had used the fifty as a decoy.

He assumed she had another weapon and a round in the chamber. He carefully unholstered his SIG.

"Youse can have it standin' like a man, or lyin' dere like a mongrel. It's yer choice." There was no hint of Irish in her accent now. She sounded pure Yooper. How the hell could she sound like two different people, clicking it on and off like a recording?

"I'll stand," he said.

"Slowly," she warned. "Use two fingers to grip the barrel of the weapon and hold it up. I want to see the other three fingers pointed up. If I don't see what I'm askin' for, youse're dead, eh?"

He had just gathered his knees under him when he heard a plop of falling snow and in what seemed like the same instant a shot exploded from the hill where he had left Gus and Grinda. He instinctively threw himself flat, held tight to his weapon and scrambled under a log, taking a load of wet snow down his neck.

The shot had come from the hill. Good old Gus, he thought as he huddled under the log, frantically piling up snow to help reduce his profile. When he felt secure, he used his hand to cut a small opening in the snow. No sign of her. Maybe she was hit, but he wasn't going to chance it by moving now. She had already snookered him once.

He spent the night under the log, trying to remain alert and think warm thoughts, and failing miserably, the cold all through his body like a blood replacement. He moved only when he heard snowmobiles approaching in the clearing behind him. McCants and Gus had waited for daylight before green-lighting help. He would have done the same. Struggling to his feet, he stayed bent over and began to approach the place where he thought he had heard Haloran's voice. As he got close he saw blood spattered on the snow for several feet.

Kate Haloran was on her left side, the top of her head gone, particles of brain and bone slung across the snow in a fan shape. A forty-millimeter SIG Sauer was two feet from her hand, mostly covered by snow. Gus's weapon.

Simon del Olmo came cautiously through the trees and Service waved for him to join him. Simon looked from the body to the hill.

"Helluva shot." Then he bent forward and sank to his knees.

Service asked for del Olmo's radio and called Grinda.

Gus Turnage answered.

"Great shot," Service said.

"Sheena," his friend said. "Not me."

"Can she talk?"

"EMS is working on her now. She refused to go with them last night when they took Carmody out." Service could hear admiration in his friend's voice.

"Put her on."

"Yeah?" Grinda said. She sounded worn out.

"Thanks," Service said.

"Is she? . . ."

"She's in custody," Service said. He would tell her the facts later.

Grinda said nothing, but he guessed she knew.

Gus came back on the radio. "Sheena's got a broken rib, maybe her sternum too. She's hurting, but she's tough."

"You?" Service asked.

"Headache. Carmody didn't have my piece."

"I've got it. How's Carmody?"

"Still alive when he left here. The tourniquet may have saved his life, but it's probably gonna cost him his leg. He lost a lot of blood, Grady. EMS took him to Marquette. That's where we're going too."

"See you there, Gus."

He took del Olmo to the fifty-cal Haloran had used to divert his attention. The bolt-action weapon was nearly six feet long and had a massive scope attached. He saw HARRIS GUNWORKS engraved on the lower barrel as he bent over to look at the weapon, careful to not touch it. The scope was a twenty-power Leupold MK-VM1, a model developed for the military. The laser sight was built into the scope, controlled by a box attached to the scope mounting. It was a lethal weapon. Service leaned down and saw that the serial number had been filed off the weapon and the area was discolored, suggesting acid had been used.

The younger officer said, "We had those suckers in Saudi. They're deadly to twenty-two hundred yards. You guys had them in 'Nam, right?"

"Not like this," Service said. "What we had we jury-rigged on the spot."

"Hey," del Olmo said. "You could be its daddy."

It was a discomfiting thought, that things spawned in Vietnam more than thirty years ago were still intervening in his life.

There were small patches of frozen blood on the snow by the fifty. They followed the drops and Haloran's tracks to her body. She had been hit twice, once up on the hill and again by the rifle. Had Carmody gotten the first round in her, or had Sheena? Forensics would have to sort it out.

The younger officer knelt and examined the body. "She's hit here," he said, pointing to the right side of the woman's chest. Service stared up at the hill across the clearing and shook his head. She had come all the way to cover with minimal bleeding. He had seen this happen before with animals and humans. It also explained why she had not pushed on. She was hit and hurting, waiting for somebody to come to her, had crawled into cover to wait, must've seen him approaching, left the fifty as a decoy, and worked her way behind him. He wondered whether, if they had all just sat tight, she would've died from the initial wound.

Simon del Olmo patted him on the back. "I predict incoming paper-work, *jeffe*."

Grady Service sat heavily on a log and lit a cigarette, watching his hand shake as if it were not part of him.

His friend sat beside him, took out a tin of Bullshido Chew and stuffed a pinch into his cheek. They sat quietly for a long time, waiting for others to arrive to take control of the body. In the distance they heard a wolf raise its voice, and a second animal answer. Wolves had settled in the Mosquito Wilderness, *his* wilderness, and as a cold and exhausted Grady Service sat with his young friend, he wondered what it was going to take to protect the animals from the only predator they needed to fear.

32

Grady Service marched into the reception area of the Emergency Services unit at Marquette General Hospital and asked a nurse to point him to the morgue. Minutes later he was standing in a room looking at a wary technician. There were two autopsy tables with stainless-steel tops and a wall of stainless-steel drawers. The room was cold.

He said, "A woman's body was brought in this morning. The head's blown off. Which drawer?"

The technician's eyes narrowed. "You can't be in here."

"Which *fucking* drawer?"

The technician pointed and Service said, "Open it."

"I have to get a pathologist," the technician said.

"Then get him."

A woman appeared in a white lab coat, the technician cowering behind her. The woman had silver hair in a bun and wore a frown.

"What's going on here, Officer?"

"Open that drawer." He pointed.

"We have procedures," she said.

"Open the drawer," he repeated.

The pathologist turned to the technician. "Call security."

Service said, "Are you going to open it or not?"

"You don't belong here," the doctor said.

Service pulled out the long drawer, unzipped the body bag, and worked it down to Haloran's waist. He used his knife to cut open Haloran's coveralls and tugged the cloth down to midthigh. He paused for a moment, then lifted the waist of her panties, looked for several seconds, stepped back, turned, grinned, and marched out of the room, leaving the doctor and technician staring at him.

Gus Turnage had a bandage wrapped around the top of his head and was sitting on the edge of a bed pulling wool socks over his union suit as he carped at a stocky nurse with the countenance of a cocker spaniel. A paper hospital gown was in shreds on the floor near his battered Danner boots. "I am *not* being admitted," Gus insisted.

"You've already *been* admitted," the nurse countered.

Irresistible force and immovable object, Service thought.

"Then I am de-admitting myself," Gus fired back at her.

Service left his friend to check on Grinda, who had just been moved into a private room. There was an I.V. stand beside the bed. Her mane of golden brown hair was mashed into the shape of a helmet, her face covered with red splotches. She looked uncomfortable and confused. He had killed enemy soldiers in Vietnam and understood what she was going through. But he had never killed anyone in the line of duty during his DNR career and he suspected that this would feel worse than in a war where killing was happening all around you.

Grinda looked at him and tried to speak. "I . . ."

He held up his hand. "You did your job, Elza. You understand the procedure now, that you'll be put on administrative leave during the investigation?"

She nodded.

He rubbed her leg. "Don't worry. They'll probably have you answering phones at the district office."

Grinda rolled her eyes.

He debated how much to tell her and how, and decided not to sugarcoat it. "You hit her twice, the first time up on the hill in the dark." He touched a place on the right side of his chest.

"I was guessing," she said. "In her place, I'd fire as I moved, so I figured I had a fifty-fifty chance if I put a quick one to each side. I guess I was lucky."

"No, I was the lucky one," Service said. "She was going to pop me."

Grinda's voice was barely audible. "I went for her head. I would've shot sooner, but I couldn't see her because of snow in the tree. When it fell, there she was. I'm sorry I took so long."

"You did great."

Sheena Grinda looked unhappy. "Alive, we could have broken the whole operation."

"With Johns gone, the operation is finished, or at least regrouping. We'll clean it up for you," he said.

"Still," she said. "I *went* for her head. I wanted her dead." She sounded appalled.

"That makes two of us," he said, earning a weak and appreciative grin.

✳   ✳   ✳

Carmody had been in surgery and was in the recovery area. Sheriff Lee and Sergeant Parker from the Newberry district office were outside the room with a Marquette County deputy Service didn't recognize. The self-serving Parker had once been his supervisor. He no longer reported to the man, but Parker remained a jerk. He was here to bask in what he perceived to be glory for DNR law enforcement. If the situation had gone badly there would be no sign of Parker.

His former sergeant perked up and smiled when he saw him. "Glad to see you, Grady!"

Service ignored Parker and turned to Lee. "Where's Carmody?"

Freddy Bear Lee nodded at the door and pushed it open. "No feds yet but they're on the way, and the doctors say he shouldn't be disturbed," the sheriff said. "I'll guard the door."

"Thanks, Freddy." Service said as he stepped into the room.

There were monitors along the ceiling above the bed. Carmody looked awake but his eyes were bloodshot and distant, his skin ashen.

"They took the bloody leg," Carmody said without emotion. " I guess it's the pirate's life for me. It is, it is a glorious thing to be a Pirate King. Or shall I become a major-general, join the righteous?" Carmody grinned and sang, "I am the very model of a modern major-general, I've information vegetable, animal, and mineral, I know the kings of England and I quote the fights historical, from Marathon to Waterloo in order categorical!"

The Irishman was loopy from drugs. "You didn't know Haloran before," Service said.

Carmody said, "Understatement from the mouth of a Yank. Your people killed the bitch."

"Funny how the past boomerangs, eh, Micnis?"

The man in the bed grinned. "I'm under the influence of pharmas, boyo. Nothing I say can be relied upon. 'You've scotched the snake, not killed it,' wrote Billy the Bard. She'd not come for me. No photos of me, nothing, I've become invisible man. 'And with bloody and invisible hand cancel and tear to pieces that great bond,'" the man in the bed mumbled. "No shame in quoting the most British of bards. Did you know dear old Willie-boy came to Papism at the moment of his passing? Timing is everything, my friend. Mine got a bit fooked, you see. As Mr. Gilbert wrote it, 'The policeman's lot is not a happy one.'"

"Haloran recognized you."

"That night, after I talked to you. She was forever at me about the old country, but I never gave her more than a sniff. Born in Boston, schooled in Dublin, returned to the bosom of Dear Old Uncle Sam like the good native son."

"Which of course your records corroborate."

"The glories of the stage of shadows, lad. I shall truly miss that leg."

"How did she find out?"

"Ah, a wee slip of the tongue, I fear. 'Twas Horace, I think, wrote, 'It is the mountaintop the lightning strikes.'" His voice trailed away.

"Minnis?"

"Aye, I'm here. The night after we spoke I found a snapshot. She was standing in front of Hadrian's Wall."

Service let him talk.

"The Caledonian tribes of northern Scotland were under one pugnacious Calgacus, who led his equally pugnacious lads against the Romans at Mons Graupius. The Roman bastards killed thirty thousand that day, but the survivors fled north, took the oath, were never subdued, fought on. Later the Emperor Hadrian built a wall to block all traffic to the north and serve as a reminder. You see the irony?" Minnis asked with a grin. "Force and walls cannot take freedom from men determined to remain free. The field below the battle site became a symbol that so long as a few survive, so long as but one lives, the battle shall never end. The place is commonly called the Field of Blood, but to some it is Heart's Field."

"Some?"

"Aye, some, the few who fight on," Minnis said disconsolately. "We were drunk. I saw the photo, made clever about grass growing on the bloody heart."

"And then she knew."

The man shrugged. "Conjecture. We were headed up the hill for the rendezvous with the wolf and she turned on me, pistol in hand. She put one into me knee and took me weapon, swearing to give me a proper finish when her work was done. A great Kraut windbag said it best, 'In revenge and love woman is more barbarous than man.'"

"She knew you were Minnis."

"Draw your own conclusions. What she knew, I believe, she knew from the rat in your ranks, that I was of *you*, not of *her*. Not Carmody of the old country, just a cop about to spoil her game."

Goddamn Allerdyce. "You took my man's weapon."

"Couldn't be helped. She'd nicked mine. The need was upon me, my blood risen, even as it gushed forth. I was forced to give the lad a wee crack on the noggin."

"We had it staked out."

"Aye, and I knew the bitch had taken my leg and intended more. I got a round into her up there on the mountain."

"You missed," Service said.

Carmody glowered, but lifted his head and looked directly at Service. "You'll tell SuRo I shan't be returning."

"You can tell her yourself."

The Irishman grunted and lowered his head. "'Light thickens and the crow makes wing to the rooky wood. The bright day is done, and we are for the dark.' For a Pom, the little bastard had the gift. Perhaps I'll write my memoirs, give Frankie McCourt a run for his money."

The door opened behind Service. Freddy Bear Lee backed into the room holding his hands in front of him like a tackle defending a pass rush.

"You can't be in here," Cassie Nevelev snapped from behind the sheriff. Wink Rector and Barry Davey stood in the doorway behind her. There was no sign of the FBI biggies.

"I was just leaving," Service said, leaning close to Nevelev as he squeezed by. "Take good care of Major-General Minnis."

Nevelev's face twisted into a look of total confusion.

Captain Grant was in a private room. His eyes lit up when he saw Service.

"Shaved it close," the captain said.

"Grinda bailed me out."

"She's a fine officer."

"What about you?" Service asked, using his foot to push a chair over to the bed.

The captain shrugged. "No permanent damage at this point. Lucky."

They sat in silence for a moment while Service gathered his thoughts. "Barry Davey gave me Carmody, who was Mouse Minnis, a killer for a fringe IRA group. Things got too hot for him in Northern Ireland and he moved to England and joined an animal rights group. He focused on British companies with links to Northern Ireland. A woman later came out of Northern Ireland and cooperated with the Brits and it got too hot for Minnis. Her name was Bridget Galway."

"Larola Brule," the captain said.

Service went on. "A second woman was sent to get the first one. That was Haloran—Wealthy Johns. In the wake of Haloran's arrival in the U.K., Minnis and the first woman ended up in the States, both of them working for Fish and Wildlife."

"Grinda shot Haloran," the captain said.

Service nodded. "Until the day she showed up in the Mosquito I knew her as Wealthy Johns and we were out to break her poaching op. But Fred Lee brought me a photo of Haloran and when I saw Johns I realized they were the same person. Haloran killed Larola Brule at Vermillion. She was the target. Her boyfriend was just in the wrong place at the wrong time."

"And the Brule woman—Galway—she was the turncoat who cooperated with the Brits?"

"Yes. I don't understand how Haloran got here, or how or why the feds would bring Minnis and Galway across the pond and end up with both of them on the Fish and Game payroll."

The captain's gaze was on the wall at the end of the bed. "Perhaps the two of them were already on a federal payroll."

This caught Service short. What had Carmody said about the records not lying? Was he an American after all?

"The wilderness of mirrors," his captain said. "Images within images and none of them real. What will you do next?"

"Gus Turnage and I will talk to Skelton Gitter, squeeze him, see if he was part of Haloran's poaching op. I'll be interested to know when and how he met her. Did she come here first and then learn about Brule, or did she come here because of Brule?"

"Some answers are not worth the effort to obtain them."

A veiled warning from his supervisor? "Gitter was or wasn't part of it and case closed, is that it?"

The captain nodded. "Done is done."

"Allerdyce was involved," Service said. "I don't know how or when he met Haloran, or what his role was other than feeding information to her about what we were doing. I thought he and I had an understanding, but he damn near got us killed."

"Arrangements with informants rarely persist. Better to limit such arrangements to one transaction at a time."

"The thing is that without Limpy's involvement we might have lost the blue wolf. And because of him we nearly lost the animal anyway. I don't know how to keep score anymore."

"Your wolf killer is no more," the captain said. "This is the only score that matters. All the rest is detail."

"Details matter in our business," Service said.

"Only until a case is closed, then you move on, Detective. The feds have impossible jobs and they're forced to do things and work with people the likes of which most of us cannot imagine. You've done your job, Grady. Now let it go and go home to Maridly. She and I have had some meaningful discussions. She has agreed to fly for the department on a contract basis until fall. Now go home, Grady. I'm pleased you're still among the living."

"I'm glad we both are," Service said, extending his hand.

He was moved by the captain's sentiments and advice, but despite the captain's view, some details did matter, and he had more to attend to.

33

Skelton Gitter's establishment sat in full view of Mount Zion north of Ironwood. The showroom walls were covered with stuffed-animal mounts; just inside the door there was an eight-foot-tall Alaskan brown bear on a pedestal, standing on its hind legs, its mouth frozen in a snarl.

Gus Turnage stared up at the animal and said, "How'd you like to deal with the likes of that?"

"No thanks," Service said. The state had enough trouble with its black bears.

There was a gun shop off one end of the showroom and a shop filled with fishing gear off the other end.

Service was accompanied by Gus Turnage, a Gogebic County deputy sheriff, and Special Agent Eddie Bernard, the BATF man from Grand Rapids who had responsibility for the U.P. Lars Hjalmquist, Betty Very, and some Ontonagon County deputies had search warrants for Gitter's camp and the camp owned by the man from Fort Wayne. Both camps were close to each other south of the Porcupine Mountains.

Service timed it so that his group arrived at the shop an hour before its scheduled opening. They were greeted by a frowning Skelton Gitter. Service introduced everyone, and Special Agent Bernard handed search warrants to Gitter.

The proprietor pointed toward an office. "Can we sit down like civilized people?"

He led them into the room and plopped down behind a polished oak table. There was a Dell computer in the corner and distressed credenza that stretched along one wall. There were photographs of Gitter and his hunting trophies in rows on the walls.

"We have some questions," Service said.

"I knew you'd be coming," the man said.

Service sat down across the table from Gitter.

"Do I need my lawyer?" the man asked.

"Be good, you call him," Service said. "We want to talk about Wealthy Johns."

Gitter stared at Service, picked up his phone, and punched in a number. "Sandy, I'm going to need you."

Tavolacci, Service thought. This was interesting. Tavolacci had tried to spring Jason Nurmanski from the Iron County Jail. Why would Gitter have Tavolacci as his lawyer? It was like hanging out a sign. If Sandy worked for Gitter, would he also work for Johns and not tell Gitter? Not likely.

"She was killing wolves and poaching deer."

"I do not poach," Gitter said.

"But you knew something was going down."

The man shook his head. "I barely knew her. I met her two years ago over to the gun club."

"That would be South Superior?"

Gitter nodded. "I never met a woman who could shoot like her, and her knowledge of weapons was astounding. I hired her."

"You barely knew her, but you hired her and then she moved in with you."

"Eventually. At first she was just an employee. Have you never made an error?"

Knowing how Haloran worked, Service doubted the relationship had evolved.

"If you knew about the poaching and didn't report her, that's conspiracy," Service said.

"I trusted her. She could sell sand to Saudis and she brought in a lot of new business."

"She was hiring freelancers to make kills for her," Gus said.

"I didn't know," Gitter said, his voice betraying frustration. "She was a unique woman."

"How so?" Service asked.

"Different, direct," Gitter said. "And unpredictable. She was wide open in some ways and totally closed in others. She refused to talk about her past and would tell me only that she was from out east. She had an accent then, Massachusetts, Maine, something out that way."

"She had an accent *then?*" Service asked.

"Right, but within weeks it was gone and she talked like she'd grown up right here."

"Do you do background checks on employees?"

"I only hire former customers. Because they've bought weapons from me I've already gotten a clean background on them and there's no need to do it again. My procedure is more efficient."

"But Johns was new to the area, an unknown. Did she buy a weapon from you?"

"No."

"So you hired her without knowing anything about her. She could have been a felon."

Gitter looked irritated. "She knew weapons and sales. I didn't want to risk losing an employee of that caliber."

"I bet," Gus said.

Service ignored Turnage. "You hired her without knowing anything about her except that she was knowledgeable."

"The law doesn't require background checks for employees selling firearms."

"She lived with you," Service said.

"As previously stated, not at first," Gitter said, exasperation beginning to show. "That came later."

"She was paying cash to hunters to take trophy deer and she was killing wolves herself."

"I don't know anything about any of that. She was the best employee I ever had."

Gus left the office and came back with the fifty-caliber weapon they had taken from Wealthy Johns and placed it on the table in front of Gitter. A DNR evidence tag dangled from the barrel.

"Recognize this?" Service asked.

"Harris Gunworks, fifty BMG, bolt-action, one of the early models, 1987 or so. They later came out with a semiautomatic version."

"This is yours."

"No," Gitter said firmly. "Not mine."

"Johns was carrying this when we confronted her. She killed wolves with it."

Gitter looked shaken. "I have no knowledge Check the serial number. There will be a paper trail. That's the law."

"The serial number's been obliterated."

Special Agent Bernard came in with a folder and placed it on the table in front of Service.

Service flipped through the pages. "The weapon came from Harris Gunworks. You sold it to a man in Indiana."

Gitter sucked in a breath and grabbed at the papers. "I did no such thing."

"Let's go through this again," Service said.

Gitter exhaled slowly. "I've never had an account with Harris Gun-works. I handle *sporting* weapons. The stuff they make is special, mostly for military and law enforcement. With specialty weapons manufacturers you have to commit to substantial inventory packages in order to be able to buy single pieces. I can't afford it. Call the people at Harris, ask them."

"We already have," Service said, tapping the paperwork, "but your own records say the fifty came from Harris."

Gitter leaned forward. "I did *not* buy that weapon from Harris Gun-works. Their records will confirm this."

"You're right," Service said. "You don't have an account with them, but your own records show that you had one of their weapons. *This* weapon."

"No!" Gitter said. "My attorney is coming. I will wait for him, as is my right."

"Our people were here before, checking on this weapon. Wealthy Johns told them that you had sold the fifty to a man in Indiana and that it had been shipped to him."

Gitter's eyes intensified. "That's nonsense! Firearms can be mailed only from one licensed dealer to another. A nondealer has to purchase a weapon in person so the proper background checks can be run."

"But you hired Johns without a background check."

"She wasn't a customer. I didn't break any law," Gitter said angrily.

Service picked up the paperwork. There was a shipping form at-tached. It showed that the fifty had been mailed by special carrier to a man named Mayhall. Service put the paper in front of Gitter. "It's against the law to ship a firearm."

Gitter glared at Service. "Listen to me. I did *not* mail a weapon to a customer. Not to that customer, not to any customer."

"You're right," Service said. "This man in Indiana never bought a weapon. He doesn't own any guns. He doesn't even hunt."

The store owner looked relieved.

"But the paperwork says a firearm was shipped." He handed the pa-pers to Gus. "Call Red Box Express and have them pull their paper-work."

"Can I use your phone book?" Gus asked Gitter, who fumbled in a drawer in the credenza along the wall and slid the book across the table.

Gus found the number, flipped open his cell phone, and tapped in the number.

He talked quietly on the phone while Service watched Gitter laboring to keep his composure.

Gus said, "Okay, thanks," and put down the phone. "R3E got a call for a pickup but when they got here, the shipment wasn't ready. They keep notes of such things in case customers bitch later. They were never recontacted."

"I don't break the law," Gitter said.

"Your paperwork says differently," Bernard said.

"You're hassling me," the gun dealer said.

Service was not about to let up. "Let's say that your girlfriend made up the story about selling the weapon so that she could keep it, and she made the paperwork look like she had sent it, and violated the law. Let's ignore the fact that she set you up for a violation. Where did she get the fifty?"

Gitter's annoyance was changing to another emotion. "I don't know, and that's the truth."

"But you knew she had it. It's not against the law to know something unless you know it to be illegal," Service said. "It's perfectly legal to own a bolt-action or semiautomatic fifty."

Gitter looked tired. "She had it when I met her," he said after a long pause. "I figured if she owned it, her record had to be clean. Harris doesn't sell to people who don't meet the rules."

"A bit blinded by his own gun," Gus said under his breath.

Service looked up at the BATF agent. "Eddie?"

The BATF man smiled at Gitter. "Sir, we took three sets of prints off the weapon, and one of them belongs to you."

Service had not been surprised at the print findings. Gitter and Johns had been passing the fifty back and forth. Carmody didn't know about the third wolf kill and the prints suggested Gitter had done it.

Gitter said, "I want my lawyer."

"Mr. Gitter," Eddie Bernard said, "we'll wait for your attorney because we're going to go through everything here and we are going to take our time doing it."

Service said, "While more officers are going through your cabin and one owned by Mr. Mayhall of Fort Wayne. If there's anything in either place, we're going to find it, Mr. Gitter. We know Wealthy shot two wolves with the fifty. We also know that another wolf was killed by the same weapon and if you did that, it would help you to tell us about it now." Service knew that if the man didn't admit to the third wolf, they would probably never get him for it. Prints on the weapon would not be sufficient.

Gitter's shoulders slumped but he said nothing more.

The conservation officers left Bernard in the store and walked outside.

"Guy's an asshole," Gus said.

"I guess he hooked up with Haloran to get a little and got a whole lot more," Service said with a grin.

"You want to grab lunch?" Gus asked.

"No thanks." Service had another visit to make, and this one he wanted to do alone.

Sandy Tavolacci pulled into the parking lot as Service got to his truck, parked, jumped out, and glared.

"Howyadoin Sandy?"

"Up yers," the lawyer shouted as he stormed toward Gitter's shop.

It took more than two hours to reach Limpy's camp. During the drive Lars Hjalmquist called on the cell phone. They had found three wolf heads in a freezer in Gitter's cabin, and eight sets of antlers, none of them tagged. At the Mayhall camp they found something else.

"There's also a bald eagle," Hjalmquist said, "mounted big as life, and a box full of eagle feathers. Gitter's signature is on the bottom of the mount."

"That's a federal rap," Service said with a grin. "Let Barry Davey know. I think Mr. Gitter has a lot of explaining to do."

The afternoon air was warming again, heading into the high fifties. Grady Service marched into the camp and pounded on the door of Allerdyce's cabin. Honeypat opened the door, and Service brushed past her to find Limpy in his rocking chair with a cup in his hand.

Service stood in front of him, his eyes dark and hard.

"Had youse a time over to da Skeeto, didjas?" the old poacher asked, flashing a crooked grin.

"You broke our deal."

Allerdyce's eyes narrowed and the pitch in his voice changed. "I din't operate in da Skeeto. I din't break nuttin' an' youse got no evidence udderwise."

"That's right. The problem is that you know all of our rules and our ways."

The old man took umbrage. "I found da blue wolf for youse."

"You found him for Wealthy Johns, too."

Allerdyce grinned. "Heard dat woman lost her head out dere. Waste of such a pretty face, eh."

"Why?" Service asked, not expecting an answer.

"She was da competition, eh? Hired freelancers for cash. I couldn't have da bitch messin' in my business. Mebbe I put her on da blue an' den put you on 'im and I knew you'd take her oot. Just like yer ole man woulda done. Dere's nothin' to show—no money passing, eh? Dis is just 'tween professionals."

"She paid you for information," Service said. "We killed her."

"Better a green-suit den a civilian like me," Limpy said with a shrug. "Dat would be murder. Dis way it's nice an' legal. No paper, eh?"

Service stared at the old man and knew Limpy had used him.

"Don't get yourself all flusterpated, Sonny. Da wolf's alive and in the Skeeto, eh? Limpy's way, we all get what we wanted."

Not quite, Service thought. "Your grandson won't be coming back," Service said.

Honeypat stepped forward. "Is Aldo hurt?"

Service looked at her. "In a manner of speaking. Your bedmate hit on Aldo's girlfriend."

The fury from Honeypat was instant and violent. She slapped Allerdyce across the side of his head and stormed out the door, slamming it with the effect of a bomb. Allerdyce struggled out of his rocker and tried to pursue her, but Service got to the porch ahead of him and blocked his way.

"You bitch!" Allerdyce shouted into the dark over Grady Service. "I'll be findin' youse and you gonna be gettin' it but good!"

Service extended his right hand and Allerdyce stared at it. When the old man stuck his hand out and grinned, Service struck him in the nose with a hard, short left jab that sent Allerdyce sprawling down the steps on his back.

"What's dat for!" the old man asked incredulously as he lay there feeling his face.

"New rules, asshole. New rules."

After a short stop at home in Gladstone, Service was on the road early in the morning, this time to the Soo for the wrap-up meeting of the investigation team.

The only people there were Ivanhoe, Sheriff Lee, Wink Rector, and Nevelev. Barry Davey. As in Marquette, there was no sign of Peterson or Phillips.

Service had a lot of questions, all of which Nevelev answered the same way.

"Where's Doctor Brule?" Service asked. He was still curious about how Bridget Galway and Minnis had come to work for Fish and Wildlife.

"That's not your concern," Nevelev said.

"Where are the Vermillion wolves?"

"Also classified."

"Where's Minnis?"

"Who?"

"Carmody."

"Special Agent Carmody is receiving medical treatment," she said. "He's no longer in Marquette."

Each time she answered, the federal prosecutor looked pleased.

Service left the meeting seething. Wink Rector overtook him on the way south and waved him up an exit ramp. They pulled onto M-28 and stopped in front of an electric power company building with an American flag made of painted hay bales propped up on the front lawn. The two men met between their parked vehicles and lit cigarettes. The temperature was in the high forties and the weather acting like winter would never come. Service stared at the lawn. No snow on the ground in December?

"Why were your people so fixated on Genova?" Service asked angrily.

Rector held up his hands in a gesture of placation. "I'm a resident agent in a backwater."

"Goddammit, Wink. Don't give me that above-your-pay-grade crap."

"You never heard any of this from me. Peterson was in the U.K. when Genova was there. He's never believed she was innocent."

"Bullshit."

"Look, Grady. Since September eleventh the heat is on all agencies for results against all terrorists, foreign and homegrown. Peterson has been predicting the animal rights lulus to go violent for years in this country. When the ballistics matched Genova's weapon that convinced him he'd predicted correctly and that she was part of it. I think he saw a promotion in the offing."

"But Genova didn't do it."

"She left her place that night and our surveillance lost her. She didn't come back until daylight. While she was gone someone could have taken her weapon and put it back. There was nobody covering the place to know this."

"Bullshit."

"The fact is that we fucked up."

"Why would Haloran take Genova's weapon?"

"All we can do is speculate. I don't know the details but Peterson seems to think that Genova had something to do with Haloran in the U.K. When he saw the stills of Haloran, he pulled out of the investigation."

"Ostrich time."

The FBI agent smiled. "Fuckups will not be tolerated in the Dubya presidency. Peterson will be retiring and Genova is in the clear."

"She should have been clear for eight years," Service said.

Rector shrugged. "Sometimes big turds clog the toilet of justice. There's more you need to know," he added. "Brule was trying to train wolves for facility security and surveillance in hostile territory. The experiment had tanked and the plug was going to be pulled for the next fiscal year. The navy trained dolphins for this purpose and the army wanted something of its own. Brule is done with wolves and is being reassigned to a facility in New Mexico," he added. "He was on Fish and Wildlife's rolls, but he took his direction from DoD."

Service said nothing.

"Minnis is headed for a VA rehab hospital in California. He'll recover, but he's being retired on a full medical."

"He's a killer, Wink."

The affable FBI agent nodded solemnly. "You think he's the only killer working for the government?"

"Did Minnis know Haloran?"

"No, and she disappeared when she left the U.K. Nobody knows how she stumbled onto Larola Brule—or should I say Bridget Galway—but Brule's husband was a gun stroker and bought several weapons from Skelton Gitter. That's the only connection we knew of, but it's only a short hop from Brule to his wife. Hell, maybe Brule introduced them. We'll never know the facts now," he added with a shrug of resignation.

Gun stroker was fed jargon for a few-degrees-past-avid gun collector. "What happened to the wolves?"

"They were disposed of."

"You mean the government killed them."

Rector pressed his lips together and raised his eyebrows.

"Where?"

"At an unnamed military installation in Alaska. The animals aren't ESA up there, Grady, if that's where you're headed with that question. It's legal to dispose of problem wolves up there."

Service understood. If government officials issued orders to destroy animals protected by the Endangered Species Act, they could be prosecuted, but in Alaska they had free rein.

"All loose ends snipped clean," he said. "What about SuRo's Walther? The ballistics matched."

"We can't explain that, but the photos proved she wasn't the shooter at Vermillion. The fact that the weapon had been wiped down suggested a setup. The theory is that Haloran took the weapon when our surveillance tanked to chase Genova. Maybe she had a grudge against Genova and there it is," Rector said. "End of story. We're at war with terrorists and nobody gives a shit about minor-league crap like this right now."

"Thanks for leveling with me."

"Hey, when elephants dance it's the grass that suffers. I figured we blades needed a little boost. Remember what we learned when we were kids, The truth shall set you free?"

Service nodded and flipped his cigarette down the road. "Does knowing all this make you feel free?" he asked the agent.

Rector flicked his cigarette away and walked back to his sedan without speaking.

Service telephoned from the truck and met Summer Rose Genova at her compound. She seemed friendly enough, but uncharacteristically subdued. He put two photographs on the table. One was the still taken from the surveillance video. The other was a glossy from the morgue.

"You knew her," he said.

Genova said, "When are you people going to leave me alone?"

"I'm here on my own. This is off the record."

"I met her at a fund-raiser in London," Genova said. "She was an actress who had several minor character roles in Irish and Brit films. She was personable, fun, and said she was 'about animal rights.' She dropped some names to establish her bona fides, but I didn't know any of them."

"Maybe you knew one," Service said. An actress? That could explain Haloran's proficiency with accents.

Genova's eyes dropped to the table and she clasped her hands. "Minnis was one of the names. She wanted to meet him and she pushed me hard."

"Minnis was the person who tipped you about impending attacks, and you didn't give her what she wanted."

"I sensed something was wrong. She had never met Minnis but swore she was in the movement. I called the Brits and told them about the contact. After that, the Brits left me alone. Just before I moved back to the States a representative of Her Majesty's government came to visit me. She told me that the information about Haloran had caused her to flee the country and that this had undoubtedly saved more lives. I was given the gratitude of Her Majesty's government—sub rosa and off the record of course."

"And you continued to see Minnis here in the States. Carmody."

She nodded. "I did."

"Haloran ended up working with Minnis. She shot him."

Genova edged forward in her chair, but said nothing.

"I'm sorry, but they amputated one of his legs, SuRo. He's done working for the government. Haloran didn't know who he was until the very end. He slipped up and made a comment that tipped her, but her target was Bridget Galway, who had come over to the Brits with information about CARP," he said. "Her name was Larola Brule here. Carmody was a bonus for Haloran but she may not have known he was Minnis."

"I told the big lug his mouth would get him in a fix," Genova said.

"You were off with your wannabe warriors the night of the killings at Vermillion."

"Yes," she said. "We were planning the next event in our campaign. Vermillion wasn't ours, Grady."

She had just intimated leading the effort that had led to all the damage done the night of the Vermillion incident, but he knew he would not use that against her. Service said, "Minnis asked me to tell you he was sorry he couldn't tell you in person."

"Where is he?"

"In a VA hospital in California and no, I don't know which one, but you're clever. If you want to find him, you can."

She gave him a hug as he prepared to leave. "You're okay, rockhead."

"We're still going to blast you for that stunt in Trout Lake," he said. "*And* the rest of it, if we develop evidence."

"Once a cop, always a prick," she said, grinning from ear to ear.

They were in the Mosquito Wilderness, nearly five miles from the spot where Grinda had shot Haloran. Service had driven to the house in Gladstone, picked up Nantz, and headed for the Mosquito.

"Where we goin', hon?" she asked.

He told her about his conversation with Rector and Genova, and she listened without asking questions.

"Genova confessed?" she asked.

"It was off the record and right now I think she's had enough heat from the government. She's a zealot, not a criminal."

As they rolled slowly down a muddy lane, an animal suddenly appeared in the headlights, paused, glanced at them, and darted into a field. Service stopped the truck. A second animal loped past, not even slowing down.

"Long tails," Nantz said. "Feline heads, rounded ears, long tails. Cougars."

Service remembered the publicity from November, stared straight ahead, and put the truck in gear. "I didn't see anything," he said.

"I saw something," Nantz said, "but they sure weren't breeding." She leaned across and kissed him on the cheek. "Though I know a pair who could use a little practice."

Service immediately jammed the accelerator down.

"Can't you make this heap go any faster?" Maridly Nantz asked, laughing.

· EPILOGUE ·

It was two weeks before Christmas, and the heavy snows that had fallen during the clash in the Mosquito had melted away under sunny skies and fifty-degree days. Service and Nantz had the truck windows down as they bumped along the eight-mile-long two-track to Gutpile Moody's camp in the swamps surrounding Duck Creek.

Nantz sat quietly, taking in the scenery. Service sensed her anxiety. Ordinarily spouses and significant others were not invited to end-of-deer-season howls, but Lisette McKower had called and invited her. She had already started one academy class and would start again next fall, and she had worked with Service in the capacity of a VCO—and the district's voluntary conservation officers were all invited. She belonged. She was already one of them.

It was nearly 11 A.M., the temperature in the midfifties, the sun brilliant in a cloudless sapphire sky.

One small piece of the puzzle had lingered until last night when Lars Hjalmquist called.

"That shirt Gus found on the dead wolf?" Lars said. "It belongs to Brakelight Bois. That day we visited Horns he took a shine to Wealthy Johns, called her up and went out with her and—"

"I get the picture," Service said. "She garked his shirt."

"Even better," Hjalmquist said. "She talked him into *giving* her one of his old ones, and then when the shit hit the fan he was scared shitless to admit what he'd done. He says it's a black mark on his career and he's going to put in his papers. I don't think it was a black mark. I think it was getting under the covers with a murderer that made his decision for him. His mind's locked in the what-if game."

Service thanked his friend. He'd told Nantz about Brakelight's shirt and she had just shaken her head and said, "That was one busy woman."

A mile from camp, they began to see vehicles parked along the ribbon of shoulder of the camp road. Farther along they encountered Joe and Kathy Ketchum walking along with their black powder rifles in cases slung over their shoulders. Joe's arm was over Kathy's shoulder, her arm around his waist. Service stopped the truck beside them.

"Hey there, armed lovebirds, what's with all the traffic?"

"Officers are in from all over the state," Joe Ketchum said. "They've even got tents set up at the camp."

From all over the state? Most howls were limited to a district's personnel with a few flop-overs from adjacent territories. He wasn't sure what to make of this.

The closest they could get to camp was a quarter of a mile. Vehicles were parked helter-skelter.

"Looks like a freeway accordion," he said. "We'll need a cop to untangle this mess when it's over." Nantz smiled and squeezed his hand.

They walked the rest of the distance to the camp gate, which was made of stripped cedar logs. Service had stopped counting vehicles at ninety. Something very strange was afoot, but he had no idea what. There was a huge weathered sign above the entrance: CAMP SWAMP COURT. The camp was one of several in the U.P. that passed from CO to CO. Service had been to Camp Swamp Court with his father when he was a boy. In those days the camp had belonged to Pegleg Riordan, a veteran with a wooden leg who had been notorious for his brutal treatment of poachers. Legend held that more than a few lawbreakers had been "interrogated" at the camp. Now the place was Gutpile Moody's. It consisted of a two-story log cabin and an outhouse. There was hand-pumped water and no electricity.

It was not yet noon, but a bonfire was already crackling and hissing from a deep pit near the cabin. The fire was being built of five-foot logs stacked in piles. More white oak was stacked in neat rows not far from the fire. Several officers were lugging fuel logs while others supervised their placement.

"Damn," Nantz said quietly to him. "I forgot the s'mores."

Service found Gus Turnage and Simon del Olmo near one of the tents.

"What is all this?" he asked Gus.

Gus looked around the gathering and said, "Got the smell of something above the working-warden level, eh?"

Simon handed beers to Service and Nantz.

"Have a nice visit to the morgue?" del Olmo whispered.

Service said, "Nurmanski wasn't lying about Kate from Wakefield." Simon began to laugh.

"What?" Nantz said.

"It's not important," Service said.

Groups of officers walked around, visiting, shouting greetings and laughing, happy to see colleagues they had not seen in a long time. The camp was built on the only significant hummock of high ground in the Duck Creek Swamp.

McCants came jogging over to them, hugged Nantz, and nodded one of her big grins at Service.

Sheena Grinda was standing with Betty Very, who worked Ontonagon County. Betty had handled more problem bears than any other officer and had scars on her face to prove it. She was known throughout the DNR as Bearclaw. Service escorted Nantz and McCants to the two women and introduced Nantz.

"You and Lars hit the jackpot at Gitter's cabin," he said. Skelton Gitter had already pled guilty to several charges surrounding the poaching operation and was trying to cut a deal with the feds on the eagles. But he refused to cop to the wolf killing.

"You found Joe?" Bearclaw asked.

Service nodded.

"Sorry. He was a helluva man."

Service had not allowed himself time to think about Joe Flap.

Nantz's hand patted his buttock.

"Died with his boots on," Bearclaw said. "Can't ask for more than that."

Service saw retired officer Eino Hultinen and left Nantz with the women.

"Yo, Marquis," Service said. During his twenty-year career Service was aware of six fistfights between conservation officers and Hultinen had been in all six of them, usually as the instigator, if not always the winner. Officers had named him Marquis for the Marquis of Queensbury.

Hultinen grinned his crooked-tooth smile and shook hands. Eino had been a horseblanket.

"Looks like Heikki Luunta's takin' 'nother vacation, eh," the retired officer said. Heikki Luunta was purported to be the Finnish god of snow.

"Heard it was a quiet season," Marquis said, choking back a laugh.

"We had an acute outbreak of lawfulness," Service said.

Sergeant "B. P." Lyrone Bolden joined them. Bolden had been one of a dozen Detroit cops who transferred to the DNR one year. The other eleven had gone back to their Detroit jobs eventually, but Bolden had stayed on in the DNR and now worked out of Grand Rapids. As a rookie he had been sent in as the point man to stop illegal commerical fishing on the Garden Peninsula. This had been a time when Indian and white fishermen and the DNR were on the verge of open warfare and bloodshed. Bolden had been wearing a black leather coat over his uniform and had marched right up to the fishermen and their boat at sunrise. They had simply stared at him with open mouths as he pulled back his jacket to show his badge and announce, "Fish cop and you motherfuckers are busted!"

The six men involved all had records of violence, but they had given up without protest as Bolden's backups streamed out of the woods. The fishermen had rarely seen a black man in the cities of the U.P., and never in a CO uniform on the Garden. When his supervisor asked how he had done what he had done, Bolden had said the men had never seen a Black Phantom before. He had become B. P. on the spot.

"Tree comin' up?" B. P. asked.

"Doubtful," Service said. "What're all you flatlanders doin' up here?"

"Word just sorta got around," B. P. said. "When I told Tina I was coming back to the Yoop, she like to have fainted." His wife had hated living in the U.P. and had been the reason B. P. moved downstate after five years in the Soo.

Venison stew simmered in pots while officers talked, swapped stories, and drank beer from kegs. CO Dutch Vohl told of his encounter with a downstate hunter who had shot a wolf out of self-defense—at seventy-seven yards, four times broadside.

Most of the officers had laughed and shaken their heads, but Vohl, a thoughtful man, didn't laugh. "People come up here to the woods and get spooked. The guy did a stupid thing, but I think he was really afraid."

Maybe, Service thought, but if he was afraid, what was he doing in the woods with a rifle?

The feed started around two in the afternoon. The officers lined up before gallons of venison stew, huge bowls of salad, and plates filled with grilled partridge and woodcock breasts, smoked whitefish, moose jerky from Ontario, smoked elk from Wyoming, all sorts of fish and game all simply prepared and washed down with beer and whiskey.

By dark the bonfire's flames were up to thirty feet, and those gathered around the flames backed up to keep from being singed.

Nantz and Grinda were hanging out together, drinking beer, laughing and talking the way women do, giving full attention to everything the other one had to say.

Lis McKower arrived just before the stew was served and wedged her way into line between Hultinen and del Olmo.

"No cuts," Hultinen complained.

"Harassment," McKower said with a grin.

The retired officer cringed. "Glad I didn't have to deal with that shit."

CO Bryan Jefferies drifted over to them and, at McKower's prompting, regaled the group with the story about the opening-day skirmish between the Amish and Mennonite hunters. By the time he finished, his audience was howling.

Turnage looked over at Service. "*Incompetent discharge of a firearm?*"

"We should write more of those."

"If it was a violation," del Olmo said, chiming in.

Service grinned. "Problematic."

His former lieutenant shook her head.

It was long after dark when vehicle lights appeared at the camp gate and pulled up to the cabin. Most of the celebrants were gathered around the fire.

Chief Lorne Driscoll got out of a green Tahoe and went back to talk to drivers of several trucks that had followed him in. People got out of the trucks, began opening doors and unloading huge cardboard boxes. Service saw Blood Hawk Chamberlin and several senior officers from Lansing.

Captain Ware Grant appeared from the other side of the Tahoe and walked unsteadily to the edge of the fire, his head up, back straight.

Nantz weaved her way through the crowd to be at Service's side. She gave him a questioning look, but he had no answers.

Service had downed only a few beers, but the alcohol and warmth of the fire had made him logy. Maybe the letdown after the incidents at Vermillion and in the Mosquito contributed. He stared at the captain and the chief and blinked several times trying to figure out what they were doing here. The chief did not approve of howls. "We're busted," he whispered to Nantz before he noticed that Grant and O'Driscoll were wearing the old wool overcoats officers had called horseblankets. The coats had been retired years before, and Service had been told several times to stop wearing his father's coat, which he had worn for years. He had reluctantly obliged only the year before.

The chief stood quietly beside the captain, the two of them silent.

Some of the people from the trucks began to move through the crowd handing out narrow-stemmed plastic glasses with DNR logos stuck on them.

Bottles of champagne were passed through the crowd. Corks popped like muted gunshots.

Gutpile Moody brought glasses to the chief and captain and poured champagne for them.

The chief held up his hands and the buzz in the crowd tailed off.

"Joe Flap died doing the thing he loved most. That he was grounded is irrelevant. Joe Flap never played games. He was a horseblanket and his passing requires a fitting tribute. Effective today, these coats are again part of the official uniforms and we will wear them with pride." He pointed toward boxes. "There is a coat for each of you. Please get one now."

Service was amazed at the orderliness of the process. Boxes were labeled with letters for last names. When Service got to the truck with the box marked "S" he saw someone step out of the shadows.

Luticious Treebone smiled and held out a new coat for his friend. Service slid it on, and noted it smelled new and felt stiff and heavy. He decided he preferred the old one his father had left to him.

Treebone and Service embraced, two old warriors who had seen so much together.

"You always crash the best parties," Service said.

"Learned it from you," his friend said. "Word's out on what went down in the Mosquito. You almost got your ass shot again."

When Nantz saw Treebone, she hugged him and introduced Service and Tree to three people in badgeless DNR shirts. "They're my classmates from the academy!" she said.

Service felt the trainees staring at him as Nantz hung on his arm and made quiet jokes with them.

Chief O'Driscoll walked over to Service and nodded for him to follow.

They stepped back into the trees. "Cigarette?" O'Driscoll asked.

Service dug out his pack, gave one to the chief, and lit it for him.

"*Filthy* habit. Been battling the damn things for years," he said. The chief lowered his voice. "I doubt Senator Timms would approve of Officer Sensitivity's behavior in the Marquette morgue."

"I can explain that, Chief."

O'Driscoll chuckled. "I'm sure you can," he said, and walked away to join Captain Grant.

Reassembled around the fire and in their new coats, Chief O'Driscoll raised a glass and looked to his right. "Ware?"

Captain Ware Grant scanned the officers until he saw Service. "Grady, you were with Joe at the end. What were his last words?"

Service started to mumble, but Nantz poked him in the side. "Sir, he asked me how close he was to the runway and when I told him he said, 'Goddamn shoulda made 'er.'"

The crowd laughed and cheered.

The captain let the noise subside. "I submit that Joe Flap did make it. He and all those like him made it by helping make us what and who we are."

His voice seemed to catch on his words and he paused to regain his composure.

"Joe made it and each of you has made it. Most people don't know what you do, but you know and that's what matters. Just as Joe and his contemporaries paved the way for you, you will set the example for those to follow. We have more than one hundred years of tradition in the force, serving people, making sacrifices, getting the job done. Tonight we are all here to say good-bye to Joe Flap and to salute each other."

Captain Ware Grant raised his glass and with a breaking voice said, "Horseblankets."

More than 150 voices roared the word, and began clicking glasses of their neighbors.

The captain threw his glass into the fire. Moments later more than a hundred plastic glasses were melting in the flames

Service whispered to Maridly Nantz, "Unlawful dumping of refuse."

She poked him in the ribs again and looked up at him, her face lit by the flames of the bonfire. "I love you, Grady Service."

He looked down at her and said, "I love you, Mar."

Lisette McKower yelled, "Hang on people, I think the earth's about to move."

· ACKNOWLEDGMENTS ·

I would like to thank my agent Betsy Nolan, who guided me into the publishing world seventeen years ago and has kept me there. And special thanks to my editor Lilly Golden at Lyons Press, who lives among the trout in the Catskills and wields the blue pencil as deftly as any surgeon to both encourage and rein in my flights of fancy

I especially want to acknowledge the assistance, time, trust, and encouragement of Michigan Department of Natural Resources Law Enforcement Division personnel: Lieutenant Tom Courchaine and Sergeants Mike Webster and Darryl Shann, COs Steve Burton, Grant Emery, Paul Higashi, Dave Painter, Tim Robson, Dave Van't Hof, and Detective Mike Johnson. Officer Robson is the first CO to check my fishing license in forty-three years of fishing in the state, doing so one muggy June night while I waded the Escanaba River, literally in the middle of nowhere, demonstrating how serious our officers are about protecting our resources. Tim materialized at sunset right after my nephew caught his first trout on a fly and a black bear swam across the river just above where we fished. It was a memorable evening on all counts

I thank our state's real "Wolf Daddy," Jim Hammill, whose passion for and curiosity about these magnificent animals knows no bounds. Jim met me after working hours, patiently and thoroughly answering my many questions about wolves and the work he and his people do.

Special gratitude goes to Department of Natural Resources Law Enforcement Division Chief Rick Asher, who has given me invaluable insights into the life of COs past and present, and to the division's spokesperson Brad Wurfel.

I am especially pleased to thank Sherie Courchaine and Sergeant Susie Webster (Michigan State Police, Retired) for their insight into the lives of spouses of COs, and for fine meals and good wine. I showed up at night late for dinner at their homes, dirty and smelly, sometimes bloody, and invariably dragging from twelve-hour patrols, and was graciously embraced as family.

I also want to thank retired CO Mike Holmes for the postseason feed at his hunting camp near Iron Mountain where I met many officers, active and retired, from Michigan and Wisconsin. They are impressive people with great senses of humor and love their stories. Special thanks also to retired BATF Special Agent Dave Mihills for his insight into federal law enforcement and for sharing driving duties in the Green Streamer II. Crystal Falls is a ten-hour drive from my home, and good conversation and company make the long sorties a hoot and a tutorial.

It is my intent in the Woods Cop series to help people understand what our officers do and to portray them as accurately as possible, but there are some procedures and working methods that I do not disclose. For poachers and violets who care to read, there will be no tips to help you.

There is no federal wolf laboratory at Vermillion, though the remains of the old storm warrior station still stand and there is protected ground for piping plovers there. The plovers were kind enough to show themselves to me in the autumn of 2001.

The Mosquito Wilderness Tract is a fictional name, but the area is real. Readers will find that its exact location is never precisely defined, and this is by design. There are some treasures you have to find on your own, the search being as delicious as the discovery.

The Michigan DNR Law Enforcement Academy is real, but funding so far has not allowed for a class to be trained every year. The architects of the academy intend for it to be a tough and grueling course that will produce dedicated and effective officers, and from what I have seen and heard, it is well on its way to meeting its objectives.

All of the characters in the Woods Cop series are fictional, but there are facets of real officers in all the characters, and many of the events and situations the fictional characters face in the stories are real. I have changed names and some details to protect privacy. Real officers demonstrate a lot more discretion than Grady Service, but they share his passion for the job.

What I've gotten right about what our COs do and how they work is due to the insight, candor, and help from these professionals and others. The mistakes are mine alone.

I have had the privilege of seeing three live gray wolves in Michigan's wilds, and I hope to see many more. Wolves have had bad PR for as long as they have been in contact with man, but the myths are just that and the animals are part of our state's natural heritage and deserve to live the way nature intends them to live.

We have about 160 COs working the woods and waters of Michigan's eighty-three counties, and our shores and shares of four Great Lakes. In my view our DNR Law Enforcement Division has too few people out there in the woods and dirt, and far too much to cover. I find it ironic that gray wolves are still listed as endangered in Michigan, yet they far outnumber our "working wardens." As we learned in the wake of the disasters of September 11, 2001, technology is a tool that can never replace the human element essential to gathering intelligence or enforcing the laws of civilized society.

Knock on wood, our gray wolf packs will continue to increase and prosper, but it's up to our government to do something about law enforcement numbers. We need more conservation officers with their boots in the dirt and we need them now.

Joseph Heywood
Portage, Michigan
March 4, 2002